Weir of Hermiston

an unfinished romance by

ROBERT LOUIS STEVENSON

Commentary and Notes by J. T. Low

Television Version by Tom Wright

Holmes McDougall

First published 1973

WEIR OF HERMISTON
was first shown on BBC2
in February/March 1973
Starring

TOM FLEMING	*as*	Adam Weir
with		
EDITH MACARTHUR	*as*	Kirstie Elliott
VIRGINIA STARK	*as*	Christina Elliott
DAVID RINTOUL	*as*	Archie Weir
and		
DAVID DUNDAS	*as*	Frank Innes

The serial was produced in Scotland
by PHARIC MACLAREN
and directed
by TINA WAKERELL

Cover pictures © BBC Television, Glasgow
Cover design by Scott McCallum, PWP

SBN 7157 1269-1

Printed by Holmes McDougall, Perth

Published by HOLMES McDOUGALL, LTD.,
30 Royal Terrace, Edinburgh, EH7 5AL

PREFACE

In recent years there has been an increasing demand both from the general public and from educational bodies for re-issues of the texts of important works of Scottish literature. This demand has been stimulated partly by the increase of the Scottish content in university and college courses in literature, partly by the activities of committees and associations concerned with encouraging the study of Scottish literature, and partly by radio and TV versions of the works themselves. This new edition of *Weir of Hermiston* is one attempt to meet that demand. Since the appearance of the first edition in 1896, apart from a single volume edition of 1925, the tendency has been to publish the novel with other works—fragments such as *The Great North Road*, *The Young Chevalier*, *Heathercat*, other novels or long short stories such as *The Master of Ballantrae* and *Dr. Jekyll and Mr. Hyde*. In the present edition *Weir* is published by itself, with a critical introduction, notes on the text, appendices, and glossary. This is a tribute long overdue to a work that is considered by many to be Stevenson's finest achievement.

In preparing the text, I have for the most part followed the two earliest editions—the first of 1896, and the Edinburgh of 1897; but I have accepted some modernised forms and spellings. I have also consulted the Pentlands edition of 1907, the Swanston edition of 1912, the Tusitala edition of 1924 (1925 reprint), the single volume edition of 1925, and three comparatively modern editions—the Dent Everyman of 1925 reprinted in 1968, the Collins of 1953 reprinted in 1965, and the Nelson of 1956 reprinted in 1963. The text of *Weir of Hermiston*, as presented in the editions I have examined, is clear and straightforward, remarkably free from ambiguities, variants or misprints. Four examples of these, however, seem to me to be of some interest—*unreverend/unreverent* in Chapter 2, *Judiciary/Justiciary* in Chapter 3, *hawse/tawse* in Chapter 5, and *howl/howf* in

3

Chapter 8—and have therefore been specially mentioned in footnotes or the general notes.

The appendices deal with the problem of the projected continuation and ending. In Appendix I, Colvin's summary of and commentary on Mrs. Strong's 'intended argument' are presented and discussed, along with references to other possible developments including M. R. Ridley's revised summary. The latest attempt to complete the story is to be found in the TV version by Tom Wright first broadcast by the BBC in February-March 1973. In Appendix II Stevenson's final sequence at the Weaver's Stone is printed side by side with Mr. Wright's version; and in Appendix III the rest of the TV script is printed in full. Readers and viewers may find it interesting, not only to compare the TV version with Stevenson's, but also to consider what is gained and what lost in transforming a work of imaginative fiction into a television recording.

Whatever may be our views about the power and effectiveness of the modern media of film and TV in presenting a novel like *Weir of Hermiston* (and there is no doubt that Stevenson's flair for dialogue and the dramatic situation makes his work excellent material for transferring to stage or screen) I think it will be agreed that it is the text itself, as Stevenson wrote it, that we must isolate and look at afresh, if we are to make a critical judgment on its worth. In the Introduction I analyse and assess *Weir* under such headings as setting, structure, characters, language, and indicate its position and uniqueness relative to the better known works of Stevenson. I need hardly add that no attempt is made to assess the overall achievement of Stevenson—as a writer of essays, travel books, short stories. novels. The reader who wishes to extend his studies into these fields may find the Select Bibliography at the end of this volume of some value.

J. T. L.

CONTENTS

The part of this book which is mine is for Anne Herd. My thanks are due to Tina, Pharic, and all who sailed in *Weir*.

T. W.

INTRODUCTION

The Author: Environment and Experience

Robert Louis Stevenson (1850-1894) is very much the Scottish topographical artist in writing, the literary man of Edinburgh and the Lothians, the Pentlands and the Borders, Galloway, Ayr, the Central Highlands and Islands. Scenes from these places feature in his essays of childhood, some of his short stories—*Thrawn Janet, Tod Lapraik, The Merry Men*—and in his historical novels *Kidnapped, Catriona, St. Ives, The Master of Ballantrae*. True there is the other side to his nature, the travelling, questing side that took him to England and America, France and the South Seas. This aspect is reflected in his early travel books like *An Inland Voyage* and *Travels with a Donkey*, in *Treasure Island* and *The Wrecker*, in some of his short stories—*The Beach of Falesa, Olalla*—and in the foreign settings he moves to in *The Master* and *Catriona*.

Although *The Beach of Falesa* (set in the South Seas) may be said to be a better short story than, say, *The Misadventures of John Nicholson* (set in Edinburgh), and although *Treasure Island* is better structured and more carefully composed in its pictorial details than, say, *St. Ives* or *The Master of Ballantrae*, there is no doubt that in overall achievement his Scottish works are his most important. *Kidnapped* reveals an awakening interest not only in the effect of history on Scottish character but also in the relationship between different kinds of Scotsmen—their affinities and conflicts. *Catriona* reveals again Stevenson's feeling for the effect of Scottish history on social patterns, but it also illustrates the awakening of an interest in the actions and psychology of women. *Dr. Jekyll and Mr. Hyde* as a long short story or a short novel is not on the face of it one of Stevenson's Scottish works, but it illustrates a Scottish obsession with moral ideas and the dual nature of

man. It concentrates on the notion of the *alter ego* in each
of us that is both nourished and suppressed by Calvinism
and that Hogg explored in *The Confessions of a Justified
Sinner*. In Stevenson this theme is most vividly presented in
the relationship between Henry and James Durie in *The
Master of Ballantrae*; but it is also latent in the study of
the psyche of Archie in *Weir of Hermiston*.

In his essays and earlier works, Stevenson is the self-
conscious artist and moralist, the experimenter with words
and with the romantic machinery of the novel of adventure.
Although his works continue to reflect the pattern of the
Romance, he becomes more and more aware of the possibilities of the historical, the psychological, and the dramatic,
especially when he returns to the mainstream of Scottish
literary traditions. The influence of the ballads and Scott,
perhaps also of Fergusson and Hogg, begins to be felt in
some of his later poems, in *Thrawn Janet*, in *Tod Lapraik*
and *The Master of Ballantrae*, above all in *Weir of Hermiston*. Perhaps the most remarkable thing is that he should
have produced *Weir*, his most mature and accomplished
work, at a time when the Scottish Novel was rapidly
declining into the Kailyard. The year in which he wrote
the last words of *Weir* was also the year of the publication
of the two prototype Kailyard novels—Ian Maclaren's
Beside the Bonnie Brier Bush and S. R. Crockett's *The Lilac
Sunbonnet*. These works were written in the same distorted,
over-sentimentalised vein as that in which Barrie wrote *A
Window in Thrums* and parts of *The Little Minister*. Stevenson corresponded with Barrie; and his letters and references
to Barrie's works show that, although he overpraised both
A Window in Thrums and *The Little Minister*, he was aware
of Barrie's besetting weakness. Writing of the happy ending
of *The Little Minister*, he says this was achieved 'at the cost
of truth to life'.[1] Stevenson was impressed also with
Crockett's Scottish stories, and wrote one of his best poems
in answer to Crockett's dedication to him of his first novel
The Stickit Minister. This poem, strangely enough, contains

1. Letter to J. M. Barrie, 1st November, 1892, quoted by Colvin in his
   Editorial Note.

three lines that conjure up something of the atmosphere of the opening of *Weir:*

> Grey recumbent tombs of the dead in desert places
> Standing Stones on the vacant wine-red moor;
> Hills of sheep, and the howes of the silent vanished races,
> And winds austere and pure!

Stevenson, in the vintage years of the Kailyard 1893-4, and despite his friendship with its leading authors, was carving out something that stood in complete contrast— a work that was able to exploit his nostalgia creatively and that could use Scottish traditions, environment, and situations to produce a study of Scottish character and family relationships that has the truth to life and the tragic vision completely beyond the range of the Kailyarders. Stevenson in *Weir* (1894) provided his own antidote to the Kailyard seven years before *The House with the Green Shutters* and twenty years before *Gillespie*.[1]

The Setting

Stevenson had resumed work on *Weir of Hermiston* in a great burst of literary activity just before he died in December 1894; and it remains one of the miracles of literature that, living so far away in the exotic surroundings of Samoa, he should have been able to make such a vivid recall of Scottish scenes and settings and to weave them into the fabric of a powerful story so essentially Scottish. The feat rivals that of Lewis Grassic Gibbon in writing *Sunset Song* from Welwyn Garden City, London. From the opening lines of the 'Introductory' in which he describes the Weaver's Stone 'in the wild end of a moorland parish' and links it with his tragic tale 'of the Justice-Clerk and of his son' to the point where the novel breaks off at a moment of temporary reconciliation between Archie and young Christina at that same Weaver's Stone, Stevenson makes us constantly aware of the power and presence of his Border etting.

1. *The House with the Green Shutters* by George Douglas Brown and *Gillespie* by John MacDougall Hay were regarded as counterblasts to the Kailyard novels, presenting as they did a harder, more realistic and tragic view of the Scots character and social life.

Even in Chapter 1 where we are concerned with an account of the 'Life and Death of Mrs. Weir', the movement of the novel is towards its Border landscape. Amidst the opening references to Flodden, Tom Dalyell, and the 'old riding Rutherfords of Hermiston', Jean Rutherford herself is oddly placed; and although there follow quick allusions to Edinburgh—George Square and the Parliament House—always the direction is back towards Hermiston. As the novel hovers over the setting that motivates and animates it, the writing glows, the pace accelerates, the cadences build up and develop with a wonderful freedom and sense of inevitability. Old Kirstie is introduced as something emanating from the landscape itself: she was—

> once a moorland Helen, and still comely as a blood horse and healthy as the hill wind. High in flesh and voice and colour, she ran the house with her whole intemperate soul, in a bustle, not without buffets.

Mrs. Weir, feckless though she is, also appears as part of the setting: she finds in its moods and views echoes of her own 'tenderness' and narrow piety. She becomes eloquent when moved by the natural scene:

> There is a corner of the policy of Hermiston, where you come suddenly in view of the summit of Black Fell, sometimes like the mere grass top of a hill, sometimes (and this is her own expression) like a precious jewel in the heavens. On such days, upon the sudden view of it, her hand would tighten on the child's fingers, her voice rise like a song. '*I to the hills!*' she would repeat.

The Weaver's Stone, in its loneliness and historical associations, is established as the focal point for meetings and inevitable climax, just as the Standing Stones become the still centre of concentrated emotion in *Sunset Song;* and it is noteworthy that women come to be closely identified with these places. It is true Chris Guthrie is more exclusively associated with the Standing Stones in Grassic Gibbon's novel; but it is significant, not only that *Weir* opens and breaks off at the Weaver's Stone, but also that both Mrs.

Weir and the young Christina are seen in Archie's mind as closely etched into its setting and atmosphere:

> He had retained from childhood a picture, now half obliterated by the passage of time and the multitude of fresh impressions, of his mother telling him, with the fluttered earnestness of her voice . . . the tale of the 'Praying Weaver', on the very scene of his brief tragedy and long repose. And now there was a companion piece; and he beheld, and he should behold for ever, Christina perched on the same tomb, in the grey colours of evening, gracious, dainty, perfect as a flower, and she also singing—

It is clear too from the note of tragic destiny struck in the Introductory that Stevenson intended the Stone to be the scene of Frank Innes's death. The three place names—The Deil's Hags, The Weaver's Stone, Francie's Cairn— strengthen the impression of a lonely remote setting where the supernatural vied with the natural to emphasise the tragic quality of the events that were destined to take place there. The first suggests happenings back in legendary times; the second places the setting historically in the Killing Time of the Covenanters; the third anticipates the central act of violence towards which Stevenson's story moves.

It is impossible—and unnecessary—to locate exactly the setting of *Weir of Hermiston*. The name occurs in places near Edinburgh and in the countryside to the south. Just outside Edinburgh on the north side of the Calder road lies the farm of East Hermiston; and beyond that a row of houses also on the north side bears the name Long Hermiston. Still farther along, off a side road that leads to Ratho, stands Hermiston House in pleasant grounds leading down to the Union Canal. Perhaps a more appropriate association would be with the farm of Hermiston on the Water of Ale, between Ettrick and Teviotdale, 'and close to the proper country of the Elliotts', as Colvin wrote in his editorial note. This farm is set in the heart of the Border country, but well within a sheltered and populated area, and well below the more remote setting of the Upper Ale and its 'wild ends of moorland'. To match some of the romantic descriptions given at the beginning of Chapter 5, this Hermiston would have had to be placed much farther up the Water of Ale:

> The road to Hermiston runs for a great part of the way up the valley of a stream . . . shaded by willows and natural woods of birch . . . All beyond and about is the great field of the hills; the plover, the curlew, and the lark cry there . . .

When Stevenson is attempting to describe his Hermiston, it is the wild nature of its surroundings that he emphasises: the building takes its character not from any architectural features but from the setting that dominated it and threatened to devour it:

> The policy . . . was of some extent, but very ill reclaimed; heather and moorfowl had crossed the boundary wall and spread and roosted within; and it would have tasked a landscape gardener to say where policy ended and unpolicied nature began . . . Standing so high and with so little shelter, it was a cold, exposed house, splashed by showers, drenched by continuous rains that made the gutters to spout, beaten upon and buffeted by all the winds of heaven; and the prospect would be often black with tempest, and often white with the snows of winter.

The Weaver's Stone and Hermiston establish the romantic Border setting, but a third place is mentioned within this setting and used to extend the action and intensify the legendary quality of the novel. This is the farm of Cauldstaneslap, occupied by the Elliotts who were notorious at one time for their thieving and brawling. Kirstie's father Gilbert had been a curious combination of religious zealot and smuggler; her brother Gilbert, quarrelsome in his cups but of immense power and courage, met his death in a manner and under circumstances almost epic and heroic: it was this death that threw the aura of legend and outlawry on his four sons—the Four Black Brothers Hob, Gib, Clem and Dand. The story of Gilbert's return home a dying man and the pursuit of his killers by the four brothers is told by Kirstie with great Scots vigour and colour.

The setting of the Cauldstaneslap is at the back of it but remains shadowy and indistinct:

> ... and the folks of Cauldstaneslap got to their feet about the table and looked at each other with white faces. The horse fell dead at the yard gate, the laird won the length of the house and fell there on the threshold ... he uttered the single command 'Brocken Dykes', and fainted ... It was three miles to Broken Dykes, down hill, and a sore road. Kirstie had seen men from Edinburgh dismounting there in plain day to lead their horses. But the four brothers rode it as if Auld Hornie were behind and Heaven in front.

The actual Cauldstaneslap of the Pentland Hills, as mentioned in the notes (p. 159) is the highest point of the track, an old drove road that is itself called Cauldstaneslap and that runs from the Lanark road near Harperrig Reservoir to the Lyne Water and West Linton. As you approach it from Edinburgh and the north, you see it on the skyline above an expanse of moorland broken by a green area beside a stream on which is set the farmstead of Harper Rig. It is an open moorland scene that has a dark look even in summer: in winter it would be exposed to all the winds; and if you lived there in that season you might well hear 'the squalls bugle on the moorland', and, like Archie, 'watch the fire prosper ... and drink deep of the pleasures of shelter'.

The church that is such an important *mis-en-scène* at the beginning of Chapter 6 recalls the area of Glencorse on the southern flanks of the Pentlands—particularly that part between Flotterstone and the Fisher's Tryst Inn, where Glencorse Old Church is situated. The kirk and manse, garden and graveyard, in *Weir*, Stevenson sets in a grove of rowans; and the kirk itself is described as 'a dwarfish, ancient place seated for fifty ... standing in a green by the burn-side among two-score gravestones'. Glencorse Old Kirk is a ruin now; but its neat tiny proportions can still be worked out, and from certain points in the graveyard the line of the Pentland Hills can be seen. There are also references in Chapter 5 to the 'Fa's o' Spango'— the name of a stream in Dumfriesshire, and to the Tweed

('Tweed had got a hold o' him'); and in Chapter 7 we read
of 'the great expanse of untenanted moorland running . . .
towards the sources of the Clyde'.

For his composite setting, then, Stevenson roams round
and selects from his favourite haunts in the Borders, in
various parts of the Pentland Hills, and also, as we have
seen, further afield in upper Tweed and Clyde. Composite
though it is, however, the setting of *Weir* remains un-
mistakably Scots, Scots of the Lammermuirs, the Pentlands
and the Borders. The descriptions are brief and impression-
istic rather than detailed; names like Cauldstaneslap, Pentlands, Rullion Green, Hermiston give the strength of
association with real places; but the power of the novel
resides more in the atmosphere created out of its setting—
the feeling for the continuity of history and race, the legendary quality, the earthiness as of the ballad, and the sense
of belonging.

Main Lines of Development: Structure

Although *Weir of Hermiston* remains unfinished, there is
a kind of brooding unity about it and an inevitable return
at the end to the opening mood and atmosphere. In the
Introductory we are at the Weaver's Stone, the cairn among
the heather 'in the wild end of a moorland parish', clearly
a place of destiny. At the end of the novel, the point at
which it breaks off, we are there again, only this time the
Weaver's Stone is a lovers' trysting place where quarrel
and reconciliation are taking place. In a curious involuntary
way Stevenson did succeed in rounding off his tale at the
Weaver's Stone before he died, although we know his
intention was to make it even more of a place of destiny—
a place of secret meetings, tragedy and death.

The first chapter—'Life and Death of Mrs. Weir'—
eventually settles down to give us a realistic enough account
of the relationship between Jean Rutherford and Adam
Weir; but throughout that first chapter there are references
back to history and legend, to the old 'riding Rutherfords
of Hermiston'; and there is alternation between the homely
and the practical on the one hand—the story of Jean's

inefficiency and füshionlessness—and, on the other, the romantic and mythic when Jean's feelings are heightened and she feels the links with the past and the timelessness of the Weaver's Stone setting. Hermiston himself is a figure on the periphery of this chapter, but his presence and influence are subtly interwoven until at the end, at the scene of his home-coming to the news of his wife's death, he comes to dominate like some remote indifferent deity. Already the two major themes are there presented side by side rather than fused—the Weaver's Stone as place of destiny, Hermiston as dominating figure.

In Chapter 2 the father-son relationship is sufficiently sketched to indicate the differences and lack of understanding between Adam Weir and Archie. Here is displayed too the friendship between Glenalmond and Archie, a friendship that serves to illuminate the strength and weakness of Hermiston himself. The sensitivity of Archie and Glenalmond is thrown against the harshness and crudity of Hermiston; but hints are thrown out of the qualities that link father and son, in particular that aloofness, that refusal to give oneself away in friendship:

> My Lord Justice-Clerk was known to many; the man Adam Weir perhaps to none . . . Innes replied, with his usual flippancy and more than usual insight: 'I know Weir, but I never met Archie.'

This chapter forms a preparation for Chapter 3—'In the Matter of the Hanging of Duncan Jopp'—where the first direct climaxes occur. Here without preliminary Stevenson presents a graphic picture of Lord Weir at work as judge—harsh, intolerant, inexorable; and here too we have the build-up to Jopp's execution and Archie's dramatic denunciation of the hanging. From these external climaxes, the movement of the novel is back towards the psychological. Stevenson explores Archie's tortured mind and illustrates how sensitive he is to criticism and outside pressure. His interview with Dr. Gregory, with its flashback to an incident in his childhood, gives him an unexpected vision of the humanity buried deep in Hermiston

himself. These inner climaxes prepare us for the change in
Archie and for his complete submission to his father in the
final scene of the chapter. That father-son exchange not
only contrasts the harshness of the father with the humility
of the son: it also marks the beginning of a change in
Archie. Something of his father's spirit—'his blameless
nobility'—affects him; and the mental change is to be
paralleled by a physical change. The move to Hermiston,
legendary place of passions and epic qualities, is adum-
brated.

Before the second part begins, however, before the novel
settles in at Hermiston, Stevenson has a final scene to play
in Edinburgh in the atmosphere of the law courts. This
episode in Glenalmond's rooms completes Archie's recovery
and marks the end of the conflict with his father. In place
of the revulsion from his father's harshness and supreme
disregard for others, there develops in Archie an admiration
for his Roman austerity—the god-like removal from
ordinary humanity, the obsession with legal duty. The toast
that is drunk almost playfully to 'The Lord Justice-Clerk,
Lord Hermiston' by Archie and Glenalmond is the resolution
of the First Movement of the novel. Although Hermiston is
physically absent, his spirit comes to dominate the finale of
that first part.

Chapter 5—'Winter on the Moors'—might be said to
constitute a Movement or Book by itself. Here we have
the heart of the Legend of Hermiston-Cauldstaneslap. In
the first section—'At Hermiston'—there is great warmth
and power in the description of the setting: here the novel
has clearly reached its topographical heart, but this is a
treatment of place as theme because the description of the
place slides imperceptively into a description of Archie as
part of that scene, drinking deep of the pleasures of shelter
and rejecting offers of society so that he becomes steeped in
the setting as the Recluse of Hermiston. At the end there is
a further development of the father-son identification theme
and a stressing of the destiny motif: in rejecting society and
avoiding 'any opportunity of pleasure', Archie shows 'a

Roman sense of duty', 'an instinctive aristocracy of manners and taste'.

In the second section of this chapter something of Stevenson's skill in handling the technique of parallelism is illustrated. Here we meet a female character to balance Hermiston, that middle-aged 'moorland Helen' Kirstie, an epic woman-figure *manquée*, homely and yet imperious. In creating her, Stevenson was breaking from his own Victorian reticence and moving towards a modern concept of character and the complexities that sex introduces into human relationships.[1] The physical attraction she feels towards her young master is clearly indicated, and her imperiousness and intolerance of neighbours are a female variation of the Adam Weir theme. From here the novel builds up to its legendary-epic core—the third part of 'Winter on the Moors', sub-titled 'A Border Family'. First from Stevenson's objective narrative and then from Kirstie's tale in Scots we have the tracing of the genealogy of the Elliotts and the evolution of the Cauldstaneslap family. Here Stevenson picks up the epic-romantic tone of the opening of the novel, but now the tone deepens and the story concentrates on a single epic figure and event—the heroic end of Gib Elliott in 1804 after being attacked on his way home to Cauldstaneslap. This story is the more dramatic and legendary for being told direct in Kirstie's supple fast-moving Scots; but for the more mundane sequel where the tension relaxes—the character sketches of the Four Black Brothers out of their legendary frame—Stevenson resorts to a more formal style, relieved by flashes of the proverbial power of Scots—'He has some of Hob's grand, whunstane sense . . .', 'If he had but twa fingers o' Gibs, he would waken them up', 'They hae a guid pride o' themsel's!' At the end of this section (and of the Second Movement of the novel) comes a transition to the young Kirstie-Archie love theme, both in the intro-

1. Lettice Cooper in *Robert Louis Stevenson* (1947) says he 'feared to offend against the taboo of sex that inhibited the British novel', and 'complained bitterly that the French did not allow themselves to be so restricted' (pp. 90-91).

duction of Christina herself and in the preliminary view
of a Hermiston church parade.

The Final Movement of the work begins at Chapter 6—
'A Leaf from Christina's Psalm-Book'—with the description
of Archie as church-goer, critic of the rural community,
and young man alerted by the sights and smells of spring
to a sense of his destiny. Here Stevenson the conscious
writer has withdrawn: we have the story out of Archie's
feelings and thoughts and consciousness—another sign of
Stevenson's developing skill. It is an apt preparation for the
scene in the church where Archie and Christina see each
other for the first time and are aware of the inevitable.
The encounter is described with a mixture of the playful
and the serious: Stevenson occasionally becomes the
avuncular author observing his bairns falling in love, but
as he warms more and more to Christina's *persona* the
essence of the story is felt as emanating out of her mind
and emotions and reactions. The climax sentence illustrates
how Stevenson in describing the 'two stealthy glances sent
out like antennae among the pews' can avoid the Kailyard
touch by setting the concrete alongside the figurative:

A charge as of electricity passed through Christina, and
behold! the leaf of her psalm-book was torn across.

(Contrast this with that touch of Kailyard fancy at the end
of Chapter 3 in S. R. Crockett's novel: "But the lilac
sunbonnet said never a word".)

This long chapter that opens the Final Movement and
develops the love motif is subtly varied in mood and pace.
We pass swiftly from the first meeting on Hermiston Brae
and the first parting to an intensification of the portrait of
Christina 'in love with herself, her destiny, the air of the
hills, the benediction of the sun'; and from there Stevenson
builds up, by way of a light-hearted dialogue in Scots
between the girl and Dand her poet-brother, to the moment
when she meets Archie at the Weaver's Stone for the first
time and 'sooths' for him Dand's ballad about 'the auld . . .
clay-cauld Elliotts'. This comes as a big internal climax in
which the historical and legendary motifs are superimposed

on the basic love theme and the whole is unified by the sense of destiny. The second chapter of this final part is headed 'Enter Mephistopheles', a title that stresses Stevenson's consciously dramatic design. This chapter and the following one 'A Nocturnal Visit' come as counterpointing contrasts to the love theme. In the first, Frank Innes is seen plotting and scheming to discredit the girl in Archie's eyes, and in the second, old Kirstie, acting with the instinct of a woman who sees the object of love being removed from her, also sows the seeds of doubt in Archie's mind. So we reach the final chapter—the climax and conclusion to the story—'At the Weaver's Stone', prepared for the break-down in the love affair, aware of the atmosphere of destiny, and ready to react to and muse over the partial reconciliation that comes at the end—a reconciliation that awakens in Archie pity and a bewildered fear, and that hints at the passion and violence to come:

> It seemed unprovoked, a wilful convulsion of brute nature . . .

Important thematic ingredients are brought together in that final chapter: the moral conflict within Archie, the forces acting against the love affair, the figure of the judge-father disapproving and condemning. It is an impressive ending not only to the third and final movement dominated as it is by the love theme, but also to the whole book as it has been structured up to that point.

The lines of development stress the two powerful forces playing upon Archie—his father's character and its influence upon him, and the power of his love for Christina; but the architecturing of the whole novel points to the importance of the legendary element, the epic nature of the story, and the underlying feeling of tragic destiny.

The Characters

There seems little doubt that Stevenson intended Adam Weir, Lord Hermiston the Justice-Clerk, to dominate the novel. The original behind this figure, Robert Macqueen, Lord Braxfield, had had a strong appeal for him: in his commentary on Raeburn's portrait of Braxfield in *Virginibus Puerisque* he tells of Macqueen's rough and cruel speech, his use of 'the pure Scotch idiom', his combination of inhumanity and intrepidity. From Henry Cockburn's *Memorials of his Time* (1856) Stevenson would have read of Braxfield's 'colloquial way of arguing, in the form of question and answer', his lack of 'taste for refined enjoyment', and his 'strength of understanding, which gave him power without cultivation', and 'encouraged him to a more contemptuous disdain of natures less coarse than his own'. Two more aspects of Braxfield's character mentioned by Cockburn obviously influenced Stevenson in portraying Hermiston—his love of indulging in rough, obscene conversation, and his way of sending his 'panel' to the gallows 'with an insulting jest'. The picture is completed by mention of his harsh and unscrupulous treatment of political offenders—radicals, liberals, those out of step with orthodox political thinking. Despite the black impression that emerges, however, it is clear Stevenson had a certain admiration for the man—for his courage and vigour and complete disregard for public opinion. In the essay 'Some Portraits by Raeburn' in *Virginibus Puerisque* he wrote:

> It is probably more instructive to entertain a sneaking kindness for any unpopular person, and, among the rest, for Lord Braxfield, than to give way to perfect raptures of moral indignation against his abstract vices.

The qualities described by Cockburn are carefully woven into the characterisation of Adam Weir. The court scene describing the trial of Duncan Jopp brings out the 'colloquial way of arguing' and the kind of 'insulting jests' with which he sent a criminal to the gallows; his conversations with Archie and Lord Glenalmond illustrate that contempt he felt for 'natures less coarse than his own'; and Glenalmond himself speaks of the after-dinner 'sculduddery' Weir indulged in. Braxfield's harshness with political offenders is humorously reflected in Weir's remark criticising the 'Raadical gigot' served up to him one day at George

Square: 'It seems rather a sore kind of business that I should be all day in court haanging Raadicals, and get nawthing to my denner'. And the lack of humanity in Braxfield-Weir is seen throughout the first part of the novel, particularly in the treatment of his wife and his harshness towards his son. Yet Stevenson, in transforming Braxfield into Weir, transmutes the materials of a real-life case-history into a rounded human portrait. There is first of all the occasional muted note of tenderness. 'Puir bitch', he says, as he looks at his wife's dead body; and, as Dr. Gregory tells Archie, he had revealed fatherly feelings when Archie had been ill as a child. Then, as Archie realises the wrong he has done in criticising his father in public, another side of Weir's nature begins to light up—his high courage, and his Roman dedication to his legal work for preserving law and order. Glenalmond, the refined fastidious old judge who represents the opposite ideals and character, confesses to being impressed by Hermiston's vigour and strong will; and the toast he and Archie drink to the Lord Justice-Clerk is a kind of ritualistic acknowledgment of the greatness of the man. It is a tribute that the timid and over-sensitive tend to pay to the courageous and over-vigorous whom they may denounce but secretly admire. This rounding out of the characterisation of Hermiston is one of the achievements of the novel.

It is certain that Weir would have returned to play a major role in the unwritten final section when his son is accused of murder and put on trial; but in the novel as we have it in its middle and final sections he moves to the background and we are more concerned with the developing character of the son Archie in his relationships with the two Kirsties. From being the little moral prig under his mother's influence, the high-principled student objecting to capital punishment and being repelled by his father's coarseness and inhumanity, and the recluse refusing to mingle with society around Hermiston, Archie changes gradually into a person who can discern admirable qualities in his father, recognise his own immaturity, and react naturally to the handsome young woman he meets at

Hermiston. In the developing character study, the struggle between his scruples and his natural instinct is dramatically depicted in his relationship with young Christina; and Stevenson illustrates his lack of subtlety and his susceptibility to moral advice in the conversations he has with Frank Innes and old Kirstie. The conflict between his moral and instinctive natures, between the virtuous Roman in him and the human being, is graphically displayed in the last chapter—the final meeting with Christina at the Weaver's Stone. As the novel progresses, we become aware more and more of the emergence of some of his father's qualities, especially that Augustan remoteness and that determination to go his own way; but it is clear that Stevenson also meant to illustrate the legacy he had inherited from the 'riding Rutherfords', the latent violence and passion that revealed itself momentarily in his public denunciation of his father and that was to emerge fully in his confrontation with Innes after Christina's seduction and bring about Innes's death at the Weaver's Stone. Despite his development and maturing, Archie's problem remains: he cannot reconcile—perhaps is not fully aware of—the two forces acting on his nature. The very last paragraph of the novel stresses this psychological dilemma:

> . . . He felt her whole body shaken by the throes of distress, and had pity upon her beyond speech. Pity, and at the same time a bewildered fear of this explosive engine in his arms, whose works he did not understand, and yet had been tampering with . . . In vain he looked back over the interview; he saw not where he had offended . . .

Archie's relationship with the three women in the story further illuminates his own character in indirect ways and extends the psychological and dramatic scope of the novel. With his mother he is precociously pious; with old Kirstie he is the 'young master', handsome, virtuous, to be cherished and adored; with young Christina he is young Hermiston, her fate, her jo, to be gently mocked and passionately loved. Mrs. Weir is finally broken by contradictory tendencies and loyalties within herself: while reacting against her husband's persecution of the righteous, she tries to justify and even support his professional out-look and actions which she cannot understand. She is not all female weakness: she has 'enthusiasm' for her religion and feels the mystery and power of the natural scene. The conflict between her tenderness and piety on the one hand and her attempt to justify her husband's diametrically opposed ways on the other brings about inevitable break-down and death. Mrs. Weir has affinities with Mrs. Gourlay of *The House with the Green Shutters*, a woman also heavily dominated by her husband, and with Mrs. Guthrie, Chris's mother, in *Sunset Song*, but Jean Guthrie has a strength—a combination of smeddum and sweetness—that the other two lack.

Old Kirstie is very fully analysed by Stevenson himself. She is superficially the managing housekeeper figure, the Scottish retainer who combines loyalty to the family with outspokenness and a proper pride in herself. Underneath all this, however, she is the 'moorland Helen'—Woman rejoicing in her physical endowments, regretting her lack of fulfilment, but still prepared at fifty to use the charms that remain to influence the young man on whom she lavishes all her care and love. Her relationship with Archie represents an attempt to enjoy vicariously some of the pleasures of a lover. Stevenson makes it clear she is physi-cally as well as spiritually attracted to Archie. We see this particularly in Chapter 8 where we have an insight into her chagrin at the developing love affair between her niece and Archie, and where we see her admiring herself in the glass as she prepares to call on Archie. At the natural-istic level she is the bustling busybody criticising her relations and keeping the household in order; at the mythic level she is the ballad-singer extolling the primitive virtues of her Four Black Nephews and the archetypal valour of her dead brother, Gilbert Elliott. She is the character who gives her creator most scope in using the narrative rhythms and vigour of the Scots tongue.

Young Kirstie is the Scottish *ingénue*, bright and attrac-tive, lacking polish and sophistication, but with a great capacity for life and a strong sense of destiny. She too has the subtleties of Everywoman which Stevenson illustrates in the scene in the kirk and in the first meeting with Archie at the Stone. She has also a Scottish pride that brings out a violence when she is hurt. It is this latent explosive quality, this hidden volatile temperament, that is so powerfully illustrated in the final Weaver's Stone scene and was intended to be exploited in later scenes when she was to succumb to Frank Innes's charms. The naiveté of the Scots she uses is frequently thrown against the formality of Archie's English; and this tends to stress her greater humanity. In her conversation with Dand, her poet brother, and in the ballad she 'sooths' to Archie she reveals a feeling for the continuity and rhythms of life and an awareness of its hidden forces. Stevenson in his portrayal of Christina, as with that of her aunt, is throwing off inhibitions that had prevented him from portraying women in earlier works. In *Catriona* he had presented two women—Barbara Grant and Catriona—as two sides of the female character, the one extrovert and witty, the other introvert and sentimental; but these are only partially realised portraits, deriving perhaps from memories of 'Claire' (Kate Drummond), the girl he fell in love with and had to reject in his youth. Christina, as Professor Daiches suggests, seems to be a more full-blooded re-creation of 'Claire'.[1]

Frank Innes, who was to have seduced Christina and was intended to die a violent death for his villainy, is an almost stock figure, a *diabolus ex machina*. He is a thoroughly anglicised Scot, spoiled, arrogant, lazy, assuming superiority, and yet capable of turning on a charm that captivates the county gentry. At the beginning of the story he shows some desire to save Archie from the consequences of his rash action; but his subsequent activities—his sponging on the Hermiston household, his systematic besmirching of Archie's character, and his Iago-like pouring of poison into Archie's ear about his relationship with Christina—all these emphasise the Morality part he was

1. David Daiches in *Robert Louis Stevenson* (pp. 90-92) deals very fully and interestingly with the possible connections between 'Claire' and these characters from *Catriona* and *Weir*.

designed to play in the novel. Stevenson allows Innes none
of the redeeming qualities he allows to his other characters:
he rather tends to play the disapproving judge to his own
creation. But in doing this, Stevenson also interpolates
some social and moral commentary. In describing (in
Chapter 7) how Innes could impress the upper strata of
society round about Hermiston while failing completely
with the ordinary country people, Stevenson is making a
valid criticism of the anglified Scottish petty aristocracy:
Frank's social activities result in his being 'taken to the
bosom of the county people as unreservedly as he had been
repudiated by the country folk'. Later in the chapter at
the end of a passage in which Stevenson has allowed his
upper-class characters to gossip—

> He had done something disgraceful, my dear. What, was not
> precisely known, but that good kind young man, Mr. Innes,
> did his best to make light of it . . .

he becomes openly the moralising author of the essays:

> How wholly we all lie at the mercy of a single prater, not
> needfully with any malign purpose!

Stevenson elsewhere stresses this lack of design in Innes's
actions: he is led by an evil tendency rather than pursuing
deliberately a carefully laid out policy or course. In this
respect he is no Iago, but rather a Steerforth, but without
Steerforth's ability to impress the lower orders.

The Four Black Brothers, whom he fails to impress,
move from their legendary role to their naturalistic role
in assessing and contemning Innes. 'Hob thought him too
light, Gib too profane'. Clem would sum him up with a
sharp economy of words—'Yon's a drone'; but it was
Dand the poet who delivered the most crushing criticism:

> 'I'm told you're quite a poet,' Frank had said.
> 'Wha tell't ye that, mannie?' had been the unconciliating
> answer.
> 'O, everybody!' says Frank.
> 'God! Here's fame!' said the sardonic poet, and he had
> passed on his way.

Stevenson himself had a sharp word to say about Innes's snobbery and arrogance. Commenting on his lack of success with the Elliott family, the author moralises:

> Condescension is an excellent thing, but it is strange how one-sided the pleasure of it is! He who goes fishing among the Scots peasantry with condescension for a bait will have an empty basket by evening.

The combination of snobbery and arrogance with treachery and evil in Frank Innes limits at this point the melodramatic scope of the novel while extending its social significance, but in the end it would have been the melodramatic potential in his character that Stevenson would have exploited structurally.

The Four Black Brothers constitute one of the most striking features of the novel. Taken together in their symbolic role as avenging forces they have something of the choric function of the Furies in Aeschylus' *Oresteia*. They indeed exist on two levels—the legendary and the naturalistic. At the legendary level they bring out the epic nature of the family story of the Elliotts: they continue or reflect the heroic pattern traced by their father in his treatment of his attackers; and in their concern for vengeance they not only act the Furies but work as a group driven on by a kind of folk morality. At the naturalistic level they become differentiated as human beings. Hob, the eldest, naturally becomes the Laird of Cauldstaneslap. He who had taken a blood oath to avenge his father's death and had ridden his horse 'to and fro' over the body of Dickieson, one of the assailants, becomes an Elder of the Kirk and 'a rather graceless model of the rustic proprieties', making money in the war, and maintaining a peaceful household. Gib becomes a weaver and espouses radical politics, much to the disgust of Hermiston himself. Eventually he becomes a member of a narrow religious sect—'God's Remnant of the True Faithful'. Clem, who had wielded the cudgel so vigorously on that fateful night, becomes a respectable Glasgow business man and the wealthiest of the family. The fourth brother is Dand, poet and shepherd. He had played an active part in tracing the criminals responsible for his father's death; and now in ordinary life, as countryman and poet, he follows the example of Burns rather than that of his more respectable brothers. He is drinking friend to Hogg, 'had figured on the stool of repentance', and enjoys a reputation for wit and sociability. Of all the brothers Dand is perhaps the most attractive and intelligent. Stevenson, after differentiating the four, stresses that they were 'united by a close bond'—deep-rooted family loyalty; and it is clear, not only from the external evidence of records and documents, but also from the way the novel was structured from the beginning, that Stevenson had intended the brothers to return to their legendary corporate role to perform a service for Archie and Christina as they had performed one for their father.

There is then a diversity of method about the characterisation in *Weir of Hermiston*. The Judge himself steps out of his Braxfield frame to become a complex character of flesh and blood. Archie and young Christina are suffering, developing characters in contrast to the more set portraits of old Kirstie and Hermiston. Innes and Mrs. Weir are perhaps more stock characters, but each is designed to fulfil a function in the dramatic scheme of the book. The four brothers in their dual characterisation exemplify the two planes on which the novel exists: in their alternation between the romantic and the mundane, the symbolic and the naturalistic, they are a means of extending and enriching the background of the work.

The Language and the Quality of the Writing

Stevenson was a conscious artist in words: sometimes we are only too aware of the careful build-up of his sentences, the calculated rhythms, the deliberate balance. These qualities are found particularly in his essays, although they push through in various parts of his novels too and are not necessarily out of place there. But in the novels and stories Stevenson is capable also of a less formal, more direct style, the narrative parts having a dramatic pace about them, and the dialogue—especially when set in

Scots—a vivid informality and flexibility. By the time Stevenson writes *Weir*, he seems to have gained complete control over his linguistic structures. The rhythmic patterns of the descriptive passages help to bring out the dramatic situation or the psychological problem or state; the narrative style varies in tone and pace, now objective and authorial, now subjective and penetrating the character's psyche, now building up the dramatic or legendary atmosphere. In dialogue Stevenson can be on occasion the formal Victorian; but for the most part in *Weir* he attains a naturalness that can present contrast, and bring out sharpness and pace in passages of repartee and argument (as in the interview between Dand and Innes quoted on page 25 above).

His flowing style proceeding from general impression to significant detail in close-up is admirably suited to produce the kind of quick dramatic touch he requires frequently in *Weir of Hermiston*. He seems sometimes to imitate the movement of a roving camera in zooming from a middle-distance shot to a close-up of an object or person. Take the opening sentence of the novel:

> In the wild end of a moorland parish, far out of the sight of any house, there stands a cairn among the heather, and a little by the east of it, in the going down of the braeside, a monument with some verses half defaced . . .

Twice in that sentence the flow is held up on an object— first the cairn among the heather, which implies a vague reference to human existence; then, after the movement of 'the going down of the braeside', we come to rest on that monument with its defaced verses—a more definite sign of human activity in the desolate scene. The last sentence of the Introductory is a remarkable *tour de force*. It telescopes the whole story, giving out the themes and the *dramatis personae*, yet doing this not as a bald summary but as a prologue to a human drama over which destiny broods. It is this quality of an almost Greek sense of something preordained that makes the audience tingle to their sense of indoor comfort as they are given a foretaste of the tragedy about to be unfolded:

> . . . To this day, of winter nights, when the sleet is on the window and the cattle are quiet in the byre, there will be told again, amid the silence of the young and the additions and corrections of the old, the tale of the Justice-Clerk and of his son, young Hermiston, that vanished from men's knowledge; of the two Kirsties and the four Black Brothers of the Cauld-staneslap; and of Frank Innes, 'the young fool advocate', that came into these moorland parts to find his destiny.

Stevenson reaches in this novel a fine balance between narrative and dialogue. His technique in the earlier part of the story is the obvious one of letting the narrative do the preliminaries and building up gradually to the intensity or intimacy that emerges from direct speech. In the first chapter he fills in the historical background of the Ruther-fords before he deals with Jean Rutherford herself; and smoothly but briskly we move to the scenes of her first meeting with Weir and the engagement. Stevenson uses only snatches of dialogue here, but these are enough to convey the casual tone and the oddness of the coupling of the two contrasting personalities:

> 'Wha's she?' he said, turning to his host; and, when he had been told, 'Ay', says he, 'she looks menseful. She minds me—'
> . . . On the very eve of their engagement, it was related that one had drawn near to the tender couple, and had overheard the lady cry out, with the tones of one who talked for the sake of talking, 'Keep me, Mr. Weir, and what became of him?' and the profound accents of the suitor reply, 'Haangit, mem, haangit'.

This restrained use of dialogue within a narrative that is presented as a report of selected instances conveys an impression of something obliquely observed, of a midway stage between pure narrative and full dialogue. Stevenson reserves his fully paragraphed dialogue in this chapter for impassioned or confidential outbursts, as for example when husband and wife discuss Archie's fight with the 'blagyard lads', and when Archie as a youngster criticises his father as the hanging judge.

At certain points Stevenson intensifies the drama and character studies by moving into whole blocks of conversation. Sometimes he does this gradually as in Chapters 1, 6, and 7, letting the narrative gradually become less general and indirect until we reach a confrontation that has to be transmitted in direct speech. In this form the language has great colloquial directness and naturalness, the Scots adding an earthy flavour that removes the last signs of the literary and brings us close to life:

> 'Her and me were never cut out for one another,' he remarked at last. 'It was a daft-like marriage.' And then, with a most unusual gentleness of tone, 'Puir bitch,' said he, 'puir bitch!' Then suddenly: 'Where's Erchie?'
>
> Kirstie had decoyed him to her room and given him 'a jeely-piece'.
>
> 'Ye have some kind of gumption, too,' observed the judge, and considered his housekeeper grimly. 'When all's said,' he added, 'I micht have done waur—I micht have been marriet upon a skirling Jezebel like you!'

This confrontation between old Kirstie and Hermiston occurs at the end of Chapter 1; and if we examine Chapter 6 we find a similar steady build-up to even more intense confrontations—between Archie and Christina; but here the passages of dialogue are placed amidst the descriptions and the narrations so that the atmosphere of the setting strengthens the dramatic quality and reintroduces the note of destiny.

Stevenson's writing glows in the passages describing the setting of Hermiston: the feeling for the open air is counterpointed against the feeling of joy in shelter (a typically Scottish attitude that goes back to Henryson); and there are occasional touches that remind us of Stevenson's experiences at sea:

> . . . All beyond and about is the great field of the hills; the plover, the curlew, and the lark cry there; the wind blows as it blows in a ship's rigging, hard and cold and pure; and the hilltops huddle one behind another, like a herd of cattle, into the sunset.

The prose is stripped down here, direct and unadorned, apart from the vivid imagery of the hilltops as cattle huddled into the sunset; and there is a rhythmic shape that gives pace and drive to the whole. When he comes to describe the house of Hermiston, Stevenson produces an almost physical sensation as he identifies his reader with his character:

> . . . and Archie might sit of an evening and hear the squalls bugle on the moorland, and watch the fire prosper in the earthy fuel, and the smoke winding up the chimney, and drink deep of the pleasures of shelter.

Sometimes he stands back and surveys his subject as an artist would, before he proceeds to move inside and let us hear the thoughts, words and music of the character. Although Hermiston was meant to dominate, at times old Kirstie seems to be the most fully displayed character, because in presenting her and letting her speak and play her apparently peripheral part Stevenson uses a variety of linguistic styles to illuminate the different aspects of her personality. First we have the artist's impression, direct, brightly coloured in its external effects, and probing below the surface to suggest inner qualities:

> Kirstie was now over fifty, and might have sat to a sculptor. Long of limb, and still light of foot, deep-breasted, robust-loined, her golden hair not yet mingled with any trace of silver, the years had but caressed and embellished her. By the lines of a rich and vigorous maternity, she seemed destined to be the bride of heroes and the mother of their children; and behold, by the iniquity of fate, she had passed through her youth alone, and drew near to the confines of age, a childless woman.

Then we have the clan view of her as loyal retainer more than half in love with her young master whom she looks upon as something set apart. This is the generalised Kirstie—atavistic and essentially feminine. The style here is formal and balanced but retains a brightness of imagery that is sometimes elevated, sometimes homely:

> Her feeling partook of the loyalty of a clanswoman,
> the hero-worship of a maiden aunt, and the idolatry due to
> a god. No matter what he had asked of her, ridiculous or tragic,
> she would have done it and joyed to do it. Her passion,
> for it was nothing less, entirely filled her. It was a rich physical
> pleasure to make his bed or light his lamp for him when he
> was absent, to pull off his wet socks or wait on him at dinner
> when he returned.

The closest, most intimate aspect of Kirstie's presentation
emerges in her story-telling in Chapter 3. Here is Kirstie
the folk-voice, recorder of the family legends, preserver of
the traditions, the link between past, present and what is
to come. First we have in a light Scots the memory of her
father who was both notorious smuggler and pious and
savage disciplinarian. Generalised picture though it is, there
is a vivid quality about it, in its strong rhythms and hard
forthright style:

> 'I mind when I was a bairn getting mony a skelp and being
> shoo'd to bed like pou'try,' she would say. 'That would be
> when the lads and their bit kegs were on the road. We've had
> the riffraff of two-three counties in our kitchen, mony's the
> time, betwix' the twelve and the three; and their lanterns
> would be standing in the forecourt, ay, a score o' them at
> once. But there was nae ungodly talk permitted at Cauld-
> staneslap; my faither was a consistent man in walk and
> conversation; just let slip an aith, and there was the door
> to ye! . . .'

Then in the description of the journey of the avenging
Black Brothers as presented in Kirstie's Scots we have the
legendary note struck—the note that is an echo from the
opening paragraph and was presumably to return in the
sequel describing the attempted vengeance of the brothers
on Archie or Frank Innes:

> 'A' nicht long they gaed in the wet heath and jennipers, and
> whaur they gaed they neither knew nor cared, but just
> followed the bluidstains and the footprints o' their faither's
> murderers. And a' nicht Dandie had his nose to the grund like
> a tyke, and the ithers followed and spak' naething, neither

> black nor white. There was nae noise to be heard, but just
> the sough of the swalled burns, and Hob, the dour yin, risping
> his teeth as he gaed.'

The ballad-like effect of 'a' nicht long they gaed' (the long
vowels) and 'There was nae noise . . . but just the sough
of the swalled burns' (the hissing sounds with their note
of menace) is striking: it balances the drama in Stevenson's
own narrative earlier in the chapter before Kirstie has
taken up the tale. Stevenson uses English here with only
an occasional Scots word, but the Scottish ballad quality
is still there in the way the drama seems to evolve out of
the setting:

> . . . That was a race with death that the laird rode! In the mirk
> night, with his broken bridle and his head swimming, he dug
> his spurs to the rowels in the horse's side, and the horse, that
> was even worse off than himself, the poor creature! screamed
> out loud like a person as he went, so that the hills echoed
> with it, and the folks at Cauldstaneslap got to their feet about
> the table and looked at each other with white faces.

The high melodramatic touch comes in Kirstie's description
of the taking of the oath of vengeance; and here Stevenson
deliberately subordinates his own part as objective narrator
to the subjective role of legend-bearer assumed by Kirstie.
Here the Scots is at its most idiomatic and sinewy:

> . . . 'Wanting the hat,' continues my author, Kirstie, whom I
> but haltingly follow, for she told this tale like one inspired,
> 'wanting guns, for there wasna twa grains o' pouder in the
> house, wi' nae mair weepons than their sticks into their
> hands, the fower o' them took the road. Only Hob, and that
> was the eldest, hunkered at the door-sill where the blood had
> rin, fyled his hand wi' it, and haddit it up to Heeven in the
> way o' the auld Border aith. "Hell shall have her ain again
> this nicht!" he raired, and rode forth upon his earrand.'

The writing in *Weir* is at its most evocative and latently
dramatic at the beginning of the great love sequences in
Chapter 6. First the scene is described in its relation to
Archie's physical state: here the character comes very close
to the earth in these evocations of the stirrings of spring:

> On this particular Sunday, there was no doubt but that the
> spring had come at last. It was warm, with a latent shiver in

B

the air that made the warmth only the more welcome. The
shallows of the stream glittered and tinkled among bunches
of primrose. Vagrant scents of the earth arrested Archie by
the way with moments of ethereal intoxication. The grey,
Quakerish dale was still only awakened in places and patches
from the sobriety of its winter colouring; and he wondered
at its beauty; an essential beauty of the old earth it seemed
to him, not resident in particulars but breathing to him from
the whole.

Then as he enters the church, the scene is transformed into
a kind of half-physical, half-mystical experience that has
in its wake a glisk of tragedy:

> . . . He could not follow the prayer, not even the heads of it.
> Brightnesses of azure, clouds of fragrance, a tinkle of falling
> water and singing birds, rose like exhalations from some
> deeper, aboriginal memory, that was not his, but belonged to
> the flesh on his bones. His body remembered; and it seemed
> to him that his body was in no way gross, but ethereal and
> perishable like a strain of music; and he felt for it an exquisite
> tenderness as for a child, an innocent, full of beautiful instincts
> and destined to an early death.

There is alternation here between deep reverberations
('deeper, aboriginal memory; no way gross') and rising
rhythms ('singing birds, ethereal like a strain of music')
that requires just the kind of expanding sentence that
Stevenson has developed, a sentence that comes to its
conclusion on the alliteratively marked note of destiny.
Later, when the meeting of Archie and Christina has taken
place and Christina is already planning to see him again,
we have another variation of this kind of heightened style,
this time describing Christina's feelings in terms of the
physical and the spiritual:

> She was in love with herself, her destiny, the air of the hills,
> the benediction of the sun. All the way home, she continued
> under the intoxication of these sky-scraping spirits. At table
> she could talk freely of young Hermiston; gave her opinion
> of him off-hand and with a loud voice, that he was a handsome
> young gentleman, real well-mannered and sensible-like, but
> it was a pity he looked doleful. Only—the moment after—a
> memory of his eyes in church embarrassed her.

The pace of the rhetoric in the opening is maintained almost to the end; but between the middle and final sections of the passage there comes a shift from the matter-of-fact to the mental, and the slackening in the last sentence stresses Christina's secret feelings. In the opening sentence, the combination of the cosmic and the fateful is strikingly thematic.

In the end it is the skill with which Stevenson counterpoints passages of dialogue with resumed narration or description of scene and situation that impresses most. This quality is illustrated in the last chapter; but it is most movingly presented within the ballad-dramatic frame of the novel in Chapter 6—'Christina's Psalm-Book':

'Have you mind of Dand's song?' she answered. 'I think he'll have been trying to say what you have been thinking.'

'No, I never heard it,' he said. 'Repeat it to me, can you?'

'It's nothing wanting the tune,' said Kirstie.

'Then sing it me,' said he.

'On the Lord's Day? That would never do, Mr. Weir!'

'I am afraid I am not so strict a keeper of the Sabbath, and there is no one in the place to hear us, unless the poor old ancient under the stone.'

'No' that I'm thinking that really,' she said. 'By my way of thinking, it's just as serious as a psalm. Will I sooth it to ye, then?'

'If you please,' said he, and, drawing near to her on the tombstone, prepared to listen.

She sat up as if to sing. 'I'll only can sooth it to ye,' she explained. 'I wouldna like to sing it loud on the Sabbath. I think the birds would carry news of it to Gilbert,' and she smiled. 'It's about the Elliotts,' she continued, 'and I think there's few bonnier bits in the book-poets, though Dand has never got printed yet.'

And she began, in the low, clear tones of her half voice, now sinking almost to a whisper, now rising to a particular note which was her best, and which Archie learned to wait for with growing emotion:—

> 'O they rade in the rain, in the days that are gane,
>   In the rain and the wind and the lave,
> They shoutit in the ha' and they routit on the hill,
>   But they're a' quaitit noo in the grave.
> Auld, auld Elliotts, clay-cauld Elliotts, dour, bauld Elliotts of
>   auld!'

The dialogue is crisp and alive; the Scots style used for Christina has a youthful naiveté and appeal; and the whole passage moves inevitably into Christina's 'soothing' of Dand's ballad in which the personal story has merged into the family legend. Against this dialogue comes a narrative commentary in an English that is vivid and direct, and combines the pictorial with the emotional:

> All the time she sang she looked steadfastly before her, her knees straight, her hands upon her knee, her head cast back and up. The expression was admirable throughout, for had she not learned it from the lips and under the criticism of the author? When it was done, she turned upon Archie a face softly bright, and eyes gently suffused and shining in the twilight, and his heart rose and went out to her with boundless pity and sympathy. His question was answered. She was a human being tuned to a sense of the tragedy of life; there were pathos and music and a great heart in the girl.

If we can overlook certain stylistic lapses ('softly bright', 'gently suffused') we may say this is a picture that captures an attitude, a frozen moment of great beauty and significance such as might be enshrined in a work of art—a painting or a piece of sculpture. (Compare T. S. Eliot's *La Figlia che piange* and Wordsworth's *The Solitary Reaper*.) There is a natural progression or extension not only into the minds of the characters but also into the tragic patterns of life. Stevenson shows insight and poetic skill in linking the ephemeral with the universal in that phrase—'a human being tuned to a sense of the tragedy of life'.

Nature of the Novel: its Achievement

In that *Weir of Hermiston* moves from its opening Edinburgh setting to a country setting where important episodes take place in the open, it is a variant of the Stevensonian novel of adventure. Archie, the leading young man in the story, has to undergo experiences in a new and romantic setting, just as Jim Hawkins has to do in *Treasure Island* and David Balfour in *Kidnapped*. There is too something of the quality of a historical novel in the treatment of its central character the hanging judge, its Border story of the Elliott family, and its frequent references to the Covenanters and the Killing Time. A mature quality emerges in the treatment of characters. What we have at the heart of the novel is an extension of the kind of thing Stevenson was trying to do in *Catriona* and *The Master of Ballantrae*—a series of studies in human relationships: between members of a family, between man and woman, between two young men, and above all between father and son. It is perhaps more of a psychological than a social novel, although we do have fleeting impressions of life in Edinburgh legal and student circles, of country life on a Sunday, of the superficialities of county life and gossip. In the end, it is a study of the plight of a young couple we are concerened with, a couple whose innermost thoughts and feelings are displayed in conflict with powerful or unscrupulous personalities who in seeking to influence them threaten to destroy them.

What we have so far is a combination of adventure story, historical romance, and psychological novel; but this does not adequately account for the power of the work. Right from the beginning we are aware of that sense of tragic destiny that unifies the whole. The scene in the court strikes the note of the inexorable harshness of legal judgment; the confrontation of father and son in Chapter 3 presents the central *agon;* and the Elliott saga placed in the heart of Chapter 5 and linking the story with a legendary past deepens the scope and introduces an epic feature that was to extend into the main story. There is too a highly dramatic, even melodramatic, quality about the main character. Hermiston has the kind of *persona* that can dominate even when off stage, just as Caesar's spirit does in Shakespeare's play. The drama in the last scene of the novel is intensified by that vision that Christina has of the 'awful figure in a wig with an ironical and bitter smile'.

At certain points Stevenson deliberately presents a dramatic attitude or pose, rather in the manner of a tableau or a dramatic pause on the stage. At the end of Chapter 6 Frank is pictured as sitting 'alone by the table . . . smiling to himself richly'. He . . . 'brooded like a deity over the strands of that intrigue which was to shatter him before the summer waned'. Young Christina, as we have seen, is caught in a similar dramatic pose as she sings the ballad for Archie. Sometimes the potentially tragic quality is pointed by a self-conscious comment as at the end of the love scene in Chapter 6—'Fate played his game artfully with this poor pair of children', or when at the end of Chapter 8 Stevenson writes of old Kirstie—'She wore a tragic mask'.

The achievement of *Weir of Hermiston* lies in the placing of all its different parts, themes and levels, within a pattern of drama and destiny. It is the sense of the inevitable that drives the novel forward; and despite the struggles and individual temperaments and actions displayed there is a Greek feeling of Fate, of something pre-ordained, of human beings caught in a sequence of events from which they cannot escape. There is no doubt that a tragic and ironic situation was to develop for Archie, his father and Christina; and there is no doubt that the Four Black Brothers were to be drawn again into the dramatic action. The outcome is so implicit in the atmosphere and structure of the novel as we have it that we hardly need to supply an ending. *Weir of Hermiston*, in throwing up its shape, themes and destiny motif so sharply, and in breaking off before coming down to an explicit conclusion, has perhaps gained something of the power of a short story deliberately cut short in full flight.

J. T. Low

Weir of Hermiston

TO MY WIFE

I saw rain falling and the rainbow drawn
On Lammermuir. Hearkening I heard again
In my precipitous city beaten bells
Winnow the keen sea wind. And here afar,
Intent on my own race and place, I wrote.
  Take thou the writing: thine it is. For who
Burnished the sword, blew on the drowsy coal,
Held still the target higher, chary of praise
And prodigal of counsel – who but thou?
So now, in the end, if this the least be good,
If any deed be done, if any fire
Burn in the imperfect page, the praise be thine.

INTRODUCTORY

In the wild end of a moorland parish, far out of the sight of any house, there stands a cairn among the heather, and a little by east of it, in the going down of the braeside, a monument with some verses half defaced. It was here that Claverhouse shot with his own hand the Praying Weaver of Balweary, and the chisel of Old Mortality has clinked on that lonely gravestone. Public and domestic history have thus marked with a bloody finger this hollow among the hills; and since the Cameronian gave his life there, two hundred years ago, in a glorious folly, and without comprehension or regret, the silence of the moss has been broken once again by the report of firearms and the cry of the dying.

The Deil's Hags was the old name. But the place is now called Francie's Cairn. For a while it was told that Francie walked. Aggie Hogg met him in the gloaming by the cairn-side, and he spoke to her, with chattering teeth, so that his words were lost. He pursued Rob Todd (if any one could have believed Robbie) for the space of half a mile with pitiful entreaties. But the age is one of incredulity; these superstitious decorations speedily fell off; and the facts of the story itself, like the bones of a giant buried there and half dug up, survived, naked and imperfect, in the memory of the scattered neighbours. To this day, of winter nights, when the sleet is on the window and the cattle are quiet in the byre, there will be told again, amid the silence of the young and the additions and corrections of the old, the tale of the Justice-Clerk and of his son, young Hermiston, that vanished from men's knowledge; of the two Kirsties and the Four Black Brothers of the Cauldstaneslap; and of Frank Innes, 'the young fool advocate,' that came into these moorland parts to find his destiny.

Chapter One

Life and Death of Mrs. Weir

THE Lord Justice-Clerk was a stranger in that part of the
country; but his lady wife was known there from a child, as
her race had been before her. The old 'riding Rutherfords of
Hermiston,' of whom she was the last descendant, had been
famous men of yore, ill neighbours, ill subjects, and ill
husbands to their wives though not their properties. Tales
of them were rife for twenty miles about; and their name
was even printed in the page of our Scots histories, not
always to their credit. One bit the dust at Flodden; one was
hanged at his peel door by James the Fifth; another fell dead
in a carouse with Tom Dalyell; while a fourth (and that was
Jean's own father) died presiding at a Hell-Fire Club, of
which he was the founder. There were many heads shaken in
Crossmichael at that judgment; the more so as the man had a
villainous reputation among high and low, and both with
the godly and the worldly. At that very hour of his demise,
he had ten going pleas before the Session, eight of them
oppressive. And the same doom extended even to his agents;
his grieve, that had been his right hand in many a left-hand
business, being cast from his horse one night and drowned
in a peat-hag on the Kye-skairs; and his very doer (although
lawyers have long spoons) surviving him not long, and
dying on a sudden in a bloody flux.

In all these generations, while a male Rutherford was in
the saddle with his lads, or brawling in a change-house, there
would be always a white-faced wife immured at home in the
old peel or the later mansion-house. It seemed this succession
of martyrs bided long, but took their vengeance in the end,
and that was in the person of the last descendant, Jean.
She bore the name of the Rutherfords, but she was the
daughter of their trembling wives. At the first she was not
wholly without charm. Neighbours recalled in her, as a
child, a strain of elfin wilfulness, gentle little mutinies, sad

43

little gaieties, even a morning gleam of beauty that was not
to be fulfilled. She withered in the growing, and (whether it
was the sins of her sires or the sorrows of her mothers)
came to her maturity depressed, and, as it were, defaced; no
blood of life in her, no grasp or gaiety; pious, anxious,
tender, tearful, and incompetent.

It was a wonder to many that she had married – seeming
so wholly of the stuff that makes old maids. But chance cast
her in the path of Adam Weir, then the new Lord Advocate,
a recognised, risen man, the conqueror of many obstacles,
and thus late in the day beginning to think upon a wife. He
was one who looked rather to obedience than beauty, yet
it would seem he was struck with her at the first look. 'Wha's
she?' he said, turning to his host; and, when he had been
told, 'Ay,' says he, 'she looks menseful. She minds me——';
and then, after a pause (which some have been daring
enough to set down to sentimental recollections), 'Is she
releegious?' he asked, and was shortly after, at his own
request, presented. The acquaintance, which it seems
profane to call a courtship, was pursued with Mr. Weir's
accustomed industry, and was long a legend, or rather a
source of legends, in the Parliament House. He was
described coming, rosy with much port, into the drawing-
room, walking direct up to the lady, and assailing her with
pleasantries, to which the embarrassed fair one responded,
in what seemed a kind of agony, 'Eh, Mr. Weir!' or 'O,
Mr. Weir!' or 'Keep me, Mr. Weir!' On the very eve of
their engagement, it was related that one had drawn near
to the tender couple, and had overheard the lady cry out,
with the tones of one who talked for the sake of talking,
'Keep me, Mr. Weir, and what became of him?' and the
profound accents of the suitor reply, 'Haangit, mem,
haangit.' The motives upon either side were much debated.
Mr. Weir must have supposed his bride to be somehow
suitable; perhaps he belonged to that class of men who
think a weak head the ornament of women – an opinion
invariably punished in this life. Her descent and her estate
were beyond question. Her wayfaring ancestors and her
litigious father had done well by Jean. There was ready

money and there were broad acres, ready to fall wholly to the husband, to lend dignity to his descendants, and to himself a title, when he should be called upon the Bench. On the side of Jean, there was perhaps some fascination of curiosity as to this unknown male animal that approached her with the roughness of a ploughman and the *aplomb* of an advocate. Being so trenchantly opposed to all she knew, loved, or understood, he may well have seemed to her the extreme, if scarcely the ideal, of his sex. And besides, he was an ill man to refuse. A little over forty at the period of his marriage, he looked already older, and to the force of manhood added the senatorial dignity of years; it was, perhaps, with an unreverend awe, but he was awful. The Bench, the Bar, and the most experienced and reluctant witness, bowed to his authority – and why not Jeannie Rutherford?

The heresy about foolish women is always punished, I have said, and Lord Hermiston began to pay the penalty at once. His house in George Square was wretchedly ill-guided; nothing answerable to the expense of maintenance but the cellar, which was his own private care. When things went wrong at dinner, as they continually did, my lord would look up the table at his wife: 'I think these broth would be better to sweem in than to sup.' Or else to the butler: 'Here, M'Killop, awa' wi' this Raadical gigot – tak' it to the French, man, and bring me some puddocks! It seems rather a sore kind of a business that I should be all day in Court haanging Raadicals, and get nawthing to my denner.' Of course this was but a manner of speaking, and he had never hanged a man for being a Radical in his life; the law, of which he was the faithful minister, directing otherwise. And of course these growls were in the nature of pleasantry, but it was of a recondite sort; and uttered as they were in his resounding voice, and commented on by that expression which they called in the Parliament House 'Hermiston's hanging face' – they struck mere dismay into the wife. She sat before him speechless and fluttering; at each dish, as at a fresh ordeal, her eye hovered toward my lord's countenance and fell again; if he but ate in silence, unspeakable relief was her

portion; if there were complaint, the world was darkened.
She would seek out the cook, who was always her *sister in the
Lord*. 'O, my dear, this is the most dreidful thing that my
lord can never be contented in his own house!' she would
begin; and weep and pray with the cook; and then the cook
would pray with Mrs. Weir; and the next day's meal would
never be a penny the better – and the next cook (when she
came) would be worse, if anything, but just as pious. It was
often wondered that Lord Hermiston bore it as he did;
indeed, he was a stoical old voluptuary, contented with
sound wine and plenty of it. But there were moments when
he overflowed. Perhaps half a dozen times in the history of
his married life – 'Here! tak' it awa', and bring me a piece of
bread and kebbuck!' he had exclaimed, with an appalling
explosion of his voice and rare gestures. None thought to
dispute or to make excuses; the service was arrested; Mrs.
Weir sat at the head of the table whimpering without
disguise; and his lordship opposite munched his bread and
cheese in ostentatious disregard. Once only, Mrs. Weir had
ventured to appeal. He was passing her chair on his way into
the study.

'O, Edom!' she wailed, in a voice tragic with tears, and
reaching out to him both hands, in one of which she held a
sopping pocket-handkerchief.

He paused and looked upon her with a face of wrath, into
which there stole, as he looked, a twinkle of humour.

'Noansense!' he said. 'You and your noansense! What do
I want with a Christian faim'ly? I want Christian broth! Get
me a lass that can plain-boil a potato, if she was a whüre off
the streets.' And with these words, which echoed in her
tender ears like blasphemy, he had passed on to his study
and shut the door behind him.

Such was the housewifery in George Square. It was better
at Hermiston, where Kirstie Elliott, the sister of a neighbouring bonnet-laird, and an eighteenth cousin of the lady's, bore
the charge of all, and kept a trim house and a good country
table. Kirstie was a woman in a thousand, clean, capable,
notable; once a moorland Helen, and still comely as a blood
horse and healthy as the hill wind. High in flesh and voice

and colour, she ran the house with her whole intemperate soul, in a bustle, not without buffets. Scarce more pious than decency in those days required, she was the cause of many an anxious thought and many a tearful prayer to Mrs. Weir. Housekeeper and mistress renewed the parts of Martha and Mary; and though with a pricking conscience, Mary reposed on Martha's strength as on a rock. Even Lord Hermiston held Kirstie in a particular regard. There were few with whom he unbent so gladly, few whom he favoured with so many pleasantries. 'Kirstie and me maun have our joke,' he would declare, in high good-humour, as he buttered Kirstie's scones, and she waited at table. A man who had no need either of love or of popularity, a keen reader of men and of events, there was perhaps only one truth for which he was quite unprepared: he would have been quite unprepared to learn that Kirstie hated him. He thought maid and master were well matched; hard, handy, healthy, broad Scots folk, without a hair of nonsense to the pair of them. And the fact was that she made a goddess and an only child of the effete and tearful lady; and even as she waited at table her hands would sometimes itch for my lord's ears.

Thus, at least, when the family were at Hermiston, not only my lord, but Mrs. Weir too, enjoyed a holiday. Free from the dreadful looking-for of the miscarried dinner, she would mind her seam, read her piety books, and take her walk (which was my lord's orders), sometimes by herself, sometimes with Archie, the only child of that scarce natural union. The child was her next bond to life. Her frosted sentiment bloomed again, she breathed deep of life, she let loose her heart, in that society. The miracle of her mother-hood was ever new to her. The sight of the little man at her skirt intoxicated her with the sense of power, and froze her with the consciousness of her responsibility. She looked forward, and, seeing him in fancy grow up and play his diverse part on the world's theatre, caught in her breath and lifted up her courage with a lively effort. It was only with the child that she forgot herself and was at moments natural; yet it was only with the child that she had conceived and

managed to pursue a scheme of conduct. Archie was to be a
great man and a good; a minister if possible, a saint for
certain. She tried to engage his mind upon her favourite
books, Rutherford's *Letters*, Scougal's *Grace Abounding*, and
the like. It was a common practice of hers (and strange to
remember now) that she would carry the child to the Deil's
Hags, sit with him on the Praying Weaver's stone, and talk
of the Covenanters till their tears ran down. Her view of
history was wholly artless, a design in snow and ink; upon
the one side, tender innocents with psalms upon their lips;
upon the other, the persecutors, booted, bloody-minded,
flushed with wine: a suffering Christ, a raging Beelzebub.
Persecutor was a word that knocked upon the woman's
heart; it was her highest thought of wickedness, and the
mark of it was on her house. Her great-great-grandfather
had drawn the sword against the Lord's anointed on the field
of Rullion Green, and breathed his last (tradition said) in
the arms of the detestable Dalyell. Nor could she blind herself to this, that had they lived in those old days, Hermiston
himself would have been numbered alongside of Bloody
Mackenzie and the politic Lauderdale and Rothes, in the
band of God's immediate enemies. The sense of this moved
her to the more fervour; she had a voice for that name of
persecutor that thrilled in the child's marrow; and when
one day the mob hooted and hissed them all in my lord's
travelling carriage, and cried, 'Down with the persecutor!
down with Hanging Hermiston!' and mamma covered her
eyes and wept, and papa let down the glass and looked out
upon the rabble with his droll formidable face, bitter and
smiling, as they said he sometimes looked when he gave
sentence, Archie was for the moment too much amazed to
be alarmed, but he had scarce got his mother by herself
before his shrill voice was raised demanding an explanation:
Why had they called papa a persecutor?

'Keep me, my precious!' she exclaimed. 'Keep me, my
dear! this is poleetical. Ye must never ask me anything
poleetical, Erchie. Your faither is a great man, my dear,
and it's no for me or you to be judging him. It would be
telling us all, if we behaved ourselves in our several stations

the way your faither does in his high office; and let me hear
no more of any such disrespectful and undutiful questions!
No that you meant to be undutiful, my lamb; and your
mother kens that – she kens it well, dearie!' And so slid
off to safer topics, and left on the mind of the child an
obscure but ineradicable sense of something wrong.

Mrs. Weir's philosophy of life was summed in one
expression – tenderness. In her view of the universe, which
was all lighted up with a glow out of the doors of hell, good
people must walk there in a kind of ecstasy of tenderness.
The beasts and plants had no souls; they were here but for a
day, and let their day pass gently! And as for the immortal
men, on what black, downward path were many of them
wending, and to what a horror of an immortality! 'Are not
two sparrows,' 'Whosoever shall smite thee,' 'God sendeth
His rain,' 'Judge not, that ye be not judged' – these texts
made her body of divinity; she put them on in the morning
with her clothes and lay down to sleep with them at night;
they haunted her like a favourite air, they clung about her
like a favourite perfume. Their minister was a marrowy
expounder of the law, and my lord sat under him with
relish; but Mrs. Weir respected him from far off; heard
him (like the cannon of a beleaguered city) usefully booming
outside on the dogmatic ramparts; and meanwhile, within
and out of shot, dwelt in her private garden which she
watered with grateful tears. It seems strange to say of this
colourless and ineffectual woman, but she was a true
enthusiast, and might have made the sunshine and the glory
of a cloister. Perhaps none but Archie knew she could be
eloquent; perhaps none but he had seen her – her colour
raised, her hands clasped or quivering – glow with gentle
ardour. There is a corner of the policy of Hermiston, where
you come suddenly in view of the summit of Black Fell,
sometimes like the mere grass top of a hill, sometimes (and
this is her own expression) like a precious jewel in the
heavens. On such days, upon the sudden view of it, her hand
would tighten on the child's fingers, her voice rise like a
song. '*I to the hills!*' she would repeat. 'And O, Erchie,

arena these like the hills of Naphtali?' and her tears would
flow.

Upon an impressionable child the effect of this continual
and pretty accompaniment to life was deep. The woman's
quietism and piety passed on to his different nature un-
diminished; but whereas in her it was a native sentiment, in
him it was only an implanted dogma. Nature and the child's
pugnacity at times revolted. A cad from the Potterrow once
struck him in the mouth; he struck back, the pair fought it
out in the back stable lane towards the Meadows, and
Archie returned with a considerable decline in the number of
his front teeth, and unregenerately boasting of the losses of
the foe. It was a sore day for Mrs. Weir; she wept and prayed
over the infant backslider until my lord was due from Court,
and she must resume that air of tremulous composure with
which she always greeted him. The judge was that day in an
observant mood, and remarked upon the absent teeth.

'I am afraid Erchie will have been fechting with some of
they blagyard lads,' said Mrs. Weir.

My lord's voice rang out as it did seldom in the privacy of
his own house. 'I'll have nonn of that, sir!' he cried. 'Do
you hear me? – nonn of that! No son of mine shall be
speldering in the glaur with any dirty raibble.'

The anxious mother was grateful for so much support;
she had even feared the contrary. And that night when she
put the child to bed – 'Now, my dear, ye see!' she said, 'I
told you what your faither would think of it, if he heard ye
had fallen into this dreidful sin; and let you and me pray
to God that ye may be keepit from the like temptation or
stren'thened to resist it!'

The womanly falsity of this was thrown away. Ice and iron
cannot be welded; and the points of view of the Justice-
Clerk and Mrs. Weir were not less unassimilable. The
character and position of his father had long been a
stumbling-block to Archie, and with every year of his age
the difficulty grew more instant. The man was mostly silent;
when he spoke at all, it was to speak of the things of the
world, always in a worldly spirit, often in language that the
child had been schooled to think coarse, and sometimes

with words that he knew to be sins in themselves. Tenderness was the first duty, and my lord was invariably harsh. God was love; the name of my lord (to all who knew him) was fear. In the world, as schematised for Archie by his mother, the place was marked for such a creature. There were some whom it was good to pity and well (though very likely useless) to pray for; they were named reprobates, goats, God's enemies, brands for the burning; and Archie tallied every mark of identification, and drew the inevitable private inference that the Lord Justice-Clerk was the chief of sinners.

The mother's honesty was scarce complete. There was one influence she feared for the child and still secretly combated; that was my lord's; and half unconsciously, half in a wilful blindness, she continued to undermine her husband with his son. As long as Archie remained silent, she did so ruthlessly, with a single eye to heaven and the child's salvation; but the day came when Archie spoke. It was 1801, and Archie was seven, and beyond his years for curiosity and logic, when he brought the case up openly. If judging were sinful and forbidden, how came papa to be a judge? to have that sin for a trade? to bear the name of it for a distinction?

'I can't see it,' said the little Rabbi, and wagged his head.

Mrs. Weir abounded in commonplace replies.

'No, I canna see it,' reiterated Archie. 'And I'll tell you what, mamma, I don't think you and me's justifeed in staying with him.'

The woman awoke to remorse; she saw herself disloyal to her man, her sovereign and bread-winner, in whom (with what she had of wordliness) she took a certain subdued pride. She expatiated in reply on my lord's honour and greatness; his useful services in this world of sorrow and wrong, and the place in which he stood, far above where babes and innocents could hope to see or criticise. But she had builded too well – Archie had his answers pat: Were not babes and innocents the type of the kingdom of heaven? Were not honour and greatness the badges of the world? And at any rate, how about the mob that had once seethed about the carriage?

'It's all very fine,' he concluded, 'but in my opinion, papa has no right to be it. And it seems that's not the worst yet of it. It seems he's called "the Hanging Judge" – it seems he's crooool. I'll tell you what it is, mamma, there's a tex' borne in upon me: It were better for that man if a milestone were bound upon his back and him flung into the deepestmost pairts of the sea.'

'O, my lamb, ye must never say the like of that!' she cried. 'Ye're to honour faither and mother, dear, that your days may be long in the land. It's Atheists that cry out against him – French Atheists, Erchie! Ye would never surely even yourself down to be saying the same thing as French Atheists? It would break my heart to think that of you. And O, Erchie, here arena *you* setting up to *judge*? And have ye no forgot God's plain command – the First with Promise, dear? Mind you upon the beam and the mote!'

Having thus carried the war into the enemy's camp, the terrified lady breathed again. And no doubt it is easy thus to circumvent a child with catchwords, but it may be questioned how far it is effectual. An instinct in his breast detects the quibble, and a voice condemns it. He will instantly submit, privately hold the same opinion. For even in this simple and antique relation of the mother and the child, hypocrisies are multiplied.

When the Court rose that year and the family returned to Hermiston, it was a common remark in all the country that the lady was sore failed. She seemed to lose and seize again her touch with life, now sitting inert in a sort of durable bewilderment, anon waking to feverish and weak activity. She dawdled about the lasses at their work, looking stupidly on; she fell to rummaging in old cabinets and presses, and desisted when half through; she would begin remarks with an air of animation and drop them without a struggle. Her common appearance was of one who has forgotten something and is trying to remember; and when she overhauled, one after another, the worthless and touching mementoes of her youth, she might have been seeking the clue to that lost thought. During this period, she gave many gifts to the neighbours and house lasses, giving them with a manner of regret that embarrassed the recipients.

The last night of all she was busy on some female work, and toiled upon it with so manifest and painful a devotion that my lord (who was not often curious) inquired as to its nature.

She blushed to the eyes. 'O, Edom, it's for you!' she said. 'It's slippers. I – I hae never made ye any.'

'Ye daft auld wife!' returned his lordship. 'A bonny figure I would be, palmering about in bauchles!'

The next day, at the hour of her walk, Kirstie interfered. Kirstie took this decay of her mistress very hard; bore her a grudge, quarrelled with and railed upon her, the anxiety of a genuine love wearing the disguise of temper. This day of all days she insisted disrespectfully, with rustic fury, that Mrs. Weir should stay at home. But, 'No, no,' she said, 'It's my lord's orders,' and set forth as usual. Archie was visible in the acre bog, engaged upon some childish enterprise, the instrument of which was mire; and she stood and looked at him a while like one about to call; then thought otherwise, sighed, and shook her head, and proceeded on her rounds alone. The house lasses were at the burnside washing, and saw her pass with her loose, weary, dowdy gait.

'She's a terrible feckless wife, the mistress!' said the one.

'Tut,' said the other, 'the wumman's seeck.'

'Weel, I canna see nae differ in her,' returned the first. 'A füshionless quean, a feckless carline.'

The poor creature thus discussed rambled a while in the grounds without a purpose. Tides in her mind ebbed and flowed, and carried her to and fro like seaweed. She tried a path, paused, returned, and tried another; questing, forgetting her quest; the spirit of choice extinct in her bosom, or devoid of sequency. On a sudden, it appeared as though she had remembered, or had formed a resolution, wheeled about, returned with hurried steps, and appeared in the dining-room, where Kirstie was at the cleaning, like one charged with an important errand.

'Kirstie!' she began, and paused; and then with conviction, 'Mr. Weir isna speeritually minded, but he has been a good man to me.'

It was perhaps the first time since her husband's elevation that she had forgotten the handle to his name, of which the tender, inconsistent woman was not a little proud. And when Kirstie looked up at the speaker's face, she was aware of a change.

'Godsake, what's the maitter wi' ye, mem?' cried the housekeeper, starting from the rug.

'I do not ken,' answered her mistress, shaking her head. 'But he is not speeritually minded, my dear.'

'Here, sit down with ye! Godsake, what ails the wife?' cried Kirstie, and helped and forced her into my lord's own chair by the cheek of the hearth.

'Keep me, what's this?' she gasped. 'Kirstie, what's this? I'm frich'ened.'

They were her last words.

It was the lowering nightfall when my lord returned. He had the sunset in his back, all clouds and glory; and before him, by the wayside, spied Kirstie Elliott waiting. She was dissolved in tears, and addressed him in the high, false note of barbarous mourning, such as still lingers modified among Scots heather.

'The Lord peety ye, Hermiston! the Lord prepare ye!' she keened out. 'Weary upon me, that I should have to tell it!'

He reined in his horse and looked upon her with the hanging face.

'Has the French landit?' cried he.

'Man, man,' she said, 'is that a' ye can think of? The Lord prepare ye: the Lord comfort and support ye!'

'Is onybody deid?' says his lordship. 'It's no Erchie?'

'Bethankit, no!' exclaimed the woman, startled into a more natural tone. 'Na, na, it's no sae bad as that. It's the mistress, my lord; she just fair flittit before my e'en. She just gi'ed a sab and was by wi' it. Eh, my bonny Miss Jeannie, that I mind sae weel!' And forth again upon that pouring tide of lamentation in which women of her class excel and over-abound.

Lord Hermiston sat in the saddle beholding her. Then he seemed to recover command upon himself.

'Weel, it's something of the suddenest,' said he. 'But she was a dwaibly body from the first.'

And he rode home at a precipitate amble with Kirstie at his horse's heels.

Dressed as she was for her last walk, they had laid the dead lady on her bed. She was never interesting in life; in death she was not impressive; and as her husband stood before her, with his hands crossed behind his powerful back, that which he looked upon was the very image of the insignificant.

'Her and me were never cut out for one another,' he remarked at last. 'It was a daft-like marriage.' And then, with a most unusual gentleness of tone, 'Puir bitch,' said he, 'puir bitch!' Then suddenly: 'Where's Erchie?'

Kirstie had decoyed him to her room and given him 'a jeely-piece.'

'Ye have some kind of gumption, too,' observed the judge, and considered his housekeeper grimly. 'When all's said,' he added, 'I micht have done waur – I micht have been marriet upon a skirling Jezebel like you!'

'There's naebody thinking of you, Hermiston!' cried the offended woman. 'We think of her that's out of her sorrows. And could *she* have done waur? Tell me that, Hermiston – tell me that before her clay-cauld corp!'

'Weel, there's some of them gey an' ill to please,' observed his lordship.

Chapter Two

Father and Son

My Lord Justice-Clerk was known to many; the man Adam Weir perhaps to none. He had nothing to explain or to conceal; he sufficed wholly and silently to himself; and that part of our nature which goes out (too often with false coin) to acquire glory or love, seemed in him to be omitted. He did not try to be loved, he did not care to be; it is probable the very thought of it was a stranger to his mind. He was an admired lawyer, a highly unpopular judge; and he looked down upon those who were his inferiors in either distinction, who were lawyers of less grasp or judges not so much detested. In all the rest of his days and doings, not one trace of vanity appeared; and he went on through life with a mechanical movement, as of the unconscious, that was almost august.

He saw little of his son. In the childish maladies with which the boy was troubled, he would make daily inquiries and daily pay him a visit, entering the sick-room with a facetious and appalling countenance, letting off a few perfunctory jests, and going again swiftly, to the patient's relief. Once, a court holiday falling opportunely, my lord had his carriage, and drove the child himself to Hermiston, the customary place of convalescence. It is conceivable he had been more than usually anxious, for that journey always remained in Archie's memory as a thing apart, his father having related to him from beginning to end, and with much detail, three authentic murder cases. Archie went the usual round of other Edinburgh boys, the High School and the College; and Hermiston looked on, or rather looked away, with scarce an affectation of interest in his progress. Daily, indeed, upon a signal after dinner, he was brought in, given nuts and a glass of port, regarded sardonically, sarcastically questioned. 'Well, sir, and what have you donn with your book to-day?' my lord might begin, and set him posers in law Latin. To a child just stumbling into Corderius,

Papinian and Paul proved quite invincible. But papa had memory of no other. He was not harsh to the little scholar, having a vast fund of patience learned upon the bench, and was at no pains whether to conceal or to express his disappointment. 'Well, ye have a long jaunt before ye yet!' he might observe, yawning, and fall back on his own thoughts (as like as not) until the time came for separation, and my lord would take the decanter and the glass, and be off to the back chamber looking on the Meadows, where he toiled on his cases till the hours were small. There was no 'fuller man' on the bench; his memory was marvellous, though wholly legal; if he had to 'advise' extempore, none did it better; yet there was none who more earnestly prepared. As he thus watched in the night, or sat at table and forgot the presence of his son, no doubt but he tasted deeply of recondite pleasures. To be wholly devoted to some intellectual exercise is to have succeeded in life; and perhaps only in law and the higher mathematics may this devotion be maintained, suffice to itself without reaction, and find continual rewards without excitement. This atmosphere of his father's sterling industry was the best of Archie's education. Assuredly it did not attract him; assuredly it rather rebutted and depressed. Yet it was still present, unobserved like the ticking of a clock, an arid ideal, a tasteless stimulant in the boy's life.

But Hermiston was not all of one piece. He was, besides, a mighty toper; he could sit at wine until the day dawned, and pass directly from the table to the bench with a steady hand and a clear head. Beyond the third bottle, he showed the plebeian in a larger print; the low, gross accent, the low, foul mirth, grew broader and commoner; he became less formidable, and infinitely more disgusting. Now, the boy had inherited from Jean Rutherford a shivering delicacy, unequally mated with potential violence. In the playing-fields, and amongst his own companions, he repaid a coarse expression with a blow; at his father's table (when the time came for him to join these revels) he turned pale and sickened in silence. Of all the guests whom he there encountered, he had toleration for only one: David Keith Carnegie, Lord

Glenalmond. Lord Glenalmond was tall and emaciated, with long features and long delicate hands. He was often compared with the statue of Forbes of Culloden in the Parliament House; and his blue eye, at more than sixty, preserved some of the fire of youth. His exquisite disparity with any of his fellow-guests, his appearance as of an artist and an aristocrat stranded in rude company, riveted the boy's attention; and as curiosity and interest are the things in the world that are the most immediately and certainly rewarded, Lord Glenalmond was attracted by the boy.

'And so this is your son, Hermiston?' he asked, laying his hand on Archie's shoulder. 'He's getting a big lad.'

'Hout!' said the gracious father, 'just his mother over again – daurna say boo to a goose!'

But the stranger retained the boy, talked to him, drew him out, found in him a taste for letters, and a fine, ardent, modest, youthful soul; and encouraged him to be a visitor on Sunday evenings in his bare, cold, lonely dining-room, where he sat and read in the isolation of a bachelor grown old in refinement. The beautiful gentleness and grace of the old judge, and the delicacy of his person, thoughts, and language, spoke to Archie's heart in its own tongue. He conceived the ambition to be such another; and, when the day came for him to choose a profession, it was in emulation of Lord Glenalmond, not of Lord Hermiston, that he chose the Bar. Hermiston looked on at this friendship with some secret pride, but openly with the intolerance of scorn. He scarce lost an opportunity to put them down with a rough jape; and, to say truth, it was not difficult, for they were neither of them quick. He had a word of contempt for the whole crowd of poets, painters, fiddlers, and their admirers, the bastard race of amateurs, which was continually on his lips. 'Signor Feedle-eerie!' he would say. 'O, for Goad's sake, no more of the Signor!'

'You and my father are great friends, are you not?' asked Archie once.

'There is no man that I more respect, Archie,' replied Lord Glenalmond. 'He is two things of price. He is a great lawyer, and he is upright as the day.'

'You and he are so different,' said the boy, his eyes dwelling on those of his old friend, like a lover's on his mistress's.

'Indeed so,' replied the judge; 'very different. And so I fear are you and he. Yet I would like it very ill if my young friend were to misjudge his father. He has all the Roman virtues: Cato and Brutus were such; I think a son's heart might well be proud of such an ancestry of one.'

'And I would sooner he were a plaided herd,' cried Archie, with sudden bitterness.

'And that is neither very wise, nor I believe entirely true,' returned Glenalmond. 'Before you are done you will find some of these expressions rise on you like a remorse. They are merely literary and decorative; they do not aptly express your thought, nor is your thought clearly apprehended, and no doubt your father (if he were here) would say, "Signor Feedle-eerie!"'

With the infinitely delicate sense of youth, Archie avoided the subject from that hour. It was perhaps a pity. Had he but talked – talked freely – let himself gush out in words (the way youth loves to do and should), there might have been no tale to write upon the Weirs of Hermiston. But the shadow of a threat of ridicule sufficed; in the slight tartness of these words he read a prohibition; and it is likely that Glenalmond meant it so.

Besides the veteran, the boy was without confidant or friend. Serious and eager, he came through school and college, and moved among a crowd of the indifferent, in the seclusion of his shyness. He grew up handsome, with an open, speaking countenance, with graceful, youthful ways; he was clever, he took prizes, he shone in the Speculative Society. It should seem he must become the centre of a crowd of friends; but something that was in part the delicacy of his mother, in part the austerity of his father, held him aloof from all. It is a fact, and a strange one, that among his contemporaries Hermiston's son was thought to be a chip of the old block. 'You're a friend of Archie Weir's?' said one to Frank Innes; and Innes replied, with his usual flippancy and more than his usual insight: 'I know Weir, but

I never met Archie.' No one had met Archie, a malady most incident to only sons. He flew his private signal, and none heeded it; it seemed he was abroad in a world from which the very hope of intimacy was banished; and he looked round about him on the concourse of his fellow-students, and forward to the trivial days and acquaintances that were to come, without hope or interest.

As time went on, the tough and rough old sinner felt himself drawn to the son of his loins and sole continuator of his new family, with softnesses of sentiment that he could hardly credit and was wholly impotent to express. With a face, voice, and manner trained through forty years to terrify and repel, Rhadamanthus may be great, but he will scarce be engaging. It is a fact that he tried to propitiate Archie, but a fact that cannot be too lightly taken; the attempt was so unconspicuously made, the failure so stoically supported. Sympathy is not due to these steadfast iron natures. If he failed to gain his son's friendship, or even his son's toleration, on he went up the great, bare staircase of his duty, uncheered and undepressed. There might have been more pleasure in his relations with Archie, so much he may have recognised at moments; but pleasure was a by-product of the singular chemistry of life, which only fools expected.

An idea of Archie's attitude, since we are all grown up and have forgotten the days of our youth, it is more difficult to convey. He made no attempt whatsoever to understand the man with whom he dined and breakfasted. Parsimony of pain, glut of pleasure, these are the two alternating ends of youth; and Archie was of the parsimonious. The wind blew cold out of a certain quarter – he turned his back upon it; stayed as little as was possible in his father's presence; and when there, averted his eyes as much as was decent from his father's face. The lamp shone for many hundred days upon these two at table – my lord, ruddy, gloomy, and unreverend,[1] Archie with a potential brightness that was always dimmed and veiled in that society; and there were

[1] As in Edinburgh, Pentlands and Swanston editions, but *unreverent* in first and Tusitala editions.

not, perhaps, in Christendom two men more radically strangers. The father, with a grand simplicity, either spoke of what interested himself, or maintained an unaffected silence. The son turned in his head for some topic that should be quite safe, that would spare him fresh evidences either of my lord's inherent grossness or of the innocence of his inhumanity; treading gingerly the ways of intercourse, like a lady gathering up her skirts in a by-path. If he made a mistake, and my lord began to abound in matter of offence, Archie drew himself up, his brow grew dark, his share of the talk expired; but my lord would faithfully and cheerfully continue to pour out the worst of himself before his silent and offended son.

'Well, it's a poor hert that never rejoices!' he would say, at the conclusion of such a nightmare interview. 'But I must get to my plew-stilts.' And he would seclude himself as usual in the back room, and Archie go forth into the night and the city quivering with animosity and scorn.

Chapter Three

In the Matter of the Hanging of Duncan Jopp

IT chanced in the year 1813 that Archie strayed one day into
the Justiciary Court.[1] The macer made room for the son of
the presiding judge. In the dock, the centre of men's eyes,
there stood a whey-coloured, misbegotten caitiff, Duncan
Jopp, on trial for his life. His story, as it was raked out
before him in that public scene, was one of disgrace and vice
and cowardice, the very nakedness of crime; and the
creature heard and it seemed at times as though he understood – as if at times he forgot the horror of the place he
stood in, and remembered the shame of what had brought
him there. He kept his head bowed and his hands clutched
upon the rail; his hair dropped in his eyes and at times he
flung it back; and now he glanced about the audience in a
sudden fellness of terror, and now looked in the face of his
judge and gulped. There was pinned about his throat a
piece of dingy flannel; and this it was perhaps that turned the
scale in Archie's mind between disgust and pity. The creature
stood in a vanishing point; yet a little while, and he was still
a man, and had eyes and apprehension; yet a little longer,
and with a last sordid piece of pageantry, he would cease to
be. And here, in the meantime, with a trait of human nature
that caught at the beholder's breath, he was tending a sore
throat.

Over against him, my Lord Hermiston occupied the bench
in the red robes of criminal jurisdiction, his face framed in
the white wig. Honest all through, he did not affect the
virtue of impartiality; this was no case for refinement;
there was a man to be hanged, he would have said, and he
was hanging him. Nor was it possible to see his lordship,
and acquit him of gusto in the task. It was plain he gloried
in the exercise of his trained faculties, in the clear sight
which pierced at once into the joint of fact, in the rude,

[1] *Judiciary* in first and Tusitala editions, corrected to *Justiciary* in Edinburgh.
Pentlands and Swanston editions.

unvarnished gibes with which he demolished every figment
of defence. He took his ease and jested, unbending in that
solemn place with some of the freedom of the tavern; and
the rag of man with the flannel round his neck was hunted
gallowsward with jeers.

Duncan had a mistress, scarce less forlorn and greatly
older than himself, who came up, whimpering and curtsey-
ing, to add the weight of her betrayal. My lord gave her the
oath in his most roaring voice, and added an intolerant
warning.

'Mind what ye say now, Janet,' said he. 'I have an e'e
upon ye, I'm ill to jest with.'

Presently, after she was tremblingly embarked on her
story, 'And what made ye do this, ye auld runt?' the Court
interposed. 'Do ye mean to tell me ye was the panel's
mistress?'

'If you please, ma loard,' whined the female.

'Godsake! ye made a bonny couple,' observed his lordship; and there was something so formidable and ferocious
in his scorn that not even the galleries thought to laugh.

The summing up contained some jewels:—

'These two peetiable creatures seem to have made up
thegither, it's not for us to explain why.' – 'The panel, who
(whatever else he may be) appears to be equally ill set-out in
mind and boady.' – 'Neither the panel nor yet the old wife
appears to have had so much common sense as even to tell a
lie when it was necessary.' And in the course of sentencing,
my lord had this *obiter dictum*: 'I have been the means, under
God, of haanging a great number, but never just such a
disjaskit rascal as yourself.' The words were strong in themselves; the light and heat and detonation of their delivery,
and the savage pleasure of the speaker in his task, made
them tingle in the ears.

When all was over, Archie came forth again into a
changed world. Had there been the least redeeming greatness
in the crime, any obscurity, any dubiety, perhaps he might
have understood. But the culprit stood, with his sore throat,
in the sweat of his mortal agony, without defence or excuse:
a thing to cover up with blushes: a being so much sunk

beneath the zones of sympathy that pity might seem harm-
less. And the judge had pursued him with a monstrous,
relishing gaiety, horrible to be conceived, a trait for nightmares. It is one thing to spear a tiger, another to crush a
toad; there are aesthetics even of the slaughter-house; and
the loathsomeness of Duncan Jopp enveloped and infected
the image of his judge.

Archie passed by his friends in the High Street with
incoherent words and gestures. He saw Holyrood in a
dream, remembrance of its romance awoke in him and
faded; he had a vision of the old radiant stories, of Queen
Mary and Prince Charlie, of the hooded stag, of the splend-
our and crime, the velvet and bright iron of the past; and
dismissed them with a cry of pain. He lay and moaned in the
Hunter's Bog, and the heavens were dark above him and
the grass of the field an offence. 'This is my father,' he said.
'I draw my life from him; the flesh upon my bones is his,
the bread I am fed with is the wages of these horrors.' He
recalled his mother, and ground his forehead in the earth.
He thought of flight, and where was he to flee to? of other
lives, but was there any life worth living in this den of
savage and jeering animals?

The interval before the execution was like a violent dream.
He met his father; he would not look at him, he could not
speak to him. It seemed there was no living creature but
must have been swift to recognise that imminent animosity;
but the hide of the Justice-Clerk remained impenetrable.
Had my lord been talkative, the truce could never have
subsisted; but he was by fortune in one of his humours of
sour silence; and under the very guns of his broadside,
Archie nursed the enthusiasm of rebellion. It seemed to
him, from the top of his nineteen years' experience, as if he
were marked at birth to be the perpetrator of some signal
action, to set back fallen Mercy, to overthrow the usurping
devil that sat, horned and hoofed, on her throne. Seductive
Jacobin figments, which he had often refuted at the Speculative, swam up in his mind and startled him as with voices:
and he seemed to himself to walk accompanied by an almost
tangible presence of new beliefs and duties.

On the named morning he was at the place of execution. He saw the fleering rabble, the flinching wretch produced. He looked on for a while at a certain parody of devotion, which seemed to strip the wretch of his last claim to manhood. Then followed the brutal instant of extinction, and the paltry dangling of the remains like a broken jumping-jack. He had been prepared for something terrible, not for this tragic meanness. He stood a moment silent, and then – 'I denounce this God-defying murder,' he shouted; and his father, if he must have disclaimed the sentiment, might have owned the stentorian voice with which it was uttered.

Frank Innes dragged him from the spot. The two handsome lads followed the same course of study and recreation, and felt a certain mutual attraction, founded mainly on good looks. It had never gone deep; Frank was by nature a thin, jeering creature, not truly susceptible whether of feeling or inspiring friendship; and the relation between the pair was altogether on the outside, a thing of common knowledge and the pleasantries that spring from a common acquaintance. The more credit to Frank that he was appalled by Archie's outburst, and at least conceived the design of keeping him in sight, and, if possible, in hand, for the day. But Archie, who had just defied – was it God or Satan? – would not listen to the word of a college companion.

'I will not go with you,' he said. 'I do not desire your company, sir; I would be alone.'

'Here, Weir, man, don't be absurd,' said Innes, keeping a tight hold upon his sleeve. 'I will not let you go until I know what you mean to do with yourself; it's no use brandishing that staff.' For indeed at that moment Archie had made a sudden – perhaps a warlike – movement. 'This has been the most insane affair; you know it has. You know very well that I'm playing the good Samaritan. All I wish is to keep you quiet.'

'If quietness is what you wish, Mr. Innes,' said Archie, 'and you will promise to leave me entirely to myself, I will tell you so much, that I am going to walk in the country and admire the beauties of nature.'

'Honour bright?' asked Frank.

C

'I am not in the habit of lying, Mr. Innes,' retorted Archie. 'I have the honour of wishing you good-day.'

'You won't forget the Spec.?' asked Innes.

'The Spec.?' said Archie. 'O no, I won't forget the Spec.'

And the one young man carried his tortured spirit forth of the city and all the day long, by one road and another, in an endless pilgrimage of misery; while the other hastened smilingly to spread the news of Weir's access of insanity, and to drum up for that night a full attendance at the Speculative, where further eccentric developments might certainly be looked for. I doubt if Innes had the least belief in his prediction; I think it flowed rather from a wish to make the story as good and the scandal as great as possible; not from any ill-will to Archie – from the mere pleasure of beholding interested faces. But for all that his words were prophetic. Archie did not forget the Spec.; he put in an appearance there at the due time, and, before the evening was over, had dealt a memorable shock to his companions. It chanced he was the president of the night. He sat in the same room where the Society still meets – only the portraits were not there: the men who afterwards sat for them were then but beginning their careers. The same lustre of many tapers shed its light over the meeting; the same chair, perhaps, supported him that so many of us have sat in since. At times he seemed to forget the business of the evening, but even in these periods he sat with a great air of energy and determination. At times he meddled bitterly, and launched with defiance those fines which are the precious and rarely used artillery of the president. He little thought, as he did so, how he resembled his father, but his friends remarked upon it, chuckling. So far, in his high place above his fellow-students, he seemed set beyond the possibility of any scandal; but his mind was made up – he was determined to fulfil the sphere of his offence. He signed to Innes (whom he had just fined, and who had just impeached his ruling) to succeed him in the chair, stepped down from the platform, and took his place by the chimney-piece, the shine of many wax tapers from above illuminating his pale face, the glow of the great red fire relieving from behind his slim figure. He had to propose, as an amendment to the next subject in the case-book, 'Whether capital punishment be consistent with God's will or man's policy?'

A breath of embarrassment, of something like aiarm, passed round the room, so daring did these words appear upon the lips of Hermiston's only son. But the amendment was not seconded; the previous question was promptly moved and unanimously voted, and the momentary scandal smuggled by. Innes triumphed in the fulfilment of his prophecy. He and Archie were now become the heroes of the night; but whereas every one crowded about Innes, when the meeting broke up, but one of all his companions came to speak to Archie.

'Weir, man! That was an extraordinary raid of yours!' observed this courageous member, taking him confidentially by the arm as they went out.

'I don't think it a raid,' said Archie grimly. 'More like a war. I saw that poor brute hanged this morning, and my gorge rises at it yet.'

'Hut-tut,' returned his companion, and, dropping his arm like something hot, he sought the less tense society of others.

Archie found himself alone. The last of the faithful – or was it only the boldest of the curious? – had fled. He watched the black huddle of his fellow-students draw off down and up the street, in whispering or boisterous gangs. And the isolation of the moment weighed upon him like an omen and an emblem of his destiny in life. Bred up in unbroken fear himself, among trembling servants, and in a house which (at the least ruffle in the master's voice) shuddered into silence, he saw himself on the brink of the red valley of war, and measured the danger and length of it with awe. He made a détour in the glimmer and shadow of the streets, came into the back stable lane, and watched for a long while the light burn steady in the Judge's room. The longer he gazed upon that illuminated window-blind, the more blank became the picture of the man who sat behind it, endlessly turning over sheets of process, pausing to sip a glass of port, or rising and passing heavily about his book-lined walls to verify some reference. He could not combine the brutal judge and the industrious, dispassionate student; the connecting link escaped him; from such a dual nature, it was impossible he should predict behaviour; and he asked himself if he had done well to plunge into a business of which the end could not be foreseen? and presently after, with a sickening decline of confidence, if he had done loyally to strike his father? For he had struck him – defied him twice over and before a cloud of witnesses – struck him a public buffet before crowds. Who had called him to judge his father in these precarious and high questions? The office was usurped. It might have become a stranger; in a son – there was no blinking it – in a son, it was disloyal. And now, between these two natures so antipathetic, so hateful to each other, there was depending an unpardonable affront: and the providence of God alone might foresee the manner in which it would be resented by Lord Hermiston.

These misgivings tortured him all night and arose with him in the winter's morning; they followed him from class to class, they made him shrinkingly sensitive to every shade of manner in his companions, they sounded in his ears through the current voice of the professor; and he brought them home with him at night unabated and indeed increased. The cause of this increase lay in a chance encounter with the celebrated Dr. Gregory. Archie stood looking vaguely in the lighted window of a book-shop, trying to nerve himself for the approaching ordeal. My lord and he had met and parted in the morning as they had now done for long, with scarcely the ordinary civilities of life; and it was plain to the son that nothing had yet reached the father's ears. Indeed, when he recalled the awful countenance of my lord, a timid hope sprang up in him that perhaps there would be found no one bold enough to carry tales. If this were so, he asked himself, would he begin again? and he found no answer. It was at this moment that a hand was laid upon his arm, and a voice said in his ear, 'My dear Mr. Archie, you had better come and see me.'

He started, turned round, and found himself face to face with Dr. Gregory. 'And why should I come to see you?' he asked, with the defiance of the miserable.

'Because you are looking exceeding ill,' said the doctor, 'and you very evidently want looking after, my young friend. Good folk are scarce, you know; and it is not every one that would be quite so much missed as yourself. It is not every one that Hermiston would miss.'

And with a nod and a smile, the doctor passed on.

A moment after, Archie was in pursuit, and had in turn, but more roughly, seized him by the arm.

'What do you mean? what did you mean by saying that? What makes you think that Hermis— my father would have missed me?'

The doctor turned about and looked him all over with a clinical eye. A far more stupid man than Dr. Gregory might have guessed the truth; but ninety-nine out of a hundred, even if they had been equally inclined to kindness would have blundered by some touch of charitable exaggeration. The doctor was better inspired. He knew the father well; in that white face of intelligence and suffering, he divined something of the son; and he told, without apology or adornment, the plain truth.

'When you had the measles, Mr. Archibald, you had them gey and ill; and I thought you were going to slip between my fingers,' he said. 'Well, your father was anxious. How did I know it? says you. Simply because I am a trained observer. The sign that I saw him make, ten thousand would have missed; and perhaps – *perhaps*, I say, because he's a hard man to judge of – but perhaps he never made another. A strange thing to consider! It was this. One day I came to him: "Hermiston," said I, "there's a change." He never said a word, just glowered at me (if ye'll pardon the phrase) like a wild beast. "A change for the better," said I. And I distinctly heard him take his breath.'

The doctor left no opportunity for anticlimax; nodding his cocked hat (a piece of antiquity to which he clung) and repeating 'Distinctly' with raised eyebrows, he took his departure, and left Archie speechless in the street.

The anecdote might be called infinitely little, and yet its meaning for Archie was immense. 'I did not know the old man had so much blood in him.' He had never dreamed this

sire of his, this aboriginal antique, this adamantine Adam,
had even so much of a heart as to be moved in the least
degree for another – and that other himself, who had
insulted him! With the generosity of youth, Archie was
instantly under arms upon the other side: had instantly
created a new image of Lord Hermiston, that of a man
who was all iron without and all sensibility within. The
mind of the vile jester, the tongue that had pursued Duncan
Jopp with unmanly insults, the unbeloved countenance that
he had known and feared for so long, were all forgotten;
and he hastened home, impatient to confess his misdeeds,
impatient to throw himself on the mercy of this imaginary
character.

He was not to be long without a rude awakening. It was
in the gloaming when he drew near the doorstep of the
lighted house, and was aware of the figure of his father
approaching from the opposite side. Little daylight lingered;
but on the door being opened, the strong yellow shine of the
lamp gushed out upon the landing and shone full on Archie,
as he stood, in the old-fashioned observance of respect, to
yield precedence. The Judge came without haste, stepping
stately and firm; his chin raised, his face (as he entered the
lamplight) strongly illumined, his mouth set hard. There was
never a wink of change in his expression; without looking
to the right or left, he mounted the stair, passed close to
Archie, and entered the house. Instinctively, the boy, upon
his first coming, had made a movement to meet him;
instinctively, he recoiled against the railing, as the old man
swept by him in a pomp of indignation. Words were needless; he knew all – perhaps more than all – and the hour of
judgment was at hand.

It is possible that, in this sudden revulsion of hope, and
before these symptoms of impending danger, Archie might
have fled. But not even that was left to him. My lord, after
hanging up his cloak and hat, turned round in the lighted
entry, and made him an imperative and silent gesture with
his thumb, and with the strange instinct of obedience,
Archie followed him into the house.

All dinner-time there reigned over the Judge's table a

palpable silence, and as soon as the solids were despatched he rose to his feet.

'M'Killop, tak' the wine into my room,' said he; and then to his son: 'Archie, you and me has to have a talk.'

It was at this sickening moment that Archie's courage, for the first and last time, entirely deserted him. 'I have an appointment,' said he.

'It'll have to be broken, then,' said Hermiston, and led the way into his study.

The lamp was shaded, the fire trimmed to a nicety, the table covered deep with orderly documents, the backs of law books made a frame upon all sides that was only broken by the window and the doors.

For a moment Hermiston warmed his hands at the fire, presenting his back to Archie; then suddenly disclosed on him the terrors of the Hanging Face.

'What's this I hear of ye?' he asked.

There was no answer possible to Archie.

'I'll have to tell ye, then,' pursued Hermiston. 'It seems ye've been skirling against the father that begot ye, and one of his Maijesty's Judges in this land; and that in the public street, and while an order of the Court was being executit. Forbye which, it would appear that ye've been airing your opeenions in a Coallege Debatin' Society'; he paused a moment: and then, with extraordinary bitterness, added: 'Ye damned eediot.'

'I had meant to tell you,' stammered Archie. 'I see you are well informed.'

'Muckle obleeged to ye,' said his lordship, and took his usual seat. 'And so you disapprove of Caapital Punishment?' he added.

'I am sorry, sir, I do,' said Archie.

'I am sorry, too,' said his lordship. 'And now, if you please, we shall approach this business with a little more parteecularity. I hear that at the hanging of Duncan Jopp – and, man! ye had a fine client there – in the middle of all the riff-raff of the ceety, ye thought fit to cry out, "This is a damned murder, and my gorge rises at the man that haangit him." '

'No, sir, these were not my words,' cried Archie.

'What were yer words, then?' asked the Judge.

'I believe I said, "I denounce it as a murder!" ' said the son. 'I beg your pardon – a God-defying murder. I have no wish to conceal the truth,' he added, and looked his father for a moment in the face.

'God, it would only need that of it next!' cried Hermiston. 'There was nothing about your gorge rising, then?'

'That was afterwards, my lord, as I was leaving the Speculative. I said I had been to see the miserable creature hanged, and my gorge rose at it.'

'Did ye, though?' said Hermiston. 'And I suppose ye knew who haangit him?'

'I was present at the trial; I ought to tell you that, I ought to explain. I ask your pardon beforehand for any expression that may seem undutiful. The position in which I stand is wretched,' said the unhappy hero, now fairly face to face with the business he had chosen. 'I have been reading some of your cases. I was present while Jopp was tried. It was a hideous business. Father, it was a hideous thing! Grant he was vile, why should you hunt him with a vileness equal to his own? It was done with glee – that is the word – you did it with glee; and I looked on, God help me! with horror.'

'You're a young gentleman that doesna approve of Caapital Punishment,' said Hermiston. 'Weel, I'm an auld man that does. I was glad to get Jopp haangit, and what for would I pretend I wasna? You're all for honesty, it seems; you couldn't even steik your mouth on the public street. What for should I steik mines upon the bench, the King's officer, bearing the sword, a dreid to evil-doers, as I was from the beginning, and as I will be to the end! Mair than enough of it! Heedious! I never gave twa thoughts to heediousness, I have no call to be bonny. I'm a man that gets through with my day's business, and let that suffice.'

The ring of sarcasm had died out of his voice as he went on; the plain words became invested with some of the dignity of the Justice-seat.

'It would be telling you if you could say as much,' the speaker resumed. 'But ye cannot. Ye've been reading some of my cases, ye say. But it was not for the law in them, it was to spy out your faither's nakedness, a fine employment in a son. You're splairging; you're running at lairge in life like a wild nowt. It's impossible you should think any longer of coming to the Bar. You're not fit for it; no splairger is. And another thing: son of mines or no son of mines, you have flung fylement in public on one of the Senators of the Coallege of Justice, and I would make it my business to see that ye were never admitted there yourself. There is a kind of a decency to be observit. Then comes the next of it – what am I to do with ye next? Ye'll have to find some kind of a trade, for I'll never support ye in indleset. What do ye fancy ye'll be fit for? The pulpit? Na, they could never get diveenity into that bloackhead. Him that the law of man whammles is no likely to do muckle better by the law of God. What would ye make of hell? Wouldna your gorge rise at that? Na, there's no room for splairgers under the fower quarters of John Calvin. What else is there? Speak up. Have ye got nothing of your own?'

'Father, let me go to the Peninsula,' said Archie. 'That's all I'm fit for – to fight.'

'All? quo' he!' returned the Judge. 'And it would be enough too, if I thought it. But I'll never trust ye so near the French, you that's so Frenchifeed.'

'You do me injustice there, sir,' said Archie. 'I am loyal; I will not boast; but any interest I may have ever felt in the French——'

'Have ye been so loyal to me?' interrupted his father.

There came no reply.

'I think not,' continued Hermiston. 'And I would send no man to be a servant to the King, God bless him! that has proved such a shaughling son to his own faither. You can splairge here on Edinburgh street, and where's the hairm? It doesna play buff on me! And if there were twenty thousand eediots like yourself, sorrow a Duncan Jopp would hang the fewer. But there's no splairging possible in a camp; and if you were to go to it, you would find out for yourself whether Lord Well'n'ton approves of caapital punishment or not. You a sodger!' he cried, with a sudden burst of scorn. 'Ye auld wife, the sodjers would bray at ye like cuddies!'

As at the drawing of a curtain, Archie was aware of some illogicality in his position, and stood abashed. He had a strong impression, besides, of the essential valour of the old gentleman before him, how conveyed it would be hard to say.

'Well, have ye no other proposeetion?' said my lord again.

'You have taken this so calmly, sir, that I cannot but stand ashamed,' began Archie.

'I'm nearer voamiting, though, than you would fancy,' said my lord.

The blood rose to Archie's brow.

'I beg your pardon, I should have said that you had accepted my affront. . . . I admit it was an affront; I did not think to apologise, but I do, I ask your pardon; it will not be so again, I pass you my word of honour. . . . I should have said that I admired your magnanimity with – this – offender,' Archie concluded with a gulp.

'I have no other son, ye see,' said Hermiston. 'A bonny one I have gotten! But I must just do the best I can wi' him, and what am I to do? If ye had been younger, I would have wheepit ye for this rideeculous exhibeetion. The way it is, I have just to grin and bear. But one thing is to be clearly understood. As a faither, I must grin and bear it; but if I had been the Lord Advocate instead of the Lord Justice-Clerk, son or no son, Mr. Erchibald Weir would have been in a jyle the night.'

Archie was now dominated. Lord Hermiston was coarse and cruel; and yet the son was aware of a bloomless nobility, an ungracious abnegation of the man's self in the man's office. At every word, this sense of the greatness of Lord Hermiston's spirit struck more home; and along with it that of his own impotence, who had struck – and perhaps basely struck – at his own father, and not reached so far as to have even nettled him.

'I place myself in your hands without reserve,' he said.

'That's the first sensible word I've had of ye the night,' said Hermiston. 'I can tell ye, that would have been the end of it, the one way or the other; but it's better ye should

come there yourself, than what I would have had to hirstle
ye. Weel, by my way of it – and my way is the best – there's
just the one thing it's possible that ye might be with decency,
and that's a laird. Ye'll be out of hairm's way at the least of
it. If ye have to rowt, ye can rowt amang the kye; and the
maist feck of the caapital punishment ye're like to come
across'll be guddling trouts. Now, I'm for no idle lairdies;
every man has to work, if it's only at peddling ballants; to
work, or to be wheeped, or to be haangit. If I set ye down at
Hermiston, I'll have to see you work that place the way it
has never been workit yet; ye must ken about the sheep like
a herd; ye must be my grieve there, and I'll see that I gain
by ye. Is that understood?'

'I will do my best,' said Archie.

'Well, then, I'll send Kirstie word the morn, and ye can go
yourself the day after,' said Hermiston. 'And just try to be
less of an eediot!' he concluded, with a freezing smile, and
turned immediately to the papers on his desk.

Chapter Four

Opinions of the Bench

LATE the same night, after a disordered walk, Archie was admitted into Lord Glenalmond's dining-room, where he sat, with a book upon his knee, beside three frugal coals of fire. In his robes upon the bench, Glenalmond had a certain air of burliness: plucked of these, it was a may-pole of a man that rose unsteadily from his chair to give his visitor welcome. Archie had suffered much in the last days, he had suffered again that evening; his face was white and drawn, his eyes wild and dark. But Lord Glenalmond greeted him without the least mark of surprise or curiosity.

'Come in, come in,' said he. 'Come in and take a seat. Carstairs' (to his servant) 'make up the fire, and then you can bring a bit of supper,' and again to Archie, with a very trivial accent: 'I was half expecting you,' he added.

'No supper,' said Archie. 'It is impossible that I should eat.'

'Not impossible,' said the tall old man, laying his hand upon his shoulder, 'and, if you will believe me, necessary.'

'You know what brings me?' said Archie, as soon as the servant had left the room.

'I have a guess, I have a guess,' replied Glenalmond. 'We will talk of it presently – when Carstairs has come and gone, and you have had a piece of my good Cheddar cheese and a pull at the porter tankard: not before.'

'It is impossible I should eat,' repeated Archie.

'Tut, tut!' said Lord Glenalmond. 'You have eaten nothing to-day, and I venture to add, nothing yesterday. There is no case that may not be made worse: this may be a very disagreeable business, but if you were to fall sick and die, it would be still more so, and for all concerned – for all concerned.'

76

'I see you must know all,' said Archie. 'Where did you hear it?'

'In the mart of scandal, in the Parliament House,' said Glenalmond. 'It runs riot below among the bar and the public, but it sifts up to us upon the bench, and rumour has some of her voices even in the divisions.'

Carstairs returned at this moment, and rapidly laid out a little supper; during which Lord Glenalmond spoke at large and a little vaguely on indifferent subjects, so that it might be rather said of him that he made a cheerful noise, than that he contributed to human conversation; and Archie sat upon the other side, not heeding him, brooding over his wrongs and errors.

But so soon as the servant was gone, he broke forth again at once. 'Who told my father? Who dared to tell him? Could it have been you?'

'No, it was not me,' said the Judge; 'although – to be quite frank with you, and after I had seen and warned you – it might have been me. I believe it was Glenkindie.'

'That shrimp!' cried Archie.

'As you say, that shrimp,' returned my lord; 'although really it is scarce a fitting mode of expression for one of the senators of the College of Justice. We were hearing the parties in a long, crucial case, before the fifteen; Creech was moving at some length for an infeftment; when I saw Glenkindie lean forward to Hermiston with his hand over his mouth and make him a secret communication. No one could have guessed its nature from your father; from Glenkindie, yes, his malice sparked out of him a little grossly. But your father, no. A man of granite. The next moment he pounced upon Creech. "Mr. Creech," says he, "I'll take a look of that sasine," and for thirty minutes after,' said Glenalmond, with a smile, 'Messrs. Creech and Co. were fighting a pretty uphill battle, which resulted, I need hardly add, in their total rout. The case was dismissed. No, I doubt if ever I heard Hermiston better inspired. He was literally rejoicing *in apicibus juris.*'

Archie was able to endure no longer. He thrust his plate away and interrupted the deliberate and insignificant stream of talk. 'Here,' he said, 'I have made a fool of myself, if I have not made something worse. Do you judge between us – judge between a father and a son. I can speak to you; it is not like . . . I will tell you what I feel and what I mean to do; and you shall be the judge,' he repeated.

'I decline jurisdiction,' said Glenalmond, with extreme seriousness. 'But, my dear boy, if it will do you any good to talk, and if it will interest you at all to hear what I may choose to say when I have heard you, I am quite at your command. Let an old man say it, for once, and not need to blush: I love you like a son.'

There came a sudden sharp sound in Archie's throat. 'Ay,' he cried, 'and there it is! Love! Like a son! And how do you think I love my father?'

'Quietly, quietly,' says my lord.

'I will be very quiet,' replied Archie. 'And I will be baldly frank. I do not love my father; I wonder sometimes if I do not hate him. There's my shame; perhaps my sin; at least, and in the sight of God, not my fault. How was I to love him? He has never spoken to me, never smiled upon me; I do not think he ever touched me. You know the way he talks? You do not talk so, yet you can sit and hear him without shuddering, and I cannot. My soul is sick when he begins with it; I could smite him in the mouth. And all that's nothing. I was at the trial of this Jopp. You were not there, but you must have heard him often; the man's notorious for it, for being – look at my position! he s my father and this is how I have to speak of him – notorious for being a brute and cruel and a coward. Lord Glenalmond, I give you my word, when I came out of that Court, I longed to die – the shame of it was beyond my strength: but I—I——' he rose from his seat and began to pace the room in a disorder. 'Well, who am I? A boy, who have never been tried, have never done anything except this twopenny impotent folly with my father. But I tell you, my lord, and I know myself, I am at least that kind of a man – or that kind of a boy, if you prefer it – that I could die in torments rather than that any one should suffer as that scoundrel suffered. Well, and what have I done? I see it now. I have made a fool of myself, as I said in the beginning; and I have gone back, and asked my father's pardon, and placed myself wholly in his hands – and he has sent me to Hermiston,' with a wretched smile, 'for life, I suppose – and what can I say? he strikes me as having done quite right, and let me off better than I had deserved.'

'My poor, dear boy!' observed Glenalmond. 'My poor dear and, if you will allow me to say so, very foolish boy! You are only discovering where you are; to one of your temperament, or of mine, a painful discovery. The world was not made for us; it was made for ten hundred millions of men, all different from each other and from us; there's no royal road there, we just have to sclamber and tumble. Don't think that I am at all disposed to be surprised; don't suppose that I ever think of blaming you; indeed I rather admire! But there fall to be offered one or two observations on the case which occur to me and which (if you will listen to them dispassionately) may be the means of inducing you to view the matter more calmly. First of all, I cannot acquit you of a good deal of what is called intolerance. You seem to have been very much offended because your father talks a little sculduddery after dinner, which it is perfectly licit for him to do, and which (although I am not very fond of it myself) appears to be entirely an affair of taste. Your father, I scarcely like to remind you, since it is so trite a commonplace, is older than yourself. At least, he is *major* and *sui juris*, and may please himself in the matter of his conversation. And, do you know, I wonder if he might not have as good an answer against you and me? We say we sometimes find him *coarse*, but I suspect he might retort that he finds us always dull. Perhaps a relevant exception.'

He beamed on Archie, but no smile could be elicited.

'And now,' proceeded the Judge, 'for "Archibald on Capital Punishment." This is a very plausible academic opinion; of course I do not and I cannot hold it; but that's not to say that many able and excellent persons have not done so in the past. Possibly, in the past also, I may have a

little dipped myself in the same heresy. My third client, or
possibly my fourth, was the means of a return in my
opinions. I never saw the man I more believed in; I would
have put my hand in the fire, I would have gone to the cross
for him; and when it came to trial he was gradually pictured
before me, by undeniable probation, in the light of so gross,
so cold-blooded, and so black-hearted a villain, that I had
a mind to have cast my brief upon the table. I was then
boiling against the man with even a more tropical tempera-
ture than I had been boiling for him. But I said to myself:
"No, you have taken up his case; and because you have
changed your mind it must not be suffered to let drop. All
that rich tide of eloquence that you prepared last night with
so much enthusiasm is out of place, and yet you must not
desert him, you must say something." So I said something,
and I got him off. It made my reputation. But an experience
of that kind is formative. A man must not bring his passions
to the bar – or to the bench,' he added.

The story had slightly rekindled Archie's interest. 'I
could never deny,' he began – 'I mean I can conceive that
some men would be better dead. But who are we to know
all the springs of God's unfortunate creatures? Who are
we to trust ourselves where it seems that God Himself
must think twice before He treads, and to do it with delight?
Yes, with delight. *Tigris ut aspera.*'

'Perhaps not a pleasant spectacle,' said Glenalmond. 'And
yet, do you know, I think somehow a great one.'

'I've had a long talk with him to-night,' said Archie.

'I was supposing so,' said Glenalmond.

'And he struck me – I cannot deny that he struck me as
something very big,' pursued the son. 'Yes, he is big. He
never spoke about himself; only about me. I suppose I
admired him. The dreadful part——'

'Suppose we did not talk about that,' interrupted Glenalmond. 'You know it very well, it cannot in any way help
that you should brood upon it, and I sometimes wonder
whether you and I – who are a pair of sentimentalists – are
quite good judges of plain men.'

'How do you mean?' asked Archie.

'*Fair* judges, I mean,' replied Glenalmond. 'Can we be just to them? Do we not ask too much? There was a word of yours just now that impressed me a little when you asked me who we were to know all the springs of God's unfortunate creatures. You applied that, as I understood, to capital cases only. But does it – I ask myself – does it not apply all through? Is it any less difficult to judge of a good man or of a half-good man, than of the worst criminal at the bar? And may not each have relevant excuses?'

'Ah, but we do not talk of punishing the good,' cried Archie.

'No, we do not talk of it,' said Glenalmond. 'But I think we do it. Your father, for instance.'

'You think I have punished him?' cried Archie.

Lord Glenalmond bowed his head.

'I think I have,' said Archie. 'And the worst is, I think he feels it! How much, who can tell, with such a being? But I think he does.'

'And I am sure of it,' said Glenalmond.

'Has he spoken to you, then?' cried Archie.

'Oh no,' replied the judge.

'I tell you honestly,' said Archie, 'I want to make it up to him. I will go, I have already pledged myself to go, to Hermiston. That was to him. And now I pledge myself to you, in the sight of God, that I will close my mouth on capital punishment and all other subjects where our views may clash, for – how long shall I say? when shall I have sense enough? – ten years. Is that well?'

'It is well,' said my lord.

'As far as it goes,' said Archie. 'It is enough as regards myself, it is to lay down enough of my conceit. But as regards him, whom I have publicly insulted? What am I to do to him? How do you pay attentions to a – an Alp like that?'

'Only in one way,' replied Glenalmond. 'Only by obedience, punctual, prompt, and scrupulous.'

'And I promise that he shall have it,' answered Archie. 'I offer you my hand in pledge of it.'

'And I take your hand as a solemnity,' replied the judge. 'God bless you, my dear, and enable you to keep your promise. God guide you in the true way, and spare your days, and preserve to you your honest heart.' At that, he kissed the young man upon the forehead in a gracious, distant, antiquated way; and instantly launched, with a marked change of voice, into another subject. 'And now, let us replenish the tankard; and I believe, if you will try my Cheddar again, you would find you had a better appetite. The Court has spoken, and the case is dismissed.'

'No, there is one thing I must say,' cried Archie. 'I must say it in justice to himself. I know – I believe faithfully, slavishly, after our talk – he will never ask me anything unjust. I am proud to feel it, that we have that much in common, I am proud to say it to you.'

The Judge, with shining eyes, raised his tankard. 'And I think perhaps that we might permit ourselves a toast,' said he. 'I should like to propose the health of a man very different from me and very much my superior – a man from whom I have often differed, who has often (in the trivial expression) rubbed me the wrong way, but whom I have never ceased to respect and, I may add, to be not a little afraid of. Shall I give you his name?'

'The Lord Justice-Clerk, Lord Hermiston,' said Archie, almost with gaiety; and the pair drank the toast deeply.

It was not precisely easy to re-establish, after these emotional passages, the natural flow of conversation. But the Judge eked out what was wanting with kind looks, produced his snuff-box (which was very rarely seen) to fill in a pause, and at last, despairing of any further social success, was upon the point of getting down a book to read a favourite passage, when there came a rather startling summons at the front door, and Carstairs ushered in my Lord Glenkindie, hot from a midnight supper. I am not aware that Glenkindie was ever a beautiful object, being short, and gross-bodied, and with an expression of sensuality comparable to a bear's.

At that moment, coming in hissing from many potations, with a flushed countenance and blurred eyes, he was strikingly contrasted with the tall, pale, kingly figure of Glenalmond. A rush of confused thought came over Archie – of shame that this was one of his father's elect friends; of pride, that at the least of it Hermiston could carry his liquor; and last of all, of rage, that he should have here under his eyes the man that had betrayed him. And then that too passed away; and he sat quiet, biding his opportunity.

The tipsy senator plunged at once into an explanation with Glenalmond. There was a point reserved yesterday, he had been able to make neither head nor tail of it, and seeing lights in the house, he had just dropped in for a glass of porter – and at this point he became aware of the third person. Archie saw the cod's mouth and the blunt lips of Glenkindie gape at him for a moment, and the recognition twinkle in his eyes.

'Who's this?' said he. 'What? is this possibly you, Don Quickshot? And how are ye? And how's your father? And what's all this we hear of you? It seems you're a most extraordinary leveller, by all tales. No king, no parliaments, and your gorge rises at the macers, worthy men! Hoot, toot! Dear, dear me! Your father's son too! Most rideeculous!'

Archie was on his feet, flushing a little at the reappearance of his unhappy figure of speech, but perfectly self-possessed. 'My lord – and you, Lord Glenalmond, my dear friend,' he began, 'this is a happy chance for me, that I can make my confession and offer my apologies to two of you at once.'

'Ah, but I don't know about that. Confession? It'll be judeecial, my young friend,' cried the jocular Glenkindie. 'And I'm afraid to listen to ye. Think if ye were to make me a coanvert!'

'If you would allow me, my lord,' returned Archie, 'what I have to say is very serious to me; and be pleased to be humorous after I am gone!'

'Remember, I'll hear nothing against the macers!' put in the incorrigible Glenkindie.

But Archie continued as though he had not spoken. 'I have played, both yesterday and to-day, a part for which I can only offer the excuse of youth. I was so unwise as to go to an execution; it seems I made a scene at the gallows; not content with which, I spoke the same night in a college society against capital punishment. This is the extent of what I have done, and in case you hear more alleged against me, I protest my innocence. I have expressed my regret already to my father, who is so good as to pass my conduct over – in a degree, and upon the condition that I am to leave my law studies.' . . .

Chapter Five

Winter on the Moors

1. *At Hermiston*

THE road to Hermiston runs for a great part of the way up the valley of a stream, a favourite with anglers and with midges, full of falls and pools, and shaded by willows and natural woods of birch. Here and there, but at great distances, a byway branches off, and a gaunt farmhouse may be descried above in a fold of the hill; but the more part of the time, the road would be quite empty of passage and the hills of habitation. Hermiston parish is one of the least populous in Scotland; and, by the time you came that length, you would scarce be surprised at the inimitable smallness of the kirk, a dwarfish, ancient place seated for fifty, and standing in a green by the burn-side among two-score gravestones. The manse close by, although no more than a cottage, is surrounded by the brightness of a flower-garden and the straw roofs of bees; and the whole colony, kirk and manse, garden and graveyard, finds harbourage in a grove of rowans, and is all the year round in a great silence broken only by the drone of the bees, the tinkle of the burn, and the bell on Sundays. A mile beyond the kirk the road leaves the valley by a precipitous ascent, and brings you a little after to the place of Hermiston, where it comes to an end in the back-yard before the coach-house. All beyond and about is the great field of the hills; the plover, the curlew, and the lark cry there; the wind blows as it blows in a ship's rigging, hard and cold and pure; and the hill-tops huddle one behind another, like a herd of cattle, into the sunset.

The house was sixty years old, unsightly, comfortable; a farmyard and a kitchen-garden on the left, with a fruit wall where little hard green pears came to their maturity about the end of October.

The policy (as who should say the park) was of some extent, but very ill reclaimed; heather and moorfowl had crossed the boundary wall and spread and roosted within;

and it would have tasked a landscape gardener to say where policy ended and unpolicied nature began. My lord had been led by the influence of Mr. Sheriff Scott into a considerable design of planting; many acres were accordingly set out with fir, and the little feathery besoms gave a false scale and lent a strange air of a toy-shop to the moors. A great, rooty sweetness of bogs was in the air, and at all seasons an infinite melancholy piping of hill birds. Standing so high and with so little shelter, it was a cold, exposed house, splashed by showers, drenched by continuous rains that made the gutters to spout, beaten upon and buffeted by all the winds of heaven; and the prospect would be often black with tempest, and often white with the snows of winter. But the house was wind and weather proof, the hearths were kept bright, and the rooms pleasant with live fires of peat; and Archie might sit of an evening and hear the squalls bugle on the moorland, and watch the fire prosper in the earthy fuel, and the smoke winding up the chimney, and drink deep of the pleasures of shelter.

Solitary as the place was, Archie did not want neighbours. Every night, if he chose, he might go down to the manse and share a 'brewst' of toddy with the minister – a hare-brained ancient gentleman, long and light and still active, though his knees were loosened with age, and his voice broke continually in childish trebles – and his lady wife, a heavy, comely dame, without a word to say for herself beyond good-even and good-day. Harum-scarum, clodpole young lairds of the neighbourhood paid him the compliment of a visit. Young Hay of Romanes rode down to call, on his crop-eared pony; young Pringle of Drumanno came up on his bony grey. Hay remained on the hospitable field, and must be carried to bed; Pringle got somehow to his saddle about 3 a.m., and (as Archie stood with the lamp on the upper doorstep) lurched, uttered a senseless view-holloa, and vanished out of the small circle of illumination like a wraith. Yet a minute or two longer the clatter of his break-neck flight was audible, then it was cut off by the intervening steepness of the hill; and again, a great while after, the renewed beating of phantom horse-hoofs, far in the valley of the Hermiston, showed that the horse at least, if not his rider, was still on the homeward way.

There was a Tuesday club at the 'Crosskeys' in Crossmichael, where the young bloods of the countryside congregated and drank deep on a percentage of the expense, so that he was left gainer who should have drunk the most. Archie had no great mind to this diversion, but he took it like a duty laid upon him, went with a decent regularity, did his manfullest with the liquor, held up his head in the local jests, and got home again and was able to put up his horse, to the admiration of Kirstie and the lass that helped her. He dined at Driffel, supped at Windielaws. He went to the New Year's ball at Huntsfield and was made welcome, and thereafter rode to hounds with my Lord Muirfell, upon whose name, as that of a legitimate Lord of Parliament, in a work so full of Lords of Session, my pen should pause reverently. Yet the same fate attended him here as in Edinburgh. The habit of solitude tends to perpetuate itself, and an austerity of which he was quite unconscious, and a pride which seemed arrogance, and perhaps was chiefly shyness, discouraged and offended his new companions. Hay did not return more than twice, Pringle never at all, and there came a time when Archie even desisted from the Tuesday Club, and became in all things – what he had had the name of almost from the first – the Recluse of Hermiston. High-nosed Miss Pringle of Drumanno and high-stepping Miss Marshall of the Mains were understood to have had a difference of opinion about him the day after the ball – he was none the wiser, he could not suppose himself to be remarked by these entrancing ladies. At the ball itself my Lord Muirfell's daughter, the Lady Flora, spoke to him twice, and the second time with a touch of appeal, so that her colour rose and her voice trembled a little in his ear, like a passing grace in music. He stepped back with a heart on fire, coldly and not ungracefully excused himself, and a little after watched her dancing with young Drumanno of the empty laugh, and was harrowed at the sight, and raged to himself that this was a world in which it was given to Drumanno to please, and to himself only to stand aside and envy. He seemed excluded, as of right, from the favour of such society – seemed to extinguish mirth wherever he came, and was quick to feel the wound, and desist, and retire into solitude. If he had but understood the figure he presented, and the impression he made on these bright eyes and tender hearts; if he had but guessed that the Recluse of Hermiston, young, graceful, well spoken, but always cold, stirred the maidens of the county with the charm of Byronism when Byronism was new, it may be questioned whether his destiny might not even yet have been modified. It may be questioned, and I think it should be doubted. It was in his horoscope to be parsimonious of pain to himself, or of the chance of pain, even to the avoidance of any opportunity of pleasure; to have a Roman sense of duty, an instinctive aristocracy of manners and taste; to be the son of Adam Weir and Jean Rutherford.

2. *Kirstie*

Kirstie was now over fifty, and might have sat to a sculptor. Long of limb, and still light of foot, deep-breasted, robust-loined, her golden hair not yet mingled with any trace of silver, the years had but caressed and embellished her. By the lines of a rich and vigorous maternity, she seemed destined to be the bride of heroes and the mother of their children; and behold, by the iniquity of fate, she had passed through her youth alone, and drew near to the confines of age, a childless woman. The tender ambitions that she had received at birth had been, by time and disappointment, diverted into a certain barren zeal of industry and fury of interference. She carried her thwarted ardours into housework, she washed floors with her empty heart. If she could not win the love of one with love, she must dominate all by her temper. Hasty, wordy, and wrathful, she had a drawn quarrel with most of her neighbours, and with the others not much more than armed neutrality. The grieve's wife had been 'sneisty'; the sister of the gardener who kept house for him had shown herself 'upsitten'; and she wrote to Lord Hermiston about once a year demanding the discharge of the offenders, and justifying the demand

by much wealth of detail. For it must not be supposed that
the quarrel rested with the wife and did not take in the
husband also – or with the gardener's sister, and did not
speedily include the gardener himself. As the upshot of all
this petty quarrelling and intemperate speech, she was
practically excluded (like a lightkeeper on his tower) from
the comforts of human association; except with her own
indoor drudge, who, being but a lassie and entirely at her
mercy, must submit to the shifty weather of 'the mistress's'
moods without complaint, and be willing to take buffets or
caresses according to the temper of the hour. To Kirstie,
thus situate and in the Indian summer of her heart, which
was slow to submit to age, the gods sent this equivocal
good thing of Archie's presence. She had known him in the
cradle and paddled him when he misbehaved; and yet, as
she had not so much as set eyes on him since he was eleven
and had his last serious illness, the tall, slender, refined, and
rather melancholy young gentleman of twenty came upon
her with the shock of a new acquaintance. He was 'Young
Hermiston,' 'the laird himsel'': he had an air of distinctive
superiority, a cold straight glance of his black eyes, that
abashed the woman's tantrums in the beginning, and therefore the possibility of any quarrel was excluded. He was
new, and therefore immediately aroused her curiosity; he
was reticent, and kept it awake. And lastly he was dark and
she fair, and he was male and she female, the everlasting
fountains of interest.

Her feeling partook of the loyalty of a clanswoman, the
hero-worship of a maiden aunt, and the idolatry due to a
god. No matter what he had asked of her, ridiculous or
tragic, she would have done it and joyed to do it. Her
passion, for it was nothing less, entirely filled her. It was a
rich physical pleasure to make his bed or light his lamp for
him when he was absent, to pull off his wet boots or wait on
him at dinner when he returned. A young man who should
have so doted on the idea, moral and physical, of any
woman, might be properly described as being in love, head
and heels, and would have behaved himself accordingly.
But Kirstie – though her heart leaped at his coming foot-

steps – though, when he patted her shoulder, her face brightened for the day – had not a hope or thought beyond the present moment and its perpetuation to the end of time. Till the end of time she would have had nothing altered, but still continue delightedly to serve her idol, and be repaid (say twice in the month) with a clap on the shoulder.

I have said her heart leaped – it is the accepted phrase. But rather, when she was alone in any chamber of the house, and heard his foot passing on the corridors, something in her bosom rose slowly until her breath was suspended, and as slowly fell again with a deep sigh, when the steps had passed and she was disappointed of her eyes' desire. This perpetual hunger and thirst of his presence kept her all day on the alert. When he went forth at morning, she would stand and follow him with admiring looks. As it grew late and drew to the time of his return, she would steal forth to a corner of the policy wall and be seen standing there sometimes by the hour together, gazing with shaded eyes, waiting the exquisite and barren pleasure of his view a mile off on the mountains. When at night she had trimmed and gathered the fire, turned down his bed, and laid out his night-gear – when there was no more to be done for the king's pleasure, but to remember him fervently in her usually very tepid prayers, and go to bed brooding upon his perfections, his future career, and what she should give him the next day for dinner – there still remained before her one more opportunity; she was still to take in the tray and say good-night. Sometimes Archie would glance up from his book with a preoccupied nod and a perfunctory salutation which was in truth a dismissal; sometimes – and by degrees more often – the volume would be laid aside, he would meet her coming with a look of relief; and the conversation would be engaged, last out the supper, and be prolonged till the small hours by the waning fire. It was no wonder that Archie was fond of company after his solitary days; and Kirstie, upon her side, exerted all the arts of her vigorous nature to ensnare his attention. She would keep back some piece of news during dinner to be fired off with the entrance of the supper tray, and form as it were the *lever de rideau* of the evening's entertainment. Once he had heard her tongue wag, she made sure of the result. From one subject to another she moved by insidious transitions, fearing the least silence, fearing almost to give him time for an answer lest it should slip into a hint of separation. Like so many people of her class, she was a brave narrator; her place was on the hearth-rug and she made it a rostrum, miming her stories as she told them, fitting them with vital detail, spinning them out with endless 'quo' he's' and 'quo' she's,' her voice sinking into a whisper over the supernatural or the horrific; until she would suddenly spring up in affected surprise, and pointing to the clock, 'Mercy, Mr. Archie!' she would say, 'whatten a time o' night is this of it! God forgive me for a daft wife!' So it befell, by good management, that she was not only the first to begin these nocturnal conversations, but invariably the first to break them off; so she managed to retire and not to be dismissed.

3. *A Border Family*

Such an unequal intimacy has never been uncommon in Scotland, where the clan spirit survives; where the servant tends to spend her life in the same service, a helpmeet at first, then a tyrant, and at last a pensioner; where, besides, she is not necessarily destitute of the pride of birth, but is, perhaps, like Kirstie, a connection of her master's, and at least knows the legend of her own family, and may count kinship with some illustrious dead. For that is the mark of the Scot of all classes: that he stands in an attitude towards the past unthinkable to Englishmen, and remembers and cherishes the memory of his forebears, good or bad; and there burns alive in him a sense of identity with the dead even to the twentieth generation. No more characteristic instance could be found than in the family of Kirstie Elliott. They were all, and Kirstie the first of all, ready and eager to pour forth the particulars of their genealogy, embellished with every detail that memory had handed down or fancy fabricated; and, behold! from every ramification of that tree there dangled a halter. The Elliotts themselves have had a chequered history; but these Elliotts deduced, besides, from three of the most unfortunate of the border clans – the Nicksons, the Ellwalds, and the Crozers. One ancestor after another might be seen appearing a moment out of the rain and the hill mist upon his furtive business, speeding home, perhaps, with a paltry booty of lame horses and lean kine, or squealing and dealing death in some moorland feud of the ferrets and the wild cats. One after another closed his obscure adventures in mid-air, triced up to the arm of the royal gibbet or the Baron's dule-tree. For the rusty blunder-buss of Scots criminal justice, which usually hurt nobody but jurymen, became a weapon of precision for the Nicksons, the Ellwalds, and the Crozers. The exhilaration of their exploits seemed to haunt the memories of their descendants alone, and the shame to be forgotten. Pride glowed in their bosoms to publish their relationship to 'Andrew Ellwald of the Laverockstanes, called "Unchancy Dand," who was justifeed wi' seeven mair of the same name at Jeddart in the days of King James the Sax.' In all this tissue of crime and misfortune, the Elliotts of Cauldstaneslap had one boast which must appear legitimate: the males were gallows-birds, born outlaws, petty thieves, and deadly brawlers; but, according to the same tradition, the females were all chaste and faithful. The power of ancestry on the character is not limited to the inheritance of cells. If I buy ancestors by the gross from the benevolence of Lyon King of Arms, my grandson (if he is Scottish) will feel a quickening emulation of their deeds. The men of the Elliotts were proud, lawless, violent as of right, cherishing and prolonging a tradition. In like manner with the women. And the woman, essentially passionate and reckless, who crouched on the rug, in the shine of the peat fire, telling these tales, had cherished through life a wild integrity of virtue.

Her father Gilbert had been deeply pious, a savage disciplinarian in the antique style, and withal a notorious smuggler. 'I mind when I was a bairn getting mony a skelp and being shoo'd to bed like pou'try,' she would say. 'That would be when the lads and their bit kegs were on the road. We've had the riffraff of two-three counties in our kitchen, mony's the time, betwix' the twelve and the three; and their

lanterns would be standing in the forecourt, ay, a score o'
them at once. But there was nae ungodly talk permitted at
Cauldstaneslap; my faither was a consistent man in walk
and conversation; just let slip an aith, and there was the door
to ye! He had that zeal for the Lord, it was a fair wonder to
hear him pray, but the faimily has aye had a gift that way.'
This father was twice married, once to a dark woman of the
old Ellwald stock, by whom he had Gilbert, presently of
Cauldstaneslap; and, secondly, to the mother of Kirstie. 'He
was an auld man when he married her, a fell auld man wi' a
muckle voice – you could hear him rowting from the top o'
the Kye-skairs,' she said; 'but for her, it appears she was
a perfit wonder. It was gentle blood she had, Mr. Archie, for
it was your ain. The countryside gaed gyte about her and
her gowden hair. Mines is no to be mentioned wi' it, and
there's few weemen has mair hair than what I have, or yet a
bonnier colour. Often would I tell my dear Miss Jeannie –
that was your mother, dear, she was cruel ta'en up about her
hair, it was unco tender, ye see – "Houts, Miss Jeannie," I
would say, "just fling your washes and your French
dentifrishes in the back o' the fire, for that's the place for
them; and awa' down to a burn side, and wash yersel' in
cauld hill water, and dry your bonny hair in the caller wind
o' the muirs, the way that my mother aye washed hers, and
that I have aye made it a practice to have wishen mines – just
you do what I tell ye, my dear, and ye'll give me news of it!
Ye'll have hair, and routh of hair, a pigtail as thick's my
arm," I said, "and the bonniest colour like the clear gowden
guineas, so as the lads in kirk'll no can keep their eyes off it!"
Weel, it lasted out her time, puir thing! I cuttit a lock of it
upon her corp that was lying there sae cauld. I'll show it ye
some of thir days if ye're good. But, as I was sayin', my
mither——'

On the death of the father there remained golden-haired
Kirstie, who took service with her distant kinsfolk, the
Rutherfords, and black-a-vised Gilbert, twenty years older,
who farmed the Cauldstaneslap, married, and begot four
sons between 1773 and 1784, and a daughter, like a post-
script, in '97, the year of Camperdown and Cape St. Vincent.

It seemed it was a tradition in the family to wind up with a belated girl. In 1804, at the age of sixty, Gilbert met an end that might be called heroic. He was due home from market any time from eight at night till five in the morning, and in any condition from the quarrelsome to the speechless, for he maintained to that age the goodly customs of the Scots farmer. It was known on this occasion that he had a good bit of money to bring home; the word had gone round loosely. The laird had shown his guineas, and if anybody had but noticed it, there was an ill-looking vagabond crew, the scum of Edinburgh, that drew out of the market long ere it was dusk and took the hill-road by Hermiston, where it was not to be believed that they had lawful business. One of the countryside, one Dickieson, they took with them to be their guide, and dear he paid for it. Of a sudden, in the ford of the Broken Dykes, this vermin clan fell on the laird, six to one, and him three parts asleep, having drunk hard. But it is ill to catch an Elliott. For a while, in the night and the black water that was deep as to his saddle-girths, he wrought with his staff like a smith at his stithy, and great was the sound of oaths and blows. With that the ambuscade was burst, and he rode for home with a pistol-ball in him, three knife wounds, the loss of his front teeth, a broken rib and bridle, and a dying horse. That was a race with death that the laird rode! In the mirk night, with his broken bridle and his head swimming, he dug his spurs to the rowels in the horse's side, and the horse, that was even worse off than himself, the poor creature! screamed out loud like a person as he went, so that the hills echoed with it, and the folks at Cauldstaneslap got to their feet about the table and looked at each other with white faces. The horse fell dead at the yard gate, the laird won the length of the house and fell there on the threshold. To the son that raised him he gave the bag of money. 'Hae,' said he. All the way up the thieves had seemed to him to be at his heels, but now the hallucination left him – he saw them again in the place of the ambuscade – and the thirst of vengeance seized on his dying mind. Raising himself and pointing with an imperious finger into the black night from which he had come, he uttered the single

command, 'Brocken Dykes,' and fainted. He had never
been loved, but he had been feared in honour. At that sight,
at that word, gasped out at them from a toothless and bleeding mouth, the old Elliott spirit awoke with a shout in the
four sons. 'Wanting the hat,' continues my author, Kirstie,
whom I but haltingly follow, for she told this tale like one
inspired, 'wanting guns, for there wasna twa grains o' pouder
in the house, wi' nae mair weepons than their sticks into
their hands, the fower o' them took the road. Only Hob, and
that was the eldest, hunkered at the door-sill where the
blood had rin, fyled his hand wi' it, and haddit it up to
Heeven in the way o' the auld Border aith. "Hell shall have
her ain again this nicht!" he raired, and rode forth upon his
earrand.' It was three miles to Broken Dykes, down hill,
and a sore road. Kirstie had seen men from Edinburgh
dismounting there in plain day to lead their horses. But the
four brothers rode it as if Auld Hornie were behind and
Heaven in front. Come to the ford, and there was Dickieson.
By all tales, he was not dead, but breathed and reared upon
his elbow, and cried out to them for help. It was at a graceless face that he asked mercy. As soon as Hob saw, by the
glint of the lantern, the eyes shining and the whiteness of the
teeth in the man's face, 'Damn you!' says he; 'ye hae your
teeth, hae ye?' and rode his horse to and fro upon that
human remnant. Beyond that, Dandie must dismount with
the lantern to be their guide; he was the youngest son,
scarce twenty at the time. 'A' nicht long they gaed in the
wet heath and jennipers, and whaur they gaed they neither
knew nor cared, but just followed the bluidstains and the
footprints o' their faither's murderers. And a' nicht Dandie
had his nose to the grund like a tyke, and the ithers followed
and spak' naething, neither black nor white. There was nae
noise to be heard, but just the sough of the swalled burns,
and Hob, the dour yin, risping his teeth as he gaed.' With
the first glint of the morning they saw they were on the
drove road, and at that the four stopped and had a dram to
their breakfasts, for they knew that Dand must have guided
them right, and the rogues could be but little ahead, hot foot
for Edinburgh by the way of the Pentland Hills. By eight

o'clock they had word of them – a shepherd had seen four
men 'uncoly mishandled' go by in the last hour. 'That's yin a
piece,' says Clem, and swung his cudgel. 'Five o' them!' says
Hob. 'God's death, but the faither was a man! And him
drunk!' And then there befell them what my author termed
'a sair misbegowk,' for they were overtaken by a posse of
mounted neighbours come to aid in the pursuit. Four sour
faces looked on the reinforcement. 'The Deil's broughten
you!' said Clem, and they rode thenceforward in the rear of
the party with hanging heads. Before ten they had found
and secured the rogues, and by three of the afternoon, as
they rode up the Vennel with their prisoners, they were
aware of a concourse of people bearing in their midst something that dripped. 'For the boady of the saxt,' pursued
Kirstie, 'wi' his head smashed like a hazel-nit, had been a'
that nicht in the chairge o' Hermiston Water, and it dunting
it on the stanes, and grunding it on the shallows, and flinging
the deid thing heels-ower-hurdie at the Fa's o' Spango; and
in the first o' the day, Tweed had got a hold o' him and
carried him off like a wind, for it was uncoly swalled, and
raced wi' him, bobbing under brae-sides, and was long
playing with the creature in the drumlie lynns under the
castle, and at the hinder end of all cuist him up on the
starling of Crossmichael brig. Sae there they were a'thegither
at last (for Dickieson had been brought in on a cart long
syne), and folk could see what mainner o' man my brither
had been that had held his head again sax and saved the
siller, and him drunk!' Thus died of honourable injuries and
in the savour of fame Gilbert Elliott of the Cauldstaneslap;
but his sons had scarce less glory out of the business. Their
savage haste, the skill with which Dand had found and
followed the trail, the barbarity to the wounded Dickieson
(which was like an open secret in the county), and the doom
which it was currently supposed they had intended for the
others, struck and stirred popular imagination. Some
centuries earlier the last of the minstrels might have
fashioned the last of the ballads out of that Homeric fight and
chase; but the spirit was dead, or had been reincarnated
already in Mr. Sheriff Scott, and the degenerate moorsmen

must be content to tell the tale in prose, and to make of the
'Four Black Brothers' a unit after the fashion of the 'Twelve
Apostles' or the 'Three Musketeers.'

Robert, Gilbert, Clement, and Andrew – in the proper
Border diminutives, Hob, Gib, Clem, and Dand Elliott –
these ballad heroes, had much in common; in particular,
their high sense of the family and the family honour; but
they went diverse ways, and prospered and failed in different
businesses. According to Kirstie, 'they had a' bees in their
bonnets but Hob.' Hob the laird was, indeed, essentially a
decent man. An elder of the Kirk, nobody had heard an
oath upon his lips, save, perhaps, thrice or so at the sheep-
washing, since the chase of his father's murderers. The
figure he had shown on that eventful night disappeared as if
swallowed by a trap. He who had ecstatically dipped
his hand in the red blood, he who had ridden down
Dickieson, became, from that moment on, a stiff and rather
graceless model of the rustic proprieties; cannily profiting by
the high war prices, and yearly stowing away a little nest-egg
in the bank against calamity; approved of and sometimes
consulted by the greater lairds for the massive and placid
sense of what he said, when he could be induced to say
anything; and particularly valued by the minister, Mr.
Torrance, as a right-hand man in the parish, and a model to
parents. The transfiguration had been for the moment only;
some Barbarossa, some old Adam of our ancestors, sleeps
in all of us till the fit circumstance shall call it into action;
and, for as sober as he now seemed, Hob had given once for
all the measure of the devil that haunted him. He was
married, and, by reason of the effulgence of that legendary
night, was adored by his wife. He had a mob of little lusty,
barefoot children who marched in a caravan the long miles
to school, the stages of whose pilgrimage were marked by
acts of spoliation and mischief, and who were qualified in
the countryside as 'fair pests.' But in the house, if 'faither
was in,' they were quiet as mice. In short, Hob moved
through life in a great peace – the reward of any one who
shall have killed his man, with any formidable and figurative
circumstance, in the midst of a country gagged and swaddled

with civilisation.

It was a current remark that the Elliotts were 'guid and bad, like sanguishes' ; and certainly there was a curious distinction, the men of business coming alternately with the dreamers. The second brother, Gib, was a weaver by trade, had gone out early into the world to Edinburgh, and come home again with his wings singed. There was an exaltation in his nature which had led him to embrace with enthusiasm the principles of the French Revolution, and had ended by bringing him under the hawse of my Lord Hermiston in that furious onslaught of his upon the Liberals, which sent Muir and Palmer into exile and dashed the party into chaff. It was whispered that my lord, in his great scorn for the movement, and prevailed upon a little by a sense of neigh-bourliness, had given Gib a hint. Meeting him one day in the Potterrow, my lord had stopped in front of him: 'Gib, ye eediot,' he had said, 'what's this I hear of you? Poalitics, poalitics, poalitics, weaver's poalitics, is the way of it, I hear. If ye arena a'thegither dozened with eediocy, ye'll gang your ways back to Cauldstaneslap, and ca' your loom, and ca' your loom, man!' And Gilbert had taken him at the word and returned, with an expedition almost to be called flight, to the house of his father. The clearest of his inheritance was that family gift of prayer of which Kirstie had boasted; and the baffled politician now turned his attention to religious matters – or, as others said, to heresy and schism. Every Sunday morning he was in Crossmichael, where he had gathered together, one by one, a sect of about a dozen persons, who called themselves 'God's Remnant of the True Faithful,' or, for short, 'God's Remnant.' To the profane, they were known as 'Gib's Deils.' Bailie Sweedie, a noted humorist in the town, vowed that the proceedings always opened to the tune of 'The Deil Fly Away with the Excise-man,' and that the sacrament was dispensed in the form of hot whisky-toddy; both wicked hits at the evangelist, who had been suspected of smuggling in his youth, and had been overtaken (as the phrase went) on the streets of Cross-michael one Fair day. It was known that every Sunday they prayed for a blessing on the arms of Bonaparte. For this,

'God's Remnant,' as they were 'skailing' from the cottage
that did duty for a temple, had been repeatedly stoned by
the bairns, and Gib himself hooted by a squadron of Border
volunteers in which his own brother, Dand, rode in a
uniform and with a drawn sword. The 'Remnant' were
believed, besides, to be 'antinomian in principle,' which
might otherwise have been a serious charge, but the way
public opinion then blew it was quite swallowed up and
forgotten in the scandal about Bonaparte. For the rest,
Gilbert had set up his loom in an outhouse at Cauldstaneslap, where he laboured assiduously six days of the week.
His brothers, appalled by his political opinions, and willing
to avoid dissension in the household, spoke but little to him;
he less to them, remaining absorbed in the study of the Bible
and almost constant prayer. The gaunt weaver was dry-
nurse at Cauldstaneslap, and the bairns loved him dearly.
Except when he was carrying an infant in his arms, he was
rarely seen to smile – as, indeed, there were few smilers in
that family. When his sister-in-law rallied him, and proposed
that he should get a wife and bairns of his own, since he
was so fond of them, 'I have no clearness of mind upon that
point,' he would reply. If nobody called him in to dinner, he
stayed out. Mrs. Hob, a hard, unsympathetic woman,
once tried the experiment. He went without food all day, but
at dusk, as the light began to fail him, he came into the house
of his own accord, looking puzzled. 'I've had a great gale of
prayer upon my speerit,' said he. 'I canna mind sae muckle's
what I had for denner.' The creed of God's Remnant was
justified in the life of its founder. 'And yet I dinna ken,' said
Kirstie. 'He's maybe no more stockfish than his neeghbours!
He rode wi' the rest o' them, and had a good stamach to
the work, by a' that I hear! God's Remnant! The deil's
clavers! There wasna muckle Christianity in the way Hob
guided Johnny Dickieson, at the least of it; but Guid kens!
Is he a Christian even? He might be a Mahommedan or a
Deevil or a Fireworshipper, for what I ken.'

The third brother had his name on a door-plate, no less, in
the city of Glasgow, 'Mr. Clement Elliott,' as long as your
arm. In his case, that spirit of innovation which had shown

itself timidly in the case of Hob by the admission of new
manures, and which had run to waste with Gilbert in
subversive politics and heretical religions, bore useful fruit
in many ingenious mechanical improvements. In boyhood,
from his addiction to strange devices of sticks and string,
he had been counted the most eccentric of the family. But
that was all by now; and he was a partner of his firm, and
looked to die a bailie. He too had married, and was rearing
a plentiful family in the smoke and din of Glasgow; he was
wealthy, and could have bought out his brother, the cock-
laird, six times over, it was whispered; and when he slipped
away to Cauldstaneslap for a well-earned holiday, which he
did as often as he was able, he astonished the neighbours
with his broadcloth, his beaver hat, and the ample plies of
his neckcloth. Though an eminently solid man at bottom,
after the pattern of Hob, he had contracted a certain
Glasgow briskness and *aplomb* which set him off. All the
other Elliotts were as lean as a rake, but Clement was
laying on fat, and he panted sorely when he must get into his
boots. Dand said, chuckling: 'Ay, Clem has the elements of a
corporation.' 'A provost and corporation,' returned Clem.
And his readiness was much admired.

The fourth brother, Dand, was a shepherd to his trade,
and by starts, when he could bring his mind to it, excelled in
the business. Nobody could train a dog like Dandie; nobody,
through the peril of great storms in the winter time, could do
more gallantly. But if his dexterity were exquisite, his
diligence was but fitful; and he served his brother for bed
and board, and a trifle of pocket-money when he asked for
it. He loved money well enough, knew very well how to
spend it, and could make a shrewd bargain when he liked.
But he preferred a vague knowledge that he was well to
windward to any counted coins in the pocket; he felt
himself richer so. Hob would expostulate: 'I'm an amature
herd.' Dand would reply, 'I'll keep your sheep to you
when I'm so minded, but I'll keep my liberty too. Thir's no
man can coandescend on what I'm worth.' Clem would
expound to him the miraculous results of compound interest,
and recommend investments. 'Ay, man?' Dand would say;

'and do you think, if I took Hob's siller, that I wouldna drink it or wear it on the lassies? And, anyway, my kingdom is no of this world. Either I'm a poet or else I'm nothing.' Clem would remind him of old age. 'I'll die young, like Robbie Burns,' he would say stoutly. No question but he had a certain accomplishment in minor verse. His 'Hermiston Burn,' with its pretty refrain –

> 'I love to gang thinking whaur ye gang linking,
> Hermiston burn, in the howe;'

his 'Auld, auld Elliotts, clay-cauld Elliotts, dour, bauld Elliotts of auld,' and his really fascinating piece about the Praying Weaver's stone, had gained him in the neighbourhood the reputation, still possible in Scotland, of a local bard; and, though not printed himself, he was recognised by others who were and who had become famous. Walter Scott owed to Dandie the text of the 'Raid of Wearie' in the *Minstrelsy*; and made him welcome at his house, and appreciated his talents, such as they were, with all his usual generosity. The Ettrick Shepherd was his sworn crony; they would meet, drink to excess, roar out their lyrics in each other's faces, and quarrel and make it up again till bedtime. And besides these recognitions, almost to be called official, Dandie was made welcome for the sake of his gift through the farmhouses of several contiguous dales, and was thus exposed to manifold temptations which he rather sought than fled. He had figured on the stool of repentance, for once fulfilling to the letter the tradition of his hero and model. His humorous verses to Mr. Torrance on that occasion – 'Kenspeckle here my lane I stand' – unfortunately too indelicate for further citation, ran through the country like a fiery cross; they were recited, quoted, paraphrased, and laughed over as far away as Dumfries on the one hand and Dunbar on the other.

These four brothers were united by a close bond, the bond of that mutual admiration – or rather mutual hero-worship – which is so strong among the members of secluded families who have much ability and little culture. Even the extremes admired each other. Hob, who had as much poetry as the tongs, professed to find pleasure in Dand's verses; Clem, who had no more religion than Claverhouse, nourished a heartfelt, at least an open-mouthed, admiration of Gib's prayers; and Dandie followed with relish the rise of Clem's fortunes. Indulgence followed hard on the heels of admiration. The laird, Clem, and Dand, who were Tories and patriots of the hottest quality, excused to themselves, with a certain bashfulness, the radical and revolutionary heresies of Gib. By another division of the family, the laird, Clem, and Gib, who were men exactly virtuous, swallowed the dose of Dand's irregularities as a kind of clog or drawback in the mysterious providence of God affixed to bards, and distinctly probative of poetical genius. To appreciate the simplicity of their mutual admiration it was necessary to hear Clem, arrived upon one of his visits, and dealing in a spirit of continuous irony with the affairs and personalities of that great city of Glasgow where he lived and transacted business. The various personages, ministers of the church, municipal officers, mercantile big-wigs, whom he had occasion to introduce, were all alike denigrated, all served but as reflectors to cast back a flattering sidelight on the house of Cauldstane-slap. The Provost, for whom Clem by exception entertained a measure of respect, he would liken to Hob. 'He minds me o' the laird there,' he would say. 'He has some of Hob's grand, whunstane sense, and the same way with him of steiking his mouth when he's no very pleased.' And Hob, all unconscious, would draw down his upper lip and produce, as if for comparison, the formidable grimace referred to. The unsatisfactory incumbent of St. Enoch's Kirk was thus briefly dismissed: 'If he had but twa fingers o' Gib's, he would waken them up.' And Gib, honest man! would look down and secretly smile. Clem was a spy whom they had sent out into the world of men. He had come back with the good news that there was nobody to compare with the Four Black Brothers, no position that they would not adorn, no official that it would not be well they should replace, no interest of mankind, secular or spiritual, which would not immediately bloom under their supervision. The excuse of their folly is in two words: scarce the breadth of a hair divided them from the peasantry. The measure of their

sense is this: that these symposia of rustic vanity were kept
entirely within the family, like some secret ancestral practice.
To the world their serious faces were never deformed by the
suspicion of any simper of self-contentment. Yet it was
known. 'They hae a guid pride o' themsel's!' was the word
in the countryside.

Lastly, in a Border story, there should be added their 'to-
names.' Hob was The Laird. 'Roy ne puis, prince ne daigne';
he was the laird of Cauldstaneslap – say fifty acres –
ipsissimus. Clement was Mr. Elliott, as upon his door-plate,
the earlier Dafty having been discarded as no longer applic-
able, and indeed only a reminder of misjudgment and the
imbecility of the public; and the youngest, in honour of his
perpetual wanderings, was known by the sobriquet of Randy
Dand.

It will be understood that not all this information was
communicated by the aunt, who had too much of the family
failing herself to appreciate it thoroughly in others. But as
time went on, Archie began to observe an omission in the
family chronicle.

'Is there not a girl too?' he asked.

'Ay: Kirstie. She was named for me, or my grandmother at
least – it's the same thing,' returned the aunt, and went on
again about Dand, whom she secretly preferred by reason of
his gallantries.

'But what is your niece like?' said Archie at the next
opportunity.

'Her? As black's your hat! But I dinna suppose she would
maybe be what you would ca' *ill-looked* a'thegither. Na,
she's a kind of a handsome jaud – a kind o' gipsy,' said the
aunt, who had two sets of scales for men and women – or
perhaps it would be more fair to say that she had three,
and the third and the most loaded was for girls.

'How comes it that I never see her in church?' said Archie.

''Deed, and I believe she's in Glesgie with Clem and his
wife. A heap good she's like to get of it! I dinna say for men
folk, but where weemen folk are born, there let them bide.
Glory to God, I was never far'er from here than Crossmichael.'

In the meanwhile it began to strike Archie as strange, that while she thus sang the praises of her kinsfolk, and manifestly relished their virtues and (I may say) their vices like a thing creditable to herself, there should appear not the least sign of cordiality between the house of Hermiston and that of Cauldstaneslap. Going to church of a Sunday, as the lady housekeeper stepped with her skirts kilted, three tucks of her white petticoat showing below, and her best India shawl upon her back (if the day were fine) in a pattern of radiant dyes, she would sometimes overtake her relatives preceding her more leisurely in the same direction. Gib of course was absent: by skreigh of day he had been gone to Crossmichael and his fellow-heretics; but the rest of the family would be seen marching in open order: Hob and Dand, stiff-necked, straight-backed six-footers, with severe dark faces, and their plaids about their shoulders; the convoy of children scattering (in a state of high polish) on the wayside, and every now and again collected by the shrill summons of the mother; and the mother herself, by a suggestive circumstance which might have afforded matter of thought to a more experienced observer than Archie, wrapped in a shawl nearly identical with Kirstie's, but a thought more gaudy and conspicuously newer. At the sight, Kirstie grew more tall – Kirstie showed her classical profile, nose in air and nostril spread, the pure blood came in her cheek evenly in a delicate living pink.

'A braw day to ye, Mistress Elliott,' said she, and hostility and gentility were nicely mingled in her tones. 'A fine day, mem,' the laird's wife would reply with a miraculous curtsey, spreading the while her plumage – setting off, in other words, and with arts unknown to the mere man, the pattern of her India shawl. Behind her, the whole Cauldstaneslap contingent marched in closer order, and with an indescribable air of being in the presence of the foe; and while Dandie saluted his aunt with a certain familiarity as of one who was well in court, Hob marched on in awful immobility. There appeared upon the face of this attitude in the family the consequences of some dreadful feud. Presumably the two women had been principals in the original encounter, and the laird had probably been drawn into the quarrel by the ears, too late to be included in the present skin-deep reconciliation.

'Kirstie,' said Archie one day, 'what is this you have against your family?'

'I dinna complean,' said Kirstie, with a flush. 'I say naething.'

'I see you do not – not even good-day to your own nephew,' said he.

'I hae naething to be ashamed of,' said she. 'I can say the Lord's prayer with a good grace. If Hob was ill, or in preeson or poverty, I would see to him blithely. But for curtchying and complimenting and colloguing, thank ye kindly!'

Archie had a bit of a smile: he leaned back in his chair. 'I think you and Mrs. Robert are not very good friends,' says he slyly, 'when you have your India shawls on?'

She looked upon him in silence, with a sparkling eye but an indecipherable expression; and that was all that Archie was ever destined to learn of the battle of the India shawls.

'Do none of them ever come here to see you?' he inquired.

'Mr. Archie,' said she, 'I hope that I ken my place better. It would be a queer thing, I think, If I was to clamjamfry up your faither's house – that I should say it! – wi' a dirty, black-a-vised clan, no ane o' them it was worth while to mar soap upon but just mysel'! Na, they're all damnifeed wi' the black Ellwalds. I have nae patience wi' black folk.' Then, with a sudden consciousness of the case of Archie, 'No that it maitters for men sae muckle,' she made haste to add, 'but there's naebody can deny that it's unwomanly. Long hair is the ornament o' woman ony way; we've good warrandise for that – it's in the Bible – and wha can doubt that the Apostle had some gowden-haired lassie in his mind – Apostle and all, for what was he but just a man like yersel'?'

Chapter Six

A Leaf from Christina's Psalm-Book

ARCHIE was sedulous at church. Sunday after Sunday he sat
down and stood up with that small company, heard the voice
of Mr. Torrance leaping like an ill-played clarionet from
key to key, and had an opportunity to study his moth-eaten
gown and the black thread mittens that he joined together in
prayer, and lifted up with a reverent solemnity in the act of
benediction. Hermiston pew was a little square box, dwarfish
in proportion with the kirk itself, and enclosing a table not
much bigger than a footstool. There sat Archie, an apparent
prince, the only undeniable gentleman and the only great
heritor in the parish, taking his ease in the only pew, for no
other in the kirk had doors. Thence he might command an
undisturbed view of that congregation of solid plaided men,
strapping wives and daughters, oppressed children, and
uneasy sheep-dogs. It was strange how Archie missed the
look of race; except the dogs, with their refined foxy faces
and inimitably curling tails, there was no one present with
the least claim to gentility. The Cauldstaneslap party was
scarcely an exception; Dandie perhaps, as he amused
himself making verses through the interminable burden of
the service, stood out a little by the glow in his eye and a
certain superior animation of face and alertness of body;
but even Dandie slouched like a rustic. The rest of the
congregation, like so many sheep, oppressed him with a
sense of hob-nailed routine, day following day – of physical
labour in the open air, oatmeal porridge, peas bannock, the
somnolent fireside in the evening, and the night-long nasal
slumbers in a box-bed. Yet he knew many of them to be
shrewd and humorous, men of character, notable women,
making a bustle in the world and radiating an influence
from their low-browed doors. He knew besides they were
like other men; below the crust of custom, rapture found a
way; he had heard them beat the timbrel before Bacchus –
had heard them shout and carouse over their whisky-toddy;

and not the most Dutch-bottomed and severe faces among them all, not even the solemn elders themselves, but were capable of singular gambols at the voice of love. Men drawing near to an end of life's adventurous journey – maids thrilling with fear and curiosity on the threshold of entrance – women who had borne and perhaps buried children, who could remember the clinging of the small dead hands and the patter of the little feet now silent – he marvelled that among all those faces there should be no face of expectation, none that was mobile, none into which the rhythm and poetry of life had entered. 'O for a live face,' he thought; and at times he had a memory of Lady Flora; and at times he would study the living gallery before him with despair, and would see himself go on to waste his days in that joyless, pastoral place, and death come to him, and his grave be dug under the rowans, and the Spirit of the Earth laugh out in a thunder-peal at the huge fiasco.

On this particular Sunday, there was no doubt but that the spring had come at last. It was warm, with a latent shiver in the air that made the warmth only the more welcome. The shallows of the stream glittered and tinkled among bunches of primrose. Vagrant scents of the earth arrested Archie by the way with moments of ethereal intoxication. The grey, Quakerish dale was still only awakened in places and patches from the sobriety of its winter colouring; and he wondered at its beauty; an essential beauty of the old earth it seemed to him, not resident in particulars but breathing to him from the whole. He surprised himself by a sudden impulse to write poetry – he did so sometimes, loose, galloping octosyllabics in the vein of Scott – and when he had taken his place on a boulder, near some fairy falls and shaded by a whip of a tree that was already radiant with new leaves, it still more surprised him that he should find nothing to write. His heart perhaps beat in time to some vast indwelling rhythm of the universe. By the time he came to a corner of the valley and could see the kirk, he had so lingered by the way that the first psalm was finishing. The nasal psalmody, full of turns and trills and graceless graces, seemed the essential voice of the kirk itself upraised in thanksgiving. 'Everything's alive,' he said; and again cried it aloud, 'thank God, everything's alive!' He lingered yet a while in the kirk-yard. A tuft of primroses was blooming hard by the leg of an old, black table tombstone, and he stopped to contemplate the random apologue. They stood forth on the cold earth with a trenchancy of contrast; and he was struck with a sense of incompleteness in the day, the season, and the beauty that surrounded him – the chill there was in the warmth, the gross black clods about the opening primroses, the damp earthy smell that was everywhere intermingled with the scents. The voice of the aged Torrance within rose in an ecstasy. And he wondered if Torrance also felt in his old bones the joyous influence of the spring morning; Torrance, or the shadow of what once was Torrance, that must come so soon to lie outside here in the sun and rain with all his rheumatisms, while a new minister stood in his room and thundered from his own familiar pulpit? The pity of it, and something of the chill of the grave, shook him for a moment as he made haste to enter.

He went up the aisle reverently, and took his place in the pew with lowered eyes, for he feared he had already offended the kind old gentleman in the pulpit, and was sedulous to offend no further. He could not follow the prayer, not even the heads of it. Brightnesses of azure, clouds of fragrance, a tinkle of falling water and singing birds, rose like exhalations from some deeper, aboriginal memory, that was not his, but belonged to the flesh on his bones. His body remembered; and it seemed to him that his body was in no way gross, but ethereal and perishable like a strain of music; and he felt for it an exquisite tenderness as for a child, an innocent, full of beautiful instincts and destined to an early death. And he felt for old Torrance – of the many supplications, of the few days – a pity that was near to tears. The prayer ended. Right over him was a tablet in the wall, the only ornament in the roughly masoned chapel – for it was no more; the tablet commemorated, I was about to say the virtues, but rather the existence of a former Rutherford of Hermiston; and Archie, under that trophy of his long descent and local greatness, leaned back in the pew and contemplated vacancy

with the shadow of a smile between playful and sad, that
became him strangely. Dandie's sister, sitting by the side
of Clem in her new Glasgow finery, chose that moment to
observe the young laird. Aware of the stir of his entrance,
the little formalist had kept her eyes fastened and her face
prettily composed during the prayer. It was not hypocrisy,
there was no one further from a hypocrite. The girl had been
taught to behave: to look up, to look down, to look unconscious, to look seriously impressed in church, and in
every conjuncture to look her best. That was the game of
female life, and she played it frankly. Archie was the one
person in church who was of interest, who was somebody
new, reputed eccentric, known to be young, and a laird,
and still unseen by Christina. Small wonder that, as she
stood there in her attitude of pretty decency, her mind
should run upon him! If he spared a glance in her direction,
he should know she was a well-behaved young lady who
had been to Glasgow. In reason he must admire her clothes,
and it was possible that he should think her pretty. At that
her heart beat the least thing in the world; and she
proceeded, by way of a corrective, to call up and dismiss a
series of fancied pictures of the young man who should now,
by rights, be looking at her. She settled on the plainest of
them – a pink short young man with a dish face and no
figure, at whose admiration she could afford to smile; but for
all that, the consciousness of his gaze (which was really
fixed on Torrance and his mittens) kept her in something of
a flutter till the word Amen. Even then, she was far too
well-bred to gratify her curiosity with any impatience. She
resumed her seat languidly – this was a Glasgow touch – she
composed her dress, rearranged her nosegay of primroses,
looked first in front, then behind upon the other side, and at
last allowed her eyes to move, without hurry, in the direction
of the Hermiston pew. For a moment, they were riveted.
Next she had plucked her gaze home again like a tame bird
who should have meditated flight. Possibilities crowded on
her; she hung over the future and grew dizzy; the image of
this young man, slim, graceful, dark, with the inscrutable
half-smile, attracted and repelled her like a chasm. 'I wonder,

will I have met my fate?' she thought, and her heart swelled.

Torrance was got some way into his first exposition, positing a deep layer of texts as he went along, laying the foundations of his discourse, which was to deal with a nice point in divinity, before Archie suffered his eyes to wander. They fell first of all on Clem, looking insupportably prosperous, and patronising Torrance with the favour of a modified attention, as of one who was used to better things in Glasgow. Though he had never before set eyes on him, Archie had no difficulty in identifying him, and no hesitation in pronouncing him vulgar, the worst of the family. Clem was leaning lazily forward when Archie first saw him. Presently he leaned nonchalantly back; and that deadly instrument, the maiden, was suddenly unmasked in profile. Though not quite in the front of the fashion (had anybody cared!), certain artful Glasgow mantua-makers, and her own inherent taste, had arrayed her to great advantage. Her accoutrement was, indeed, a cause of heart-burning, and almost of scandal, in that infinitesimal kirk company. Mrs. Hob had said her say at Cauldstaneslap. 'Daft-like!' she had pronounced it. 'A jaiket that'll no meet! Whaur's the sense of a jaiket that'll no button upon you, if it should come to be weet? What do ye ca' thir things? Demmy brokens, d'ye say? They'll be brokens wi' a vengeance or ye can win back! Weel, I have naething to do wi' it – it's no good taste.' Clem, whose purse had thus metamorphosed his sister, and who was not insensible to the advertisement, had come to the rescue with a 'Hoot, woman! What do you ken of good taste that has never been to the ceety?' And Hob, looking on the girl with pleased smiles, as she timidly displayed her finery in the midst of the dark kitchen, had thus ended the dispute: 'The cutty looks weel,' he had said, 'and it's no very like rain. Wear them the day, hizzie; but it's no a thing to make a practice o'.' In the breasts of her rivals, coming to the kirk very conscious of white under-linen, and their faces splendid with much soap, the sight of the toilet had raised a storm of varying emotion, from the mere unenvious admiration that was expressed in a long-drawn 'Eh!' to the angrier feeling that found vent in an emphatic 'Set her up!' Her frock was of straw-coloured jaconet muslin, cut low at the bosom and short at the ankle, so as to display her *demi-broquins* of Regency violet, crossing with many straps upon a yellow cobweb stocking. According to the pretty fashion in which our grandmothers did not hesitate to appear, and our great-aunts went forth armed for the pursuit and capture of our great-uncles, the dress was drawn up so as to mould the contour of both breasts, and in the nook between, a cairngorm brooch maintained it. Here, too, surely in a very enviable position, trembled the nosegay of primroses. She wore on her shoulders – or rather, on her back and not her shoulders, which it scarcely passed – a French coat of sarsenet, tied in front with Margate braces, and of the same colour with her violet shoes. About her face clustered a disorder of dark ringlets, a little garland of yellow French roses surmounted her brow, and the whole was crowned by a village hat of chipped straw. Amongst all the rosy and all the weathered faces that surrounded her in church, she glowed like an open flower – girl and raiment, and the cairngorm that caught the daylight and returned it in a fiery flash, and the threads of bronze and gold that played in her hair.

Archie was attracted by the bright thing like a child. He looked at her again and yet again, and their looks crossed. The lip was lifted from her little teeth. He saw the red blood work vividly under her tawny skin. Her eye, which was great as a stag's, struck and held his gaze. He knew who she must be – Kirstie, she of the harsh diminutive, his housekeeper's niece, the sister of the rustic prophet, Gib – and he found in her the answer to his wishes.

Christina felt the shock of their encountering glances, and seemed to rise, clothed in smiles, into a region of the vague and bright. But the gratification was not more exquisite than it was brief. She looked away abruptly, and immediately began to blame herself for that abruptness. She knew what she should have done, too late – turned slowly with her nose in the air. And meantime his look was not removed, but continued to play upon her like a battery of cannon constantly aimed, and now seemed to isolate her alone

with him, and now seemed to uplift her, as on a pillory,
before the congregation. For Archie continued to drink
her in with his eyes, even as a wayfarer comes to a well-head
on a mountain, and stoops his face, and drinks with thirst
unassuageable. In the cleft of her little breasts the fiery eye
of the topaz and the pale florets of primrose fascinated him.
He saw the breasts heave, and the flowers shake with the
heaving, and marvelled what should so much discompose the
girl. And Christina was conscious of his gaze – saw it,
perhaps, with the dainty plaything of an ear that peeped
among her ringlets; she was conscious of changing colour,
conscious of her unsteady breath. Like a creature tracked,
run down, surrounded, she sought in a dozen ways to give
herself a countenance. She used her handkerchief – it was a
really fine one – then she desisted in a panic: 'He would
only think I was too warm.' She took to reading in the
metrical psalms, and then remembered it was sermon-time.
Last she put a 'sugar-bool' in her mouth, and the next
moment repented of the step. It was such a homely-like
thing! Mr. Archie would never be eating sweeties in kirk;
and, with a palpable effort, she swallowed it whole, and her
colour flamed high. At this signal of distress Archie awoke
to a sense of his ill-behaviour. What had he been doing? He
had been exquisitely rude in church to the niece of his
housekeeper; he had stared like a lackey and a libertine at a
beautiful and modest girl. It was possible, it was even likely,
he would be presented to her after service in the kirk-yard,
and then how was he to look? And there was no excuse. He
had marked the tokens of her shame, of her increasing
indignation, and he was such a fool that he had not understood them. Shame bowed him down, and he looked
resolutely at Mr. Torrance; who little supposed, good,
worthy man, as he continued to expound justification by
faith, what was his true business: to play the part of derivative to a pair of children at the old game of falling in love.

Christina was greatly relieved at first. It seemed to her that
she was clothed again. She looked back on what had passed.
All would have been right if she had not blushed, a silly
fool! There was nothing to blush at, if she *had* taken a

sugar-bool. Mrs. MacTaggart, the elder's wife in St. Enoch's, took them often. And if he had looked at her, what was more natural than that a young gentleman should look at the best-dressed girl in church? And at the same time, she knew far otherwise, she knew there was nothing casual or ordinary in the look, and valued herself on its memory like a decoration. Well, it was a blessing he had found something else to look at! And presently she began to have other thoughts. It was necessary, she fancied, that she should put herself right by a repetition of the incident, better managed. If the wish was father to the thought, she did not know or she would not recognise it. It was simply as a manoeuvre of propriety, as something called for to lessen the significance of what had gone before, that she should a second time meet his eyes, and this time without blushing. And at the memory of the blush, she blushed again, and became one general blush burning from head to foot. Was ever anything so indelicate, so forward, done by a girl before? And here she was, making an exhibition of herself before the congregation about nothing! She stole a glance upon her neighbours, and behold! they were steadily indifferent, and Clem had gone to sleep. And still the one idea was becoming more and more potent with her, that in common prudence she must look again before the service ended. Something of the same sort was going forward in the mind of Archie, as he struggled with the load of penitence. So it chanced that, in the flutter of the moment when the last psalm was given out, and Torrance was reading the verse, and the leaves of every psalm-book in church were rustling under busy fingers, two stealthy glances were sent out like antennae among the pews and on the indifferent and absorbed occupants, and drew timidly nearer to the straight line between Archie and Christina. They met, they lingered together for the least fraction of time, and that was enough. A charge as of electricity passed through Christina, and behold! the leaf of her psalm-book was torn across.

Archie was outside by the gate of the graveyard, conversing with Hob and the minister and shaking hands all round with the scattering congregation, when Clem and Christina

were brought up to be presented. The laird took off his hat
and bowed to her with grace and respect. Christina made her
Glasgow curtsey to the laird, and went on again up the road
for Hermiston and Cauldstaneslap, walking fast, breathing
hurriedly with a heightened colour, and in this strange frame
of mind, that when she was alone she seemed in high
happiness, and when any one addressed her she resented it
like a contradiction. A part of the way she had the company
of some neighbour girls and a loutish young man; never
had they seemed so insipid, never had she made herself so
disagreeable. But these struck aside to their various destina-
tions or were out-walked and left behind; and when she
had driven off with sharp words the proffered convoy of
some of her nephews and nieces, she was free to go on alone
up Hermiston brae, walking on air, dwelling intoxicated
among clouds of happiness. Near to the summit she heard
steps behind her, a man's steps, light and very rapid. She
knew the foot at once and walked the faster. 'If it's me he's
wanting, he can run for it,' she thought, smiling.

   Archie overtook her like a man whose mind was made up.
   'Miss Kirstie,' he began.
   'Miss Christina, if you please, Mr. Weir,' she interrupted.
'I canna bear the contraction.'
   'You forget it has a friendly sound for me. Your aunt is an
old friend of mine, and a very good one. I hope we shall
see much of you at Hermiston?'
   'My aunt and my sister-in-law doesna agree very well. Not
that I have much ado with it. But still when I'm stopping in
the house, if I was to be visiting my aunt, it would not look
considerate-like.'
   'I am sorry,' said Archie.
   'I thank you kindly, Mr. Weir,' she said. 'I whiles think
myself it's a great peety.'
   'Ah, I am sure your voice would always be for peace!' he
cried.
   'I wouldna be too sure of that,' she said. 'I have my days
like other folk, I suppose.'
   'Do you know, in our old kirk, among our good old grey
dames, you made an effect like sunshine.'

'Ah, but that would be my Glasgow clothes!'

'I did not think I was so much under the influence of pretty frocks.'

She smiled with a half look at him. 'There's more than you!' she said. 'But you see I'm only Cinderella. I'll have to put all these things by in my trunk; next Sunday I'll be as grey as the rest. They're Glasgow clothes, you see, and it would never do to make a practice of it. It would seem terrible conspicuous.'

By that they were come to the place where their ways severed. The old grey moors were all about them; in the midst a few sheep wandered; and they could see on the one hand the straggling caravan scaling the braes in front of them for Cauldstaneslap, and on the other, the contingent from Hermiston bending off and beginning to disappear by detachments into the policy gate. It was in these circumstances that they turned to say farewell, and deliberately exchanged a glance as they shook hands. All passed as it should, genteelly; and in Christina's mind, as she mounted the first steep ascent for Cauldstaneslap, a gratifying sense of triumph prevailed over the recollection of minor lapses and mistakes. She had kilted her gown, as she did usually at that rugged pass; but when she spied Archie still standing and gazing after her, the skirts came down again as if by enchantment. Here was a piece of nicety for that upland parish, where the matrons marched with their coats kilted in the rain, and the lasses walked barefoot to kirk through the dust of summer, and went bravely down by the burn-side, and sat on stones to make a public toilet before entering! It was perhaps an air wafted from Glasgow; or perhaps it marked a stage of that dizziness of gratified vanity, in which the instinctive act passed unperceived. He was looking after! She unloaded her bosom of a prodigious sigh that was all pleasure, and betook herself to run. When she had overtaken the stragglers of her family, she caught up the niece whom she had so recently repulsed, and kissed and slapped her, and drove her away again, and ran after her with pretty cries and laughter. Perhaps she thought the laird might still be looking! But it chanced the little scene came under the view

of eyes less favourable; for she overtook Mrs. Hob marching
with Clem and Dand.

'You're shürely fey, lass!' quoth Dandie.

'Think shame to yersel', miss!' said the strident Mrs. Hob.
'Is this the gait to guide yersel' on the way hame frae kirk?
You're shürely no sponsible the day! And anyway I would
mind my guid claes.'

'Hoot!' said Christina, and went on before them head in
air, treading the rough track with the tread of a wild doe.

She was in love with herself, her destiny, the air of the
hills, the benediction of the sun. All the way home, she
continued under the intoxication of these sky-scraping
spirits. At table she could talk freely of young Hermiston;
gave her opinion of him offhand and with a loud voice, that
he was a handsome young gentleman, real well mannered
and sensible-like, but it was a pity he looked doleful. Only –
the moment after – a memory of his eyes in church
embarrassed her. But for this inconsiderable check, all
through meal-time she had a good appetite, and she kept
them laughing at table, until Gib (who had returned before
them from Crossmichael and his separative worship)
reproved the whole of them for their levity.

Singing 'in to herself' as she went, her mind still in the
turmoil of a glad confusion, she rose and tripped upstairs to
a little loft, lighted by four panes in the gable, where she
slept with one of her nieces. The niece, who followed her,
presuming on 'Auntie's' high spirits, was flounced out of the
apartment with small ceremony, and retired, smarting and
half tearful, to bury her woes in the byre among the hay. Still
humming, Christina divested herself of her finery, and put
her treasures one by one in her great green trunk. The last
of these was the psalm-book; it was a fine piece, the gift of
Mistress Clem, in distinct old-faced type, on paper that
had begun to grow foxy in the warehouse – not by service –
and she was used to wrap it in a handkerchief every Sunday
after its period of service was over, and bury it end-wise at
the head of her trunk. As she now took it in hand the book
fell open where the leaf was torn, and she stood and gazed
upon that evidence of her bygone discomposure. There

returned again the vision of the two brown eyes staring at her, intent and bright, out of that dark corner of the kirk. The whole appearance and attitude, the smile, the suggested gesture of young Hermiston came before her in a flash at the sight of the torn page. 'I was surely fey!' she said, echoing the words of Dandie, and at the suggested doom her high spirits deserted her. She flung herself prone upon the bed, and lay there, holding the psalm-book in her hands for hours, for the more part in a mere stupor of unconsenting pleasure and unreasoning fear. The fear was superstitious; there came up again and again in her memory Dandie's ill-omened words, and a hundred grisly and black tales out of the immediate neighbourhood read her a commentary on their force. The pleasure was never realised. You might say the joints of her body thought and remembered, and were gladdened, but her essential self, in the immediate theatre of consciousness, talked feverishly of something else, like a nervous person at a fire. The image that she most complacently dwelt on was that of Miss Christina in her character of the Fair Lass of Cauldstaneslap, carrying all before her in the straw-coloured frock, the violet mantle, and the yellow cobweb stockings. Archie's image, on the other hand, when it presented itself was never welcomed – far less welcomed with any ardour, and it was exposed at times to merciless criticism. In the long vague dialogues she held in her mind, often with imaginary, often with unrealised interlocutors, Archie, if he were referred to at all, came in for savage handling. He was described as 'looking like a stirk,' 'staring like a caulf,' 'a face like a ghaist's.' 'Do you call that manners?' she said; or, 'I soon put him in his place.' ' "*Miss Christina, if you please, Mr. Weir!*" says I, and just flyped up my skirt tails.' With gabble like this she would entertain herself long whiles together, and then her eye would perhaps fall on the torn leaf, and the eyes of Archie would appear again from the darkness of the wall, and the voluble words deserted her, and she would lie still and stupid, and think upon nothing with devotion, and be sometimes raised by a quiet sigh. Had a doctor of medicine come into that loft, he would have diagnosed a healthy, well-

developed, eminently vivacious lass lying on her face in a fit
of the sulks; not one who had just contracted, or was just
contracting, a mortal sickness of the mind which should yet
carry her towards death and despair. Had it been a doctor
of psychology, he might have been pardoned for divining
in the girl a passion of childish vanity, self-love *in excelsis*,
and no more. It is to be understood that I have been painting
chaos and describing the inarticulate. Every lineament that
appears is too precise, almost every word used too strong.
Take a finger-post in the mountains on a day of rolling mists;
I have but copied the names that appear upon the pointers,
the names of definite and famous cities far distant, and now
perhaps basking in sunshine; but Christina remained all
these hours, as it were, at the foot of the post itself, not
moving, and enveloped in mutable and blinding wreaths of
haze.

The day was growing late and the sunbeams long and
level, when she sat suddenly up, and wrapped in its handkerchief and put by that psalm-book which had already played
a part so decisive in the first chapter of her love-story. In
the absence of the mesmerist's eye, we are told nowadays
that the head of a bright nail may fill his place, if it be
steadfastly regarded. So that torn page had riveted her
attention on what might else have been but little, and
perhaps soon forgotten; while the ominous words of Dandie
– heard, not heeded, and still remembered – had lent to her
thoughts, or rather to her mood, a cast of solemnity, and
that idea of Fate – a pagan Fate, uncontrolled by any
Christian deity, obscure, lawless, and august – moving
indissuadably in the affairs of Christian men. Thus even that
phenomenon of love at first sight, which is so rare and seems
so simple and violent, like a disruption of life's tissue, may
be decomposed into a sequence of accidents happily
concurring.

She put on a grey frock and a pink kerchief, looked at
herself a moment with approval in the small square of glass
that served her for a toilet mirror, and went softly down-
stairs through the sleeping house that resounded with the
sound of afternoon snoring. Just outside the door, Dandie

was sitting with a book in his hand, not reading, only honouring the Sabbath by a sacred vacancy of mind. She came near him and stood still.

'I'm for off up the muirs, Dandie,' she said.

There was something unusually soft in her tones that made him look up. She was pale, her eyes dark and bright; no trace remained of the levity of the morning.

'Ay, lass? Ye'll have yer ups and downs like me, I'm thinkin',' he observed.

'What for do ye say that?' she asked.

'O, for naething,' says Dand. 'Only I think ye're mair like me than the lave of them. Ye've mair of the poetic temper, tho' Guid kens little enough of the poetic taalent. It's an ill gift at the best. Look at yoursel'. At denner you were all sunshine and flowers and laughter, and now you're like the star of evening on a lake.'

She drank in this hackneyed compliment like wine, and it glowed in her veins.

'But I'm saying, Dand' – she came nearer him – 'I'm for the muirs. I must have a braith of air. If Clem was to be speiring for me, try and quaiet him, will ye no?'

'What way?' said Dandie. 'I ken but the ae way, and that's leein'. I'll say ye had a sair heed, if ye like.'

'But I havena,' she objected.

'I daursay no',' he returned. 'I said I would say ye had; and if ye like to nay-say me when ye come back, it'll no mateerially maitter, for my chara'ter's clean gane a'ready past reca'.'

'O, Dand, are ye a leear?' she asked, lingering.

'Folks say sae,' replied the bard.

'Wha says sae?' she pursued.

'Them that should ken the best,' he responded. 'The lassies, for ane.'

'But, Dand, you would never lee to me?' she asked.

'I'll leave that for your pairt of it, ye girzie,' said he. 'Ye'll lee to me fast eneuch, when ye hae gotten a jo. I'm tellin' ye and it's true; when you have a jo, Miss Kirstie, it'll be for guid and ill. I ken: I was made that way mysel', but the deil was in my luck! Here, gang awa wi' ye to your muirs, and let me be; I'm in an hour of inspiraution, ye upsetting tawpie!'

But she clung to her brother's neighbourhood, she knew not why.

'Will ye no gie's a kiss, Dand?' she said. 'I aye likit ye fine.'

He kissed her and considered her a moment; he found something strange in her. But he was a libertine through and through, nourished equal contempt and suspicion of all womankind, and paid his way among them habitually with idle compliments.

'Gae wa' wi' ye!' said he. 'Ye're a dentie baby, and be content wi' that!'

That was Dandie's way; a kiss and a comfit to Jenny – a bawbee and my blessing to Jill – and good-night to the whole clan of ye, my dears! When anything approached the serious, it became a matter for men, he both thought and said. Women, when they did not absorb, were only children to be shoo'd away. Merely in his character of connoisseur, however, Dandie glanced carelessly after his sister as she crossed the meadow. 'The brat's no that bad!' he thought with surprise, for though he had just been paying her compliments, he had not really looked at her. 'Hey! what's yon?' For the grey dress was cut with short sleeves and skirts, and displayed her trim strong legs clad in pink stockings of the same shade as the kerchief she wore round her shoulders, and that shimmered as she went. This was not her way in undress; he knew her ways and the ways of the whole sex in the countryside, no one better; when they did not go barefoot, they wore stout 'rig and furrow' woollen hose of an invisible blue mostly, when they were not black outright; and Dandie, at sight of this daintiness, put two and two together. It was a silk handkerchief, then they would be silken hose; they matched – then the whole outfit was a present of Clem's, a costly present, and not something to be worn through bog and briar, or on a late afternoon of Sunday. He whistled. 'My denty May, either your heid's fair turned, or there's some ongoings!' he observed, and dismissed the subject.

She went slowly at first, but ever straighter and faster for the Cauldstaneslap, a pass among the hills to which the farm owed its name. The Slap opened like a doorway between two rounded hillocks; and through this ran the short cut to Hermiston. Immediately on the other side it went down through the Deil's Hags, a considerably marshy hollow of the hill tops, full of springs, and crouching junipers, and pools where the black peat-water slumbered. There was no view from here. A man might have sat upon the Praying Weaver's stone a half century, and seen none but the Cauldstaneslap children twice in the twenty-four hours on their way to the school and back again, an occasional shepherd, the irruption of a clan of sheep, or the birds who haunted about the springs, drinking and shrilly piping. So, when she had once passed the Slap, Kirstie was received into seclusion. She looked back a last time at the farm. It still lay deserted except for the figure of Dandie, who was now seen to be scribbling in his lap, the hour of expected inspiration having come to him at last. Thence she passed rapidly through the morass, and came to the farther end of it, where a sluggish burn discharges, and the path for Hermiston accompanies it on the beginning of its downward way. From this corner a wide view was opened to her of the whole stretch of braes upon the other side, still sallow and in places rusty with the winter, with the path marked boldly, here and there by the burn-side a tuft of birches, and – two miles off as the crow flies – from its enclosures and young plantations, the windows of Hermiston glittering in the western sun.

Here she sat down and waited, and looked for a long time at these far-away bright panes of glass. It amused her to have so extended a view, she thought. It amused her to see the house of Hermiston – to see 'folk'; and there was an indistinguishable human unit, perhaps the gardener, visibly sauntering on the gravel paths.

By the time the sun was down and all the easterly braes lay plunged in clear shadow, she was aware of another figure coming up the path at a most unequal rate of approach, now half running, now pausing and seeming to hesitate. She watched him at first with a total suspension of thought. She held her thought as a person holds his breathing. Then she consented to recognise him. 'He'll no be coming here, he canna be; it's no possible.' And there began to grow upon her a subdued choking suspense. He *was* coming; his hesitations had quite ceased, his step grew firm and swift; no doubt remained; and the question loomed up before her instant: what was she to do? It was all very well to say that her brother was a laird himself; it was all very well to speak of casual intermarriages and to count cousinship, like Auntie Kirstie. The difference in their social station was trenchant; propriety, prudence, all that she had ever learned, all that she knew, bade her flee. But on the other hand the cup of life now offered to her was too enchanting. For one moment, she saw the question clearly, and definitely made her choice. She stood up and showed herself an instant in the gap relieved upon the sky line; and the next, fled trembling and sat down glowing with excitement on the Weaver's stone. She shut her eyes, seeking, praying for composure. Her hand shook in her lap, and her mind was full of incongruous and futile speeches. What was there to make a work about? She could take care of herself, she supposed! There was no harm in seeing the laird. It was the best thing that could happen. She would mark a proper distance to him once and for all. Gradually the wheels of her nature ceased to go round so madly, and she sat in passive expectation, a quiet, solitary figure in the midst of the grey moss. I have said she was no hypocrite, but here I am at fault. She never admitted to herself that she had come up the hill to look for Archie. And perhaps after all she did not know, perhaps came as a stone falls. For the steps of love in the young, and especially in girls, are instinctive and unconscious.

In the meantime Archie was drawing rapidly near, and he at least was consciously seeking her neighbourhood. The afternoon had turned to ashes in his mouth; the memory of the girl had kept him from reading and drawn him as with cords; and at last, as the cool of the evening began to come on, he had taken his hat and set forth, with a smothered ejaculation, by the moor path to Cauldstaneslap. He had no hope to find her; he took the off chance without expectation of result and to relieve his uneasiness. The greater was his surprise, as he surmounted the slope and came into the hollow of the Deil's Hags, to see there, like an answer to his wishes, the little womanly figure in the grey dress and the pink kerchief sitting little, and low, and lost, and acutely solitary, in these desolate surroundings and on the weather-beaten stone of the dead weaver. Those things that still smacked of winter were all rusty about her, and those things that already relished of the spring had put forth the tender and lively colours of the season. Even in the unchanging face of the death-stone, changes were to be remarked; and in the channelled lettering, the moss began to renew itself in jewels of green. By an after-thought that was a stroke of art, she had turned up over her head the back of the kerchief; so that it now framed becomingly her vivacious and yet pensive face. Her feet were gathered under her on the one side, and she leaned on her bare arm, which showed out strong and round, tapered to a slim wrist, and shimmered in the fading light.

Young Hermiston was struck with a certain chill. He was reminded that he now dealt in serious matters of life and death. This was a grown woman he was approaching, endowed with her mysterious potencies and attractions, the treasury of the continued race, and he was neither better nor worse than the average of his sex and age. He had a certain delicacy which had preserved him hitherto unspotted, and which (had either of them guessed it) made him a more dangerous companion when his heart should be really stirred. His throat was dry as he came near; but the appealing sweetness of her smile stood between them like a guardian angel.

For she turned to him and smiled, though without rising. There was a shade in this cavalier greeting that neither of them perceived; neither he, who simply thought it gracious and charming as herself; nor yet she, who did not observe (quick as she was) the difference between rising to meet the laird, and remaining seated to receive the expected admirer.

'Are ye stepping west, Hermiston?' said she, giving him

his territorial name after the fashion of the countryside.

'I was,' said he, a little hoarsely, 'but I think I will be about the end of my stroll now. Are you like me, Miss Christina? The house would not hold me. I came here seeking air.'

He took his seat at the other end of the tombstone and studied her, wondering what was she. There was infinite import in the question alike for her and him.

'Ay,' she said. 'I couldna bear the roof either. It's a habit of mine to come up here about the gloaming when it's quaiet and caller.'

'It was a habit of my mother's also,' he said gravely. The recollection half startled him as he expressed it. He looked around. 'I have scarce been here since. It's peaceful,' he said, with a long breath.

'It's no like Glasgow,' she replied. 'A weary place, yon Glasgow! But what a day have I had for my hame-coming, and what a bonny evening!'

'Indeed, it was a wonderful day,' said Archie. 'I think I will remember it years and years until I come to die. On days like this – I do not know if you feel as I do – but everything appears so brief, and fragile, and exquisite, that I am afraid to touch life. We are here for so short a time; and all the old people before us – Rutherfords of Hermiston, Elliotts of the Cauldstaneslap – that were here but a while since riding about and keeping up a great noise in this quiet corner – making love too, and marrying – why, where are they now? It's deadly commonplace, but, after all, the commonplaces are the great poetic truths.'

He was sounding her, semi-consciously, to see if she could understand him; to learn if she were only an animal the colour of flowers, or had a soul in her to keep her sweet. She, on her part, her means well in hand, watched, woman-like, for any opportunity to shine, to abound in his humour, whatever that might be. The dramatic artist, that lies dormant or only half awake in most human beings, had in her sprung to his feet in a divine fury, and chance had served her well. She looked upon him with a subdued twilight look that became the hour of the day and the train

pair of children. The generations were prepared, the pangs were made ready, before the curtain rose on the dark drama.

In the same moment of time that she disappeared from Archie, there opened before Kirstie's eyes the cup-like hollow in which the farm lay. She saw, some five hundred feet below her, the house making itself bright with candles, and this was a broad hint to her to hurry. For they were only kindled on a Sabbath night with a view to that family worship which rounded in the incomparable tedium of the day and brought on the relaxation of supper. Already she knew that Robert must be within-sides at the head of the table, 'waling the portions'; for it was Robert in his quality of family priest and judge, not the gifted Gilbert, who officiated. She made good time accordingly down the steep ascent, and came up to the door panting as the three younger brothers, all roused at last from slumber, stood together in the cool and the dark of the evening with a fry of nephews and nieces about them, chatting and awaiting the expected signal. She stood back; she had no mind to direct attention to her late arrival or to her labouring breath.

'Kirstie, ye have shaved it this time, my lass,' said Clem. 'Whaur were ye?'

'O, just taking a dander by mysel',' said Kirstie.

And the talk continued on the subject of the American War, without further reference to the truant who stood by them in the covert of the dusk, thrilling with happiness and the sense of guilt.

The signal was given, and the brothers began to go in one after another, amid the jostle and throng of Hob's children.

Only Dandie, waiting till the last, caught Kirstie by the arm. 'When did ye begin to dander in pink hosen, Mistress Elliott?' he whispered slyly.

She looked down; she was one blush. 'I maun have forgotten to change them,' said she; and went into prayers in her turn with a troubled mind, between anxiety as to whether Dand should have observed her yellow stockings at church, and should thus detect her in a palpable falsehood, and shame that she had already made good his prophecy. She remembered the words of it, how it was to be when she had gotten a jo, and that that would be for good and evil. 'Will I have gotten my jo now?' she thought with a secret rapture.

And all through prayers, where it was her principal business to conceal the pink stockings from the eyes of the indifferent Mrs. Hob – and all through supper, as she made a feint of eating and sat at the table radiant and constrained – and again when she had left them and come into her chamber, and was alone with her sleeping niece, and could at last lay aside the armour of society – the same words sounded within her, the same profound note of happiness, of a world all changed and renewed, of a day that had been passed in Paradise, and of a night that was to be heaven opened. All night she seemed to be conveyed smoothly upon a shallow stream of sleep and waking, and through the bowers of Beulah; all night she cherished to her heart that exquisite hope; and if, towards morning, she forgot it a while in a more profound unconsciousness, it was to catch again the rainbow thought with her first moment of awaking.

Chapter Seven

Enter Mephistopheles

Two days later a gig from Crossmichael deposited Frank Innes at the doors of Hermiston. Once in a way, during the past winter, Archie, in some acute phase of boredom, had written him a letter. It had contained something in the nature of an invitation, or a reference to an invitation – precisely what, neither of them now remembered. When Innes had received it, there had been nothing further from his mind than to bury himself in the moors with Archie; but not even the most acute political heads are guided through the steps of life with unerring directness. That would require a gift of prophecy which has been denied to man. For instance, who could have imagined that, not a month after he had received the letter, and turned it into mockery, and put off answering it, and in the end lost it, misfortunes of a gloomy cast should begin to thicken over Frank's career? His case may be briefly stated. His father, a small Morayshire laird with a large family, became recalcitrant and cut off the supplies; he had fitted himself out with the beginnings of quite a good law library, which, upon some sudden losses on the turf, he had been obliged to sell before they were paid for; and his bookseller, hearing some rumour of the event, took out a warrant for his arrest. Innes had early word of it, and was able to take precautions. In this immediate welter of his affairs, with an unpleasant charge hanging over him, he had judged it the part of prudence to be off instantly, had written a fervid letter to his father at Inverauld, and put himself in the coach for Crossmichael. Any port in a storm! He was manfully turning his back on the Parliament House and its gay babble, on porter and oysters, the racecourse and the ring; and manfully prepared, until these clouds should have blown by, to share a living grave with Archie Weir at Hermiston.

To do him justice, he was no less surprised to be going than Archie was to see him come; and he carried off his wonder with an infinitely better grace.

'Well, here I am!' said he, as he alighted. 'Pylades has come to Orestes at last. By the way, did you get my answer? No? How very provoking! Well, here I am to answer for myself, and that's better still.'

'I am very glad to see you, of course,' said Archie. 'I make you heartily welcome, of course. But you surely have not come to stay, with the Courts still sitting; is that not most unwise?'

'Damn the Courts!' says Frank. 'What are the Courts to friendship and a little fishing?'

And so it was agreed that he was to stay, with no term to the visit but the term which he had privily set to it himself – the day, namely, when his father should have come down with the dust, and he should be able to pacify the book-seller. On such vague conditions there began for these two young men (who were not even friends) a life of great familiarity and, as the days drew on, less and less intimacy. They were together at meal times, together o' nights when the hour had come for whisky-toddy; but it might have been noticed (had there been any one to pay heed) that they were rarely so much together by day. Archie had Hermiston to attend to, multifarious activities in the hills, in which he did not require, and had even refused, Frank's escort. He would be off sometimes in the morning and leave only a note on the breakfast table to announce the fact; and sometimes, with no notice at all, he would not return for dinner until the hour was long past. Innes groaned under these desertions; it required all his philosophy to sit down to a solitary breakfast with composure, and all his unaffected good-nature to be able to greet Archie with friendliness on the more rare occasions when he came home late for dinner.

'I wonder what on earth he finds to do, Mrs. Elliott?' said he one morning, after he had just read the hasty billet and sat down to table.

'I suppose it will be business, sir,' replied the housekeeper dryly, measuring his distance off to him by an indicated curtsey.

'But I can't imagine what business!' he reiterated.

'I suppose it will be *his* business,' retorted the austere Kirstie.

He turned to her with that happy brightness that made the charm of his disposition, and broke into a peal of healthy and natural laughter.

'Well played, Mrs. Elliott!' he cried; and the house-keeper's face relaxed into the shadow of an iron smile. 'Well played indeed!' said he. 'But you must not be making a stranger of me like that. Why, Archie and I were at the High School together, and we've been to College together, and we were going to the Bar together, when – you know! Dear, dear me! what a pity that was! A life spoiled, a fine young fellow as good as buried here in the wilderness with rustics; and all for what? A frolic, silly, if you like, but no more. God, how good your scones are, Mrs. Elliott!'

'They're no mines, it was the lassie made them,' said Kirstie; 'and, saving your presence, there's little sense in taking the Lord's name in vain about idle vivers that you fill your kyte wi'.'

'I dare say you're perfectly right, ma'am,' quoth the imperturbable Frank. 'But as I was saying, this is a pitiable business, this about poor Archie; and you and I might do worse than put our heads together, like a couple of sensible people, and bring it to an end. Let me tell you, ma'am, that Archie is really quite a promising young man, and in my opinion he would do well at the Bar. As for his father, no one can deny his ability, and I don't fancy any one would care to deny that he has the deil's own temper——'

'If you'll excuse me, Mr. Innes, I think the lass is crying on me,' said Kirstie, and flounced from the room.

'The damned, cross-grained, old broomstick!' ejaculated Innes.

In the meantime, Kirstie had escaped into the kitchen, and before her vassal gave vent to her feelings.

'Here, ettercap! Ye'll have to wait on yon Innes! I canna haud myself in. "Puir Erchie!" I'd "puir Erchie" him, if I

had my way! And Hermiston with the deil's ain temper!
God, let him take Hermiston's scones out of his mouth first.
There's no a hair on ayther o' the Weirs that hasna mair
spunk and dirdum to it than what he has in his hale dwaibly
body! Settin' up his snash to me! Let him gang to the black
toon where he's mebbe wantit – birling in a curricle – wi'
pimatum on his heid – making a mess o' himsel' wi' nesty
hizzies – a fair disgrace!' It was impossible to hear without
admiration Kirstie's graduated disgust, as she brought forth,
one after another, these somewhat baseless charges. Then
she remembered her immediate purpose, and turned again to
her fascinated auditor. 'Do ye no hear me, tawpie? Do ye no
hear what I'm tellin' ye? Will I have to shoo ye in to him?
If I come to attend to ye, mistress!' And the maid fled the
kitchen, which had become practically dangerous, to attend
on Innes's wants in the front parlour.

Tantaene irae? Has the reader perceived the reason? Since
Frank's coming there were no more hours of gossip over the
supper tray! All his blandishments were in vain; he had
started handicapped on the race for Mrs. Elliott's favour.

But it was a strange thing how misfortune dogged him in
his efforts to be genial. I must guard the reader against
accepting Kirstie's epithets as evidence; she was more
concerned for their vigour than for their accuracy. Dwaibly,
for instance; nothing could be more calumnious. Frank was
the very picture of good looks, good humour, and manly
youth. He had bright eyes with a sparkle and a dance to
them, curly hair, a charming smile, brilliant teeth, an
admirable carriage of the head, the look of a gentleman, the
address of one accustomed to please at first sight and to
improve the impression. And with all these advantages, he
failed with every one about Hermiston; with the silent
shepherd, with the obsequious grieve, with the groom who
was also the ploughman, with the gardener and the
gardener's sister – a pious, down-hearted woman with a
shawl over her ears – he failed equally and flatly. They did
not like him, and they showed it. The little maid, indeed,
was an exception; she admired him devoutly, probably
dreamed of him in her private hours; but she was

accustomed to play the part of silent auditor to Kirstie's
tirades and silent recipient of Kirstie's buffets, and she had
learned not only to be a very capable girl of her years, but a
very secret and prudent one besides. Frank was thus
conscious that he had one ally and sympathiser in the midst
of that general union of disfavour that surrounded, watched,
and waited on him in the house of Hermiston; but he had
little comfort or society from that alliance, and the demure
little maid (twelve on her last birthday) preserved her own
counsel, and tripped on his service, brisk, dumbly responsive,
but inexorably unconversational. For the others, they were
beyond hope and beyond endurance. Never had a young
Apollo been cast among such rustic barbarians. But perhaps
the cause of his ill-success lay in one trait which was habitual
and unconscious with him, yet diagnostic of the man. It
was his practice to approach any one person at the expense
of some one else. He offered you an alliance against the
some one else; he flattered you by slighting him; you were
drawn into a small intrigue against him before you knew
how. Wonderful are the virtues of this process generally; but
Frank's mistake was in the choice of the some one else. He
was not politic in that; he listened to the voice of irritation.
Archie had offended him at first by what he had felt to be
rather a dry reception, had offended him since by his
frequent absences. He was besides the one figure continually
present in Frank's eye; and it was to his immediate depend-
ants that Frank could offer the snare of his sympathy. Now
the truth is that the Weirs, father and son, were surrounded
by a posse of strenuous loyalists. Of my lord they were vastly
proud. It was a distinction in itself to be one of the vassals
of the 'Hanging Judge,' and his gross, formidable joviality
was far from unpopular in the neighbourhood of his home.
For Archie they had, one and all, a sensitive affection and
respect which recoiled from a word of belittlement.

Nor was Frank more successful when he went farther
afield. To the Four Black Brothers, for instance, he was
antipathetic in the highest degree. Hob thought him too
light, Gib too profane. Clem, who saw him but for a day or
two before he went to Glasgow, wanted to know what the

fule's business was, and whether he meant to stay here all session time! 'Yon's a drone,' he pronounced. As for Dand, it will be enough to describe their first meeting, when Frank had been whipping a river and the rustic celebrity chanced to come along the path.

'I'm told you're quite a poet,' Frank had said.

'Wha tell 't ye that, mannie?' had been the unconciliating answer.

'O, everybody!' says Frank.

'God! Here's fame!' said the sardonic poet, and he had passed on his way.

Come to think of it, we have here perhaps a truer explanation of Frank's failures. Had he met Mr. Sheriff Scott he could have turned a neater compliment, because Mr. Scott would have been a friend worth making. Dand, on the other hand, he did not value sixpence, and he showed it even while he tried to flatter. Condescension is an excellent thing, but it is strange how one-sided the pleasure of it is! He who goes fishing among the Scots peasantry with condescension for a bait will have an empty basket by evening.

In proof of this theory Frank made a great success of it at the Crossmichael Club, to which Archie took him immediately on his arrival; his own last appearance on that scene of gaiety. Frank was made welcome there at once, continued to go regularly, and had attended a meeting (as the members ever after loved to tell) on the evening before his death. Young Hay and young Pringle appeared again. There was another supper at Windielaws, another dinner at Driffel; and it resulted in Frank being taken to the bosom of the county people as unreservedly as he had been repudiated by the country folk. He occupied Hermiston after the manner of an invader in a conquered capital. He was perpetually issuing from it, as from a base, to toddy parties, fishing parties, and dinner parties, to which Archie was not invited, or to which Archie would not go. It was now that the name of The Recluse became general for the young man. Some say that Innes invented it; Innes, at least, spread it abroad.

'How's all with your Recluse to-day?' people would ask.

'O, reclusing away!' Innes would declare, with his bright air of saying something witty; and immediately interrupt the general laughter which he had provoked much more by his air than his words, 'Mind you, it's all very well laughing, but I'm not very well pleased. Poor Archie is a good fellow, an excellent fellow, a fellow I always liked. I think it small of him to take his little disgrace so hard and shut himself up. "Grant that it is a ridiculous story, painfully ridiculous," I keep telling him. "Be a man! Live it down, man!" But not he. Of course it's just solitude, and shame, and all that. But I confess I'm beginning to fear the result. It would be all the pities in the world if a really promising fellow like Weir was to end ill. I'm seriously tempted to write to Lord Hermiston, and put it plainly to him.'

'I would if I were you,' some of his auditors would say, shaking the head, sitting bewildered and confused at this new view of the matter, so deftly indicated by a single word. 'A capital idea!' they would add, and wonder at the *aplomb* and position of this young man, who talked as a matter of course of writing to Hermiston and correcting him upon his private affairs.

And Frank would proceed, sweetly confidential: 'I'll give you an idea, now. He's actually sore about the way that I'm received and he's left out in the county – actually jealous and sore. I've rallied him and I've reasoned with him, told him that every one was most kindly inclined towards him, told him even that *I* was received merely because I was his guest. But it's no use. He will neither accept the invitations he gets, nor stop brooding about the ones where he's left out. What I'm afraid of is that the wound's ulcerating. He had always one of those dark, secret, angry natures – a little underhand and plenty of bile – you know the sort. He must have inherited it from the Weirs, whom I suspect to have been a worthy family of weavers somewhere; what's the cant phrase? – sedentary occupation. It's precisely the kind of character to go wrong in a false position like what his father's made for him, or he's making for himself, whichever

you like to call it. And for my part, I think it a disgrace,'
Frank would say generously.

Presently the sorrow and anxiety of this disinterested
friend took shape. He began in private, in conversations of
two, to talk vaguely of bad habits and low habits. 'I must
say I'm afraid he's going wrong altogether,' he would say.
'I'll tell you plainly, and between ourselves, I scarcely like
to stay there any longer; only, man, I'm positively afraid
to leave him alone. You'll see, I shall be blamed for it
later on. I'm staying at a great sacrifice. I'm hindering my
chances at the Bar, and I can't blind my eyes to it. And what
I'm afraid of is that I'm going to get kicked for it all round
before all's done. You see, nobody believes in friendship
nowadays.'

'Well, Innes,' his interlocutor would reply, 'it's very good
of you, I must say that. If there's any blame going, you'll
always be sure of *my* good word, for one thing.'

'Well,' Frank would continue, 'candidly, I don't say it's
pleasant. He has a very rough way with him; his father's
son, you know. I don't say he's rude – of course, I couldn't
be expected to stand that – but he steers very near the wind.
No, it's not pleasant; but I tell ye, man, in conscience I
don't think it would be fair to leave him. Mind you, I don't
say there's anything actually wrong. What I say is that
I don't like the looks of it, man!' and he would press the
arm of his momentary confidant.

In the early stages I am persuaded there was no malice. He
talked but for the pleasure of airing himself. He was
essentially glib, as becomes the young advocate, and
essentially careless of the truth, which is the mark of the
young ass; and so he talked at random. There was no
particular bias, but that one which is indigenous and
universal, to flatter himself and to please and interest the
present friend. And by thus milling air out of his mouth, he
had presently built up a presentation of Archie which was
known and talked of in all corners of the county. Wherever
there was a residential house and a walled garden, wherever
there was a dwarfish castle and a park, wherever a quadruple
cottage by the ruins of a peel-tower showed an old family

going down, and wherever a handsome villa with a carriage
approach and a shrubbery marked the coming up of a new
one – probably on the wheels of machinery – Archie began
to be regarded in the light of a dark, perhaps a vicious
mystery, and the future developments of his career to be
looked for with uneasiness and confidential whispering. He
had done something disgraceful, my dear. What, was not
precisely known, and that good kind young man, Mr. Innes,
did his best to make light of it. But there it was. And Mr.
Innes was very anxious about him now; he was really
uneasy, my dear; he was positively wrecking his own
prospects because he dared not leave him alone. How
wholly we all lie at the mercy of a single prater, not needfully
with any malign purpose! And if a man but talks of himself
in the right spirit, refers to his virtuous actions by the way,
and never applies to them the name of virtue, how easily his
evidence is accepted in the court of public opinion!

All this while, however, there was a more poisonous
ferment at work between the two lads, which came late
indeed to the surface, but had modified and magnified their
dissensions from the first. To an idle, shallow, easy-going
customer like Frank, the smell of a mystery was attractive. It
gave his mind something to play with, like a new toy to a
child; and it took him on the weak side, for like many
young men coming to the Bar, and before they have been
tried and found wanting, he flattered himself he was a
fellow of unusual quickness and penetration. They knew
nothing of Sherlock Holmes in those days, but there was a
good deal said of Talleyrand. And if you could have caught
Frank off his guard, he would have confessed with a smirk
that, if he resembled any one, it was the Marquis de
Talleyrand-Périgord. It was on the occasion of Archie's first
absence that this interest took root. It was vastly deepened
when Kirstie resented his curiosity at breakfast, and that
same afternoon there occurred another scene which clinched
the business. He was fishing Swingleburn, Archie accom-
panying him, when the latter looked at his watch.

'Well,goodbye,' said he. 'I have something to do. See you
at dinner.'

'Don't be in such a hurry,' cries Frank. 'Hold on till I get my rod up. I'll go with you; I'm sick of flogging this ditch.'

And he began to reel up his line.

Archie stood speechless. He took a long while to recover his wits under this direct attack; but by the time he was ready with his answer, and the angle was almost packed up, he had become completely Weir, and the hanging face gloomed on his young shoulders. He spoke with a laboured composure, a laboured kindness even; but a child could see that his mind was made up.

'I beg your pardon, Innes; I don't want to be disagreeable, but let us understand one another from the beginning. When I want your company, I'll let you know.'

'O!' cries Frank, 'you don't want my company, don't you?'

'Apparently not just now,' replied Archie. 'I even indicated to you when I did, if you'll remember – and that was at dinner. If we two fellows are to live together pleasantly – and I see no reason why we should not – it can only be by respecting each other's privacy. If we begin intruding——'

'O, come! I'll take this at no man's hands. Is this the way you treat a guest and an old friend?' cried Innes.

'Just go home and think over what I said by yourself,' continued Archie, 'whether it's reasonable, or whether it's really offensive or not; and let's meet at dinner as though nothing had happened. I'll put it this way, if you like – that I know my own character, that I'm looking forward (with great pleasure, I assure you) to a long visit from you, and that I'm taking precautions at the first. I see the thing that we – that I, if you like – might fall out upon, and I step in and *obsto principiis*. I wager you five pounds you'll end by seeing that I mean friendliness, and I assure you, Francie, I do,' he added, relenting.

Bursting with anger, but incapable of speech, Innes shouldered his rod, made a gesture of farewell, and strode off down the burnside. Archie watched him go without moving. He was sorry, but quite unashamed. He hated to

be inhospitable, but in one thing he was his father's son.
He had a strong sense that his house was his own and no
man else's; and to lie at a guest's mercy was what he refused.
He hated to seem harsh. But that was Frank's lookout. If
Frank had been commonly discreet, he would have been
decently courteous. And there was another consideration.
The secret he was protecting was not his own merely; it
was hers: it belonged to that inexpressible she who was fast
taking possession of his soul, and whom he would soon
have defended at the cost of burning cities. By the time he
had watched Frank as far as the Swingleburnfoot, appearing
and disappearing in the tarnished heather, still stalking at
a fierce gait but already dwindled in the distance into less
than the smallness of Lilliput, he could afford to smile at
the occurrence. Either Frank would go, and that would be
a relief – or he would continue to stay, and his host must
continue to endure him. And Archie was now free – by
devious paths, behind hillocks and in the hollow of burns –
to make for the trysting-place where Kirstie, cried about by
the curlew and the plover, waited and burned for his coming
by the Covenanter's stone.

Innes went off down-hill in a passion of resentment, easy
to be understood, but which yielded progressively to the
needs of his situation. He cursed Archie for a cold-hearted,
unfriendly, rude, rude dog; and himself still more
passionately for a fool in having come to Hermiston when he
might have sought refuge in almost any other house in
Scotland. But the step, once taken, was practically irretriev-
able. He had no more ready money to go anywhere else; he
would have to borrow from Archie the next club-night; and
ill as he thought of his host's manners, he was sure of his
practical generosity. Frank's resemblance to Talleyrand
strikes me as imaginary; but at least not Talleyrand himself
could have more obediently taken his lesson from the facts.
He met Archie at dinner without resentment, almost with
cordiality. You must take your friends as you find them, he
would have said. Archie couldn't help being his father's son,
or his grandfather's, the hypothetical weaver's grandson.
The son of a hunks, he was still a hunks at heart, incapable

of true generosity and consideration; but he had other
qualities with which Frank could divert himself in the
meanwhile, and to enjoy which it was necessary that Frank
should keep his temper.

So excellently was it controlled that he awoke next
morning with his head full of a different, though a cognate
subject. What was Archie's little game? Why did he shun
Frank's company? What was he keeping secret? Was he
keeping tryst with somebody, and was it a woman? It would
be a good joke and a fair revenge to discover. To that task he
set himself with a great deal of patience, which might have
surprised his friends, for he had been always credited not
with patience so much as brilliancy; and little by little,
from one point to another, he at last succeeded in piecing
out the situation. First he remarked that, although Archie
set out in all the directions of the compass, he always
came home again from some point between the south and
west. From the study of a map, and in consideration of the
great expanse of untenanted moorland running in that
direction towards the sources of the Clyde, he laid his
finger on Cauldstaneslap and two other neighbouring farms,
Kingsmuirs and Polintarf. But it was difficult to advance
farther. With his rod for a pretext, he vainly visited each of
them in turn; nothing was to be seen suspicious about this
trinity of moorland settlements. He would have tried to
follow Archie, had it been the least possible, but the nature
of the land precluded the idea. He did the next best,
ensconced himself in a quiet corner, and pursued his move-
ments with a telescope. It was equally in vain, and he soon
wearied of his futile vigilance, left the telescope at home,
and had almost given the matter up in despair, when, on the
twenty-seventh day of his visit, he was suddenly confronted
with the person whom he sought. The first Sunday Kirstie
had managed to stay away from kirk on some pretext of
indisposition, which was more truly modesty; the pleasure
of beholding Archie seeming too sacred, too vivid for that
public place. On the two following, Frank had himself
been absent on some of his excursions among the neighbouring families. It was not until the fourth, accordingly, that

Frank had occasion to set eyes on the enchantress. With the first look, all hesitation was over. She came with the Cauldstaneslap party; then she lived at Cauldstaneslap. Here was Archie's secret, here was the woman, and more than that – though I have need here of every manageable attenuation of language – with the first look, he had already entered himself as rival. It was a good deal in pique, it was a little in revenge, it was much in genuine admiration: the devil may decide the proportions! I cannot, and it is very likely that Frank could not.

'Mighty attractive milkmaid,' he observed, on the way home.

'Who?' said Archie.

'O, the girl you're looking at – aren't you? Forward there on the road. She came attended by the rustic bard; presumably, therefore, belongs to his exalted family. The single objection! for the four black brothers are awkward customers. If anything were to go wrong, Gib would gibber, and Clem would prove inclement; and Dand fly in danders, and Hob blow up in gobbets. It would be a Helliott of a business!'

'Very humorous, I am sure,' said Archie.

'Well, I am trying to be so,' said Frank. 'It's none too easy in this place, and with your solemn society, my dear fellow. But confess that the milkmaid has found favour in your eyes, or resign all claim to be a man of taste.'

'It is no matter,' returned Archie.

But the other continued to look at him, steadily and quizzically, and his colour slowly rose and deepened under the glance, until not impudence itself could have denied that he was blushing. And at this Archie lost some of his control. He changed his stick from one hand to the other, and – 'O, for God's sake, don't be an ass!' he cried.

'Ass? That's the retort delicate without doubt,' says Frank. 'Beware of the homespun brothers, dear. If they come into the dance, you'll see who's an ass. Think now, if they only applied (say) a quarter as much talent as I have applied to the question of what Mr. Archie does with his evening hours, and why he is so unaffectedly nasty when the subject's touched on——'

'You are touching on it now,' interrupted Archie, with a wince.

'Thank you. That was all I wanted, an articulate confession,' said Frank.

'I beg to remind you——' began Archie.

But he was interrupted in turn. 'My dear fellow, don't. It's quite needless. The subject's dead and buried.'

And Frank began to talk hastily on other matters, an art in which he was an adept, for it was his gift to be fluent on anything or nothing. But although Archie had the grace or the timidity to suffer him to rattle on, he was by no means done with the subject. When he came home to dinner, he was greeted with a sly demand, how things were looking 'Cauldstaneslap ways.' Frank took his first glass of port out after dinner to the toast of Kirstie, and later in the evening he returned to the charge again.

'I say, Weir, you'll excuse me for returning again to this affair. I've been thinking it over, and I wish to beg you very seriously to be more careful. It's not a safe business. Not safe, my boy,' said he.

'What?' said Archie.

'Well, it's your own fault if I must put a name on the thing; but really, as a friend, I cannot stand by and see you rushing head down into these dangers. My dear boy,' said he, holding up a warning cigar, 'consider! What is to be the end of it?'

'The end of what?' – Archie, helpless with irritation, persisted in this dangerous and ungracious guard.

'Well, the end of the milkmaid; or, to speak more by the card, the end of Miss Christina Elliott of the Cauldstaneslap.'

'I assure you,' Archie broke out, 'this is all a figment of your imagination. There is nothing to be said against that young lady; you have no right to introduce her name into the conversation.'

'I'll make a note of it,' said Frank. 'She shall henceforth be nameless, nameless, nameless, Gregarach! I make a note besides of your valuable testimony to her character. I only want to look at this thing as a man of the world. Admitted she's an angel – but, my good fellow, is she a lady?'

This was torture to Archie. 'I beg your pardon,' he said, struggling to be composed, 'but because you have wormed yourself into my confidence——'

'O, come!' cried Frank. 'Your confidence? It was rosy but unconsenting. Your confidence, indeed? Now look! This is what I must say, Weir, for it concerns your safety and good character, and therefore my honour as your friend. You say I wormed myself into your confidence. Wormed is good. But what have I done? I have put two and two together, just as the parish will be doing to-morrow, and the whole of Tweeddale in two weeks, and the black brothers – well, I won't put a date on that; it will be a dark and stormy morning! Your secret, in other words, is poor Poll's. And I want to ask of you as a friend whether you like the prospect? There are two horns to your dilemma, and I must say for myself I should look mighty ruefully on either. Do you see yourself explaining to the four black brothers? or do you see yourself presenting the milkmaid to papa as the future lady of Hermiston? Do you? I tell you plainly, I don't!'

Archie rose. 'I will hear no more of this,' he said, in a trembling voice.

But Frank again held up his cigar. 'Tell me one thing first. Tell me if this is not a friend's part that I am playing?'

'I believe you think it so,' replied Archie. 'I can go as far as that. I can do so much justice to your motives. But I will hear no more of it. I am going to bed.'

'That's right, Weir,' said Frank heartily. 'Go to bed and think over it; and I say, man, don't forget your prayers! I don't often do the moral – don't go in for that sort of thing – but when I do there's one thing sure, that I mean it.'

So Archie marched off to bed, and Frank sat alone by the table for another hour or so, smiling to himself richly. There was nothing vindictive in his nature; but, if revenge came in his way, it might as well be good, and the thought of Archie's pillow reflections that night was indescribably sweet to him. He felt a pleasant sense of power. He looked down on Archie as on a very little boy whose strings he pulled – as on a horse whom he had backed and bridled by sheer power of intelligence, and whom he might ride to glory or the grave at pleasure. Which was it to be? He lingered long, relishing the details of schemes that he was too idle to pursue. Poor cork upon a torrent, he tasted that night the sweets of omnipotence, and brooded like a deity over the strands of that intrigue which was to shatter him before the summer waned.

Chapter Eight

A Nocturnal Visit

KIRSTIE had many causes of distress. More and more as we grow old – and yet more and more as we grow old and are women, frozen by the fear of age – we come to rely on the voice as the single outlet of the soul. Only thus, in the curtailment of our means, can we relieve the straitened cry of the passion within us; only thus, in the bitter and sensitive shyness of advancing years, can we maintain relations with those vivacious figures of the young that still show before us and tend daily to become no more than the moving wall-paper of life. Talk is the last link, the last relation. But with the end of the conversation, when the voice stops and the bright face of the listener is turned away, solitude falls again on the bruised heart. Kirstie had lost her 'cannie hour at e'en'; she could no more wander with Archie, a ghost if you will, but a happy ghost, in fields Elysian. And to her it was as if the whole world had fallen silent; to him, but an unremarkable change of amusements. And she raged to know it. The effervescency of her passionate and irritable nature rose within her at times to bursting point.

This is the price paid by age for unseasonable ardours of feeling. It must have been so for Kirstie at any time when the occasion chanced; but it so fell out that she was deprived of this delight in the hour when she had most need of it, when she had most to say, most to ask, and when she trembled to recognise her sovereignty not merely in abeyance but annulled. For, with the clairvoyance of a genuine love, she had pierced the mystery that had so long embarrassed Frank. She was conscious, even before it was carried out, even on that Sunday night when it began, of an invasion of her rights; and a voice told her the invader's name. Since then, by arts, by accident, by small things observed, and by the general drift of Archie's humour, she had passed beyond all possibility of doubt. With a sense of justice that Lord Hermiston might have envied, she had that day in church

considered and admitted the attractions of the younger
Kirstie; and with the profound humanity and sentimentality
of her nature, she had recognised the coming of fate. Not
thus would she have chosen. She had seen, in imagination,
Archie wedded to some tall, powerful, and rosy heroine of
the golden locks, made in her own image, for whom she
would have strewed the bride-bed with delight; and now
she could have wept to see the ambition falsified. But the
gods had pronounced, and her doom was otherwise.

She lay tossing in bed that night, besieged with feverish
thoughts. There were dangerous matters pending, a battle
was toward, over the fate of which she hung in jealousy,
sympathy, fear, and alternate loyalty and disloyalty to either
side. Now she was reincarnated in her niece, and now in
Archie. Now she saw, through the girl's eyes, the youth on
his knees to her, heard his persuasive instances with a
deadly weakness, and received his overmastering caresses.
Anon, with a revulsion, her temper raged to see such utmost
favours of fortune and love squandered on a brat of a girl,
one of her own house, using her own name – a deadly
ingredient – and that 'didna ken her ain mind an' was as
black's your hat.' Now she trembled lest her deity should
plead in vain, loving the idea of success for him like a
triumph of nature; anon, with returning loyalty to her own
family and sex, she trembled for Kirstie and the credit of the
Elliotts. And again she had a vision of herself, the day over
for her old-world tales and local gossip, bidding farewell to
her last link with life and brightness and love; and behind
and beyond, she saw but the blank butt-end where she must
crawl to die. Had she then come to the lees? she, so great, so
beautiful, with a heart as fresh as a girl's and strong as
womanhood? It could not be, and yet it was so; and for a
moment her bed was horrible to her as the sides of the
grave. And she looked forward over a waste of hours, and
saw herself go on to rage, and tremble, and be softened, and
rage again, until the day came and the labours of the day
must be renewed.

Suddenly she heard feet on the stairs – his feet, and soon
after the sound of a window-sash flung open. She sat up with

her heart beating. He had gone to his room alone, and he had not gone to bed. She might again have one of her night cracks; and at the entrancing prospect a change came over her mind; with the approach of this hope of pleasure, all the baser metal became immediately obliterated from her thoughts. She rose, all woman, and all the best of woman, tender, pitiful, hating the wrong, loyal to her own sex – and all the weakest of that dear miscellany, nourishing, cherishing next her soft heart, voicelessly flattering, hopes that she would have died sooner than have acknowledged. She tore off her nightcap, and her hair fell about her shoulders in profusion. Undying coquetry awoke. By the faint light of her nocturnal rush, she stood before the looking-glass, carried her shapely arms above her head, and gathered up the treasures of her tresses. She was never backward to admire herself; that kind of modesty was a stranger to her nature; and she paused, struck with a pleased wonder at the sight. 'Ye daft auld wife!' she said, answering a thought that was not; and she blushed with the innocent consciousness of a child. Hastily she did up the massive and shining coils, hastily donned a wrapper, and with the rushlight in her hand, stole into the hall. Below stairs she heard the clock ticking the deliberate seconds, and Frank jingling with the decanters in the dining-room. Aversion rose in her, bitter and momentary. 'Nesty, tippling puggy!' she thought; and the next moment she had knocked guardedly at Archie's door and was bidden enter.

Archie had been looking out into the ancient blackness, pierced here and there with a rayless star; taking the sweet air of the moors and the night into his bosom deeply; seeking, perhaps finding, peace after the manner of the unhappy. He turned round as she came in, and showed her a pale face against the window-frame.

'Is that you, Kirstie?' he asked. 'Come in!'

'It's unco late, my dear,' said Kirstie, affecting unwillingness.

'No, no,' he answered, 'not at all. Come in, if you want a crack. I am not sleepy, God knows!'

She advanced, took a chair by the toilet-table and the

candle, and set the rushlight at her foot. Something – it
might be in the comparative disorder of her dress, it might
be the emotion that now welled in her bosom – had touched
her with a wand of transformation, and she seemed young
with the youth of goddesses.

'Mr. Erchie,' she began, 'what's this that's come to ye?'

'I am not aware of anything that has come,' said Archie,
and blushed, and repented bitterly that he had let her in.

'O, my dear, that'll no dae!' said Kirstie. 'It's ill to blend
the eyes of love. O, Mr. Erchie, tak' a thocht ere it's ower
late. Ye shouldna be impatient o' the braws o' life, they'll a'
come in their saison, like the sun and the rain. Ye're young
yet; ye've mony cantie years afore ye. See and dinna wreck
yersel' at the outset like sae mony ithers! Hae patience – they
told me aye that was the owercome o' life – hae patience,
there's a braw day coming yet. Gude kens it never cam' to
me; and here I am, wi' nayther man nor bairn to ca' my
ain, wearying a' folks wi' my ill tongue, and you just the
first, Mr. Erchie!'

'I have a difficulty in knowing what you mean,' said
Archie.

'Weel, and I'll tell ye,' she said. 'It's just this, that I'm
feared. I'm feared for ye, my dear. Remember, your faither is
a hard man, reaping where he hasna sowed and gaithering
where he hasna strawed. It's easy speakin', but mind! Ye'll
have to look in the gurly face o'm, where it's ill to look, and
vain to look for mercy. Ye mind me o' a bonny ship pitten
oot into the black and gowsty seas – ye're a' safe still,
sittin' quait and crackin' wi' Kirstie in your lown chalmer;
but whaur will ye be the morn, and in whatten horror o' the
fearsome tempest, cryin' on the hills to cover ye?'

'Why, Kirstie, you're very enigmatical tonight – and very
eloquent,' Archie put in.

'And, my dear Mr. Erchie,' she continued, with a change
of voice, 'ye maunna think that I canna sympathise wi' ye.
Ye maunna think that I havena been young mysel'. Lang
syne, when I was a bit lassie, no twenty yet——' She paused
and sighed. 'Clean and caller, wi' a fit like the hinney bee,'
she continued. 'I was aye big and buirdly, ye maun under-

stand; a bonny figure o' a woman, though I say it that
suldna – built to rear bairns – braw bairns they suld hae
been, and grand I would hae likit it! But I was young, dear,
wi' the bonny glint o' youth in my e'en, and little I dreamed
I'd ever be tellin' ye this, an auld, lanely, rudas wife! Weel,
Mr. Erchie, there was a lad cam' courtin' me, as was but
naetural. Mony had come before, and I would nane o' them.
But this yin had a tongue to wile the birds frae the lift and
the bees frae the foxglove bells. Deary me, but it's lang syne.
Folk have dee'd sinsyne and been buried, and are forgotten,
and bairns been born and got merrit and got bairns o' their
ain. Sinsyne woods have been plantit, and have grawn up
and are bonny trees, and the joes sit in their shadow; and
sinsyne auld estates have changed hands, and there have
been wars and rumours of wars on the face of the earth.
And here I'm still – like an auld droopit craw – lookin' on
and craikin'! But, Mr. Erchie, do ye no think that I have
mind o' it a' still? I was dwalling then in my faither's house;
and it's a curious thing that we were whiles trysted in the
Deil's Hags. And do ye no think that I have mind of the
bonny simmer days, the lang miles o' the bluid-red heather,
the cryin' o' the whaups, and the lad and the lassie that was
trysted? Do ye no think that I mind how the hilly sweetness
ran about my hairt? Ay, Mr. Erchie, I ken the way o' it – fine
do I ken the way – how the grace o' God takes them, like
Paul of Tarsus, when they think it least, and drives the pair
o' them into a land which is like a dream, and the world
and the folks in 't are nae mair than clouds to the puir lassie,
and heeven nae mair than windle-straes, if she can but
pleesure him! Until Tam dee'd – that was my story,' she
broke off to say, 'he dee'd, and I wasna at the buryin'. But
while he was here, I could take care o' mysel'. And can yon
puir lassie?'

Kirstie, her eyes shining with unshed tears, stretched out
her hand towards him appealingly; the bright and the dull
gold of her hair flashed and smouldered in the coils behind
her comely head, like the rays of an eternal youth; the pure
colour had risen in her face; and Archie was abashed alike
by her beauty and her story. He came towards her slowly

from the window, took up her hand in his and kissed it.

'Kirstie,' he said hoarsely, 'you have misjudged me sorely. I have always thought of her, I wouldna harm her for the universe, my woman!'

'Eh, lad, and that's easy sayin',' cried Kirstie, 'but it's nane sae easy doin'! Man, do ye no comprehend that it's God's wull we should be blendit and glamoured, and have nae command over our ain members at a time like that? My bairn,' she cried, still holding his hand, 'think o' the puir lass! have pity upon her, Erchie! and O, be wise for twa! Think o' the risk she rins! I have seen ye, and what's to prevent ithers! I saw ye once in the Hags, in my ain howf,[1] and I was wae to see ye there – in pairt for the omen, for I think there's a weird on the place – and in pairt for pure nakit envy and bitterness o' hairt. It's strange ye should forgather there tae! God! but yon puir, thrawn, auld Covenanter's seen a heap o' human natur' since he lookit his last on the musket-barrels, if he never saw nane afore,' she added, with a kind of wonder in her eyes.

'I swear by my honour I have done her no wrong,' said Archie. 'I swear by my honour and the redemption of my soul that there shall none be done her. I have heard of this before. I have been foolish, Kirstie, but not unkind and, above all, not base.'

'There's my bairn!' said Kirstie, rising. 'I'll can trust ye noo, I'll can gang to my bed wi' an easy hairt.' And then she saw in a flash how barren had been her triumph. Archie had promised to spare the girl, and he would keep it; but who had promised to spare Archie? What was to be the end of it? Over a maze of difficulties she glanced, and saw, at the end of every passage, the flinty countenance of Hermiston. And a kind of horror fell upon her at what she had done. She wore a tragic mask. 'Erchie, the Lord peety you, dear, and peety me! I have buildit on this foundation' – laying her hand heavily on his shoulder – 'and buildit hie, and pit my hairt in the buildin' of it. If the hale hypothec were to fa', I think, laddie, I would dee! Excuse a daft wife that loves ye, and that kenned your mither. And for His name's sake keep

---

[1] *howl* in first edition, glossed as 'hovel.'

yersel' frae inordinate desires; haud your heart in baith your hands, carry it canny and laigh; dinna send it up like a bairn's kite into the collieshangie o' the wunds! Mind, Maister Erchie dear, that this life's a' disappointment, and a mouthfu' o mools is the appointed end.'

'Ay, but Kirstie, my woman, you're asking me ower much at last,' said Archie, profoundly moved, and lapsing into the broad Scots. 'Ye're asking what nae man can grant ye, what only the Lord of heaven can grant ye if He see fit. Ay! And can even He? I can promise ye what I shall do, and you can depend on that. But how I shall feel – my woman, that is long past thinking of!'

They were both standing by now opposite each other. The face of Archie wore the wretched semblance of a smile; hers was convulsed for a moment.

'Promise me ae thing,' she cried, in a sharp voice. 'Promise me ye'll never do naething without telling me.'

'No, Kirstie, I canna promise ye that,' he replied. 'I have promised enough, God kens!'

'May the blessing of God lift and rest upon ye, dear!' she said.

'God bless ye, my old friend,' said he.

Chapter Nine

At the Weaver's Stone

IT was late in the afternoon when Archie drew near by the
hill path to the Praying Weaver's stone. The Hags were in
shadow. But still, through the gate of the Slap, the sun shot a
last arrow, which sped far and straight across the surface of
the moss, here and there touching and shining on a tussock,
and lighted at length on the gravestone and the small figure
awaiting him there. The emptiness and solitude of the great
moors seemed to be concentred there, and Kirstie pointed
out by that figure of sunshine for the only inhabitant. His
first sight of her was thus excruciatingly sad, like a glimpse
of a world from which all light, comfort, and society were on
the point of vanishing. And the next moment, when she had
turned her face to him and the quick smile had enlightened
it, the whole face of nature smiled upon him in her smile of
welcome. Archie's slow pace was quickened; his legs hasted
to her though his heart was hanging back. The girl, upon her
side, drew herself together slowly and stood up, expectant;
she was all languor, her face was gone white; her arms
ached for him, her soul was on tip-toes. But he deceived
her, pausing a few steps away, not less white than herself,
and holding up his hand with a gesture of denial.

'No, Christina, not to-day,' he said. 'To-day I have to talk
to you seriously. Sit ye down, please, there where you were.
Please!' he repeated.

The revulsion of feeling in Christina's heart was violent.
To have longed and waited these weary hours for him,
rehearsing her endearments – to have seen him at last come –
to have been ready there, breathless, wholly passive, his to
do what he would with – and suddenly to have found herself
confronted with a grey-faced, harsh schoolmaster – it was
too rude a shock. She could have wept, but pride withheld
her. She sat down on the stone, from which she had arisen,
part with the instinct of obedience, part as though she had
been thrust there. What was this? Why was she rejected?

Had she ceased to please? She stood here offering her wares, and he would none of them! And yet they were all his! His to take and keep, not his to refuse though! In her quick petulant nature, a moment ago on fire with hope, thwarted love and wounded vanity wrought. The schoolmaster that there is in all men, to the despair of all girls and most women, was now completely in possession of Archie. He had passed a night of sermons, a day of reflection; he had come wound up to do his duty; and the set mouth, which in him only betrayed the effort of his will, to her seemed the expression of an averted heart. It was the same with his constrained voice and embarrassed utterance; and if so – if it was all over – the pang of the thought took away from her the power of thinking.

He stood before her some way off. 'Kirstie, there's been too much of this. We've seen too much of each other.' She looked up quickly and her eyes contracted. 'There's no good ever comes of these secret meetings. They're not frank, not honest truly, and I ought to have seen it. People have begun to talk; and it's not right of me. Do you see?'

'I see somebody will have been talking to ye,' she said sullenly.

'They have, more than one of them,' replied Archie.

'And whae were they?' she cried. 'And what kind o' love do ye ca' that, that's ready to gang round like a whirligig at folk talking? Do ye think they havena talked to me?'

'Have they indeed?' said Archie, with a quick breath. 'That is what I feared. Who were they? Who has dared——?'

Archie was on the point of losing his temper.

As a matter of fact, not any one had talked to Christina on the matter; and she strenuously repeated her own first question in a panic of self-defence.

'Ah, well! what does it matter?' he said. 'They were good folk that wished well to us, and the great affair is that there are people talking. My dear girl, we have to be wise. We must not wreck our lives at the outset. They may be long and happy yet, and we must see to it, Kirstie, like God's rational creatures and not like fool children. There is one thing we must see to before all. You're worth waiting for,

Kirstie! worth waiting for a generation; it would be enough
reward.' – And here he remembered the schoolmaster again,
and very unwisely took to following wisdom. 'The first
thing that we must see to, is that there shall be no scandal
about for my father's sake. That would ruin all; do ye no
see that?'

Kirstie was a little pleased, there had been some show of
warmth of sentiment in what Archie had said last. But the
dull irritation still persisted in her bosom; with the aboriginal
instinct, having suffered herself, she wished to make Archie
suffer.

And besides, there had come out the word she had always
feared to hear from his lips, the name of his father. It is not
to be supposed that, during so many days with a love
avowed between them, some reference had not been made
to their conjoint future. It had in fact been often touched
upon, and from the first had been the sore point. Kirstie
had wilfully closed the eye of thought; she would not argue
even with herself; gallant, desperate little heart, she had
accepted the command of that supreme attraction like the
call of fate, and marched blindfold on her doom. But
Archie, with his masculine sense of responsibility, must
reason; he must dwell on some future good, when the present
good was all in all to Kirstie; he must talk – and talk lamely,
as necessity drove him – of what was to be. Again and again
he had touched on marriage; again and again been driven
back into indistinctness by a memory of Lord Hermiston.
And Kirstie had been swift to understand and quick to
choke down and smother the understanding; swift to leap
up in flame at a mention of that hope, which spoke volumes
to her vanity and her love, that she might one day be Mrs.
Weir of Hermiston; swift, also, to recognise in his stumbling
or throttled utterance the death-knell of these expectations,
and constant, poor girl! in her large-minded madness, to go
on and to reck nothing of the future. But these unfinished
references, these blinks in which his heart spoke, and his
memory and reason rose up to silence it before the words
were well uttered, gave her unqualifiable agony. She was
raised up and dashed down again bleeding. The recurrence

of the subject forced her, for however short a time, to open
her eyes on what she did not wish to see; and it had invariably ended in another disappointment. So now again, at the
mere wind of its coming, at the mere mention of his father's
name – who might seem indeed to have accompanied them
in their whole moorland courtship, an awful figure in a wig
with an ironical and bitter smile, present to guilty consciousness – she fled from it head down.

'Ye havena told me yet,' she said, 'who was it spoke?'

'Your aunt for one,' said Archie.

'Auntie Kirstie?' she cried. 'And what do I care for my
Auntie Kirstie?'

'She cares a great deal for her niece,' replied Archie, in
kind reproof.

'Troth, and it's the first I've heard of it,' retorted the girl.

'The question here is not who it is, but what they say,
what they have noticed,' pursued the lucid schoolmaster.
'That is what we have to think of in self-defence.'

'Auntie Kirstie, indeed! A bitter, thrawn auld maid that's
fomented trouble in the country before I was born, and will
be doing it still, I daur say, when I'm deid! It's in her nature;
it's as natural for her as it's for a sheep to eat.'

'Pardon me, Kirstie, she was not the only one,' interposed
Archie. 'I had two warnings, two sermons, last night, both
most kind and considerate. Had you been there, I promise
you you would have grat, my dear! And they opened my
eyes. I saw we were going a wrong way.'

'Who was the other one?' Kirstie demanded.

By this time Archie was in the condition of a hunted
beast. He had come, braced and resolute; he was to trace
out a line of conduct for the pair of them in a few cold,
convincing sentences; he had now been there some time,
and he was still staggering round the outworks and undergoing what he felt to be a savage cross-examination.

'Mr. Frank!' she cried. 'What nex', I would like to ken?'

'He spoke most kindly and truly.'

'What like did he say?'

'I am not going to tell you; you have nothing to do with that,' cried Archie, startled to find he had admitted so much.

'Oh, I have naething to do with it?' she repeated, springing to her feet. 'A'body at Hermiston's free to pass their opinions upon me, but I have naething to do wi' it! Was this at prayers like? Did ye ca' the grieve into the consultation? Little wonder if a'body's talking, when ye make a'body yer confidants! But as you say, Mr. Weir – most kindly, most considerately, most truly, I'm sure – I have naething to do with it. And I think I'll better be going. I'll be wishing you good evening, Mr. Weir.' And she made him a stately curtsey, shaking as she did so from head to foot, with the barren ecstasy of temper.

Poor Archie stood dumbfounded. She had moved some steps away from him before he recovered the gift of articulate speech.

'Kirstie!' he cried. 'Oh, Kirstie woman!'

There was in his voice a ring of appeal, a clang of mere astonishment that showed the schoolmaster was vanquished.

She turned round on him. 'What do ye Kirstie me for?' she retorted. 'What have ye to do wi' me? Gang to your ain freends and deave them!'

He could only repeat the appealing 'Kirstie!'

'Kirstie, indeed!' cried the girl, her eyes blazing in her white face. 'My name is Miss Christina Elliott, I would have ye to ken, and I daur ye to ca' me out of it. If I canna get love, I'll have respect, Mr. Weir. I'm come of decent people, and I'll have respect. What have I done that ye should lightly me? What have I done? What have I done? O, what have I done?' and her voice rose upon the third repetition. 'I thocht – I thocht – I thocht I was sae happy!' and the first sob broke from her like the paroxysm of some mortal sickness.

Archie ran to her. He took the poor child in his arms, and she nestled to his breast as to a mother's, and clasped him in hands that were strong like vices. He felt her whole body shaken by the throes of distress, and had pity upon her beyond speech. Pity, and at the same time a bewildered fear of this explosive engine in his arms, whose works he did not understand, and yet had been tampering with. There arose from before him the curtains of boyhood, and he saw for the first time the ambiguous face of woman as she is. In vain he looked back over the interview; he saw not where he had offended. It seemed unprovoked, a wilful convulsion of brute nature. . . .

NOTES

42 **Claverhouse:** John Graham of Claverhouse, Viscount Dundee (1649-89), was defeated by the Covenanters at Drumclog, but crushed them at Bothwell Bridge (1679). In the following year he routed a company of 'rebels' at Aird's Moss and killed the leader Richard Cameron. He became notorious for his unrelenting treatment of Covenanters. Scott depicts him in *Old Mortality*.

Praying Weaver of Balweary: this seems to be a fictitious character carved out of history. Claverhouse had many Covenanters shot in the course of his military career, amongst them the Richard Cameron referred to above and John Brown of Priesthill who, with his nephew, was chased over the moors of Lanarkshire and Ayrshire. In James K. Hewison's book *The Covenanters* there are several references to weavers who were martyred for the Covenanting cause, including one Andrew Sword from Borgue who was hanged in chains on Magus Moor, and one Laurence Hay, a Fife man, who was hanged in the Grassmarket. Weavers seem to have been associated with radical causes. Gib, one of the Four Black Brothers in *Weir*, was weaver, radical, and member of the religious sect 'God's Remnant'. Hermiston, in denouncing his espousal of the principles of Liberalism, said: 'Gib, ye eediot, what is this I hear of you? Poalitics, . . . weaver's poalitics, is the way of it, I hear'.

Balwearie is in Abbotshall Parish, Fife, the remains of an ancient baronial fortalice reputed to have been at one time the residence of the wizard Michael Scott.

Old Mortality: this is a reference to Robert Paterson, an old Covenanter, who wandered about Scotland cleaning up the tombstones of the Cameronians. Scott opens the novel of this name by giving an account of Paterson's life and ways.

Cameronian: a strict Covenanter, a follower of that Richard Cameron who was killed at Aird's Moss near Auchinleck in Ayrshire in 1680.

42 Cauldstaneslap: Cauldstane Slap gives its name to a well-known drove road that crosses the Pentlands at a height of 1,430 ft. under the slopes of the East and the West Cairn Hills. Strictly speaking it is the actual pass (Scots 'slap') between these two hills. It is not difficult to reconcile the setting of the real Cauldstane Slap with that of the fictitious one. See the text p. 121, and the Introduction p. 13.

43 One bit the dust at Flodden: Flodden Hill on the banks of the Till in Northumberland was the scene of a bloody battle in 1513 in which the English under the Earl of Surrey defeated the Scots under James IV. It is appropriate that a 'riding Rutherford' should be numbered amongst the Scottish dead at this historic battle.

one was hanged at his peel door by James the Fifth: the peel door is the door to a fortified watch-tower. James V (1513-1542), having subdued the rebellious Douglases, tried to bring law and order to the Borders by suppressing chiefs like John Armstrong. The Rutherfords would have suffered with others in this process.

a carouse with Tom Dalyell: it would appear that the Rutherfords were associated with the anti-Covenanting cause. Sir Thomas Dalziel, a harsh royalist who had served in Russia, routed a band of Covenanters at Rullion Green in the Pentland Hills near Flotterstone in 1666.

Hell-Fire Club: Hell-Fire Clubs originated in London, drawing their members from groups of men noted for their blasphemy and drunkenness. An Order in Council issued in 1721 described their gatherings as 'scandalous meetings held for the purpose of ridiculing religion and morality'. Branches formed in Edinburgh and Dublin.

Crossmichael: parish and village in Kirkcudbright about four miles north-west of Castle Douglas. Sidney Colvin says in his Editorial Note to *Weir* (Edinburgh edition p. 303) that Crossmichael may be taken 'as standing for Peebles' where there was a well-known club similar to the one described here.

the Kye-skairs: skairs are hillsides, bare and steep, where wandering cattle (kye) would have found meagre grazing.

44 the Parliament House: this dates from 1632-40 and is
situated in Parliament Square, Edinburgh, just behind
St. Giles Cathedral. The Courts of Session are held here;
and in the Parliament Hall itself the Scottish Parliament
met from 1639 until 1707, the year of the union with
England.

45 George Square: this square in Edinburgh was designed by
James Brown in the second half of the eighteenth century
as a 'parallelogram'. Sir Walter Scott lived in No. 25
until his marriage in 1796. The University now occupy
many of the buildings and have erected two towers—
the Appleton and the Hume, as well as a vast library and
a theatre.

48 Rutherford's Letters: Samuel Rutherford (1600-1661),
Scottish minister of religion, was born near Jedburgh,
studied theology at Edinburgh and was ordained
minister at Anwoth in Galloway. He was a member of
Covenanting assemblies, and rector of St. Andrews
University. He published a treatise against arminianism,
but was deprived of his offices for opposing the treaty
with Charles II. His great work is reckoned to be the
Letters, published 1664.

Scougal's Grace Abounding: Henry Scougal (1650-1678)
was the author of a number of religious essays and
sermons, including the religious classic *The Life of God
in the Soul of Man* (1677). He was born in Fife, educated
at King's College, Aberdeen, and was at one time a
parish minister at Auchterless. He eventually became
professor of Divinity at Aberdeen. *Grace Abounding*
(1666) is the title of a work by John Bunyan: in ascribing
it to Scougal, Stevenson may be gently mocking Mrs.
Weir's muddled enthusiasm.

Bloody Mackenzie . . . the politic Lauderdale and Rothes:
Sir George Mackenzie (1636-1691) was given the nick-
name 'Bloody Mackenzie' after the battle of Bothwell
Bridge (1679) because of his savage treatment of the
Covenanters. Lauderdale, originally a supporter of the
Covenanters and then their harsh opponent, was
Secretary of the Privy Council for Scotland under
Charles II, and later Commissioner representing Charles.
His 'reign' as Commissioner ended in 1679 after Both-

well Bridge. His one-time associate the Earl of Rothes
had held the Commissionership before him from 1663-8.

49 Black Fell: Stevenson might have been thinking of Black
or Bleak Law (1,460 ft.), nine miles south-west of West
Linton and above the hamlet of Dunsyre. Here is
situated the grave of a nameless Covenanter slain at
Rullion Green.

50 Naphtali: the territory of Naphtali lies north and west of
the Sea of Galilee, and became incorporated in the
Northern Kingdom (Israel). Naphtali as border territory
is said to have bred hardy men who took part in various
battles. (Naphthali was the name of the sixth son of
Jacob, Rachel's husband; he was reputed to be the
ancestor of one of the Twelve Tribes of Israel.)

Potterrow . . . Meadows: the Potterrow runs from near
the old University in South College Street south towards
Chapel Street in the neighbourhood of George Square.
The Meadows, bounded by Melville Drive, the Royal
Infirmary, and the ends of George Square and Buccleuch
Place, are on the site of what was once a lake—the
Borough Loch. Thomas Hope of Rankeillor in about
1722 had the bed of the loch drained and the area
enclosed with hedges and trees. The Meadows now form
a pleasant open space for sport and relaxation.

55 Jezebel: the daughter of Ethbaal of Tyre and wife of Ahab,
king of Israel. As champion of Baal worship, Jezebel
led the king and Israel into gross immoralities. Her
name became synonymous with feminine wickedness.
(See I Kings XVI, 31-33, and II Kings IX, 7-10.)

**56-7 To a child just stumbling into Corderius, Papinian and
Paul proved quite invincible:** Corderius—Mathurin
Cordier (1480-1564), a French schoolmaster who taught
Calvin in Paris at one time, and later became famous
at Geneva for his skill in teaching Latin. His graduated
dialogues for beginners *Colloquiorum scholasticorum
libri quattuor* were still being used in the nineteenth
century. Papinian—Aemilius Paullus Papinianus—was a
Roman jurist and Praetorian prefect under Septimius
Severus. He accompanied the emperor to Britain in
203 A.D., and tried to keep the peace between the sons
Caracalla and Geta. He was executed by Caracalla after
the fratricide of 212 A.D. He was one of the greatest of

F

Roman jurists, producing thirty-seven books of *Quaes-tiones* (legal questions) and nineteen books of *Responsa* (decisions). Paul V—Camillo Borghese (1552-1621)—was one of the great canonists of the Church, thoroughly trained in jurisprudence.

58 **Forbes of Culloden:** Duncan Forbes (1685-1747), Scottish statesman and jurist, took an active part in suppressing the Rising of 1715. His activities on behalf of the Hanoverian dynasty succeeded in reducing support amongst the clans for the Jacobite cause in 1745.

59 **Cato and Brutus were such:** Cato—Marcus Porcius Priscus (234-149 B.C.)—was a Roman soldier and statesman renowned for his extreme severity and conservatism, his integrity, and the simplicity of his way of living. His stern sense of duty and discipline, his patriotism and dislike of Hellenic culture, suggest qualities in Adam Weir. Brutus—Marcus Junius (79-42 B.C.)—one of the assassins of Julius Caesar—practised as an advocate and was brought up on the principles of the aristocratic party. He seems to have been an idealist rather than a practical politician, opposed to the idea of one-man rule. Perhaps Glenalmond is thinking of Brutus' aloofness and austere attitude to life in associating him with Hermiston.

the Speculative Society: a debating society connected with Edinburgh University. Henry Cockburn in his *Memorials* describes it as 'an institution which has trained more young men to public speaking, talent, and liberal thought, than all the other private institutions in Scotland'.

60 **a malady most incident to only sons:** an echo of a phrase from Perdita's speech in *The Winter's Tale*, IV. iii, 124-5—'a malady Most incident to maids'.

Rhadamanthus: according to Greek legend he was the son of Zeus and Europa, and brother of Minos, King of Crete. Rhadamanthus laid the foundations of the Cretan code of laws which was completed by Minos. After his death he was made a judge in the kingdom of Pluto or Islands of the Blessed.

62 **Justiciary Court:** this is the High Court of Justiciary, the supreme court for criminal causes in Scotland. It sits permanently in Edinburgh, but its judges go on circuit

to Glasgow, Aberdeen, Dundee and Perth, Ayr, Dumfries, Inveraray, Inverness, Jedburgh and Stirling. Special sessions may also be held at any convenient town. For the significance of the circuit town in the projected final part of the novel, see Appendix I—Continuation and Ending, p. 169.

63 **Obiter dictum:** a remark added by the way or cursorily.

64 **He saw Holyrood in a dream . . . he had a vision of the old radiant stories, of Queen Mary and Prince Charlie, of the hooded stag . . .:** Robert Kiely in his book *Robert Louis Stevenson and the Fiction of Adventure*, pp. 251-2, says that Archie here tries to escape from the sordidness of the court scene 'into a romantic vision of history', but feels his close blood connection with the judge prevents him from being identified with 'the honourable Scottish past'. Kiely goes on to say that this concept of history, being 'almost void of humanity', prevents Archie at this point from making peace with his father and with himself. The 'hooded stag' refers to the story of how David I was attacked by a stag near Arthur's Seat but saved by a fragment of the Holy Rood that was miraculously placed in his hand.

Hunter's Bog: the valley between Arthur's Seat and Salisbury Crags in the King's Park, Edinburgh.

Jacobin figments: the Jacobins were a revolutionary political society formed during the French Revolution. They took their name from the building in which they met in the Rue S. Honoré in Paris.

68 **the celebrated Dr. Gregory:** James Gregory (1753-1821), a native of Aberdeen and professor of medicine at Edinburgh, was a member of the illustrious Gregory family of distinguished mathematicians and doctors. He was a great lecturer, Latin scholar, and talker; and he was frequently involved in professional controversies. He was the author of *Conspectus medicinae theoreticae* (1788) and *Literary and Philosophical Essays* (1792).

73 **the Peninsula:** in the Peninsular War (1808-1814) a British army under Sir Arthur Wellesley, afterwards the Duke of Wellington, fought alongside the Spaniards and the Portuguese to drive the French from the Iberian Peninsula.

77   **in apicibus juris:** in the (fine) points of the law.

79   **major and sui juris:** of full age and with full legal capacity to act.

    Capital Punishment: punishment by death. Much controversy has raged about the moral or ethical justification for capital punishment. It was abolished in Great Britain in 1965.

80   **Tigris ut aspera:** just like a cruel tigress.

83   **Don Quickshot:** Glenkindie is presumably using this malapropism for Don Quixote to emphasise both the foolhardiness and the impetuosity of Archie's attack on his father.

96   **as they rode up the Vennel:** presumably this describes the entry into Edinburgh of the posse of neighbours with their prisoners after the pursuit and struggles in the Pentlands. The Vennel is a narrow lane that runs up out of the Grassmarket at its west end.

97   **some Barbarossa . . . devil that haunted him:** the Barbarossa brothers, Horuk and Khair-ed-Din, were Turkish corsairs notorious for plundering and terrorising Christian fleets sailing the Mediterranean in the early sixteenth century. Stevenson, in speaking of the two sides of Hob's nature—the lawless and the respectable, is revealing his great interest in the *alter ego* concept of human psychology that he had explored in *Dr. Jekyll and Mr. Hyde* (1886).

98   **the principles of the French Revolution:** the triple notion of *liberté*, *égalité*, *fraternité*, embraced by Gib the weaver, would obviously be anathema to such an authoritarian as my Lord Hermiston.

    under the hawse: 'hawse' may well be, as M. R. Ridley suggests, a mistake—a misprint for 'tawse'. Certainly in this context 'under the lash' makes better sense than 'under the throat'.

99   **'antinomian in principle':** holding the belief that Christians or the elect of God are exempt from the moral law.

101   **The Ettrick Shepherd was his sworn crony:** James Hogg (1770-1835), shepherd and poet, would have been an ideal friend for Dand Elliott. He published a collection of his early ballads *The Mountain Bard* in 1807; and his celebrated work *The Queen's Wake*, which includes

'Kilmeny' and 'The Witch of Fife', appeared in 1813. The last period of his life he spent at the farm of Altrive in Yarrow combining his farming with his writing activities.

101 **stool of repentance . . . his hero and model:** the hero and model, Robert Burns, had himself sat on the stool of repentance—a place or pew in the Kirk set aside for those who had sinned or in any way offended the moral law.

103 **Hob was The Laird. 'Roy ne puis, prince ne daigne':** Stevenson is poking fun at Hob's pretensions as the little laird by quoting a curtailed version of the family motto of the Rouhans of Brittany. The original and complete version is: *Roy ne puis, duc ne daigne, Rouhan suis*—I cannot be a king, a duke I would not want to be, I am a Rouhan.

110 **that deadly instrument, the maiden:** a Stevensonian conceit. The 'deadly instrument' is the Scottish beheading machine as well as the attractive young woman.

112 **to play the part of a derivative:** 'derivative' seems to be used here in the sense of an agency that brings two forces together which are normally separated, presumably from the medical use of the word in the phrase 'derivative circulation'. According to the Shorter Oxford Dictionary, it is a term applied to the direct communication which exists between arteries and veins in some parts of the body.

M. R. Ridley suggests that 'derivative' here might mean something like 'go-between', but adds that this 'is not, on examination, satisfactory'.

118 **that idea of Fate—a pagan Fate, uncontrolled by any Christian diety . . . moving indissuadably in the affairs of Christian men:** Stevenson sets the pagan notion of destiny against conventional Christian belief and background to heighten the drama here.

119 **'only I think ye're mair like me than the lave of them':** this dialogue between poet and young sister in love is so composed and developed as to mark their affinity and bring out another aspect of family relationship.

126 **'of old, unhappy far-off things . . .':** the lines from Wordsworth's poem *The Solitary Reaper* emphasise the drama-

tic fusing of past and present in the family background
that is an important *leitmotif* of the novel.

128 Beulah: a land of rest—the name given to Palestine after
the Exile when it was re-peopled and restored to God's
favour. In *The Pilgrim's Progress* Beulah lies 'beyond
the valley of the Shadow of Death and out of the reach
of Giant Despair'. Here the pilgrims were said to be
within sight of the Heavenly City.

130 'Pylades has come to Orestes at last': Orestes was the son
of Agamemnon, who returned with his close friend
Pylades from Phocis to Argos and killed his mother,
Clytemnestra, to avenge his father's death. He was later
pursued by the Furies and driven mad before being
acquitted by the Court of the Areopagus. In the second
play of Aeschylus' Oresteian trilogy—*The Choephori*—
Pylades breaks silence only to urge Orestes not to
weaken but to go on with his resolve to kill Clytemnestra.

Although there was no real friendship between Archie and
Frank, there is something in the analogy: Frank's inter-
vention in the affairs of Archie and Christina was to
lead to Archie's passionate outburst and fatal attack on
Frank.

132 tantaene irae: are there such violent passions? An ab-
breviated version of *tantaene animis caelestibus irae?*
Are there such violent passions in celestial minds?
(from Virgil: *Aeneid* I, 11).

137 the Marquis de Talleyrand-Perigord: a French statesman
(1754-1838) of great ability and opportunism. At one
time he acted as foreign minister for the Revolutionary
Directory, and later supported Napoleon's policies.
Subsequently he turned against Napoleon and worked
for the restoration of the Bourbons. There seems little
resemblance between Innes and Talleyrand; but one
thing they have in common, as Stevenson points out
on p. 139: each accepts the situation and uses it for his
own purpose and advantage.

138 obsto principiis: I resist the first beginnings (from Ovid:
Remedia Amoris, where the actual form of the expression
is *principiis obsta:* resist the first beginnings). Archie is
determined not to allow Frank to establish the right to
intrude on his privacy.

141 **the retort delicate:** perhaps a playful echo from Touchstone's analysis of the seven causes or degrees in a verbal quarrel —'retort courteous', 'quip modest', 'reply churlish', and so on. See *As You Like It*, V. iv, 69-109.

143 **She shall henceforth be nameless, nameless, nameless Gregarach!:** M. R. Ridley notes here that when the clan Macgregor was proscribed, even the use of the name was forbidden. In the context of the novel, however, the point seems to be that Innes is mockingly misquoting a line from Scott's 'MacGregor's Gathering':

We're landless, landless, landless, Grigalach.

149 **'there was a lad cam' courtin' me ... whiles trysted in the Deil's Hags':** In Kirstie's tale of her own love affair there is deliberate parallelism and stressing of the destiny motif associated with the setting.

150 **she ... saw ... the flinty countenance of Hermiston. And a kind of horror fell upon her at what she had done. She wore a tragic mask:** the sense of Greek tragedy emerges starkly here: Kirstie becomes a kind of Cassandra-prophetess figure seeing clearly the tragic consequences of her egotistical action.

155 **at the mere mention of his father's name ... an awful figure in a wig with an ironical and bitter smile:** we see conjured up in this dramatic vision the figure of the hanging judge who had dominated the first part of the novel and was to return to mark its tragic pattern in the final stages.

156 **'My name is Miss Christina Elliott . . .' and she nestled to his breast . . .:** the juxtaposition of young Kirstie's outburst to assert herself and her emotional breakdown produces pathos and a temporary reconciliation. Here at the point where the novel breaks off is evidence of Stevenson's developing skill and insight in portraying the relationship between a man and a woman.

APPENDIX I

Continuation and Ending: Stevenson's Intentions

Sidney Colvin in his editorial note to the first and Edinburgh editions outlines the intended continuation and conclusion of the novel 'so far as it was known at the time of the writer's death to his stepdaughter and devoted amanuensis, Mrs. Strong':

> Archie persists in his good resolution of avoiding further conduct compromising to young Kirstie's good name. Taking advantage of the situation thus created, and of the girl's unhappiness and wounded vanity, Frank Innes pursues his purpose of seduction; and Kirstie, though still caring for Archie in her heart, allows herself to become Frank's victim. Old Kirstie is the first to perceive something amiss with her, and believing Archie to be the culprit, accuses him, thus making him aware for the first time that mischief has happened. He does not at once deny the charge, but seeks out and questions young Kirstie, who confesses the truth to him; and he, still loving her, promises to protect and defend her in her trouble. He then has an interview with Frank Innes on the moor, which ends in a quarrel, and in Archie killing Frank beside the Weaver's Stone. Meanwhile the Four Black Brothers, having become aware of their sister's betrayal, are bent on vengeance against Archie as her supposed seducer. But their vengeance is forestalled by his arrest for the murder of Frank. He is tried before his own father, the Lord Justice-Clerk, found guilty, and condemned to death. Meanwhile the elder Kirstie, having discovered from the girl how matters really stand, informs her nephews of the truth; and they, in a great revulsion of feeling in Archie's favour, determine on an action after the ancient manner of their house. They gather a following, and after a great fight break the prison where Archie lies confined, and rescue him. He and young Kirstie thereafter escape to America. But the ordeal of taking part in the trial of his own son has been too much for the Lord Justice-Clerk, who dies of the shock. 'I do not know,' adds the amanuensis, 'what becomes of old Kirstie, but that character grew and strengthened so in the writing that I am sure he had some dramatic destiny for her.'

Colvin, commenting on this summary, makes the point that Stevenson might well have changed his mind about some of the lines of development 'originally traced'. There is no doubt however that Stevenson intended that Archie should kill Frank at the Weaver's Stone: the Introductory prepares us for this. What there is doubt about is the exact point at which Archie becomes aware of the truth about Frank's seduction of Christina. Does he know it when he kills Frank at the Stone? Or is this a quarrel stirred up by suspicions and fanned by Archie's latent passion? This would fit in with the story of how Stevenson in the spring of 1894 'rehearsed in conversation' with Sidney Lysaght 'a scene where the girl was to confess to her lover in prison that she was with child by the man he had killed'. There would be great dramatic power, as M. R. Ridley points out in the Everyman edition (pp. 289-290), in Archie's learning the truth when he is on the verge of being tried for his life.

The great flaw in Mrs. Strong's summary was pointed out by Sidney Colvin himself. Archie could not have been tried and condemned by his own father:

> . . . I am assured on the best legal authority of Scotland that no judge, however powerful either by character or office, could have insisted on presiding at the trial of a near kinsman of his own.

Stevenson was aware of this problem himself. In the letter to his friend Charles Baxter dated October 1892 in which he asks for materials—reports of trials, the text of the Scots judiciary oath—he makes it clear he knows that there would have to be two trials and that the judge-father would have to be excluded from the second:

> The Justice-Clerk tries some people capitally on circuit. Certain evidence cropping up, the charge is transferred to the Justice-Clerk's own son. Of course in the next trial the Justice-Clerk is excluded, and the case is called before the Lord Justice-General. Where would this trial have to be? I fear in Edinburgh, which would not suit my view. Could it be again at the circuit town?

Stevenson was very happy to be assured by Mr. Graham Murray that there would be no difficulty in making the new trial take place at the circuit town: his projected rescue of Archie by the Four Black Brothers could now be legitimately fitted in to the later parts of the novel.

Certain problems remain. Who are the people who are tried first of all for the murder before Archie? Tom Wright with

considerable insight and plausibility concentrates on one person
and casts Dand the poet for the role (see Appendix III). A greater
problem is to bring Hermiston into the forefront of the tragedy.
Both Sidney Colvin and M. R. Ridley postulate that Hermiston's
part would be limited to presiding at the first trial and then
unflinchingly allowing the law to take its course, fully aware that
the evidence pointed directly to his son. It is certain that Stevenson intended this tragic situation to develop out of the relationship and conflict between father and son. Colvin writes:

> The situation and fate of the judge, confronting like a
> Brutus, but unable to survive, the duty of sending his own
> son to the gallows, seems clearly to have been destined to
> furnish the climax and tragedy of the tale.

This is supported by Ridley in his 'revised summary' in the
Everyman edition (p. 292). He speaks of the strain being too
much 'for even Hermiston's iron resolution', and concludes:

> He knows that his duty, as a minister of the law, had been
> inescapable—being what he was he 'could have done no
> other'; but he knows also that he has brought his own son
> to the foot of the gallows. And he dies.

The final problem concerns the fate of Archie and Christina.
Would it have been fitting that they should have escaped and
gone to live in America in happiness and peace? Ridley envisages
this end; and Stevenson in his letter to J. M. Barrie (1st November 1892) hints that this is how he would like the novel to
end:

> Why should not young Hermiston escape clear out of the
> country? and be happy, if he could, with his—but soft! I will
> not betray my secret or my heroine.

Yet earlier in the letter he speaks of his 'heavy case of conscience . . . about my Braxfield story':

> Braxfield—only his name is Hermiston—has a son who is
> condemned to death; plainly there is a fine tempting fitness
> about this; and I meant he was to hang.

Tom Wright in the TV version printed in Appendix III takes
Stevenson at his word and works out a tragic ending for both
Christina and Archie. This seems in accordance with the note
of destiny that pervades the novel. On the other hand tragedy
need not imply a whole series of deaths: too many deaths might

well blur the sharp lines of a genuine tragic situation. The build-up to the single death of Hermiston, after all the ironical twists in the father-son relationship, would provide, I think, a far more memorable ending to an epic novel: the death of Hermiston would resound—like the death of Antony. Such an ending— clear-cut and inevitable—would justify the title and preserve the tragic unity of the whole work, if we must have an ending and an explicit final part.

J. T. L.

APPENDIX II

Original Text of Robert Louis Stevenson

'No, Christina, not today,' he said. 'Today I have to talk to you seriously. Sit ye down, please, there where you were. Please!' he repeated.

He stood before her some way off. 'Kirstie, there's been too much of this. We've seen too much of each other.' She looked up quickly and her eyes contracted.

'There's no good ever comes of these secret meetings. They're not frank, not honest truly, and I ought to have seen it. People have begun to talk; and it's not right of me. Do you see?'

Television Script by Tom Wright

EPISODE 2

TELECINE

30. EXTERIOR. THE CAIRN. DAY.

Christina is waiting happily at the cairn. She sees Archie approach, rises and waves. Archie's face is gloomy but the gloom leaves him and his pace quickens. She comes to meet him and they embrace with growing warmth. Archie, realising the danger, breaks off. Christina is slightly annoyed till she sees his troubled face.

CHRISTINA: What is it, Archie? What's the matter?

ARCHIE: We have to talk very seriously about the future, Christina.

He sits and pulls her down beside him. She sits rather stiffly fearing what is to come. He tries to choose his words carefully and makes a mess of it.

ARCHIE: I think we've been seeing too much of each other.

She rises.

CHRISTINA: That's no' very hard to put right, Archie. Good-day to you.

He catches her arm.

ARCHIE: Please hear me out. (*He draws her back down beside him.*) It's not that my feeling for you has changed in any way, but I've realised that no good can come of these secret meetings.

'I see somebody will have been talking to ye,' she said sullenly.

'They have—more than one of them,' replied Archie.

'And whae were they?' she cried. 'And what kind o' love do ye ca' that, that's ready to gang round like a whirligig at folk talking? Do ye think they havena talked to me?'

'Have they indeed?' said Archie, with a quick breath. 'That is what I feared. Who were they? Who has dared—?'

Archie was on the point of losing his temper.

As a matter of fact, not any one had talked to Christina on the matter; and she strenuously repeated her own first question in a panic of self-defence.

'Ah well! what does it matter?' he said. 'They were good folk that wished well to us, and the great affair is that there are people talking. My dear girl, we have to be wise. We must not wreck our lives at the outset. They may be long and happy yet, and we must see to it, Kirstie, like God's rational creatures and not like fool children. There is one thing we must see to before all. You're worth waiting for, Kirstie! worth waiting for a generation; it would be enough reward.'—And here he remembered the schoolmaster again, and very unwisely took to following wisdom. 'The first thing that we must see to is that there shall be no scandal about for my father's sake. That would ruin all; do ye no see that?'

'Ye havena told me yet,' she said, 'who was it spoke?'

'Your aunt for one,' said Archie.

'Auntie Kirstie?' she cried. 'And what do I care for my Auntie Kirstie?'

'She cares a great deal for her niece,' replied Archie, in kind reproof.

'Troth, and it's the first I've heard of it,' retorted the girl.

'The question here is not who it is, but what they say, what they have noticed,' pursued the lucid schoolmaster. 'That is what we have to think of in self-defence.'

CHRISTINA. (*rising angrily*) And whose fault is it that they're secret? I'd have met you at my front door or yours, or at the kirk door afore the minister and the haill congregation if you'd asked me!

ARCHIE: (*Now feeling completely in the wrong*) If there's been a fault it's mine. I know that. I'm older than you; I should have seen the danger.

CHRISTINA: I'm sorry if you find yourself in danger through me, Mr. Weir, but, as I said, it's soon repaired.

ARCHIE: (*angrily*) For God's sake, let me finish! I was speaking of the danger to you. People have begun to talk.

CHRISTINA: And what kind o' love is it that goes round like a whirligig at folks' talking?

ARCHIE: (*not without male pomposity*) I haven't changed; I've realised that we haven't been wise.

CHRISTINA: I never tried to be wise. I thought it better just to be happy. Who's talking?

ARCHIE: People who wished us well.

CHRISTINA: Who?

ARCHIE: Your aunt for one.

'Auntie Kirstie, indeed! A bitter, thrawn auld maid that's fomented trouble in the country before I was born, and will be doing it still, I daur say, when I'm deid! It's in her nature; it's as natural for her as it's for a sheep to eat.'

'Pardon me, Kirstie, she was not the only one,' interposed Archie. 'I had two warnings, two sermons, last night, both most kind and considerate. Had you been there, I promise you you would have grat, my dear! And they opened my eyes. I saw we were going a wrong way.'
'Who was the other one?' Kirstie demanded.

By this time Archie was in the condition of a hunted beast. He had come, braced and resolute; he was to trace out a line of conduct for the pair of them in a few cold, convincing sentences; he had now been there some time, and he was still staggering round the outworks and undergoing what he felt to be a savage cross-examination.

'Mr. Frank!' she cried. 'What nex', I would like to ken?'
'He spoke most kindly and truly.'
'What like did he say?'

'I am not going to tell you; you have nothing to do with that,' cried Archie, startled to find he had admitted so much.
'O, I have naething to do with it? she repeated, springing to her feet. 'A'body at Hermiston's free to pass their opinions upon me, but I have naething to do wi' it! Was this at prayers like? Did ye ca' the grieve into the consultation? Little wonder if a'body's talking, when ye make a'body yer confidants! But as you say, Mr. Weir—most kindly, most considerately, most truly, I'm sure—I have naething to do with it. And I think I'll better be going. I'll be wishing you good evening, Mr. Weir.' And she made him a stately curtsey, shaking as she did so from head to foot, with the barren ecstasy of temper.
Poor Archie stood dumbfounded. She had moved some steps away from him before he recovered the gift of articulate speech.
'Kirstie!' he cried. 'O, Kirstie woman!'

She turned round on him. 'What do ye Kirstie me for?' she retorted. 'What have ye to do wi' me? Gang to your ain freends and deave them!'
He could only repeat the appealing 'Kirstie!'

CHRISTINA: (*laughing harshly*) Her! A bitter thrawn old maid that's been fomenting trouble since before I was born. What do I care for her?

ARCHIE: There were others.

CHRISTINA: Who else?

ARCHIE: (*evasively*) Does it matter who else? The important thing is that people have noticed and are talking.

CHRISTINA: If it's me they're talking about, it matters to me who's talking. Who was it?

ARCHIE: Frank Innes.

CHRISTINA: And what did he say?

Archie doesn't answer. Her anger increases.

CHRISTINA: A'body at Hermiston is free to pass an opinion on me, but I'm never to know what it is. Is that the way of it? I'll be wishing you good-day.

ARCHIE: (*hopeless and anguished*) Kirstie!

'Kirstie, indeed!' cried the girl, her eyes blazing in her white face. 'My name is Miss Christina Elliott, I would have ye to ken, and I daur ye to ca' me out of it. If I canna get love, I'll have respect, Mr. Weir. I'm come of decent people, and I'll have respect. What have I done that ye should lightly me? What have I done? What have I done? O, what have I done?' and her voice rose upon the third repetition. 'I thocht—I thocht—I thocht I was sae happy!' and the first sob broke from her like the paroxysm of some mortal sickness.

CHRISTINA: (*flaring up*) My name is Miss Christina Elliott, I'd have you ken. If I cannae get love, I'll get respect, Mr. Weir. I'm come of decent folk and I'll hae respect! What have I done to you that you should lightly me? (*Gradually breaking down*) What have I done? What have I done? What have I done?

He puts his arms round her and holds her till her sobbing subsides.

ARCHIE: Kirstie, love. Listen to me, please. We can't go on like this forever. There must be no scandal; for your sake, for our sake, for my father's sake.

At the mention of Weir she becomes grave.

CHRISTINA: A'body here speaks of your father, but this is the first time you've ever done it. It made a shudder in my blood. I feel as though we've been walking here thinking we were alone and all the time we've been watched by a terrible old man with a hanging face.

ARCHIE: I know that's how men see him. It's how I've seen him myself. Doling out justice like a God that has no love in him, but there's something about him that makes him bigger than other men. He's given himself wholly to the law; he scavenges the rubbish of mankind to stop their plague from spreading. But there's something buried in him that I'll reach out and touch one day. Till then we must be careful.

CHRISTINA: What's he to do with us, Archie?

ARCHIE: I'm a half-trained lawyer with nothing else I can turn my hand to. It's only because I'm his son I'm not in jail, it's only because I'm his son I've a roof over my head. How can I ask you to marry me when I've nothing to offer you?

CHRISTINA: (*surprised although she has always hoped for this impossibility*) Marry me? Oh, Archie, would you marry me?

ARCHIE: With us it has to be that or nothing.

CHRISTINA: I'm afraid if it depends on Lord Weir it'll be nothing.

ARCHIE: If I can prove to him that there's some sense in me he might let me finish my studies. Then, if we must we could live our own lives. That's why we must avoid scandal; to protect our future.

CHRISTINA: Will we stop seeing each other then?

ARCHIE: I couldn't do that, but we must see less of each other.

CHRISTINA: When will I see you?

All Archie's wisdom disappears.

ARCHIE: The day after tomorrow.

Suddenly the humour of this strikes them and they begin to laugh.

APPENDIX III

Television Script by Tom Wright

Episode 2 (*continued*)

Scene 31. INTERIOR. HERMISTON. NIGHT.

Archie is reading. Innes, dressed for outdoors, enters.

ARCHIE: Are you bound for Crossmichael again?

INNES: I'm dining with the Pringles. It will be a scene of wild rustic revelry. (*He takes a letter from his pocket and hands it to Archie.*) By the way, this came for you. I'm afraid I put it in my pocket and forgot it.

Archie looks at it.

ARCHIE: The seal is broken.

INNES: I expect it's had some rough handling en route and I've been carrying it for a while.

Archie nods and opens the letter.

INNES: Now look here, Weir, you don't think I would open a letter addressed to you, do you?

Archie is staring at the letter.

INNES: Not bad news, I hope.

ARCHIE: I don't know. It's a summons to meet my father in Edinburgh tomorrow. The delay has left me very little time.

INNES: (*coldly*) I'm sorry, old man, but—

Archie waves this aside.

ARCHIE: It wasn't your fault. You couldn't know what was in it.

INNES: (*quite insincerely*) I suppose if you're going, I shall have to go with you. But, dammit, I can't go to Edinburgh. Not with that damned bookseller thirsting for my money or my blood.

ARCHIE: Of course not. You must stay here and make as free with the house as if I were still in it.

A sardonic smile flickers across Innes's face and disappears.

181

INNES: There's a problem there, old man. I hate to mention it. Dash it all, I've borrowed quite enough from you already.

ARCHIE: **Don't** mention it, Innes, I wouldn't go without seeing you were provided for.

INNES: Now that is damned decent of you, Weir.

ARCHIE: (*ringing the bell rope*) I may be gone for a day or so, but I'll see you when I return.

INNES: And I hope, whatever it is your father wants, he hasn't heard of— (*He inclines his head towards the moors and goes out as Kirstie enters*).

ARCHIE: Kirstie, my father has sent for me.

KIRSTIE: Oh!

ARCHIE: Could he have heard about Christina and me?

KIRSTIE: No' frae me, he couldnae. I'll no' say I approve o' the likes o' you foregathering wi' the sister o' a wee bonnet laird that's your own tenant, but if he's heard, it must be frae the common gossip or frae yon Innes man.

ARCHIE: Gossip from Hermiston rarely causes a great stir in Edinburgh and Frank Innes means me no harm.

KIRSTIE: Nor any good either. Yon's a drone, Mr. Archie. He's neither the energy nor the will to do you any harm, but if the chance comes his way don't be too sure he'll pass it by.

ARCHIE: Why should he harm me, Kirstie? I've always helped him when I could.

KIRSTIE: There's them that would forgive you right away for kicking at their dowp that'll never forgie ye for helpin' them.

ARCHIE: (*amused*) You've as low an opinion of human nature as my father, Kirstie.

KIRSTIE: Well, we've both seen mair o' it than you have.

ARCHIE: Will you do something for me? Something important.

KIRSTIE: If it's important, it'll be to do with my niece.

He nods.

KIRSTIE: Then I don't know that I can.

ARCHIE: In that case I'll go to Cauldstaneslaps myself.

KIRSTIE: (*surrendering*) What do you want me to do?

ARCHIE: If I'm not back by then, meet her the day after tomorrow at the cairn and tell her what has happened. Tell her if I'm not home soon I'll write to her.

KIRSTIE: Not at Cauldstaneslaps, man. Have you lost your reason?

ARCHIE: Then I'll write to this address and you must see the letters are delivered. Probably it would be best if she didn't reply. I can't be gone for long. And, Kirstie—tell her I'll be thinking of our future.

KIRSTIE: What does that mean, Mr. Archie?

ARCHIE: She'll know.

32. INTERIOR. WEIR'S HOUSE, AND GEORGE SQUARE. NIGHT.

Glenalmond and Weir are drinking wine. There is a noise in the hall. The door opens and Archie enters aggressively. Weir grins at him.

WEIR: So you got here at last.

ARCHIE: Your letter was delayed and my horse went lame. I came as fast as I could.

Weir looks at him critically. Archie toughens under the scrutiny.

WEIR: There's a change in you. I cannae just place it, but I hope it's for the better.

ARCHIE: If there is anything in my conduct that displeases you, father, please tell me at once.

WEIR: (*raising his eyebrows and joining battle happily and evenly*) At once, is it? The first thing about your conduct that displeases me, if ye'd ca' a notion to take my hand across your lug 'displeasure', is your damned bad manners. Oh, no' to me, I'd never ask ye to exercise your poe-faced gentility in my direction. But to Lord Glenalmond here who's been a better friend to you than you deserve.

ARCHIE: (*conscience-stricken*) Forgive me, Lord Glenalmond. I've ridden far and hard to answer my father's summons.

WEIR: Summons! That's why you're so thin-skinned, is it? You thought you were summoned here to answer for some misconduct at Hermiston. If you had been, you could have served your case better than by coming ram-stam through that door and blustering before ye'd even passed the time of day. He hasnae changed, Glenalmond. He's still a splairger.

GLENALMOND: (*smiling*) Good evening, Archie. Your father, like most lawyers, can't resist the opportunity to play-act, but I think he's almost as pleased to see you as I am myself. (*He rises and shakes Archie by the hand.*) Your father thought—

WEIR: No, no, Davie, it was **you** that thought it.

GLENALMOND: (*amused*) Perhaps, but I rather thought it was **you** that led me to think, or at least to say, it was time we saw him again. We've missed you, Archie.

WEIR: I like the way you always feel fit to speak for the entire company, Davie.

GLENALMOND: Only when the entire company is incapable of speaking for itself, Adam. Archie, the entire company feel it is now safe to recall you from your banishment. It thinks it would now even be possible to resume your studies in law.

Archie looks stricken.

ARCHIE: But, Sir—

WEIR: (*blandly*) No doubt you're thinking that the College would never take you back, and, if they'd any sense, you'd have the right of it. But you're a lucky man for Lord Glenalmond there is well up in legal circles and is no' above using his influence to force their hand.

ARCHIE: Is this true?

GLENALMOND: As your father says, I am a vicious and corrupt old man.

ARCHIE: When would I begin?

WEIR: Tomorrow.

ARCHIE: Thank you both for your good intentions.

He falls into a painful silence.

WEIR: My Lord Glenalmond, would you not say that Mr. Archie Weir's heartfelt speech of thanks left a wee doubt hanging in the air?

GLENALMOND: I confess, Lord Weir, I expected a little more enthusiasm.

ARCHIE: It's not that I'm not grateful, but I need time to put things in order at Hermiston.

WEIR: There are those that are paid to keep things in order at Hermiston. Do you suggest they're not fit for the job?

ARCHIE: I must go back, Sir, if only for a few days.

WEIR: Now here's a thing that's no' canny, Davie. A while back we sent a young man off to the country looking as if we'd signed his death warrant. For he's a right cultured young fellow. But all that's changed. Does that suggest anything to your keen legal brain?

GLENALMOND: He wouldn't be the first man who was surprised to find country life congenial.

WEIR: You mean wi' a' thae cultured pigs and cows and the like— (*with an air of discovery*) Glenalmond, it's a woman!

ARCHIE: Sir!—

WEIR: Wheesht, wheesht! Can you no' see that two senators o' the College of Justice are considering a weighty matter!

ARCHIE: (*keeping his temper with difficulty*) If you ask me directly I could spare you the effort of deliberation.

WEIR: Oh, deliberation's no' the effort for the likes of us that are used to it, that it is to the likes of you that have never tried it. (*He becomes serious.*) Well, is it a woman?

ARCHIE: Yes, father, it is.

To his surprise and annoyance, Weir roars with laughter.

ARCHIE: You think it's funny?

WEIR: Aye, and peetiful, but it's no' unexpected.

Archie is puzzled.

GLENALMOND: We had a visit from Lord Muirfell and his daughter last week.

ARCHIE: And how is his Lordship?

WEIR: Well enough, but I'd a notion his daughter's no' at her best.

ARCHIE: I never heard that Lady Flora was ill.

WEIR: Aye, it's an affliction quite common in young women that's buried in the country. Heart trouble. Is it this Lady Flora? Is that the way the wind's blowing?

ARCHIE: No, Sir, it is not.

WEIR: I'm no' sorry to hear that. She's bonny enough and her expectations are good, but she's a dwaibly body like your mither was.

Archie suppresses his indignation at this.

ARCHIE: If you wish, I'll tell you everything. I've done nothing that I'm ashamed of.

Weir dismisses the offer.

WEIR: If you've done nothing to be ashamed of, you've done nothing at all—and if you've done nothing at all there's nothing to tell.

ARCHIE: I think I've behaved as a man of honour should.

WEIR: (*his interest sharpening*) Honour, eh? Honour, is it? That has a sound that brings a cauld grue to my banes, Glenalmond. (*To Archie.*) You wouldnae hae some idea o' mairriage, would you?

ARCHIE: Yes, father.

WEIR: Well, get it out of your head.

ARCHIE: What have you against marriage, father?

WEIR: Naething, it's a legal institution, and you'll no' hear me railing against legal institutions. I was mairrit myself once— in a manner of speaking—which is no bad thing for you. It's no' marriage I object to, it's you getting married. You've shown nae sign that you're fit to make a considered judgment on anything else; I'll no' let you blunder into an ill-considered mairrage, if I can help it. A bad mairrage is a life sentence, and I've always thought it a barbarian trick to shut a man up for life. A good hangin's better than a bad mairrage any day.

ARCHIE: (*calm and stiff*) Father, I'll not let you stand between my happiness and the happiness of the woman I love.

WEIR: Hear that, Davie. Godsakes, you've a lot to answer for letting him read those bluidy nouvelles. He's started talking like them.
(*To Archie*) If you mean by that you're set on mairrying, I cannae stop ye. Get on wi'it if you're fool enough, but ye'll no' hae my blessing and you'll no' hae my support for you, nor her, nor any daft-like brats that come out o' your union.

ARCHIE: My mind is made up, father.

WEIR: And so is mine. Davie, see if ye can talk some sense into him. And if ye cannae, tell him to fill his belly in my kitchen and get to hell out of my house and off my hands for good.

Episode 3

1. INTERIOR. ROOM IN WEIR'S HOUSE. GEORGE SQUARE. EDINBURGH. NIGHT.

Archie and Glenalmond.

GLENALMOND: Your father's right, Archie. You're still splairging. The way you handled that interview showed clearly that you still lack self control.

ARCHIE: Was he not in the least at fault?

GLENALMOND: That is of no matter, Archie. If you had used a little tact and consideration, you might have got your way in time. He's worked hard to get you reinstated at the college and you come in and throw this new problem in his face like a gauntlet. He's a man that could never resist a challenge.

ARCHIE: (*in despair*) What will I do, Lord Glenalmond?

GLENALMOND: You must stay here and work and prove to him you are capable of other things before he will believe you to be capable of choosing a wife.

ARCHIE: I must go back to Hermiston!

GLENALMOND: Then you will shut this door and the door of Hermiston to yourself for a very long time, if not forever, Archie. And you will prove your father right. You will not lose the young lady because you do not see her every day, and if you do you have been mistaken in her. In which case, you will have been fortunate in learning it in time. If you stay and do well, I'm sure your father will let you go to Hermiston when the term ends.

ARCHIE: It's a lifetime till the term ends!

GLENALMOND: When you are as old as I am, you will know that even a lifetime is not so very long.

TELECINE

2. EXTERIOR. THE WEAVER'S CAIRN. DAY.

Christina is waiting. She sees Kirstie approach and affects to be there for no particular purpose.

CHRISTINA: Good day to ye, Auntie Kirstie. It's no' often I see you taking a walk in these parts.

KIRSTIE: There's nae need to play games wi' me, my lassie. I know you're waiting on Mr. Archie.

CHRISTINA: And what if I am; what is it to you?

KIRSTIE: (*with satisfaction*) He'll no' be coming. He's mair important things to attend to.

CHRISTINA: Is that what he said?

Kirstie savours Christina's disappointment.

KIRSTIE: It's what I say. His faither's called him back to Edinburgh. If he's kept there, he says, he'll write.

CHRISTINA: Is that all?

KIRSTIE: And he said he'd be thinking about your future. (*Christina lights up.*) And that pleases ye, does it?

CHRISTINA: Why should it no'?

KIRSTIE: If he mentions you to Lord Weir he'll get disowned.

CHRISTINA: Because of me? You're awful sure his Lordship'll think I'm no' good enough for his son.

KIRSTIE: And so would you if you werenae puffed up wi' vanity and pride. Would you say Bridie Morrison was good enough for him?

Christina looks disgusted at the thought.

KIRSTIE: Why no' when she's the sister o' a wee bonnet-laird like yoursel?

CHRISTINA: Archie thinks I am and that's a' that matters to me.

KIRSTIE: And maybe it's a' that matters to him for the moment but will it never matter? Can ye just see yoursel as lady o' Hermiston, playing the hostess to Lord Muirfell and his daughter and the like while your auntie's serving up their vittles.

CHRISTINA: If that's a' that's worrying you, ye'll be hoping his father cuts him off. Then I'll never be the lady o' Hermiston for he'll never be the Laird.

KIRSTIE: And what will he be?

Christina, who does not want to think of this, is silent.

KIRSTIE: Your brothers hold their land frae Hermiston, they couldnae take him in. And even if they could it can hardly feed the mouths that are in it as it is. Two mair would make them a' poor. What will he be? A labourer in some farm? He's no' been trained for that. Or maybe Clem would get him set up as a wee hand loom weaver in Glesgie? Is that the life ye see for him?

CHRISTINA: Things will come right, Auntie Kirstie! You'll see!

KIRSTIE: (*a little softened by the appeal in Christina's voice*) I wish I knew how! Sometimes I think there's a curse on the women o' our family! (*She is beginning to enjoy the drama of the situation.*) Gie him up, lassie! For his good and for your ain! (*She finds Christina looking steadily at her.*)

CHRISTINA: If you could see yoursel, Auntie Kirstie, ye'd know what the curse was. 'Gie him up' ye say and your eyes light up at the great part you're playing. It's easy to say when it costs you nothing, is it no'? You've no' had ower muckle frae this life and it sticks bitter in your thrapple that ane o' the same name and the same condition could get so much as is promised me.

KIRSTIE: Is that what ye think o' me, Miss Christina Elliott?

CHRISTINA: It's what a'body thinks of you, Miss Christina Elliott.

KIRSTIE: Does a'body think I'd harm Mr. Archie? There's nothing I wouldnae do to see him happy.

Her sincerity is clear.

CHRISTINA: Except to let him be happy wi' somebody else. Oh, ye could thole it if it was some great lady, but no' if it was wi' me. Can ye no' let yoursel see it? You're in love wi' him yoursel.

For a moment the truth of this astonishes Kirstie. Then she dismisses it.

CHRISTINA: Aye, it's easy for you to make me see what you think's the truth, but can ye no' face it yoursel?

KIRSTIE: I've always loved Mr. Archie—like the son I never had.

CHRISTINA: (*bitterly*) Aye, and like the man you never had.

KIRSTIE: I've tried to be a frien' to you and a frien' to Mr. Archie at the same time, but I see that what's good for one of you is no' good for the other. I've kept my word and brought his message. And there's an end to any business there can ever be between us.

Kirstie turns away. Christina's triumph fades.

CHRISTINA: Supposing he writes! He'll no' write to Cauld-staneslaps.

KIRSTIE: He'll send it through me. (*She savours Christina's fear for a moment.*) I'll see it's left for you on the big stone in the cairn, but I'll have nae mair truck wi' you whatever.

She goes.

TELECINE
3. EXTERIOR. THE MOORS. DAY.

Innes is walking. He sees the young maid coming towards him and accosts her. She carries a letter.

INNES: Where are you going to my pretty maid?

She blushes and drops her eyes.

INNES: Oh, come, surely at your age you're not meeting your lover out here.

She becomes more confused.

MAID: Miss Kirstie said I wasn't to speak to anyone about it.

Innes is intrigued by the mystery.

INNES: But surely you don't think of me as just anybody?
MAID: Oh, no, Mr. Innes.
INNES: Then tell me where you are going?
MAID: I'm taking a letter for Mistress Kirstie.
INNES: To whom?
MAID: I dinnae ken.
INNES: Then how do you expect to find them?
MAID: I'm not to find them, Mr. Frank. I've to leave it for them. At the Praying Weaver's Cairn.
INNES: How very mysterious, my pretty. Is it not addressed?
MAID: I think so, Mr. Frank. But I cannae read.
INNES: (*to her horror taking the letter from her hand*) Let me see it. (*He looks at the envelope which is marked 'Christina'. He whistles and smiles.*) I wonder what Mistress Kirstie was thinking about? To send you out on the moors alone on such an errand. It isn't safe, my dear! And to the Weaver's Cairn? You know, of course, that it's haunted?
MAID: I've heard it, Mr. Frank.
INNES: I really can't let you do this.
MAID: (*frightened*) Oh, sir, I've got to!
INNES: Are you not afraid of meeting the Praying Weaver's ghost?
MAID: Oh, aye, sir. But I'm mair afraid o' Mistress Kirstie!
INNES: There's only one thing to be done then. I'll deliver the letter.
MAID: Oh, no, sir! Mistress Kirstie would kill me if she knew.
INNES: Then she must never know. Don't be afraid. I promise I'll protect you. Off you go. And by the way—

She stops.

INNES: If she gives you any more of these, be sure you pass them on to me. Otherwise I'll have to scold Kirstie for exposing you to danger—and it might come out that you had given me this.

She goes unhappily. He puts the letter in his pocket, smiles and moves off jauntily.

4. INTERIOR. HERMISTON KIRK. DAY.

The congregation is leaving. Christina is stopped by Innes.

INNES: Excuse me, Miss Christina. We have never met, but Archie spoke of you so often that I feel we are old friends.

CHRISTINA: You are no friend to me, Mr. Innes.

INNES: I can't think what makes you say that, Miss Christina.

CHRISTINA: Archie said you talked about me.

INNES: (*calmly*) And did he tell you what I said?

CHRISTINA: No. He didn't.

INNES: I'm not surprised. Few men repeat conversations that are—in however small a measure—discreditable to themselves.

Christina scoffs at this.

INNES: If you persist in disbelieving in my friendship, you will force me to reveal the content of our conversation.

CHRISTINA: I've no wish to force you to anything, Mr. Innes.

INNES: Nevertheless, you do. I told Archie that your secret meetings could come to no good.

CHRISTINA: Oh? And who asked your opinion?

INNES: Why, Archie, of course.

This angers her a little against Archie.

INNES: Do you think I'd have volunteered an opinion on so delicate a matter?

CHRISTINA: And who told you about our meetings?

INNES: Archie, who else?

She is taken aback.

CHRISTINA: (*confused*) I thought it would be Auntie Kirstie!

INNES: I'm afraid I'm not in favour with that good lady who, by the way, is not your friend. It was she who doubted the wisdom of your relationship and put him in a state of doubt. That is why he raised the matter with me. I am, after all, his oldest friend.

CHRISTINA: And you advised him not to meet me.

INNES: I advised him not to meet you in secret. I told him— and if it brings a blush to your cheek the fault is your own for compelling me to speak plainly—I told him that it was cowardly and quite unworthy of him to meet you furtively as if he were ashamed to own your friendship openly—and that if I had been fortunate enough to find favour with so beautiful a lady I would shout it from the rooftops.

She looks away.

INNES: I'm sorry if I seem forward, but you left me no option. Since my company is repugnant to you, I'll not press it on you, but, believe me, if there is anything I can ever do to serve you, you have only to ask.

CHRISTINA: Mr. Innes! I don't think I deserve such kindness at your hands.

INNES: Kindness! (*His tone implies that his feelings are deeper than that.*) Tell me, have you heard from Archie?

She shakes her head. He looks deeply concerned.

INNES: I'm afraid— (*He appears to shrug off a doubt as absurd.*)

CHRISTINA: What is it you're afraid of?

INNES: I was about to say I was afraid he had deserted us. He is so given to sudden enthusiasms that leave him as suddenly. But no man could lose his enthusiasm for you. It's only a few weeks since he left and no doubt he has been kept very busy. If I have any news of him, I promise I'll bring it to you.

CHRISTINA: (*quickly*) Not to Cauldstaneslaps!

INNES: To where then?

CHRISTINA: To the Weaver's Cairn.

INNES: But how will you know to be there?

CHRISTINA: I'm there every day. Looking for a letter from Archie.

INNES: Then I shall be there every day—to report to you.

5. INTERIOR. CAULDSTANESLAPS. DAY.

Dand is composing. Hob is reading the Bible. Christina enters.

HOB: I think it's time you were back in Glesgie, my girl.

CHRISTINA: Why?

HOB: I saw you passing the time wi' that man, Innes. Yon's a drone.

DAND: Yon's worse than a drone.

CHRISTINA: (*on her high horse*) Have either of you spoken to the gentleman?

DAND: Just the once and it was once too often.

CHRISTINA: Then we've both spoken to him the same number of times and I think differently of him.

HOB: And what do you think of him?

CHRISTINA: That he's a kind young man without a bit of malice.

DAND: I'd say he'd something mair dangerous than malice and that's a great conceit of himself and a great idleness.
HOB: And the deil ay finds something for idle hands to do.

Christina tosses her head and goes out.

HOB: Have you noticed the way she's changed?
DAND: Aye!
HOB: I think she's sickening for something.
DAND: (*knowingly*) Or somebody that's no' here.
HOB: I'll write Clem and ask him to come and fetch her soon.

TELECINE

6. EXTERIOR. THE WEAVER'S CAIRN. DAY.

Christina's hand searching among the stones of the cairn and emerging disappointed.

INNES: (*voice over*) Good day, Christina.

Christina starts and looks up sadly.

CHRISTINA: Good day, Mr. Frank.
INNES: No letter yet?

She shakes her head.

INNES: I wish you would call me Frank. Titles like 'Miss' and 'Mr.' have no place between such old friends as we are.
CHRISTINA: We're not such old friends as that.
INNES: They have no place between friends at all. I begin to believe you still doubt my friendship.
CHRISTINA: Oh, no, Mr. Frank!
INNES: I had news from Edinburgh today.
CHRISTINA: About Archie?
INNES: He was mentioned.

His inflection makes her concerned.

CHRISTINA: He's not ill?
INNES: To the best of my knowledge, he is in good health. And I'm told he is back in his father's favour. Now please don't jump to conclusions.
CHRISTINA: (*who had no intention of jumping to conclusions*) Conclusions, Mr. Frank. What conclusions? Tell me!

G

INNES: When Archie was called back so suddenly, we supposed that it could only be because his father had heard of—you.

CHRISTINA: I see. I see it now!

INNES: I should never have mentioned it.

CHRISTINA: No, I should have seen it for myself. He's back in favour because he's promised to give me up.

She turns away.

INNES: (*surprised*) Where are you going?

CHRISTINA: Back home. And back to Glasgow as soon as I can. Does it matter where I go?

INNES: It matters to me.

CHRISTINA: (*with a wan smile*) I'll always be beholden to you, Mr. Frank.

She turns away. He catches her arm roughly and she turns surprised. He releases it and looks ashamed.

INNES: I'm sorry. But you mustn't go.

His plan has misfired and his powers of invention are taxed.

INNES: Even if he has promised he does not necessarily intend to keep his promise. Only to profit by it and qualify as a lawyer. Suppose he returns and finds you have gone?

CHRISTINA: It'll be easy for him to find me in Glasgow if he wants to.

INNES: But how will he know you want him to find you?

CHRISTINA: You can tell him.

INNES: No, Christina. If you go, I shall go too; it would be too painful for me—to stay here and feel your absence every day. (*He's almost sincere.*) You cannot imagine how empty this place would be without you.

CHRISTINA: I think I can.

He moves towards her hopefully.

CHRISTINA: I know how empty it is without Archie.

A flush of anger crosses his face and is suppressed.

7. INTERIOR. ROOM IN GEORGE SQUARE. NIGHT. (WEIR'S HOUSE)

Glenalmond and Weir are reading Archie's written work while Archie fidgets. Weir puts his papers down with grim satisfaction.

WEIR: God, Davie, between us we've managed to ram some law into this young eediot's thick skull. He'll no' be far behind the worst o' them at college now.

GLENALMOND: Don't you think some praise is due to our pupil as well?

WEIR: I cannae say I do. Wi' teachers like us a neep would have learned as much. (*He empties his wine glass.*) I'll say goodnight to the both of ye. No' that I'm tired, but now the work's done you'll start your feedleerie and I'd rather go to sleep in my bed than sitting in that chair.

ARCHIE: Goodnight, father.

GLENALMOND: Goodnight, Adam.

Weir takes a glass of wine with him.

GLENALMOND: He's pleased with you, Archie. And so am I.

ARCHIE: I can't go on much longer, Lord Glenalmond. I must go to Hermiston.

GLENALMOND: And waste all your effort? He knows you are anxious to go back there. Every day you spend here without complaining proves to him that you are learning patience as well as law. Consolidate your gains and when you go to Hermiston it will be with his permission. Perhaps even his blessing.

ARCHIE: I doubt that, Lord Glenalmond. I doubt it very much. Not when he knows who I intend to marry.

GLENALMOND: (*calmly*) Why? Has she slandered His Majestie's Judges too? Or merely committed murder?

ARCHIE: Neither of you has asked about her. Don't you want to know?

GLENALMOND: I'm sure he is as curious as I am, but first he wishes to know if you are fit to marry at all.

ARCHIE: She is the sister of a very small Laird on my father's own estate.

GLENALMOND: Would that be the only ground for his objection to her?

ARCHIE: Is it not enough?

GLENALMOND: (*with some severity*) When will you stop mis-
judging your father, Archie. He neither claims nor affects
gentility. You've heard his opinion of the nobility, the gentility,
the literati, and what he calls 'the hale bastard tribe o'
amatures'.

ARCHIE: Very often.

GLENALMOND: And yet you think he'd make you marry into
them. Archie, his worst enemy would not accuse him of
hypocrisy. Prove to him you're fit to choose for yourself
and he'll let you do it. Indeed, I think he would be disappointed in you if you did not insist on doing it.

TELECINE

8. EXTERIOR. THE WEAVER'S CAIRN. DAY.

*Innes is waiting impatiently. His face is resolute. At Christina's
approach he drops his cigar, grinds it savagely underfoot and
assumes a look of tender concern.*

CHRISTINA: You didn't come these last two days.

INNES: I've been away from Hermiston.

CHRISTINA: To Edinburgh? (*He nods*) You've seen Archie,
then?

INNES: He refused point blank to see me.

CHRISTINA: Oh!

INNES: (*bitterly*) He is completely under his father's thumb
now. How could he treat you this way!   (*She is absorbing
the shock.*) I'm sorry, I've failed you.

CHRISTINA: It isn't **you** that's failed me. I'd like to be alone now,
if you please.

INNES: Let me stay. Let me help you.

*He puts his arm round her and she breaks down. He makes her
sit and tries to comfort her by caressing her soothingly.
Gradually the quality and tempo of his caresses change and
she becomes alarmed.*

CHRISTINA: No, Frank.

*He does not stop. She tries to push him away but he draws her
closer to him and her fear becomes panic.*

CHRISTINA: No, Frank! No! No! No!

The camera pans up to the cairn.

9. INTERIOR. GEORGE SQUARE. NIGHT.

Archie is writing and scoring out and writing. Suddenly he sweeps the pen, paper and inkwell savagely from the table.

10. INTERIOR. CAULDSTANESLAPS. DAY.

Dand and Gib are sitting in tense silence. Mrs. Hob is looking out of the window.

MRS. HOB: It's Hob wi' Clem!

Hob and Clem come in.

CLEM: Where is she?

HOB: In by.

MRS. HOB: She's sleeping now.

GIB: And thank the Lord for it.

MRS. HOB: I'd leave her be. She's no' slept much this while back.

CLEM: What's the matter wi' her?

HOB: We don't know.

CLEM: What does the doctor say?

HOB: We never called him in.

DAND: She wouldnae have it, Clem.

GIB: You might as well have said you'd bring the deil as bring the doctor to her. It's her heid that's sick, you see.

CLEM: How bad is she?

MRS. HOB: Sometimes she's clean out of her mind.

GIB: And she's no' much sense the rest o' the time.

CLEM: What did it? Something must have done it.

HOB: I couldnae say. Maybe she'll talk easier to you. You've been mair o' a father than a brother to her.

GIB: The only faither that she's known except her heavenly faither.

Clem moves towards the door.

MRS. HOB: Be gentle wi' her.

CLEM: What else could I be?

11. INTERIOR. BEDROOM. DAY.

Clem enters and looks down at Christina. Her eyes open and she sits up in terror.

CHRISTINA: Clem!

CLEM: There, there, I've come to make everything all right.

Her voice is high with fear.

CHRISTINA: Go home, go home. I've seen this in my sleep.

She becomes pleading.

You're to be a baillie, Clem, and syne a provost. And we'll a'
be that proud of you. Go home. If ye care for me dinnae tak
the road wi' your brothers again! They'll hang ye this time!
They'll hang ye all!

She falls back sobbing.

CLEM: Wheesht, wheesht, my hinny! That was long ago, when
we were young and daft. It's a' past, I tell ye.

*She lies with her face turned from him. He pats her shoulder
awkwardly.*

Sleep. You'll be the better for it.

He turns away.

12. INTERIOR. CAULDSTANESLAPS. DAY.

Clem emerges shaking his head.

CLEM: She thinks we'll be hangit for riding after the murderin'
thieves that killed our faither!

DAND: I've heard her on that. There's nae sense in it.

CLEM: It's time she saw a doctor.

DAND: A doctor! You're as gyte as she is! All that doctors
ever do is bleed and purge you. If I was to treat my sheep like
that they'd a' be mutton in a week.

MRS. HOB: It didnae come on all at once, Clem. First off she
started going out on the moors for hours on end quite happily
and then she started moping. Then one day she came in all
wild and never spoke for days and took to her bed till yesterday. Then she went down to Crossmichael. When she came
back she was worse than ever.

DAND: The best thing we could do is to find the cause and it's
no' far to seek.

MRS. HOB: I suppose you think you've found it?

DAND: (*calmly*)   Aye, it's a man. Did ye not know she used to
meet Archie Weir up at the cairn?

Their surprise makes him smug.

DAND: Your ignorance fair astounds me. Did ye not notice that she started moping when he went to Edinburgh?

HOB: If you knew this why did you not tell us?

DAND: It was none of your damned business and none of mine. But it is now, for if that's the cause the cure's as easy. (*He pauses for effect.*) We just tell her Archie's back.

GIB: But that would be a lie.

DAND: Aye and a mortal sin into the bargain. I'll just go in and do it.

He goes into the bedroom.

13. INTERIOR. BEDROOM. DAY.

Christina is sobbing quietly. Dand enters and sits on the bed and they begin to talk at cross purposes.

DAND: There, there, lassie. I know what's the matter wi' you.

She stops crying and sits up.

CHRISTINA: Do you, Dand? Do you?

DAND: Sure I do. And it's no' the end o' the world.

CHRISTINA: Oh, Dand, it is to me!

DAND: You're making ower much o' a thing that happens every day.

CHRISTINA: I never thought it could happen to me. Does Clem know? And Hob?

DAND: I've just telt them.

CHRISTINA: (*surprised*) And they're no' mad?

DAND: (*laughing*) It's been the way o' men and women for a long time. I've got good news for you.

CHRISTINA: Good news?

DAND: Aye, about Archie Weir.

CHRISTINA: (*suddenly very apprehensive*) What about him?

DAND: (*like a man bringing a rabbit out of a hat*) He's back!

Christina is silent for a moment and then begins to scream.

14. INTERIOR. CAULDSTANESLAPS. DAY.

Christina's screams bring Clem to his feet. As he moves towards the door, Dand emerges very shaken.

DAND: My God, it's worse than I thought!

GIB: I think we'd best be offering up a prayer to the Lord to take frae us this cross.

DAND: Aye, do that, Gib. I'm for Crossmichael to fetch Dr. Gow!

15. INTERIOR. HERMISTON. DAY.

Innes, looking haggard, is smoking a cigar tensely. Kirstie enters.

KIRSTIE: Will ye be home all day again today?

INNES: Yes, have you some objection?

KIRSTIE: It's no' for me to object to you staying here under my feet like a rabbit that's feart to leave its hole.

INNES: Can you suggest somewhere else I can go when I'm so damned hard up?

KIRSTIE: And it's no' for me to suggest where ye can go, Mr. Innes.

INNES: (*letting this pass*) Is there any improvement in Miss Elliott's health?

KIRSTIE: You're taking a great interest in my family's business these days.

INNES: What else is there for me to take an interest in? (*He assumes a judicial gravity.*) It's a bad thing when people lose their reason. Not only for the person affected but for everyone around them. (*He laughs lightly, but his uneasiness shows through.*) They're liable to say anything at all. Make accusations and that sort of thing. There was one odd chap in Edinburgh who used to accuse everyone of murdering his wife. Lucky for everyone, he was a life-long bachelor.

KIRSTIE: You'll forgive me if I don't see my niece's illness as a joking matter, Mr. Innes.

INNES: I was trying to show how unfortunate this sort of thing can be.

KIRSTIE: I think we ken fine already that it's unfortunate.

INNES: (*with the air of a man of feeling*) This has taken all the joy out of my stay here, Mistress Kirstie. It's upset me damnably. It's time I was moving on.

KIRSTIE: I daresay there'll be somebody that's sorry to see you go, Mr. Innes.

INNES: But it won't be you, eh? I'd oblige you by leaving this minute, but I've no money. Absolutely none!

KIRSTIE: That's a pity, for I'm sure there are those that'll be sorry to see you stay.

INNES: (*openly agitated*) If Archie were here, he wouldn't see me in this predicament! He wasn't always the best of company, but he was always willing to help a friend with money. He helped me often in the past you know. If there's any money about the place, I'm sure he wouldn't mind if you gave it to me.

KIRSTIE: I'm sure he wouldnae, but there's no such thing.

INNES: Are you sure?

KIRSTIE: If you mean am I lying, I've no call to lie to the likes of you. You've talked about nothing but leaving for weeks now. You're no' a cripple, can ye no' just walk away?

INNES: And starve? Without money where could I go? (*A thought strikes him.*) Pringle and Hay! They might help me out! I should have thought of them before! (*Hope brings back some of his old poise.*) An evening with those provincial bores is a small price to pay for bailing me out of this prison.

The sound of galloping hooves wrecks his composure.

INNES: Do you hear that?

The horse stops.

INNES: If it's anyone looking for me, tell them I'm not at home. Tell them I've gone to Edinburgh and won't be back.

KIRSTIE: And why should I tell them that?

INNES: Can't you see my nerves are in a damnable state? I couldn't talk to anyone! Please, Kirstie, tell them I've gone.

The appeal softens Kirstie.

KIRSTIE: Quieten yourself. I'll tell them.

INNES: Even if it's your own flesh and blood.

KIRSTIE: (*with puzzled suspicion*) What would my ain flesh and blood want wi' you, Mr. Innes?

INNES: I meant no matter who it was—

The front door bangs. Terror seizes Innes.

INNES: Don't let them in, Kirstie! For God's sake don't let them in.

The door opens briskly and Archie comes in smiling.

KIRSTIE: (*delighted*) Oh, Mr. Archie, you're back!

ARCHIE: I am, Kirstie. Hello Innes. God, you look ill!

INNES: It's the shock of seeing you. I thought you'd write if you
were coming. You should have warned us.

ARCHIE: (*amused and puzzled*) 'Shock', 'warned'; these are
scarcely welcoming words, Frank. My father said I could come.
I've almost broken my horse's wind. How is Christina?

The joy leaves Kirstie. She looks at the floor.

ARCHIE: Is something wrong, Kirstie? Answer me.

She begins to cry.

ARCHIE: Innes, what has happened to Christina?

INNES: It's very sad. I'm told she's suffering from a brain fever.

Archie turns towards the door.

INNES: Wait! Don't go to Cauldstaneslaps! There's no good in
you going there. She's mad. Quite mad—raving and making
wild accusations against you and everybody else! Archie!

But Archie has gone.

TELECINE

16. EXTERIOR. THE MOORS. DAY.

Archie is walking.
He looks towards the cairn and sees a woman's figure there.
He hurries towards the cairn.

TELECINE

17. EXTERIOR. WEAVER'S CAIRN. DAY.

Christina's back is to Archie. She does not turn.

ARCHIE: Christina, love!

He goes to her.

ARCHIE: I was coming to you. They told me you were ill!

He puts his hands on her shoulders.
She turns quickly throwing them off.
*He recoils at the sight of her ravaged face, then moves towards
her.*
She shrinks back.

CHRISTINA: Don't touch me!

ARCHIE: Don't you know me?

CHRISTINA: Oh, I know you, Mr. Archie Weir o' Hermiston. Dand said you had come back, so I came up here. For the caller air.

ARCHIE: Christina!

CHRISTINA: 'Miss Christina Elliott' an' you please. I'll hae respect, Mr. Weir. I'll hae respect!

ARCHIE: I'll stand here and not come near you. But surely you know I'd never harm you!

Her laugh is like a girn.

ARCHIE: I came to tell you that I've gone a long way towards winning my father's favour.

CHRISTINA: Aye, I heard as much.

ARCHIE: If things go on this way, I don't think he will stand in our way.

CHRISTINA: **Our** way? Our way, Mr. Weir? What way is that? There's your way—and there's my way. But where's the way that's ours?

ARCHIE: I thought I was bringing good news.

CHRISTINA: There can be nae news that's good to me now— except that you're away frae here.

ARCHIE: Christina!

CHRISTINA: Dinnae use my christian name. I'll hae respect. If I cannae hae letters, I'll hae respect. (*Suddenly lucid.*) Oh, Archie, you said you'd write to me. Why did ye no'?

ARCHIE: I **did** write. Don't you remember? Your Aunt gave them to you!

CHRISTINA: She gied me nothing from you. Except your promise. She gied me nothing.

ARCHIE: I can't believe it!

CHRISTINA: (*flaring*) So now I'm leein' is it? Or do you think I'm mad, as well? I think I've **been** mad. But I'm no' mad now.

ARCHIE: Christina, if there's anything I can say or do—

CHRISTINA: There's naething man can do for me. I hoped you'd come here. It was here I gied you my love—and it's here I gie you my curse! Ye can go now.

ARCHIE: Christina—

CHRISTINA: (*suddenly screaming with something like hate*) Go! Go! Go! Go!

He covers his ears and turns away distracted. Her screams follow him down the hill.

18. INTERIOR. CAULDSTANESLAPS. LATE IN DAY.

Clem, Hob, his wife and Gib.

MRS. HOB: It'll be dark soon and Dand not back yet wi' the doctor.

GIB: I hope he's all right. He went off like the fiends o' hell were on his tail.

HOB: The moors'll no' hurt Dand.

CLEM: She's been very quiet.

MRS. HOB: Leave her be till they come.

CLEM: Shouldn't somebody be wi' her?

GIB: Her maker's wi' her. She's in his gentle care.

CLEM: It's no' been all that gentle up till now.

The door opens and Dand enters.

MRS. HOB: Could ye no' find the doctor.

DAND: Oh, I found him easy enough.

MRS. HOB: Then why did ye no' bring him?

DAND: There was no need. He'd seen her when she was in Crossmichael and diagnosed her complaint.

CLEM: What was it?

But Dand with a story will not be hurried.

DAND: He wouldnae tell me at first, said it would be violatin' his hypocritic oath. So I picked him up and shook him till his hypocritic oath fell out.

GIB: For God's sake, man, what's wrong wi' her?

DAND: I wish ye wouldnae blaspheme at a time like this. There's nothing wrong wi' her condition that marriage won't cure.   Marriage to the right man of course—Archie Weir.

MRS. HOB: Supposing he'll no' mairry her. He's the Laird's son.

HOB: If it was Weir himself, he'd marry her.

CLEM: By God, he will.

MRS. HOB: But he's in Edinburgh.

DAND: He can be fetched. Clem, you'd best inform the bride.

Clem tries to open the door. It is bolted.

CLEM: It's bolted.

HOB: (*moving towards it*) I'll soon open it.

DAND: Leave it to me. A window's sooner mended than a door.

He goes out. They wait. The bedroom door opens and Dand comes out.

DAND: She's gone! Out the window!
GIB: In her state, there's no tellin' where she's gone!
MRS. HOB: Dand telt her Archie Weir was back. She'll have gone looking for him.
HOB: We'd better start for Hermiston.
DAND: You go there. We'll take a look at the Deil's Hags. She's as likely to be at the Weaver's Cairn.

19. INTERIOR. HALL AT HERMISTON. EARLY EVENING.

Archie enters looking wild and dishevelled. He calls:

ARCHIE: Kirstie! Kirstie!

Kirstie enters.

KIRSTIE: Heavens, Mr. Archie, what's a' the steer?
ARCHIE: (*with brutal directness*)   I sent you letters for Christina. Were they delivered?

Kirstie nods.

ARCHIE: She tells me they were not.
KIRSTIE: The lassie's no' right in her head. She doesnae ken what she's sayin'.
ARCHIE: (*very much the master*)   I must be sure of this Kirstie. **You** delivered them?

She nods stubbornly.

ARCHIE: With your own hand?
KIRSTIE: Well, no' exactly—
ARCHIE: How were they delivered?
KIRSTIE: I sent them by the wee kitchen maid.
ARCHIE: Bring her here.

Kirstie goes out. Archie paces impatiently till she returns dragging the maid and throws her forward.

KIRSTIE: Tell Mr. Archie what ye did wi' the letters. Come on my wee tawpie, or ye'll feel the weight o' my hand on your lug.

MAID: I gied them to Mr. Innes. He **made** me do it!

ARCHIE: (*now totally commanding*) Fetch Mr. Innes.

MAID: He's no' here, sir. He's gone. He took his things and flittit. Wi' one o' your horses frae the stable.

KIRSTIE: And good riddance to bad rubbish!

ARCHIE: Where did he go?

MAID: He never said.

Archie dismisses her with a wave.

KIRSTIE: Back to the kitchen, miss; you've no' heard the last o' this.

ARCHIE: Do **you** know where he's gone?

KIRSTIE: Not for sure, but he said all that was keeping him here was that he'd nae siller. He talked about getting it from thae daft young lairds at Crossmichael.

Archie takes a flat case from a drawer and opens it to reveal two pistols.

Kirstie does not see this.

KIRSTIE: I hope he gets it and goes out of our lives for good.

Archie is priming the pistols.

ARCHIE: Not till I've had a word with him.

Kirstie realises what he is doing and is alarmed.

KIRSTIE: Promise me you'll dae nothing foolish, Mr. Archie!

ARCHIE: (*bitterly*) I've tried your kind of wisdom and God knows what evil has come of it. I'll never be wise again.

He checks the pistols.

KIRSTIE: What do you want thae for? It's against the law to fight.

ARCHIE: When the law gives us no satisfaction, we must go outside the law, Kirstie.

KIRSTIE: Your father'll no' take kindly to that. What would your mother say if she was alive?

ARCHIE: These are the shadows that have lived in me for the whole of my life. I've rebelled against them stupidly and submitted to them stupidly. Now I mean to live by my own lights.

KIRSTIE: He'll no' fight ye. That's no' the way o' mister Innes. And you'll no' shoot a man that'll no' defend himself!

ARCHIE: I'm beginning to agree with my father that there are men who'll be none the worse of a hanging.

> *He closes the case decisively. As he does so there is a loud knocking. He nods to Kirstie. She opens the door. Hob and Clem enter pushing past her.*

KIRSTIE: Clem!

CLEM: My business is with Mr. Archie.

ARCHIE: You're welcome, Mr. Elliott.

> *He holds out his hand but Clem does not take it. Archie stiffens.*

ARCHIE: What do you want? I have important matters to attend to in Crossmichael.

> *Clem confronting Archie with stolid aggression.*

CLEM: You've important matters to attend to here.

ARCHIE: Tell me what it is, or get out of my way.

CLEM: Where's Christina?

ARCHIE: Is she not at Cauldstaneslaps? Then we'd be better employed in looking for her.

CLEM: My brothers are doing that. When they find her, they'll bring her here. And then they'll fetch a minister.

KIRSTIE: What are ye havering about, Clem Elliott?

HOB: We're here to see our sister married.

> *Archie looks surprised, then smiles.*

ARCHIE: To me?

HOB: Aye, Mr. Weir.

KIRSTIE: You're mad, Hob. Lord Hermiston would hang you for that.

HOB: He can hang us if he likes, but he cannae undo what we've done.

ARCHIE: (*smiling*) I'll be glad to marry your sister if she'll have me. There's been a serious misunderstanding between us, but now I can prove to her that I was not at fault.

HOB: We're no' concerned wi' blame for you or blame for her, Mr. Weir, just so ye marry her and undo the harm you've done her.

ARCHIE: You must be mad to think I'd harm Christina.

CLEM: We Elliotts are no' born mad, Mr. Weir, but we can be driven that way.

> *Hooves are heard.*

HOB: That'll be them!

He moves towards the door. The horses stop. Kirstie intervenes.

KIRSTIE: Since when were you the housekeeper o' Hermiston, Hob Elliott? I'll answer the door, if you please.

She opens the door and waits, then falls back in horror as Dand and Gib enter carrying Christina's body. They put it on the floor and step back.

KIRSTIE: Goodness, what happened to the lass?

DAND: We found her at the foot o' the Deil's Hags.

Archie kneels beside Christina and wipes the hair back from her face gently. His whole being is numb.

ARCHIE: (*numbly*)   She's dead!

The brothers stand round him like executioners.

DAND: Aye, she's deid. And so is the bairn inside her. The bairn you put there.

ARCHIE: Bairn?

HOB: That's two o' our blood that has died through your fault this night.

ARCHIE: It can't be! You must be wrong!

HOB: (*bitterly*)   And so must she and Dr. Gow.

Archie realises what has happened.

ARCHIE: (*soft as a snake hiss*)   Innes!

Hob puts his hand on Archie's shoulder firmly. Archie knocks it aside and rises. His face is as terrible as theirs.

HOB: We're going to hang you, Mr. Weir. Out there where your ancestors were hangit. They were right hard men, but they'll spew in disgust when you join them. Get a rope, Gib.

DAND: On my horse, Gib.

Gib goes out.

KIRSTIE: Ye'll no' dae this?

HOB: Aye, and we'll joy in it. And if there's Elliott blood in you, you'll do the same.

KIRSTIE: You'll hang me first.

HOB: An we hae to, we will.

KIRSTIE: Then you'll surely hae to.

She throws herself kicking and scratching on Hob. He tries to control her and fails. Dand and Chem drag her off and hold her with difficulty. They turn to Archie and are startled to see him white with anger pointing the pistols at them.

KIRSTIE: For God's sake, Mr. Archie, dinnae kill them.

Archie moves to the side of the door. Gib enters with the rope, follows his brothers' eyes to Archie and lets the rope fall as if getting rid of evidence. Archie gestures him into the hall.

ARCHIE: I'm going to Crossmichael, Kirstie. If you want them to live, keep them here. I'll come back when I've finished my business, and my life will be theirs or anyone's that wants it.

He goes out; they hear him shout and there is the sound of hooves. Dand goes to the door.

DAND: He's driving off the horses!

HOB: Then we'll go after him on foot.

KIRSTIE: Save your legs. Just wait till he gets back.

GIB: He'll no' be back.

KIRSTIE: Why would he keep away from his own house? For the likes of you?

GIB: Because there's black sin on his conscience.

KIRSTIE: (*contemptuously*) You're no' Elliotts, you're eediots! Archie would never harm that lassie.

HOB: Then she wasnae pregnant and she's no' deid.

KIRSTIE: Can ye no' see what happened?

20. INTERIOR. CROSS KEYS INN. NIGHT.

In the company are Pringle and Hay and Innes.

INNES: What I'll miss most is the pleasure of your company, gentlemen. I swear there are not two men in Edinburgh with your wit, manners and deportment. Still it will only be for a short time and the legacy my poor father has left me will compensate for a short absence.

PRINGLE: How big would you say it is?

INNES: Oh, I wouldn't say. Never count your legacies before they're hatched. But my father was a man of means. Fairly substantial means. I'd say it was large. I'm sorry I can't offer you security for this money.

They make deprecating noises.

PRINGLE: We wouldn't ask it, would we, Hay?

HAY: We're gentlemen and you're a gentleman and that's enough for us.

INNES: If Archie Weir had been in as much of a hurry to return my money as he was to borrow it, I wouldn't have been placed in this embarrassing predicament. Still, the fact that I'm his guest should guarantee you against loss. Whatever his faults— and we all know he has them, Weir is a gentleman. (*They make fuddled noises of assent. Innes rises.*) I'm truly sorry to leave you, but the sooner I'm gone, the sooner I'll be back. No, don't see me off—I swear I'd cry if you did.

TELECINE

21. EXTERIOR. DOOR OF THE CROSS KEYS. NIGHT.

Innes becomes framed by the doorway. He chuckles and lights a cigar. Archie's voice is heard:

ARCHIE: Innes!

Innes starts and frowns.

INNES: Who is it?

ARCHIE: Archie Weir. Don't make a noise.

INNES: What's this about?

ARCHIE: I've come to get you away from here.

INNES: Where to?

ARCHIE: To safety. I have our horses here. There's no time to waste.

INNES: (*suspiciously*) Why should I go with you?

ARCHIE: Don't play the fool, man. The Elliott brothers are after you; and they'll be here soon.

INNES: How will they know I'm here?

ARCHIE: The same way as I did. Kirstie'll tell them. You can go alone if you wish, but if you keep to the roads, they'll find you; and if you take to the moors without me, you'll go round in circles or break your neck.

Innes drops his cigar and tramples it.

INNES: Come on, Archie. We'd better get started.

22. INTERIOR. HALL OF HERMISTON. NIGHT.

Kirstie and the brothers.

KIRSTIE: So you can thank your maker you did no harm to Archie Weir.

HOB: Then we'd better be after Innes.

KIRSTIE: I pray to God Archie hasnae found him first.

HOB: If he hasnae, Dand will.

DAND: Aye, **Dand** will. On his own.

CLEM: I'll no' have that.

DAND: D'you think I cannae do it on my own.

HOB: It's family business and the family will do it.

DAND: And the family will hang for it. One Elliott's more than enough to pay for yon drone, Hob.

HOB: There's truth in that, but as head o' the family—

DAND: As head o' the family, you'll take the rest back to Cauldstaneslaps.

CLEM: Dand, it's no' your ploy. I raised the lassie. I'm responsible for her. If blood's to be shed or given, it's for me to do it.

DAND: Clem, you're doted. If there's ever going to be an Elliott that's a baillie or a provost it's you. We're no' that well off for dignitaries that we can spare you.

HOB: He's right, Clem. We couldnae let you go, but as head o' the family—

DAND: I've told you your duties as head o' the family. And what about your own family?

HOB: You would look after them.

DAND: No, No, Hob. I'm a poet, no' a farmer. While you were fertilisin' the prison cemetery, I'd be in a tavern liquidatin' Cauldstaneslaps. You know that's true.

GIB: There's one you havenae mentioned.

DAND: I never like to blaspheme, for ye cannae talk about God behind his back, but he's put such a load of religion on you that he's taken away your capacity for every day things like killing Frank Innes. You'd be that busy saving his soul, you'd probably get killed yoursel! Now, I'm just a God-forsaken poet, and poets are no' long for this world. If it's no' this that takes me, it'll be something else.

He rises in a leisurely fashion.

DAND: Besides, I'll brain any of you that tries to come wi' me.

He goes.

TELECINE

23. EXTERIOR. THE MOORS. NIGHT.

Archie and Innes riding.

INNES: Where are we?
ARCHIE: On the moors.
INNES: Are you sure you won't get lost here?
ARCHIE: I spent all of my childhood on the moors. They don't change.

They ride in silence.

INNES: You haven't told me what the Elliotts want with me.
ARCHIE: To kill you.
INNES: But why?
ARCHIE: Don't you know?
INNES: I've done them no harm.
ARCHIE: Will we go back and tell them that?
INNES: No, God knows what their sister might have said to them—and they're as mad as she is.
ARCHIE: Shut up, Innes! (*He corrects his tone.*) Dand Elliott can pick a whisper out of the wind.

24. INTERIOR. CROSS KEYS INN. NIGHT.

Dand enters pushing the landlord who is trying to keep him out ahead of him, quite good-naturedly. Hay and Pringle and another member approach in their role as officials.

PRINGLE: (*to landlord*) We'll attend to this.

The landlord nods and goes out.

PRINGLE: This room is reserved for members of the Tuesday Club.

DAND: Aye, so I've heard. I've often wondered why, since you're in here every night, you call it Tuesday—I suppose it's because when you've nothing to do every day's the same.

HAY: We'll have to ask you to leave.

DAND: I wasnae thinking of **joining**, Mr. Hay. I've business wi' one of your members. An Edinburgh tyke called 'Innes'.

PRINGLE: **Mr.** Innes has gone.

DAND: Wi' your permission I'll make sure.

PRINGLE: You don't have our permission, does he, Hay?

HAY: By God he doesn't!

DAND: My business is awfully important.

PRINGLE: What important business could the likes of you have with a gentleman like Mr. Innes?

DAND: (*very calmly*) I'm going to kill him.

In their surprise they allow him to push past them. He surveys the room, goes to one man whose back is to him and who resembles Innes and puts a hand on his shoulder. The man looks up.

DAND: I humbly beg your pardon for the interruption. Just go on wi' the nonsense you're talking.

He retires to the door and nods to Hay and Pringle.

DAND: Your pardon, gentlemen. I should have taken your word, but you've got such awful leear's faces.

TELECINE

25. EXTERIOR. WEAVER'S CAIRN. NIGHT.

Archie and Innes walk up to it. Innes becomes alarmed.

INNES: It's the Weaver's Cairn! Why have you brought me here? They're bound to find us here.

ARCHIE: You've no need to fear the Elliotts now.

INNES: I find you unbearably solemn at the best of times, Weir, but you're beginning to sound like a damned oracle. I've been through a lot, I'm tired and I'd appreciate it if you'd speak plainly.

ARCHIE: You've no one to fear now but me.

INNES: God, has that bitch poisoned your mind against me as well.

ARCHIE: Bitch?

INNES: The milkmaid. But you never really knew her, did you?
You know so little of life. After you left she was up here with
every grieve and every bonnet laird in the shire. If you'd been
more experienced you'd have known right away the kind she
is. (*He pauses but cannot gauge Archie's reaction in the dark.*)
It was painful for me to stand by and watch the best friend I
have in the world getting more and more entangled with her.
I tried to tell you, but you wouldn't listen. You should have
trusted me more, Archie. (*He pauses, but gets no lead from
Archie.*) You saw her today didn't you?

ARCHIE: (*tonelessly*) I saw her.

INNES: Quite mad I believe?

ARCHIE: Quite.

INNES: Did the bitch say anything against me? (*Silence.*)
Sorry, I shouldn't have said that. But did she?

ARCHIE: You were never mentioned.

INNES: (*relieved*) I shouldn't feel so bitterly against her, but
watching her play fast and loose when you were gone—

ARCHIE: You're a great one for watching people, Innes.

INNES: It amuses me.

ARCHIE: Did it amuse you to watch her playing fast and loose?

INNES: God, man, why do you keep twisting my words?

ARCHIE: I'm untwisting them, Innes.

INNES: (*beginning to crack.*) For pity's sake stop this, Archie.
Everything I've done has been done for your own good.

ARCHIE: Everything?

INNES: What if I did amuse myself with her a little? I wasn't
the only one—and, whatever she said, she was more than
willing. (*He pulls himself together.*) I'm sick of this inquisition.
Do you hear me? I won't be interrogated any longer.

ARCHIE: There's no need. I have two pistols here.

INNES: (*incredulously*) For you and me? (*He laughs.*) A
duel? Between old friends like us? I'll never fight with you.
And certainly not over a rustic whore.

ARCHIE: Then I shall kill you.

INNES: Why?

ARCHIE: (*suddenly releasing his anger*) Because the 'milkmaid,'
the 'bitch', the 'rustic whore' is dead. (*He shoots Innes with
both pistols, killing him at once, and stands looking down at him
with a face as dead as Innes's. Dand appears beside him. He
examines Innes's body.*)

DAND: There's nothing more we can do to him. You'd best go home and leave this to me.

ARCHIE: Home?

DAND: To Hermiston. And forget everything that's happened the night.

ARCHIE: No, I'll wait here till they find me.

DAND: Then what?

ARCHIE: I'll stand my trial.

DAND: You'll do no such thing. I think I can speak for my brothers when I say we're beholden to you for the trouble you've saved us. You'd better be on your way. We'll see you never suffer for this. (*He stoops and picks up one of the pistols Archie has let fall.*)

ARCHIE: I'll not suffer, I'm past feeling now.

DAND: Then this'll no' hurt you all that much.

He brings the pistol down on Archie's head, stunning him.

26. INTERIOR. HALL OF HERMISTON. DAY.

Adam Weir is pacing the floor. Dr. Gow and Kirstie come down.

GOW: Just carry on wi' the treatment, Kirstie. It's hopeful treatment, but where there's hope there's life.

WEIR: It's all right, Kirstie. I'll see the doctor out.

She goes back up and Weir interrogates the doctor silently.

GOW: He's had a sair dunt, Hermiston. The skull's broken.

WEIR: (*masking his concern*) It would take a sore dunt to crack a skull as thick as his. Is there anything mair that we can do?

GOW: What you're dying to ask me, Hermiston, is would you be better to take him to Edinburgh and turn the hale college o' surgeons loose on him. Is that no' right?

WEIR: An' if it is?

GOW: If you move him, he'll be deid before he gets to Edinburgh.

WEIR: And what if I was to bring them to him?

Gow: Ye'd be wasting your time and theirs. This isn't one of
   thae fancy diseases they invent in Edinburgh so they can
   invent a miraculous cure. It's a broken head and there's been
   broken heads in these parts since Adam and Eve invented the
   whale o' sins and the whale o' pleasures. I've seen more of
   them in my time than the hale college o' surgeons put thegither. There's two things cure a broken head—time and
   Providence and neither of them'll be hurried.
Weir: There's nothing I can do, then?
Gow: Ye can try a wee prayer. If it does him nae good, it'll
   dae him nae harm.

   There is a knocking at the door. Weir opens it.

Weir: Sheriff Walker! Come in, man.

   The Sheriff comes in.   Kirstie appears on the stairs.

Weir: What is it, Sheriff?
Walker: You'd better baith come. A man's been found murdered up at the Weaver's Cairn.

TELECINE

27.   EXTERIOR.   WEAVER'S CAIRN.   DAY.

   *Innes's body has been laid out by Dand on the cairn like a man
   crucified. Weir, Gow, and Walker are looking at it with some
   others looking on.*

Weir: The one that did this wasnae anxious to keep it a
   secret. He was shot here and lifted up there. You'd think the
   murderer was feared that nobody would notice it.

   Gow looks at the body.

Weir: How long since it happened?
Gow: Two days, three at the most.
Weir: Goad! The accuracy o' medical science fair fills me wi'
   admiration. Does anybody ken who he is?
Man: He's no frae these parts.
Weir: Thank you for your shrewd observation, but if he was
   frae these parts it's likely that I wouldnae have to ask. Now
   that we've heard wha he's no'—does anybody ken wha he was?
Second Man: I think I ken. He's an Edinburgh chiel that was
   stopping at Hermiston. I think his name was Innes.

WEIR: (*his memory stirring*) Innes? (*He looks more closely at the body.*) I've seen him before. He was at the High School wi' Archie.

GOW: I suppose he's changed.

WEIR: Aye, he wasnae deid then.

GOW: He's been shot twice. So it was either one man wi' twa guns or twa wi' one each.

WEIR: Aye, or a firing squad where the most o' them missed.

GOW: (*indignantly*) Would it no' be better if instead o' being comical, you got a posse thegither and went after him or them as the case may be.

WEIR: If ye'll just be so good as to tell me wha he is—or them as the case may be—and point us in the direction he, or they went, I'd be mair than happy to oblige you.

GOW: How can I do that? I wasnae here when it happened. Could we no' follow the tracks?

WEIR: If ye feel like the exercise, but it seems likely to me that you'd only follow every one of the people here back to where they came from. Here, you four, (*he points to Innes*) get this thing out of here afore it frichtens the bairns.

They go to the body.

MAN: Where will we take it, my Lord?

WEIR: If it came frae Hermiston, ye'd better take it back there. The rest of you can stop gawkin' and get back to your business. It's nae wonder we're a poor country if we're relying on the likes of you for our daily bread.

They disperse except for Gow, Walker and Weir. Weir takes out a bottle and drinks from it, passing to Gow.

WEIR: It's a gey drouthy business looking at corpses, doctor.

GOW: (*taking it*) Aye, and I've had mair nor my fill of it these past few days.

WEIR: Oh, wha else?

WALKER: Well, there was the Laird o' Cauldstaneslaps' sister, Christina Elliott by name.

WEIR: I mind her as a bairn.

GOW: And your Archie—that counts as a half.

WEIR: What did Miss Elliott die of?

GOW: Heart failure—brought on by her lowpin' ower the Deil's Hags.

WEIR: And what made her do a daft-like thing like that?

Gow: She was having a bairn. It does things to their minds betimes—especially when it's out o' wedlock.

Weir: I see. And who was the faither?

Gow: There's no way a doctor can tell that.

Weir: I'm glad to hear that medical science has its limitations like anythin' else. But ye get about the country, doctor. Was there no' a wee whisper in the wind?

Gow: I hear a lot of what goes on in Crossmichael, but the folks up here keep themselves to themselves and enjoy lamentably good health. Oh, they get their heads bashed in, and shot, and jump off mountains, but they're no' often ill.

Walker: Did her brothers know about it?

Gow: One of them did—Dand.

Weir: And how did he know?

Gow: Because I telt him.

Weir: Was that no' a breach o' medical etiquette?

Gow: Dand wasnae paying much heed to ony kind of etiquette. They're black-tempered bodies, thae Elliotts.

Walker: He threatened you.

Gow: He laid hands on me. I thought it best to humour him.

Weir: And when ye telt him did he laugh? There seems to have been a lot going on in these parts, Sheriff Walker. An Elliott gets pregnant, the doctor gets threatened, a man that's the guest of my son gets shot, and my son gets a broken head. Can you see a connection?

Walker: Aye, I think I can.

Gow: It's as plain as the nose on your face.

Weir: There's nothing plain in my face, Gow. And there's nothing plain in law. It's my opinion, but no' my judicial opinion that yon bonnie thing they're carrying to Hermiston is the faither o' that child. It narrows down the suspects.

Walker: Aye, to just one man.

Gow: Then you'll be gathering a posse?

Weir takes the bottle back, drinks from it and hands it to the Sheriff.

Weir: We'll be gathering more evidence first.

Gow: You've got enough of that.

Weir: We've only got a motive, doctor. If you could hang a man because he had a motive, the hale population o' Scotland would be swinging on trees.

Episode 4

1. INTERIOR. HERMISTON. DAY.

Weir and Sheriff Walker.

WALKER: I have depositions from the landlord of the Cross
Keys in Crossmichael and from two gentlemen of the Tuesday
Club called Hay and Pringle that make the case against Dand
Elliott a formality, Lord Weir. The landlord deposes that
Dand Elliott, brother of the deceased Christina Elliott, forced
his way into the room that's reserved for the Tuesday Club, in
the Cross Keys.

Mr. Hay and Mr. Pringle, two officials o' the said club, depose
that Andrew, or Dand, Elliott forced his way into their meeting
place and refused to leave until he was sure that Mr. Innes
wasnae among those present. And what is more, when asked
what his business was wi' the said Innes, answered he was
going to kill him. The said Innes.

WEIR: He said that? Before witnesses?

WALKER: And no' under his breath. This was the night his
sister died and the last time Mr. Innes was seen alive.

WEIR: He must have a kind heart to make our job this easy.
Let's see what we have. We've got it from Dr. Gow that Miss
Elliott was pregnant by a person at present unknown, but
assumed for the moment to be one Francis Innes. We also
have it from the doctor that Dand Elliott had discovered her
condition, by the subtle method o' half-strangling the doctor.
Which might be taken by a jury to indicate he had a violent
nature. It's well-kenned in these parts that the Elliotts have a
short way wi' them when they're offendit. As soon as she
knows o' her condition, the said Miss Elliott puts an end to
hersel' by loupin' ower the Deil's Hags. On the day o' her
demise her brother goes looking for Mr. Innes and utters
threats against his life. The next time Innes is seen he's been
shot. And he's been draped over the Weaver's Cairn like Jesus
hung outside a Papist kirk.

WALKER: And his murder's no' in furtherance o' a robbery,
for he borrowed siller at the Cross Keys and it's still on his
person.

WEIR: Is that a fair summation o' the evidence?

WALKER: I'd say it was.

WEIR: But ye'll admit it stands or falls on the assumption that this Innes was the faither o' the child, or that Dand thought he was.

WALKER: Aye.

WEIR: So what's the evidence for that? This Innes is a guest in my house. He leaves, to say the least, abruptly—though he's been in an agitated condition for some time and talked about leaving if he had the money. That, however, wouldnae account for the suddenness o' his departure without taking leave of his host, nor Kirstie. On top of that he takes a horse from the stables without a by your leave.

WALKER: It seems too he invented a cock and bull story about his father dying, to get money off those idiots at the Cross Keys. He seems to have been in a hurry to get away.

WEIR: A hell of a hurry.

WALKER: We can conclude he had a guilty conscience and was on the run frae the black brothers, for we've evidence o' Innes's involvement and we've found a motive for Dand killing him.

WEIR: There's just one thing that sticks in my gullet. Or two related things. One is that my son, Archie, should pick that very night to fall off his horse and break his heid—the which is no' a habit of his. And the second is that there's no other mark on him. We've got a murder and a suicide and a broken head. Two o' them seem to tie thegither. I wonder if the third does as well. I'd like to know what **did** happen to Archie.

WALKER: It might be interesting but we don't need any more evidence and the poor lad's in no condition to tell us.

WEIR: But maybe there's someone that can but doesnae want to. (*He pulls the bell rope.*)

Kirstie enters.

WEIR: You should have waited longer, woman. The mark o' the keyhole is still on your lug.

KIRSTIE: (*testily*) What is it now, Hermiston? Is it no' enough that you fill the house wi' clarty strangers—no offence to you, Sheriff—but you've got to drag me in here when I'm clearing up the mess they've made.

WEIR: Give us some straight answers and you can go back to it. You say Archie fell off his horse and got that dunt.

Kirstie nods.

WEIR: Did he tell ye that?

Kirstie hesitates.

WEIR: Well, did he? Did he break his skull and wait till he got home to tell you about it afore he went unconscious?

KIRSTIE: The man that brought him said it.

WEIR: And who was the man that brought him? Was it your nephew Dand?

Kirstie nods.

WEIR: That doesnae surprise me. I hear your niece came to a bad end, Kirstie—and I'm sorry for it—but can ye put a name to the man in the case?

KIRSTIE: Christina and me were no' that close that she'd confide in me.

WEIR: Would ye like to guess? Well, suppose I gie you a name —Innes.

Kirstie gasps.

WEIR: Is it the name that suprises you? Or is it that you thought I wouldnae know.

KIRSTIE: Why are ye meddling wi' this, Hermiston?

WEIR: Dand was covered in blood was he no'?

KIRSTIE: Who says?

WEIR: I do, for one. And if ye don't care to admit it here, ye can do it under oath in court wi' the Bible in your hand.

KIRSTIE: What if there was blood on him, he'd been carrying Archie.

WEIR: Aye, but Archie wasnae bleeding to speak of and Dand looked as if he'd been carrying a pig wi' its throat cut.

KIRSTIE: Maybe that's what he had been doing.

WEIR: Aye, maybe. I've no' heard muckle good o' Frank Innes. Now tell me this. Was Dand in this house earlier? Looking for Innes, maybe?

Kirstie is stubbornly silent.

WEIR: Would you like me to ask the grieve, or the gardener, or the wee kitchen maid?

KIRSTIE: (*sullenly*) Aye. He was here.

WEIR: So Archie could have known o' Dand's intention to kill Innes.

KIRSTIE: Wha says he intendit to kill Innes?

WEIR: He said it himsel'. And he said it aloud afore witnesses.

KIRSTIE: You're a cunning old devil, Hermiston! A bitter twisted auld devil that would make a woman testify against her own flesh and blood! I'll say nae mair.

WEIR: You've said enough, Kirstie. And more than enough. Sheriff, if Elliott had a' that blood on him when he brought Archie back he must have killed Innes first. And if he'd just murdered Innes, you'd think he'd be too busy getting away to play the Good Samaritan. Unless his conscience was bothering him. It wouldnae surprise me if Archie never did fall off his horse. Maybe he was even there or thereabouts when Innes got himsel' killed.

KIRSTIE: Naethin'll bring back them that are dead, Hermiston. For God's sake leave it be. Your son is lying up there at death's door. Is the likes of Innes worth the ruinin' of decent folks?

WEIR: There's mair than one answer to that. There's the legal answer that the law's the law and it's no' to be mocked by any man. There's the fact that Innes was a guest in my house, which puts me under a social obligation. And it doesnae show a fitting respect for the Lord Justice Clerk's office to go killing his guest. And if that's no' enough there's my son lying up there out of his mind and like to die.

KIRSTIE: You'll no' help him by meddling in this.

WEIR: There's no way I can help him, Kirstie. That's for the doctors and the divinity—and one's as much beyond my control as the other. I think, Sheriff, it's time we got a posse thegither and took a wee dauner over to Cauldstaneslaps for a word wi' Dand Elliott. Ye see, Kirstie, I think it was Dand that gied Archie that dunt.

KIRSTIE: Why would Dand do that?

WEIR: Because Archie was trying to protect his friend. I'm no' a Border man mysel' but if Archie dies, or if he doesnae get his wits back you'll see it's no' just the Elliotts o' Cauldstaneslaps that know how to pay their debts. By God, I promise you I'll spare neither man nor woman, nor kith nor kin till the one that did it is jumping at the end of a rope. Come on, Sheriff. We've to arrest Dand Elliott on a charge of murder.

TELECINE

2. EXTERIOR. CAULDSTANESLAPS. DAY.

A posse led by Weir, Walker and Gow ride up. Before they can dismount, Hob, Gib and Clem emerge and confront them. Walker goes off with some men to search the barns.

WEIR: If Dand Elliott's no' here, when did ye last see him?

There is no reply.

WEIR: Then maybe you'll tell me where we can find him.

HOB: He never said and we never asked. Dand comes and goes as he pleases.

WEIR: At one time or another I've had a hand in keeping you all from jail or the rope. I've saved you, Gib, twice over. Do you know where he is?

GIB: It's no' that I dinnae appreciate no' being hangit, Lord Weir, but my memory's no' what it was.

WEIR: (*grinning ferociously*) Is that a fact? Then I'll gie you some free advice. Gin anybody comes to you in a legal capacity and speirs after something, never make it so bloody clear that you're obstructing them. Especially if it's a murder they're speirin' about. Ye might be taken up as art and part to it—and to be art and part to a murder's a hangin' matter.

HOB: There's none of us had any part in any murder.

WEIR: That's as it may be, but if I was a man given to suspicion, I'd suspicion that you'd some knowledge o' one you were withholding. I'm ower auld to go on the hot-trod after a young fellow like Dand Elliott. The longer we've to hunt him, the more I'll get rheumatic twinges; and the more I get rheumatic twinges the less I'm going to like him. So the best thing you can do to help him is to tell us whaur we'll find him.

HOB: You'll find him in hell when you get there, Hermiston.

WEIR: Nae doubt we'll find all our friends there, Elliott.

The Sheriff approaches with one of the men who is carrying a bundle of bloodstained clothes.

WALKER: We found these in the barn!

WEIR: (*puzzled, therefore irritated*) Now what possessed him to leave these behind? It wouldnae have been hard to burn them. I always thought Dand's daftness was all on the outside, but it seems he's daft through and through. (*He shrugs this off.*) Oh, well, if he's in that much of a hurry to get himsel' hangit, it would be a pity if we didnae do all we could to help him on wi' it.

TELECINE

3. EXTERIOR. A SMALL RIVER. DAY.

Dand is fishing contentedly. There is the sound of hooves. He does not move till the posse arrive and Weir and Walker are looking down at him.

Dand pulls in his line, puts the rod down, rises and turns to face them.

DAND: Whatever took you so long? I thought you were never coming.

4. INTERIOR. ROOM IN WEIR'S HOUSE, GEORGE SQUARE, EDINBURGH. NIGHT.

Glenalmond, Glenkindie and Weir are drinking. There is a knock at the door.

WEIR: Aye?

McKillop enters with a letter.

MCKILLOP: This just came from Hermiston.

Weir takes the letter and dismisses McKillop with a nod. He stands grimfaced staring at the letter, afraid to open it.

GLENALMOND: Pray God it's good news, Adam.

WEIR: (*opening it*) Pray God it is, Davie.

He reads the letter impassively and replaces it in the envelope deliberately.

GLENALMOND: How is he?

WEIR: Doctor Gow says if he gets peace and rest his life is out of danger.

GLENALMOND: Is he conscious?

WEIR: Sometimes, but he's no' just in his right mind yet—if he ever was.

GLENKINDIE: Aye, the best thing that could happen would be that he stayed out of his mind.

WEIR: (*grimly*) It's for me to say the likes o' that. No' for you, Glenkindie.

Glenkindie laughs.

GLENKINDIE: Caught ye, Adam! Ye walked straight into the trap. Own up now, you're no' just the Lord Justice Clerk. There's a faither somewhere in you as well.

WEIR: I'd have thought it was a thing that could be taken for granted.

GLENKINDIE: As a learned judge wi' your experience o' child murder, I don't see how you can take it for granted.

WEIR: I was talking about **me,** Glenkindie. Could ye no' take it for granted in **me?**

GLENKINDIE: I wouldnae say for sure. Mind you I was aye sure you wouldnae murder him. Because it's against the law and you've always upheld the law. In any case you've got to feel something the one way or the other to commit murder. I wouldnae have put it past ye to hang him if the occasion arose.

WEIR: Did ye no' think I'd any feelings for Archie?

GLENKINDIE: If I'd been a jury deliberating the matter, I'd have been inclined to return a verdict of not proven.

WEIR: Did you feel the same, Davie?

GLENALMOND: Of course not. But I think Archie did sometimes.

WEIR: God, man, did I no' keep him out of the jail? Did I no' sit up night after night showing him the mistakes in his Latin and hammering the law into him? Did I no' point out to him when he was being glaikit? Would I have taken all that trouble wi' him if I felt nothing for him?

GLENALMOND: (*almost amused by the examples Weir has chosen*) There are signs that the old read easily enough, Adam, that the young can't even see. Did you ever say or do anything that would make clear to him what you were feeling?

Weir stands for a moment in dark agony, then he bursts out:

WEIR: No, Davie, I didnae! Ye see, I cannae! I don't know how! God knows I've wanted to, but I never could. (*He pauses and reflects bitterly.*) And I'll tell you this, if he were to walk in that door this minute, as fit and as well as he's ever been, I still couldnae—for I still wouldnae know how!

5. INTERIOR. ARCHIE'S BEDROOM. DAY.

Archie is asleep in bed. He wakens. Realisation of where he is comes to him and with it confusion. He pulls the bell rope and calls like a frightened child, his accent broadening to that of his childhood.

ARCHIE: Kirstie! Kirstie!

Kirstie comes in. He's relieved.

Oh, Kirstie, it's yoursel'!

KIRSTIE: Mr. Archie, you know me! You're getting well again!

Archie puts his hands to his bandaged head and speaks in the boy's voice that he maintains throughout the scene.

ARCHIE: Oh, Kirstie!—My head's sair!—What's happened to me? I've had awful bad dreams, Kirstie.—But I cannae remember them.

KIRSTIE: (*apprehensively*) Dinnae you try, Mr. Archie. Just you lie down and rest yoursel'!

ARCHIE: Is my faither in Edinburgh?

KIRSTIE: Aye, dearie, he is.

ARCHIE: Hangin' folk and persecutin' them?

KIRSTIE: He's got his work to do and he's doing it.

ARCHIE: And where's my mither?

KIRSTIE: She's sleeping, lad. You should be sleeping too. Lie down now, lie down.

He lies down obediently.

ARCHIE: Kirstie, is your name Christina Elliott of Cauldstane-slaps? Was your hair ever black?

KIRSTIE: My hair? Black? Whatever gied you that idea? I was born wi' gowden hair and heaven be thanked it's been gowden ever since.

ARCHIE: I dreamed it was. I dreamed about a black-haired Kirstie Elliott.

He goes to sleep.

KIRSTIE: And please God, ye'll dream again some day.

6. INTERIOR. RETIRING ROOM. THE HIGH COURT. NIGHT.

Glenkindie, Glenalmond and Weir are removing wigs and robes. Fyfe enters looking very pleased with himself. Glenkindie nudges Weir and they proceed to bait him.

GLENKINDIE: God, I thought we'd be sitting the whole night, Davie. Our Lord Advocate has a gift for making a short case last a long time.

GLENALMOND: I think tonight's case would illustrate what Prince Hamlet meant when he spoke of the law's delays.

WEIR: I'm no' well read in these foreign cases, but I see what ye mean.

FYFE: I had necessary evidence to lead and I led it.

GLENKINDIE: I think ye can hang a man for a murder he committed this year without showing that afore he could walk he beat his mother to death wi' his rattle.

FYFE: If your Lordships had been paying more attention to the pleading and less to your own private jokes, you might have noticed that it had a marked effect on the jury.

GLENKINDIE: I noticed. One or two o' them were yawning.

WEIR: There's them that never learn that no matter how long they talk you can only hang a man the once.

GLENKINDIE: You'll no' by any chance be prosecutin' this Dand Elliott in person when his case comes up?

FYFE: Naturally. It's too important to leave to my subordinates.

GLENKINDIE: I was afraid you'd say that.

WEIR: The brither o' a wee laird is accused of murdering a conceited young puppy that was no great loss to anybody. Now what's important in that?

GLENKINDIE: Ye know fine, Adam. That Elliott is a' the rage in Edinburgh the now. The weemin, maist o' them what ye ca' 'ladies', are payin' the jailer to get keekin at him through the bars. A' the riff-raff are buyin broadsheets o' his ballads. The papers are printing a' his daft sayings, one o' thae artists is doing a portrait o' him and the rest are complaining that they cannae all get into his cell at the one time. Is that no' right, Glenalmond.

GLENALMOND: Indeed. He's becoming quite a figure among the literati. Creech is talking of bringing out a book of his poems and no musical evening is complete unless some Italian gentleman has done violence to one of his songs.

WEIR: Aye, the feedleeries ay loved a human sacrifice.

GLENKINDIE: There'll be a great rush to see his trial. The court'll be packed wi' the gentry that day. It'll be a rare chance for Fyfe to show off in front o 'them.

FYFE: There are times when I feel your Lordships' sense of humour is, to say the least, misguided.

7. INTERIOR. DAND'S CELL IN THE TOLBOOTH. DAY.

Dand is being sketched by an artist and interviewed by a reporter from the Courier.

DAND: I've never been drawn afore so that'll be the only record o' my physiognomy that'll be left for posterity. I wouldnae ask ye to make it flattering, but be sure to make it very accurate. For would it no' be an awful thing if generations to come never knew the true beauty that was cut off when Dand Elliott went to the gallows?

The artist laughs and goes on sketching.

REPORTER: (*indicating the artist*) You don't seem to mind this.

DAND: Why should I mind being drawn and hung when afterwards I'm likely to be hung and drawn.

REPORTER: You're quite sure that you'll be hanged, then Mr. Elliott?

DAND: That's the purpose o' my visit to Edinburgh, after all. They'll hang me all right, unless I'm given a Royal pardon for my good looks and my talent and my modesty.

REPORTER: If it was up to the Edinburgh folks, you could be sure of a pardon. You've given them a lot of pleasure since you came here.

DAND: In that case, I don't know that I could accept a pardon. You see I've got a suit o' clothes that's being made especial for my last appearance and I've never had a suit made specially for me afore. The lassies'll greet like mad when they see me in it and think I'm being wasted. And then I'm making up a song for the occasion that will dae for a duet if the public executioner's got any voice at all. It wouldnae do to cheat the poor folks o' all that, now would it? So if the pardon comes, I'll just write back a wee note saying, Dear Majesty, It's no' that I'm no' sensible o' the honour your Royal Germanship has done me—the which is by no means undeservit, but I cannae disappoint the folk o' Edinburgh that have been sae good to me.

REPORTER: I hope when the time comes, they appreciate what you've done for them.

DAND: Oh, it's no' just for them. There's my immortality to be considered. Scotland's had Royal poets and gaberlunzie poets, ploughman poets and milkmaid poets—Jamie Hogg has beat me to the title o' Shepherd poet—but have we ever had a hangit poet?

REPORTER: Not that I'm aware of.

DAND: Well, then, what's a wee jig at the end of a rope to my prospects o' immortality?

REPORTER: (*shaking his head in admiration*) Frankly, Mr. Elliott, I don't know how, in your present position, you can take everything with such good humour.

DAND: How else is there to take it?

8. INTERIOR. ARCHIE'S BEDROOM. NIGHT.

A candle is burning. Kirstie is reading the Bible by it and Archie is mumbling in his sleep restlessly. Suddenly he screams and wakes. Kirstie goes to him.

KIRSTIE: Wheesht, wheesht.

ARCHIE: (*relieved to see her*) Kirstie! Oh, Kirstie, it came again! The nightmare.

KIRSTIE: Lie down! Lie down and sleep.

ARCHIE: Kirstie, I dreamed I was one o' the black brithers riding the moor! We killed a man, Kirstie!

KIRSTIE: You're no' to upset yoursel', Mr. Archie.

ARCHIE: We were up at the Weaver's Cairn—your nephew Dand and me—and we were going to kill a man. I kenned his face, but couldnae mind his name. And faither was there wi' a gallows, grinning like a fiend and waiting for the end of it.

KIRSTIE: Lie down, dearie, the doctor says you're no' to move. You'll do yoursel' a hurt.

ARCHIE: I'm feared, Kirstie, I'm feared!

KIRSTIE: Oh, Mr. Archie, you're no' to move! The doctor says you'll kill yoursel' if you dinnae rest.

He lies down. Slowly, as if he is waking up, his expression matures. He sits up.

ARCHIE: (*in his own voice*)   Kirstie, why am I here?

KIRSTIE: Because you're no' weel.

ARCHIE: Christina! Where's Christina?

KIRSTIE: Wheesht, Mr. Archie, wheesht.

ARCHIE: Where is she?

KIRSTIE: She's back in Glesgie wi her brother, Clem.

ARCHIE: And Innes? Where's Frank Innes?

KIRSTIE: He didnae find your company to his liking so he left.

Archie relaxes.

ARCHIE: I must write to Christina. I promised her I'd write to her.

KIRSTIE: You can write to her in the morning.

ARCHIE: (*firmly*)   No, Kirstie. I'll write to her tonight.

He sits up resolutely and clutches his head as the pain stabs through it. His boyish voice returns.

ARCHIE: Oh, Kirstie! My heid! My heid! My heid!

She pushes him down gently. Her face is very troubled.

9.   INTERIOR.   DAND'S CELL.   NIGHT.

Dand is writing by candlelight. He stops and begins to read his lines softly.

DAND: 'And wha'd hae thought a poet chiel,
             That asked nae mair than you can see
             In drink or bonnie woman's e'e,
             Would set this city in a reel?
             And people that would pay nae heed,
             If they'd been asked to hear him sing,
             Will fight and rabble till they're deid,
             For room enough to see him hing.
             But when the wonder o't is o'er,
             A day, a week, a month, no more,
             Will they pay heed to the remains,
             The craws leave on the gibbet chains.'

He shudders.

10. INTERIOR. HERMISTON HALL. DAY.

Gow is leaving. Weir and Kirstie are present.

GOW: The damage to his skull is beginning to mend. I wouldnae be surprised if his mind started clearing soon.

Kirstie gasps and, noting their surprise, covers up.

WEIR: What's this? Would you be sorry to see him like a man again?

GOW: Women are a' the same. They ay need something to mither.

KIRSTIE: Ay, and men are a' the same. No' happy unless they're jumping to conclusions about women. I was thinking if he's himsel' again it'll be hard to keep him in his bed.

GOW: Ye'll have to see to it if it means breaking his legs, for ye cannae very well hit him on the head. If he starts rattlin' his brain like a pea in a drum I wouldnae give you that for his life. (*He snaps his fingers.*) He'll need rest and plenty o't for a long time to come. It's the only miracle worker I know.

WEIR: But if he gets it, he'll get well?

GOW: I'm a doctor, no' a spey wife, but I've every hope for him. If he's taken bad in the next day or two, and I very much doubt if he will be, send to Crossmichael for Willie Fletcher. He's mended a lot of broken bones in his time—horses' and cows' and sheeps' for the maist part, but a broken bone's a broken bone.

KIRSTIE: You're going to Edinburgh for Dand's trial.

He nods discreetly.

WEIR: Then you'll be seeing me in my professional capacity.

GOW: Aye, just so.

WEIR: Don't look so worried, doctor, I never hanged a witness yet.

He realises Kirstie's position and coughs gruffly.

GOW: I heard Dand's causing quite a steer up there.

WEIR: From all accounts he's in his glory.

GOW: It says very little for the human race that a man can tend his sheep and make his wee songs or slave away at healing the sick a' his days and a' body pays never a heed. But just let him up and kill one o' his fellow creatures and his name's on everybody's lips up and down the country and he's the toast o' the Athens o' the North.

Kirstie Turns away. Gow is a bit embarrassed.

GOW: I'll say good-day to you, Hermiston, and to you, Kirstie.

He looks helplessly at her for a moment and goes out.

WEIR: Dand's happy enough, what are you greetin' for?

KIRSTIE: For my nephew, Hermiston! For my brither's son! For a wee boy I've played with and for a man that never hurt a living soul.

WEIR: Except Frank Innes, and Archie, if he counts at all.

KIRSTIE: Aye, he counts, Hermiston. He counts to me mair than anything in the world, but does that mean I cannae greet for my ain brither's son that you're for hanging the morrow?

WEIR: I'll take no pleasure in it, Kirstie.

KIRSTIE: Oh, that'll make a difference! If he knew that he'd be glad to be hangit.

WEIR: Dand kill'd a man and there's a penalty for that in law. God, woman, if greetin' would change that the High Court would be floating on salt water like Noah's Ark. (*Weir softens.*) There's naethin' I can see that would get him off and there's naethin' to mitigate the offence. Revenge is no' permitted legally and a blood feud is nae better than a law, for everyone's got blood kin—even Innes—so it never ends until a name's wiped off the face of the earth. There's naithin' you or anybody else can do for Dand Elliott now.

He almost touches her, but doesn't.

I'm for Edinburgh—just you look after Archie.

He goes.

KIRSTIE: God take pity on you, Hermiston, and keep Archie mad till Dand's been hanged.

11. INTERIOR. DAND'S CELL. NIGHT.

Clem and Hob are with him.

DAND: I once heard that an English doctor said if a man knew he was to be hanged in the morning it would fair concentrate his mind. He'd a lot of sense for an Englishman. Ever since I came here the muses have been at me like it was years since they'd had a poet. They should pass a law for the good o' the arts that a' the poets should be kept in the Tolbooth and told every wee while they're to be hangit this week.

CLEM: Man, why did you no' keep that laywer I sent you? He was the best that money could buy.

DAND: Nae man's life is worth the money he was asking, Clem.

CLEM: I'm no' poor, Dand, but if I was, d'you think I wouldnae gie all I've got to save your life.

DAND: It's just possible that I'd let you spend your money if I was sure it would get me off, but I'll no' let you waste it. I asked your lawyer what the chances were and he wasnae exactly hopeful.

HOB: We could get another one.

DAND: You mean try every lawyer in Edinburgh till you find one that thinks he can get me off?

HOB: Aye.

DAND: A lawyer that's that daft isnae fit to represent me, Hob. But if you do find one, try to get him to prosecute. A real idiot prosecuting is the only chance I've got.

CLEM: There must be somebody.

DAND: (*sharply*) There's naebody! Now listen to me. My mind's made up. I'm to be hanged and that's the only way. It wasnae easy to settle to the idea but I've managed it. I've carried this through so far. I've even done it wi' a bit of style— and I can do it to the end. There's only one thing that'll destroy me and that's hope. So don't try to gie me it now or ever. I could have got away if I'd wanted to and they'd never have found me, but somebody has to be tried and found guilty to put an end to this case. I want no lawyers!

The old buffoonery comes back.

Why should a lawyer have a' the profit and a' the fun while a' we get is the loss? The morrow's morn I'll go to that court and speak for mysel' and break a' the lassies' hearts. By God, if my life's to be short, I'll make sure that it's merry. Where's Gib?

HOB: He's away hame to pray.

DAND: Could he no' have seen me first?

CLEM: You know how soft he is. He'd have burst out greetin'.

DAND: He might have known that before he came all this way.

CLEM: Well—

He stops and Dand notices.

DAND: Well what? If you dinnae tell me now, it'll be a while afore ye get the chance again.

HOB: We had a notion to come and look at this place and see
        if we could break you out after the trial. But we just got as
        far as the door.

DAND: (*nodding*) Aye, and Gib decided prayer was the only
        thing for it. And he was right. The last time anyone was
        broken out of here it took the hale population o' Edinburgh
        and they had to burn the gate down.

CLEM: There's other ways we could try.

DAND: (*firmly*) I want nae mair o' that foolishness from any
        of ye. Innes is deid and any man's big toe nail's enough to pay
        for his life. It doesnae need the lives o' the hale family.

HOB: It's hard for us to stand by and let this happen to you,
        Dand.

DAND: It's no' that easy for me either.

CLEM: Just tell me one thing, Dand. Was it really you that
        killed him?

DAND: It was for me to dae it, and it was for me to pay. And
        if I never did it, it's still for me to pay. You understand,
        Clem? (*Clem nods.*) And you, Hob? (*Hob nods.*) Then
        there's an end to it. You'll no' be waitin' for the hangin' I
        hope? Good! It's easier to put a show on for folk that don't
        know ye. But I'll wear my new clothes for the trial and let
        ye all see what a bonny gentleman I might have been.

12. INTERIOR. HALL, HERMISTON. NIGHT.

*Archie, fully dressed, is reaching the foot of the stairs with
difficulty. Kirstie enters and is shocked.*

KIRSTIE: Oh, Mr. Archie, ye know you should be up there in
        your bed!

ARCHIE: Kirstie, I'm trying to understand what has really
        happened. The dreams I've had. It's my head. The truth and
        the dreams are so mixed up in it. Is Christina really in Glasgow
        or is . . .

KIRSTIE: (*quickly*) She's in Glasgow. Did I no' tell you she
        was?

ARCHIE: I wasn't sure if that was a dream as well. And Innes.
        Is he well?

KIRSTIE: He was the last time I set eyes on him. Oh, Archie,
        you must stop all this and go to your bed.

ARCHIE: I must see Christina. It's the only way to stop the nightmares!

KIRSTIE: You'll see her. Just as soon as you're well.

ARCHIE: I must see her now!

KIRSTIE: (*humouring him*) Ye cannae see her now. She's in Glesgie.

ARCHIE: Then I'll go there.

KIRSTIE: You're no' fit to go there. Oh, Mr. Archie, if you was to cross this threshold it could be the death of ye. Why do ye no' just sit down and write to her? I'll see it goes off right away.

This acts on Archie like a shock.

ARCHIE: I did write to her, didn't I, Kirstie?

KIRSTIE: That was in your dream, Archie. Don't go upsetting yoursel' again.

ARCHIE: I wrote to her, but she never got my letters.

KIRSTIE: (*nearly desperate*) You've been ill, dearie, awful ill. You've been at death's door and you're no' far from it now. Your mind wasnae right. It's made things up.

ARCHIE: Was I mad? Like Christina?

KIRSTIE: Wha says she was mad?

ARCHIE: She was in my dream, if it was a dream.

KIRSTIE: It was! It was!

ARCHIE: Why did I kill Frank Innes? Was I mad?

KIRSTIE: You're mad to think you did. You never killed anybody. Oh, Mr. Archie, come awa to your bed! These are just nightmares that have stayed on through the day!

ARCHIE: Then help me get rid of them. Let me go to Christina.

KIRSTIE: (*moving between him and the door*) Ye'll no' leave here. If I have to I'll get help to keep you. I cannae let you do yoursel' a mortal hurt!

Archie screams and clutches his head.

ARCHIE: My God! My head is bursting open!

Kirstie is panic stricken.

KIRSTIE: Wait here, Mr. Archie, I'll no be long. Just wait. I'll send for somebody frae Crossmichael.

She rushes out. Archie takes his hand from his head and makes his way to the drawer where the pistol case is kept. He takes it out, opens it and finding it empty knows what has happened. He staggers out of the house.

TELECINE

13. EXTERIOR. THE CAIRN. NIGHT.

Archie reconstituting his memory of the murder of Innes.

14. INTERIOR. CAULDSTANESLAPS. NIGHT.

Gib, Hob's wife and the children. The door opens and Archie enters looking ghastly.

ARCHIE: Where's Dand? I must speak to him!

MRS. HOB: Mr. Weir! You're no' well, lad! Sit down.

ARCHIE: I've no time, Mistress Elliott. Where's Dand?

MRS. HOB: He's no' here.

ARCHIE: Will he be back soon?

GIB: He'll no' be back. He's in the Tolbooth o' Edinburgh. He'll come out to be tried the morrow, and he'll come out to be hangit. Then he'll go to his Maker, but he'll never come back here.

ARCHIE: What has he done?

MRS. HOB: He's rid the earth o' yon trash Innes.

ARCHIE: No! If Innes is dead, I killed him.

MRS. HOB: It's in your head, Mr. Weir. Dand telt us himsel' how it was. You meant to kill him, but your horse tripped and threw you off. The intentions no' the deed. It was Dand that killed him.

GIB: And the Lord have mercy on his soul!

ARCHIE: I killed him! Will you not believe me?

She shakes her head sadly. Archie turns to the door.

MRS. HOB: Where are you going?

ARCHIE: To Edinburgh. If no one else will believe me, my father will.

MRS. HOB: Ye cannae go to Edinburgh. No like that, man!

But the door has shut behind Archie leaving an eerie silence.

15. INTERIOR. RETIRING ROOM IN THE HIGH COURT. MORNING.

Glenalmond, Glenkindie and Weir about to prepare for the trial of Dand Elliott. Glenkindie pours three large glasses of wine.

GLENKINDIE: Fortify yourselves, gentlemen. We're in for a long day, and if Fyfe has his way, a long night forbye.

GLENALMOND: I hope you are wrong, Glenkindie. Elliott's pleading guilty.

WEIR: That'll no' stop Fyfe. He's got a court room full of the notabilities o' this fair city and a case he cannae lose. Fyfe's a dog wi' two tails the day and he'll wag them as long as he can.

He chuckles to himself.

If I've got to sit all though this trial I'd rather be conductin' the defence than sittin' on the bench.

GLENKINDIE: You'd have little enough to do in either case.

GLENALMOND: Adam, I've a feeling you think there might be some grounds on which the case could be defended?

WEIR: There are.

GLENKINDIE: And might we ask just what your defence would be?

WEIR: That he's protecting somebody, of course. And there's only the one snag wi' that—the only people he'd protect are his brithers and they wouldnae let him.

The judges are almost fully robed and wigged. An officer of the court enters.

OFFICER: Lord Weir, there's a lady who says she is your house-keeper asking to see you.

Weir stiffens with shock.

GLENALMOND: Send her in at once.

The officer goes.

Adam, it may be good news.

WEIR: (*shaking his head*) No.

He empties the wine glass.

Guid news can ay wait. The ither kind is always in a hurry.

They wait in silence till the officer shows Kirstie in and closes the door. Weir stands looking at her, but she is speechless.

Well, woman, out with it.

KIRSTIE: Oh, Hermiston, it's Mr. Archie!

He nods and turns away.

He's gone out of the house.

Weir's relief shows itself in anger.

WEIR: And what the hell dae ye expect me to dae about it?
Leave the court and rush back to Hermiston to find him?

KIRSTIE: He's no' at Hermiston. Hob Elliott's wife says he's
come here to find you.

WEIR: Then he'll be in my house in George Square. I suggest
you get along there and keep him company until we're finished
trying your Dand.

KIRSTIE: He'll maybe come here.

WEIR: What would he do that for?

KIRSTIE: To try to tell you something.

WEIR: Something about this case?

KIRSTIE: Ay, but you're no' to pay ony heed to it. He's no'
in his right mind yet.

Weir looks at her steadily for a moment.

WEIR: If you're worried in case anythin' Erchie might say will
make things worse for your nephew, you're daft. There's
nothing anyone can say that'll make things worse for him—
and nothing that'll stop him hangin'.

KIRSTIE: Naethin'?

Weir nods.

Thank God!

WEIR: (*puzzled*) For what?

KIRSTIE: (*covering up*) That Erchie'll have had nae hand in
hangin' Dand.

There is an uproar in the passage.

GLENKINDIE: I'll see to it.

He goes out.

KIRSTIE: I thought I heard Mr. Erchie's voice.

WEIR: Stay where you are, woman. If it's him we'll know soon
enough.

*Glenkindie enters supporting Archie. Glenalmond goes to his
aid. They seat Archie at the table. He is looking into space
like a ventriloquist's dummy.*

GLENKINDIE: He's been fighting the macers to get to see you.

WEIR: Stay with him, Kirstie, and I'll send for a surgeon. Gentlemen, there's a man out there waitin' to be hangit. I suggest we attend to his business.

ARCHIE: (*dully*) You can't hang Dand Elliott. I'll not let you.

GLENKINDIE: Even when he's ravin', Weir, he takes after his father for damned impidence. It could get him hangit one of these days.

ARCHIE: (*rising with difficulty*) I fully intend to get myself hanged today.

They stare at him for a moment, then Glenkindie laughs.

GLENKINDIE: Well, now, you'll hae to find yourself anither court for that. We're hangin' someone else the day.

ARCHIE: You're not hanging anyone—unless it's me.

Archie sways and Kirstie moves to him. She looks pleadingly at the judges.

KIRSTIE: Can ye no' see how sick he is, Your Lordships? Juist leave him wi' me—I'll see to him.

Weir nods. They turn to go.

ARCHIE: I killed Frank Innes.

GLENKINDIE: (*shaking his head*) It's worse than I thought.

GLENALMOND: Archie, don't say any more—rest till we get back.

ARCHIE: It will be too late then, Lord Glenalmond. I killed Frank Innes. You must believe me.

GLENALMOND: I can't, Archie.

ARCHIE: Because you don't want to!

GLENALMOND: You're quite right—I don't want to, but even if I did I could not do so. As a judge, because the case against another person seems unshakeable. As a man because I know you have been—and still are—a very sick boy.

ARCHIE: Why should my sickness make me say I killed a man if I did not, Lord Glenalmond?

GLENALMOND: (*quietly*) Do you not know, my boy?

Archie shakes his head stubbornly. Glenalmond speaks to Weir and Glenkindie.

May I have your indulgence for a moment?

They nod. He goes to Archie.

Listen to me very carefully, Archie. Frank Innes was your friend, was he not?

ARCHIE: I thought he was.

GLENALMOND: And your guest?

Archie nods.

And he was in danger from Dand Elliott—you knew that didn't you—and you wanted to protect him?

ARCHIE: No!

GLENALMOND: I submit, Archie, that you did.

ARCHIE: No! No!—I wanted to kill him.

GLENALMOND: Why, Archie?

ARCHIE: I can't tell you!

GLENALMOND: Then tell me this. How did you come by that injury to your head?

Archie does not answer.

Archie, was it inflicted by Dand Elliott? You **must** answer me, Archie.

ARCHIE: Yes, it was!

GLENALMOND: Need we hear more, gentlemen?

ARCHIE: Yes, you must—why should I lie to you?

GLENALMOND: Oh, Archie, I never for a moment suggested that you did—only that you were deluded. You set out to save the life of your friend and you failed. The guilt this fostered is the root of your delusion.

Archie becomes confused and bewildered.

ARCHIE: Is that possible?

GLENALMOND: It is not only possible but natural—

KIRSTIE: His Lordship's right, Mr. Erchie. You know that since you were hurt you've never known the difference between your waking and dreaming.

Archie covers his face with his hands.

ARCHIE: Oh, God!

Glenalmond nods to his fellow judges. They prepare to leave.

Wait! Lord Glenalmond! The girl I spoke of! The girl I loved and wanted to marry was Christina Elliott.

Glenalmond stops and looks very serious for a moment. Then lies very gravely.

GLENALMOND: That in no way affects the issue, Archie.

GLENKINDIE: And if it did, it would hardly be part of our immediate business. You're no' mentioned in the indictment.

ARCHIE: Is it only law you care about? Is justice none of your business?

WEIR: As a matter of fact, it's no'. You'll make a bonny lawyer if ye cannae see that. Justice is too big a thing for ony man to dispense. One man arrests ye, anither defends you and yet anither prosecutes you. The jury decides if you're guilty or no', we pass the sentence and if it's that sort of case the hangman completes the process. If ony one man did it a' on the basis o' what he thought was justice, there'd be nae law and damned little justice either. So juist calm yoursel' and wait here till we've done our wee bit of the job and we'll enlighten you on all the ither things the coallege has omitted from your education.

ARCHIE: Father, I'm not talking about abstractions. Do none of you care if justice is done on Dand Elliott?

GLENKINDIE: As judges we've got to see that a verdict is reached on the basis of the evidence at our disposal. Beyond that we've no more right to go than ony ither man.

ARCHIE: I'm offering you new evidence, Lord Glenkindie.

GLENKINDIE: And what might that be?

ARCHIE: My confession.

GLENKINDIE: D'ye call that evidence? If a' the confessions made were taken as evidence we'd hing half the lunatics in Edinburgh. And we'd still hing Dand Elliott—for he's confessed to the murder o' Innes as well.

ARCHIE: He's lying!

GLENKINDIE: Well, it would certainly appear that somebody's lying. Unless of course, ye baith killt him. He was shot twice.

WEIR: Save your jokes for the court room, Glenkindie; we're going to need them when the Lord Advocate Fyfe gets started.

GLENALMOND: And speaking of Fyfe, I should imagine that this delay will have put his temper out of joint.

Weir nods.

WEIR: (*to Kirstie*) Look to Erchie—and if ye want ony help use my name as ye would your own.

ARCHIE: Father!—No, don't look away from me—I've not been much of a son to you—

WEIR: (*with a hint of pleading*) Archie—

ARCHIE: No, hear me out. I've opposed you, disobeyed you, been disloyal to you, attacked you and everything you stand for. I think it was partly because I was afraid.

WEIR: I could always get people to fear me. I never asked for much else, and I never got it.

ARCHIE: You're blind, father. You might never have asked for it, but you've got respect, aye, and even—there's got to be a time to use the word—love. You've got both from everyone in this room—Glenalmond, Glenkindie, Kirstie and even from me. It wasn't you I was afraid of, Father, it was me. I was afraid I could never make you as proud of me as I was of you. And if I couldn't make you see me as worthy of being your son, then, by God, I had to destroy the worth of your opinion.

WEIR: You bloody eediot!

ARCHIE: I'm trying to tell you something important, father. I respect you, I'm proud of you—not because of your beliefs, but because I know that for your own life and soul you could not fail to carry them out. I killed Frank Innes. I think you believe me. What would be left of you tomorrow if you go in there today and pass sentence on Dand Elliott? Every Duncan Jopp and every other kind of mean, vicious, miserable beast you ever rid the world of would howl in derision from their graves at the travesty you'd made of your life. But you can't do it, father, I know you can't.

WEIR: You're asking to be tried, Archie. Well, you'll be tried. No' out there in the court-room. That isnae possible. We'll try you. Here and now.

GLENALMOND: Is this wise, Adam?

WEIR: No, Davie. It's no' wise. It's inevitable. Glenkindie, you'll be judge. Glenalmond, you'll defend. Kirstie, you'll have to be the jury. Oh, dinnae worry, we'll no' ask you for a verdict. It's juist to gie us something to address.

KIRSTIE: (*with quiet horror*) And what will you dae, Hermiston.

WEIR: What Erchie wants me to dae. I'll prosecute.

His professional manner begins to enfold him.

My Lord, since the circumstances of this trial are, to say the least, unusual, the procedure is likely to be by-ordinary.

GLENALMOND: My Lord, I move that under these circumstances a fair trial is impossible—not on the grounds that it is unusual, but on the grounds that witnesses for the defence cannot be called.

WEIR: I take it that the defence you intend to offer is an impeachment of Dand Elliott for the murder of which your client stands accused?

GLENALMOND: It is.

WEIR: Then we're all familiar with the evidence your witnesses would present and I'm prepared to accept every word of it as the gospel truth. Does that meet your objection, Davie?

Glenalmond looks at Archie and is forced to be honest.

GLENALMOND: It does.

GLENKINDIE: Then get on with it before Fyfe decides to come and join us.

GLENALMOND: (*to Kirstie*) Madame, the defence we offer is simply that the accused could not have murdered Frank Innes since we have established beyond a reasonable doubt that Andrew—known as Dand—Elliott of Cauldstaneslaps committed the crime in question. We have established a predisposition in Dand Elliott to undertake violent revenge. We have established that revenge was his motive. We have shown that he evinced the intention to kill Innes and have his confession to show that he carried out this intention. I see no reason to add anything to this except to say that no evidence against my client exists except a confession which, since it proceeds from a man whose skull is fractured and whose mind has wandered into delirium, cannot be given the least credence. There is no evidence against Mr. Archibald Weir and, therefore, no case for him to answer.

He sits and Glenkindie nods approvingly.

GLENKINDIE: I can only hope that when it's Fyfe's turn he'll be as commendably brief. What have you to say to that Adam?

WEIR: Only that I wish I could be as brief as Davie and as sure as you are that Fyfe's turn will come. But it's my duty to take the case against Dand Elliott point by point. Firstly, there's no evidence that he was over predisposed to unlawful violence. We know that he and his black brothers set out in pursuit of his father's murderers—I would like to point out that I personally pursued these same men and hope the court will not conclude therefore that I am predisposed to unlawful action.

Secondly, Dand Elliott is presumed to be motivated by revenge on the grounds that Frank Innes was the father of his sister's child. If this is so, we have all heard the accused admit that he loved and intended to marry that same woman. Could we not say that he would be motivated by revenge to an equal or even greater degree?

Thirdly, there is all the rest of the evidence against Elliott. His announcement in the Cross Keys and his so-called flight from justice. Is it not clear to all of us that there would be no case against Dand Elliott if he hadn't presented us with one? There was no need for him to go to the Cross Keys and tell the world he meant to kill Frank Innes. He could have killed Innes as quiet as ye like and when he did he could have buried him some place he'd no' be found for long enough, but no, he hangs him up high on the Weaver's Cairn for a' the world to see. He could have burned his bloodstained clothes but he leaves them where they cannae but be found, and he could have rode like hell for the Border but he goes off twa or three miles and sits and waits for us to find him. There's no' a shred of evidence against Dand Elliott that isnae o' his ain making. A blind man could see he wanted to be thought a murderer, and to be caught, and to be hangit.

GLENALMOND: While I'd be the first to admit that many people have strange ways of taking their pleasure, Adam, I'd find this fiction rather more convincing if you could give some reason why a man as fond of living as Dand Elliott is reputed to be should suddenly become so anxious to be hanged.

WEIR: To protect my son out of a sense of obligation.

GLENKINDIE: For saving him the bother of killing Innes, eh?

He chuckles.

Oh, Adam, that was as good a try at making bricks without straw as I've heard these many years. It's ingenious, I'll no' say that it's no', but it's conjecture—every word of it.

Weir turns and meets Archie's eye relentlessly.

WEIR: I've done my best to get ye hangit, Erchie, but his Lordship will hae nane o' it and neither would a jury.

Archie looks at Kirstie.

ARCHIE: Kirstie, you know it's true. You know I said I'd kill Innes. You know I left for the Cross Keys before Dand and you know why I killed him at the Weaver's Cairn. Tell them you know I killed Innes. Tell them your nephews can corroborate most of what you say. Oh, Kirstie, if you let Dand die for me I'll hate you till the end of my days.

WEIR: (*to Kirstie*) Is this true? Answer me, woman. Is it true? Speak up or I'll have you dragged into that court and get it from you if I have to take your tongue out by the roots.

KIRSTIE: Oh, Mr. Erchie—

ARCHIE: Look at her! Can you not see it's true?

Cut to the faces of the judges with realisation creeping over them.

16. INTERIOR. COURT ROOM. DAY.

Dand, elegantly dressed in the dock. His brothers are in the crowd. Fyfe is waiting impatiently for the trial to begin. The cry, 'The Court will stand' is heard. They rise and the three judges enter and take their places. All sit and Fyfe looks at Weir whose face is set like granite. Weir signs to him to approach. Fyfe goes to him looking puzzled. They exchange a few words. Fyfe seems to be protesting, but his protests are quelled. He returns to his place.

FYFE: Your Lordships, the Crown begs to desert the case against Dand Elliott.

There is a hubbub in the courtroom.

On the grounds that another man is about to be arrested and charged with the crimes of which he is accused.

The hubbub breaks out again. It is quelled by Weir's ferocious glare.

WEIR: The court will grant the Crown's request.

The judges rise and the others rise with them and stand as the judges begin to leave their places.

17. INTERIOR. RETIRING ROOM. HIGH COURT. DAY.

Archie is sprawled unconscious over the table and Kirstie is weeping over him.

18. INTERIOR. COURT ROOM. DAY.

The faces of Glenkindie and Glenalmond are deeply moved. Cut to Weir whose face is set in a tragic mask as he moves down from the bench.

SELECT BIBLIOGRAPHY

Texts of Weir of Hermiston

First edition: Chatto & Windus, London, 1896

Edinburgh edition: Romances Vol. VII: Longmans Green, Cassell, Seeley, Chas. Scribner's Sons, Chatto & Windus, London, 1897

Pentlands edition: Vol. XVIII: Cassell, Chatto & Windus, Heinemann, Longmans Green, London, 1907

Swanston edition: Vol. XIX: Chatto & Windus, in association with Cassell, Heinemann, Longmans Green, London, 1912

Tusitala edition: Vol. XVI: William Heinemann in association with Chatto & Windus, Cassell, and Longmans, London, 1924, 3rd reprint 1925

Single volume edition: Chatto & Windus, London, 1925

Everyman's Library edition, with introduction by M. R. Ridley: Dent, London, 1925, reprint 1968

Collins edition, with introduction by Louis J. McQuilland: London and Glasgow, 1953, reprint 1965

Nelson edition: London and Edinburgh, 1956, reprint 1963

Other Works by Stevenson

The Black Arrow Cassell, London, 1905

Catriona Cassell, London, 1905

Dr. Jekyll and Mr. Hyde and other stories with an introduction by John Kelman Collins, London and Glasgow, 1953

The Ebb-Tide (by Robert Louis Stevenson and Lloyd Osbourne) Heinemann, London, 1905

Essays in the Art of Writing Chatto & Windus, London, 1908

Essays of Travel Chatto & Windus, London, 1905

Familiar Studies of Men and Books Chatto & Windus, London, 12th edition 1897

An Inland Voyage Cassell, London, 1905

Island Nights' Entertainments Cassell, London, 1905

Kidnapped Cassell, London, 1905

Lay Morals and other Papers (new edition with preface by Mrs. Stevenson) Chatto & Windus, London, 1911

The letters of Robert Louis Stevenson to his Family and Friends ed. Sidney Colvin, 2 vols. Methuen, London, 1902

The Master of Ballantrae and *Weir of Hermiston* with introduction by M. R. Ridley Everyman's Library, Dent, London, 1925, reprint 1968

Memories and Portraits Chatto & Windus, London, 1909

The Merry Men and other tales and fables Chatto & Windus, London, 5th edition, 1896

New Arabian Nights Chatto & Windus, London, 1901

Prince Otto Chatto & Windus, London, 1906

St. Ives with introduction by M. R. Ridley Dent, London, 1934, reprint 1958

The Silverado Squatters Chatto & Windus, London, 1901

The Suicide Club and *The Rajah's Diamond* Chatto & Windus, London, 1897

Tales and Fantasies Chatto & Windus, London, 1905

Travels with a Donkey Cassell, London, 1905

Treasure Island Cassell, London, 1906

Virginibus Puerisque and other papers Chatto & Windus, London, 1908

Virginibus Puerisque/Familiar Studies of Men and Books Dent, London, 1925, reprint 1948

The Waif Woman Chatto & Windus, London, 1916

The Wrecker (by R. L. Stevenson and Lloyd Osbourne) O.U.P. (World's Classics), London, 1950, reprint 1954

The Wrong Box (by Robert Louis Stevenson and Lloyd Osbourne) Longmans Green, London, 1903

General

ALDINGTON, RICHARD *Portrait of a Rebel* Evans Bros., London, 1957

BAILDON, H. BELLYSE *Robert Louis Stevenson* Chatto & Windus, London, 1901

BALFOUR, GRAHAM, *The Life of Robert Louis Stevenson* Methuen, London, 1901, 5th edition 1910

BBC *Robert Louis Stevenson* 1850-1950 a radio commemoration BBC, London, 1950

BERMANN, RICHARD A. *Home from the Sea—Robert Louis Stevenson in Samoa* The Bobbs-Merrill Co., Indianapolis and New York, 1939

BLAKE, GEORGE *Barrie and the Kailyard School* Arthur Barker, London, 1951

BROWN, P. HUME *A Short History of Scotland* New edition by Henry W. Meikle Oliver & Boyd, Edinburgh and London, 1908, revised edition 1955

BUTTS, DENNIS *R. L. Stevenson* (a Bodley Head monograph) The Bodley Head, London, 1966

CALDWELL, ELSIE NOBLE *Last Witness for Robert Louis Stevenson* University of Oklahoma Press, Norman, 1960

CHESTERTON, G. K. *Robert Louis Stevenson* Hodder & Stoughton, London, 1927

COCKBURN, HENRY *Memorials of his Time* T. N. Foulis, Edinburgh and London, 1910

COOPER, LETTICE *Robert Louis Stevenson* Arthur Barker, London, 1947, 2nd edition 1967

COWELL, H. J. *Robert Louis Stevenson* Epworth, London, 1945

CROCKETT, S. R. *The Raiders* and *The Lilac Sunbonnet* with introduction by George Blake Collins, London and Glasgow, 1954

DAICHES, DAVID *Robert Louis Stevenson* Macmillan, Glasgow, 1947

DALGLISH, DORIS N. *Presbyterian Pirate—A Portrait of Stevenson* O.U.P., London, 1937

EIGNER, EDWIN M. *Robert Louis Stevenson and the Romantic Tradition* Princeton University Press, Princeton, New Jersey, 1966

ELLISON, JOSEPH W. *Tusitala of the South Seas* Hastings House, New York, 1953

FURNAS, J. C. *Voyage to Windward* Faber & Faber, London, 1952

GUTHRIE, LORD *Robert Louis Stevenson—Some Personal Recollections* W. Green & Son, Edinburgh, 1920

HAMMERTON, J. A. (ed.) *Stevensoniana* Grant Richards, London, 1903

HAYES, CARLTON J. H. *A Political and Cultural History of Modern Europe* (two volumes) New York, The Macmillan Co., 1939

HEWISON, JAMES KING *The Covenanters* (two volumes) John Smith & Son, Glasgow, 1913

HOWIE, JOHN *The Scots Worthies* Oliphant, Anderson & Ferrier, Edinburgh and London (undated)

JAPP, A. H. *Robert Louis Stevenson—A Record, an Estimate, and a Memorial* Werner Laurie, London, 1905

KELMAN, JOHN *The Faith of Robert Louis Stevenson* Oliphant Anderson & Ferrier, Edinburgh and London, 1903

KIELY, ROBERT   *Robert Louis Stevenson and the Fiction of Adventure*   Harvard University Press, Cambridge, Massachusetts, 1964

LANG, JEAN   *A Land of Romance—The Border, its History and Legend*   T. C. & E. C. Jack, London and Edinburgh (undated)

LUCAS, E. V.   *The Colvins and their Friends*   Methuen, London, 1928

MACLAREN, IAN   *Beside the Bonnie Brier Bush*   Hodder & Stoughton, London, 1895

MCLAREN, MORAY   *Stevenson and Edinburgh* (Centenary Study)   Chapman & Hall, London, 1950

RALEIGH, WALTER   *Robert Louis Stevenson*   Edward Arnold, London, 1927

SIMPSON, E. BLANTYRE   *Robert Louis Stevenson's Edinburgh Days*   Hodder & Stoughton, London, 1913

SMITH, JANET ADAM   *R. L. Stevenson* (Great Lives)   Duckworth, London, 1937

STERN, G. B.   *Robert Louis Stevenson* (Writers and their Work No. 27)   Longmans Green, London, 1952, reprint 1961

STEUART, J. A.   *Robert Louis Stevenson—Man and Writer* (2 vols.)   Sampson Low, Marston & Co., London, 1924

SWINNERTON, FRANK   *R. L. Stevenson, A Critical Study*   Martin Secker, London, 1924

WATT, L. MACLEAN   *The Hills of Home*   T. N. Foulis, London and Edinburgh, 1913

WILSON, JOHN M.   *The Gazeteer of Scotland*   W. & A. K. Johnston, Edinburgh, 1882

WITTIG, KURT   *The Scottish Tradition in Literature*   Oliver & Boyd, Edinburgh and London, 1958

GLOSSARY

a'body	everybody
ae	one
ain	own
aith	oath, swearword
arena	aren't
Auld Hornie	the Devil
bairns	children
ballants	ballads
bauchles	old down-at-heel shoes or slippers
bauld	bold
bawbee	halfpenny, a trifle
besoms	bunches of twigs (brooms for sweeping)
bide	stay
birling	whirling
black-avised	dark-complexioned
blagyard	blackguard
blend(it)	blind(ed)
bonnet-laird	small landed proprietor, yeoman, one who farms his own land
braw	fine, pleasant
braws	finery, fine things
brewst	a brewing, a making
brig	bridge
buirdly	fine-looking, well-made, stalwart
burn	a stream
butt-end	far end of a house, (end of a) single-roomed cottage
byre	cow-house
ca'	drive, work (at), call
caller	fresh, bracing, cool
cannie	gentle, comfortable, beneficial ('cannie hour at e'en')
canny	careful(ly)
cantie	lively, happy, cheerful
carline	old woman
chalmer	room, bedroom, chamber
claes	clothes
clamjamfry	to crowd, fill with a rabble
clavers	idle talk, gossip
cock-laird	small landed proprietor (bonnet-laird)
collieshangie	turmoil, uproar
colloguing	talking confidentially
cracking	talking, chatting
craiking	croaking
cuddy	donkey

251

cuist	cast, throw
curtchying	curtseying
cutty	short stumpy girl; child, lass, brat (playfully, affectionately)
daft-like	giddy, foolish, crazy, eccentric in appearance
dander	a gentle stroll, to saunter
danders	clinkers, cinders
daurna	dare not
deave	deafen
dee'd	died
demmy brokens	low shoes (demi-broquins)
dentie	comely, dainty
dirdum	vigour, passion
disjaskit	forlorn, exhausted, broken-down, wretched-looking
doer	law agent
dour	hard, obstinate
dozened	benumbed, stupefied
drumlie	thick, dark, muddy
dule-tree	gallows, hanging tree, tree of lamentation
dunting	knocking
dwaibly	infirm, weakly, feeble
ettercap	vixen, wretch, angry person (*lit.* a spider, an ant)
far'er	further
fechting	fighting
feck	amount, quantity, portion, abundance
feckless	powerless, feeble, ineffective
fell	grim, strong
fey	unlike oneself, 'strange', having premonitions, acting unnaturally as if fated
flittit	departed
flyped	folded up, turned inside out
forbye	besides, in addition to
formalist	an expert in legal forms and styles, here applied playfully in sense of a young person observing the correct forms of behaviour
fower	four
fry	set, clique, a number (generally of children)
füshionless	weak, feeble, flabby, spiritless
fyled	defiled, dirtied, besmirched
fylement	defilement, calumny
gaed gyte	went silly
gait	way, fashion
gang	go
gey an' ill	very difficult, very badly
ghaist	ghost
girzie	a diminutive of Grizel, a name for a servant lass, a playful nickname, 'hussy'
glamoured	(*glammered*) bewitched, beguiled

glaur	mud
glint	glance, glimpse, sparkle
gloaming	twilight
glowered	scowled
gowden	golden
gowsty	tempestuous, stormy (gusty)
grat	wept
grieve	land-steward, farm-overseer
grunding	grinding, grounding
guddling	catching (fish) by the hand by groping under the water
gumption	common-sense
gurly	surly, threatening
ha'	hall, house
haddit	held
hae	have, take (this)
hale	whole, entire
haud	hold
heels-ower-hurdie	heels over buttocks, head over heels
hie	high
hinder-end	the end, (at) last
hinney	honey
hirstle	push, move on, nudge
hizzie	wench, lass (hussy)
howe	hollow, glen
howf	haunt
hunkered	crouched, lingered in a crouching position
hunks	curmudgeon, miser
hypothec	strictly—legal security for rent or money due colloquially—concern or collection (i.e. 'whole lot')
idleset	idleness
infeftment	(Scots law) legal possession, investiture
jaud	jade, a woman not to be trusted
Jeddart	Jedburgh
jeely-piece	a slice of bread spread with jelly or jam
jennipers	junipers
jo	sweetheart
justifeed	made subject to justice, executed
jyle	jail
kebbuck	(a whole) cheese
ken	know
kenspeckle	conspicuous, notable, easily recognised
kilted	tucked up
kirk	church
kye	cattle
kyte	stomach
laigh	low
lane	alone
lang syne	long ago

lave	(the) rest
lift	sky, air
lightly	to undervalue, treat disrespectfully, disparage
linking	tripping along, flowing
lown	lonely, still
lynn	waterfall, pool under a waterfall
Lyon King of Arms	the chief of the Court of Heraldry in Scotland
macers	officers of the supreme court, officers who keep order in law-courts, mace-bearers
maun	must
menseful	well-mannered, respectful, respectable
minds	reminds
mirk	dark
misbegowk	a mishap, a disappointment
mishandled	maltreated, beaten up
mools	mould, earth
muckle	much
nowt	cattle
ower	over, too
owercome	refrain (of a song), motto
palmering	walking clumsily or feebly
panel	(Scots law) the accused person in a criminal action
plew-stilts	plough-handles (i.e. 'work')
policy	the grounds surrounding a country house, generally ornamented in some way
puddocks	frogs
puggy	a monkey, a drunken man
quait	quiet
quean	girl, lassie
rair	to roar
risping	grating
routh	abundance, plenty
rowt	bellow, rant, roar
rudas	rough, ugly, haggard
runt	old cow past breeding (an old man or woman)
sasine	(in Scots law) the deed or document proving legal possession, investiture
sclamber	scramble
sculduddery	filthy or gross talk, obscenity
session	Court of Session, the supreme court of Scotland
shauchling	shuffling, slipshod
shoo	chase away
siller	money, silver
sinsyne	since then
skailing	dispersing, breaking up
skelp	smack
skirling	screaming

skreigh	(of day) daybreak
snash	abuse, vituperation
sneisty	supercilious, scornful, sneering
sooth	hum, croon
speiring	asking
speldering	sprawling
splairging	splashing, bespattering
spunk	spirit
steik	close, shut
sterling	(*starling*) a pile or piling protecting a bridge pier
stirk	a young bullock
stockfish	hard, dull, dried up
stopping	staying
sugar-bool	round sugar-plum (*lit.* sugar-ball)
suld	should
swalled	swollen
syne	ago, since
tawpie	slut, (playfully) monkey, foolish idle girl
thir	these
thocht	thought
thrawn	cross-grained, twisted
to-names	nick-names, special names added to surname to distinguish from another or others of same name
trysted	engaged to meet
unchancy	unlucky
unco	very
uncoly	very much, very badly, extremely, strangely
upsitten	impertinent, indifferent, callous
vennel	a narrow lane
vivers	food, provisions
wae	sad, woeful, unhappy
waling	selecting, picking out
warrandise	surety, warranty
waur	worse
weird	doom, destiny, curse, prediction
whae	who
whammle	to upset
whatten	what, what kind of
whaups	curlews
wheepit	whipped
whiles	sometimes
whunstane	(whinstone) hard
whüre	whore, prostitute
windle-straes	stalks of withered grass, crested dog's-tail grass
wishen	washed
withinsides	inside
wunds	winds
yin	one

B